ALSO BY ARTHUR PHILLIPS

The Egyptologist
Prague

Angelica

Angelica

A Novel

ARTHUR PHILLIPS

RANDOM HOUSE

NEW YORK

Copyright © 2007 by Arthur Phillips

Published in the United States by Random House,
an imprint of The Random House Publishing Group,
a division of Random House, Inc., New York.

RANDOM HOUSE and colophon are registered
trademarks of Random House, Inc.

ISBN-13: 978-0-7394-8904-8

Printed in the United States of America
Book design by Dana Leigh Blanchette

for Jan, of course

Scientific examination of the spiritual or "occultist" experience demonstrates that haunting can emerge from the forgotten depths of our own past, and assume physical and externalized form, now independent of the memories that spawned it, as Athena sprang from the head of Zeus, of him but at once free of him. Memories and ghosts are not so easily distinguished as previous generations have assumed.

—SIR EVERETT D'OYLY, 1889

Contents

PART ONE

Constance Barton

I suppose my prescribed busywork should begin as a ghost story, since that was surely Constance's experience of these events. I fear, however, that the term arouses unreasonable expectations in you. I scarcely expect to frighten you of all people, even if you should read this by snickering candle and creaking floorboards. Or with me lying at your feet.

So. A ghost story! The scene opens in unthreatening daylight, the morning Joseph cast the child out of their bedroom. The horror tales Constance kept at her bedside always opened peacefully, and so shall hers:

The burst of morning sunlight startled the golden dust off the enfolded crimson drapery and drew fine black veins at the edges of the walnut-brown sill. The casement wants repainting, she thought. The distant irregular trills of Angelica's uncertain fingers stumbling across the piano keys downstairs, the floury aroma of the first loaves rising from the kitchen: from within this thick foliage of domestic safety his coiled rage found her unprepared.

"I have suffered this insult too long," he said. "I cannot countenance a single night more of this—this *reversal of nature*. You encourage this upending of my authority. You delight in it," he accused. "It ends now. Angelica has a bedroom and shall sleep in it. Am I understood? You have made us ridiculous. Are you blind to this? Answer me. Answer!"

"If she should, my dear, after all, call out for me in the night?"

"Then go to her or not. The question is of no significance to me, and I strongly doubt that it is of any to her." Joseph pointed at the small bed, unobtrusive at the foot of their own, as if noticing it for the first time, as if its very existence justified his cruelty. The sight of it refreshed his anger, and he kicked it, pleased to see his boot spoil the bedding. He had calculated the gesture to affect Constance, and she retreated. "Look at me when I am speaking. Would you have us live as a band of Gypsies?" He was shouting now, though she had not contradicted him, had never once in seven years contemplated such rebellion. "Or are you no longer capable of even a single act of obedience? Is that, then, where we have arrived? Move her before I return. Not a word more."

Constance Barton held her tongue before her husband's hectoring. In his imperial mood, when he imagined himself most English even as he strutted like an Italian *bravo,* reason could sustain no hope of gaining a foothold. "For how long would you have delayed this, if I did not at last relieve you of the womanly decision?" Against the acquiescence of her silence still he raved, intending to lecture her until she pronounced him wise.

But Constance would have been seeing farther than he was: even if Joseph could deceive himself that he was merely moving a child's bed, she knew better. He was blind (or would feign blindness) to the obvious consequences of his decision, and Constance would pay for his intemperance. If he could only be coaxed into waiting a bit longer, their trouble would pass entirely of its own accord. Time would establish a different, cooler sympathy between them. Such was the fate of all husbands and wives. True, Constance's weakened condition (and Angelica's) had demanded that she and Joseph adapt themselves more hurriedly than most, and she was sorry for him in this. She always intended that Angelica would be exiled downstairs, of course, but later, when she no longer required the child's protective presence. They were not distant from that safer shore.

But Joseph would not defer. "You have allowed far too much to elude you." He buttoned his collar. "The child is spoiling. I have allowed you too much rein."

Only with the front door's guarantee that he had departed for his work did Constance descend to the kitchen and, betraying none of her pain at the instruction, asked Nora to prepare the nursery for Angelica, to call in a man to dismantle the child's outgrown bed and haul the blue silk Edwards chair up from the parlor to her new bedside. "For when I read to her," Constance added and fled the Irish girl's mute examination of her.

"Watch, Con—she will celebrate the change," Joseph had promised before departing, either failed kindness or precise cruelty (the child celebrating a separation from her mother). Constance ran her fingers over Angelica's clothing, which hung lightly in her parents' wardrobe. Her playthings occupied such a paltry share of the room's space, and yet he had commanded, "All of this. All of it. Not one piece when I return." Constance transmitted these excessive orders to Nora, as she could not bear to execute them herself.

She escaped with Angelica, found excuses to stay away from the disruption until late in the afternoon. She brought her weekly gifts of money, food, and conversation to the widow Moore but failed to drown her worries in the old woman's routine, grateful tears. She dallied at market, at the tea shop, in the park, watching Angelica play. When they at last returned, as the long-threatened rain broke and fell in warm sheets, she busied herself downstairs, never looking in the direction of the staircase but instead correcting Nora's work, reminding her to air out the closets, inspecting the kitchen. She poked the bread, criticized the slipshod stocking of the pantry, then left Nora in mid-scold to place Angelica at the piano to practice "The Wicked Child and the Gentle." She sat across the room and folded the napkins herself. "Which child are you, my love?" she murmured, but found only sadness in the practiced reply: "The gentle, Mamma."

As the girl's playing broke and reassembled itself, Constance finally forced herself up to the second floor and walked back and forth before the closed door of Angelica's new home. No great shock greeted her inside. In truth, the room's transformation hardly registered, for it had sat six years now in disappointed expectation. Six years earlier, with his new wife seven months expectant, Joseph had without apparent resentment dismantled his beloved home laboratory to make space for a nursery. But God demanded of Constance three efforts before a baby survived to occupy the room. Even then it remained empty, for in the early weeks of Angelica's life, mother and daughter both ailed, and it was far wiser that the newborn should sleep beside her sleepless mother.

In the months that followed, Constance's childbed fever and Angelica's infant maladies ebbed and flowed in opposition, as if between the two linked souls there were only health enough for one, so that a year had passed without it ever being advisable to send the child downstairs to the nursery. Even when Angelica's health restored itself, Dr. Willette had been particularly insistent on the other, more sensitive issue, and so—Constance's solution—it seemed simplest and surest to keep Angelica tentatively asleep within earshot.

Nora had placed the chair beside the bed. She was powerful, the Irish girl, more brawn than fat to have hoisted it by herself. She had arranged Angelica's clothing in the child-sized cherry-wood wardrobe. Bleak, this new enclosure to which Angelica had been sentenced. The bed was too large; Angelica would feel lost in it. The window was loose in its setting, and the noise of the street would surely prevent her sleeping. The bedclothes were tired and dingy in the rain-gray light, books and dolls cheerless in their new places. No wonder he had kept his laboratory here; it was by any standard a dark, nasty room, fit only for the stink and scrape of science. The Princess Elizabeth reclined in a favored position atop the pillows, her legs crossed at the ankle; of course Nora knew Angelica's favorite doll and would make just such a display of her affection for the girl.

The blue chair was too far from the bed. Constance pressed her back against it until it clattered a few inches forward. She sat again, smoothed her dress, then rose and straightened the Princess Elizabeth's legs into a more natural position. She had raised her voice often at Angelica during their day out, barked sharp commands (just as Joseph had done to her) when kindness would have served better. The day she was destined to lose a piece of her child, the day she wished to hold her ever closer and unchanging—that very day, how easily Angelica had irritated her.

This shift of Angelica's residence—this cataclysmic shift of *everything*—coming so soon after her fourth birthday, likely marked the birth of the girl's earliest lasting memories. All that had come before—the embraces, sacrifices, moments of slow-blinking contentment, the defense of her from some icy cruelty of Joseph's—none of this would survive in the child as conscious recollection. What was the point of those forgotten years, all the unrecorded kindness? As if life were the telling of a story whose middle and end were incomprehensible without a clearly recalled beginning, or as if the child were ungrateful, culpable for its willful forgetfulness of all the generosity and love shown to it over four years of life, eight months of carrying her, all the agony of the years before.

This, today, marked the moment Angelica's relations with the world changed. She would collect her own history now, would gather from the seeds around her the means to cultivate a garden: these panes of bubbled glass would be her "childhood bedroom window," as Constance's own, she recalled now, had been a circle of colored glass, sliced by wooden dividers into eight wedges like a tart. This would be the scrap of blanket, the texture of which would calibrate Angelica's notion of "soft" for the rest of her life. Her father's step on the stair. His scent. How she would comfort herself in moments of fear.

A stuttered song usurped unfinished scales, but then it, too, stopped short, abandoned in the midst of its second repetition. The unresolved harmony made Constance shudder. A moment later, she heard Angelica's light step on the stair. The girl ran into her new room and leapt upon the bed, swept her doll into her arms. "So here is where the princess secluded herself," she said. "We searched high and low for Your Highness." She ceremoniously touched each of the bed's dark posts in turn, then examined the room from ceiling to floor, playing a prim courtier. She visibly struggled to ask a question, moved her lips silently as she selected her words. Constance could almost read her daughter's thoughts, and at length Angelica said, "Nora says I shall sleep here now."

Constance held her child tightly to her. "I am very sorry, my love."

"Why sorry? Must the princess stay up with you and Papa?"

"Of course not. You are her lady-in-waiting. She would be lost upstairs."

"Here she shall be free of royal worries, for a spell": Angelica unknowingly quoted a storybook. She crossed to the tiny dressing table, dragged its small chair over her mother's protests, stood upon it to peer out the front window. "I can see the *road*." She stood on her toes at the very edge of the chair's scarlet seat, pressed her hands and nose against the window's loose pane.

"Please be careful, my love. You must not do that."

"But I *can* see the road. That's a chestnut mare."

"Come to me, please, for a moment. You must promise me that if you need me, you will not hesitate to call or even come and rouse me. I will never be angry if you need me. It shall be just like it was, truly. Sit upon my lap. Yes, the princess too. Now tell, are you pleased with these arrangements your father has dictated for us or no?"

"Oh, yes. He is kind. Is this a tower, because of the window?"

"Not a tower, no. If it is a tower you desire, you slept in a higher point with us, upstairs. It is I, up in the tower."

"But you have no tower window looking at the horses far below, so this is the tower." So the child was happy.

"Will you not be frightened to be alone when you sleep?"

"Oh, Mamma, yes! I will! It's very frightening," and her face reflected the thought of her dark night ahead, but then brightened at once. "But I will be brave as the shepherdess. 'When the woods crow dark / and by faint stars impale / God's light leave its mark / then does her heart wail / God's light leave its mark. . . . When the woods crow dark . . .' "

Constance smoothed the girl's hair, touched the small soft cheeks, brought the round face close. " 'When the woods *grow* dark / and by faint stars and pale / does God's light leave its mark / then does her heart *quail*. But . . .' "

" 'But her faith's like a lamp,' " Angelica interrupted proudly, but then stumbled again at once. " 'And God . . . God slow, God sl . . .' I can't recall."

" 'And God's *love* is brighter . . . still . . . than . . . ,' " her mother prompted.

"Shall I see a moon through the tower window?"

11

Angelica's excitement was unmistakable as night approached. Twice she looked closely at Constance and said with great seriousness, "I am frightened to be alone tonight, Mamma." But Constance did not believe her. Angelica claimed to be afraid only because she could sense—for reasons beyond her understanding—that her mother wished she *were* frightened. Her claim of fear was an unwanted gift—a child's scribbled drawing—offered in perceptive love.

Still, those transparent lies were the exception to her candid anticipation. Constance washed her, and Angelica spoke of the princess's adventures alone in her tower. Constance brushed her hair while Angelica brushed the princess's, and Angelica asked if she could please go to bed yet. Constance read to her from the blue chair, and in mid-sentence Angelica uncharacteristically claimed fatigue, then sweetly refused her mother's offer to sit with her until she fell asleep.

"Should I leave the door open, my love?"

"No, thank you, Mamma. The princess desires her solitudary."

Constance likely waited in the narrow hall, tidied the linens in the armoire, straightened paintings, lowered lamps, but heard no protest, only muttering court intrigue until that, too, faded.

Downstairs Joseph had still not returned. "Is all well in the child's bedroom, madam?" the maid asked.

"In the *nursery,* Nora. Yes, thank you."

When Joseph did arrive, he did not inquire but assumed his dictates had been smoothly instituted. He spoke of his day and did not mention Angelica at all, did not even—as they extinguished the downstairs gas and rose to the third story—stop on the second to look upon his child in her new situation. His cold triumph was understood. "Angelica resisted the new arrangements," Constance allowed herself in mild rebellion.

He showed no concern, seemed even to take a certain pleasure in this report or, at least, in Constance carrying out his will despite resistance. She was curious if any description would inspire him even to mere sympathy, let alone a retraction of the deadly orders. Besides, the child's actual satisfaction tonight was surely temporary, and Constance wondered what sort of response he would offer when the child's courage finally broke, and so she said, "Angelica wept herself to sleep, so isolated she feels."

"She shall adjust, I imagine," he replied. "No choice in the matter, and where there is no choice, one adjusts. She shall learn this readily. Or not." He took her hand. New whiskers were emerging, a spreading shadow at the edges of his beard. He put his lips upon her brow. He released her hand, rose to the basin and looking glass. "She shall adjust," he repeated and examined himself. "Further to all this, I have been giving thought to her education."

It seemed he would not be satisfied with his victory today, as a dam that has held for years before yielding to its first crack will then collapse in minutes. "Surely there is no urgency to act upon that as well," Constance attempted.

"Surely I might speak before you indulge your passion to contradict me."

"I apologize." No longer regretting her lie, wishing only that his child's weeping could cause him any pain at all, she occupied herself with a hairbrush.

"I have not concerned myself sufficiently with her education. She has achieved an age where her formation as a thinking person should be monitored."

"You believe she has suffered under my eye?"

"You must not start at shadows, my dear. More of her father's influence is necessary. I mean to give more thought whether a tutor is in order or if she should go to Mr. Dawson's. I will decide presently."

"You would have her spend her days away from me? She is too young."

"I cannot recall opening a debate on the point." He crossed to her, took her hand. "The day may yet come when she considers me her friend."

"When she considers me her friend": a familiar phrase, spoken as it had been to a stationer's girl not so many years before, though Constance had then had the face of a woman far younger. "You may in time consider me a friend," Joseph had said to the girl he meant to win.

And he gazed at her tonight, his desire unblinking. This then was how rapidly he meant to breach their long-standing agreement—this very night. Though the child wept below stairs (as far as he knew), he would charge hungrily forward, no thought for Constance's risks, betraying by his very appetite the absence of all tender love for her.

"I must look in on Angelica," she said. He did not reply. "It is her first evening separated from me. From us. She was upset. She will be a bit adrift, you must be patient with her." He did not speak—his intent to charm her likely wrestling with his irritation—but he made no move to stop her. "You are quite understanding," she concluded, and left when he turned away.

She sat below and watched Angelica sleep. Surely he could not intend so soon, so purposefully, to menace Constance's safety. Surely a fatal disregard for her was not possible. Yet he had long been losing interest in her; indifference even to her well-being could certainly result from such extended coldness.

Constance returned when she felt certain he must be asleep. She watched him silently from the threshold then lay down beside him. She did wish to be affectionate and dutiful, but without inflaming him. She dozed then awoke, fully awake in an instant, cast out from sleep. A quarter past three. She slid from under Joseph's grasp, lifted a candle and matches from the ebony side table, and in the lightless night stepped onto the thick crimson carpet.

The stairs croaked under her so insistently that she could scarcely believe the noise did not rouse both Joseph above her and Angelica beneath her. She lit her candle and walked the corridor to Angelica's oversized chamber. Nora slept below: tonight Angelica slept nearer to the maid-of-all-work than to her own mother.

She was so small in this giant's bed, in the clouds of linen. Constance brought the candle closer to the round face and the black hair. She was terribly pale. She touched the high forehead, and Angelica did not stir. She brought the candle closer still. The girl was not breathing.

Of course she was breathing. These relentless fears from the moment she was born! The girl was fine and well. There was no longer anything to fear for her health. Constance could be forgiven if old habits of thought still troubled her, but the truth was evident: Angelica was sturdy, Joseph's old term for her.

"Sturdy," he had reassured Constance on their holiday the summer before, when he forced Angelica to stay out after dusk, poking at insects until she fell deathly ill, and it had taken the local doctor (whom Joseph had resisted summoning) all his skill to save the girl, while Joseph clucked about the expense and behaved as if the whole matter were a source of amusement. "A sturdy girl," he had jabbered at Constance, as if she were an imbecile to question him.

The candle unfurled a spiral of smoke, and its wax wept and froze into marble tears, and from the blue chair Constance watched. Such a depth of sleep, a kitten's sleep. How enviable to allow sleep to cradle you so deeply that you seem to approach that other dark state—no adult can sleep like that, she thought, only the innocent child. Constance's own brothers and sister had allowed themselves to sleep too deeply.

Her head snapped forward, and she blinked at the cone of candlelight, a full inch lower than it had floated a moment before. The old nonsense, "slept too deeply"—that seed her own mother had planted in her when she was not much older than Angelica, the phrase Constance had then clung to in terror for so many years, fearing the dark and sleep. She felt that childish fear for an instant even now, grown and in her own daughter's room, then let it leave her as the years returned. It had been twenty years or more since her mother held her, wetting her face with tears, squeezing so fiercely that Constance's shoulders ached: "You mustn't let yourself sleep like that, Connie, you mustn't, mustn't leave me." The facts, though, squatted unimpressed by maternal notions: Alfred had died of typhus, George and Jane both of cholera from the bad well.

Years later, in a chapter of their courtship, I know that Constance—during a walk they had stretched over hours, city to park to café to park—confessed to her suitor that she was an orphan. She felt this admission would likely be the end of their brief time in each other's company, and that her fantasies of his love for her (furtively enjoyed even in solitude) faced certain doom. Still she spoke, as if offering a hanging judge the extenuations of her stained character. She told Joseph of her siblings, and in her description of death after death she said, "They slept too deeply. My mother used to tell me that." He did not banish her, only asked if she would accompany him to his home; he wished to show her something. It should have been out of the question—but it was an insult she recognized but did not feel, for she would by then have sunk to any depth for his approval. She gladly entered his grand home and was led into his study, this very room where her daughter now slept by candlelight. "These are your enemies," he said and bid her look inside the black cylinder of his microscope at loops and threads. "These are the beasts that steal lives. Your brothers and sister did not sleep too deeply. On the contrary, they likely prayed for it. Sleepless, brows damp with anguish, sickness most violent and unremitting, torment for patient and parent alike." Quite a lecture to a young woman he was courting. The biology lesson had ended with his taking her hand. They had very nearly come to an understanding right then, surrounded by laboratory apparatus and restored memories of her family's destruction, the handsome scientist explaining the cruelties of Nature, while she felt no sorrow, only a prickly warmth in her fingers and cheeks, and a desire for his hand to stay wrapped around hers.

She knew Joseph's descriptions were accurate, but she could not *recall* events as he painted them. Her most certain recollections (though certainly false) glowed as incontrovertible as holy relics or newspaper reports: wishing her healthy, strong elder brother Alfred good night, then sitting at his bedside, watching him fall asleep, deeper, deeper, until he simply all at once turned white and cold, and a last visible puff of steam escaped from between his cracked and blackened lips. By the light of Joseph's slow instructive conversation, she could prove that this fantastic memory was impossible: she had been younger by far than Alfred, would never have put him to bed or watched him fall asleep, and, of course, that was simply not how human souls were called to their reward. She must have seen his body at burial, ashen and cold. Perhaps that was one of the fragments from which she had created this figment: her own breath in the November cold steaming on his behalf, her own lips cracked in the dry air.

She had been younger than Angelica was now when Alfred died, and he was the first to go. Alfred, George, Jane, Father, Mother. Invisible string-beasts steal into the blood and devour us. Joseph laughed when she asked, "How ever are doctors expected to catch such tiny devils as these?" She recalled that at the time she thought his laughter kindly. "They cannot be caught. One can only deny them the conditions that favor their growth," he said lightly.

What could a mother expect to do in a world where enemies such as these assaulted children? What could she prevent, if not the illnesses that had caused her own mother such suffering, child after child after child melting away from her? What could Constance's weak arm accomplish against germs or murderers or the black men who, she read in the newspaper this evening, slaughtered fifty-six defenseless English women and children in their homes in a faraway land? The truth blazed brightly against this black London night: she could not protect Angelica from threats large or small, human or inhuman. To be a mother was to be sentenced simply to watch, never to prevent, only to wait for something horrible to happen to her child, and then to sit by, wailing and useless. To think now, as a grown woman with her own beloved child, what her mother must have felt: it was neither surprise nor sin that she had finally fled the heartbreaks of this world, left Constance alone.

She lit another candle and melted its base onto the head of its stumpy predecessor. Her hair had come loose. She meant to gather it, but the next moment Angelica was a bridge, her legs on her bed and her hands on her mother's knees, the room gray and yellow throughout. "Mother, mother, mother, mother!" Angelica laughed at Constance's difficulty waking, mimicked her rapid blinks, her confusion at the wick, black in a pool of grease. The girl shouted with morning joy, squeaking as much as speaking. "Hush, mouse," said Constance. "I love your little face in morning light."

"You slept here with me," marveled the girl. "In a chair!"

"I did," said Constance, crawling under the bedclothes next to Angelica.

"You were asleep, and I woke you."

"I was, and you did."

"Where's Papa?"

"Still abed, I should think. Shall we rouse him?"

"No," said Angelica. "Mamma and baby."

Constance kissed her child's hair. "Yes indeed and very nice."

"Mamma and baby very nice."

III

Angelica resembled her mother less every day. More painful still, this divergence accelerated during separations. Lately, when Constance was forced to leave Angelica in Nora's care, she could, upon returning, fancy the hateful alteration had progressed even in hours, like some terrifying fairy story.

As a newborn with a map of veins under her translucent skin, turning her blind eyes towards Constance's essential breast, with her stiff limbs and squall of unsatisfied appetite, Angelica had begun life as an unfamiliar animal, but so quickly did drinking of Constance instill in the child some element of her mother that admirer after admirer soon remarked their growing similarity in aspect. On the street, in the shops, and from visitors, the chorus grew daily louder: "She is your very image." No—not essential at all, Constance recalled, for she had been forced to share her life's joy with that filthy wet nurse for two stolen months.

Of course, Joseph had, at some meanly early stage, flashed one of his fleeting but urgent sparks of intrusive interest in Angelica and presented some plan ("from the finest medical advice") insisting this fragile little child should be torn screaming from her mother's breast and shoved at once before plates of food. "Would you have her choke on macaroni so soon?" she had demanded, silencing him and winning a few months more to plump her imitator with the magical product designed to draw them to each other in temperament and appearance. Even when his will prevailed, she smuggled Angelica secret nourishing embraces, for some long time whenever Nora was far away, and none could report upon her loving disobedience. Still the change came. The less she nursed, the more pronounced the transformation. Before long, Angelica's metamorphosis accelerated: her hair crossed forests of chestnut to arrive at fields of jet, and over the cold northern seawater of her eyes swept slicks of Italian ink.

Today, when the rain subsided, Constance accepted the deceitful promise of blue sky and led Angelica to the park where the girl engaged in a concentrated exchange of views with a small boy dressed as a seaman. She could not hear them from where she sat, but saw her daughter grow adamant in conversation. Whatever could these two children deliberate with such passion? The sailor, ginger-haired and pale, seemed ready to collapse into tears. He would someday be a stout, ruddy Englishman. Would he then have such emotional interviews with ladies? He stamped his foot in its neat black shoe, and his anger made Angelica laugh, that sound Constance held as by far the finest moment of a day.

They whisper in each other's ears, cupping their secrets with unnecessary drama, the sideways subtlety of novice conspirators. They pretend they must keep their words even from Constance. How can this charmless stranger without the slightest exertion draw forth those expressions on Angelica's face, winning a prize the value of which eludes the dullard entirely? What remarks does Angelica already compose only for others, so cruelly soon, never to share or even summarize for Constance, who once—only yesterday—served as her only confidante? Now whispering under the tree to him, Angelica reserves her thoughts instead for the males who will soon spread out their patient predator smiles before the old mother while one of them dances Angelica away into a crowd of spinning couples.

And what precisely, at that tender age, does the naval man see when he looks at the dark princess? Cool Englishman's blood he obviously carries, unexcitable, barely able to tint his pale face, though the sun has flung freckles across it in an effort to add color. But that blood—Constance's own, of course—sweeps like helpless tidewater before the soft, shimmering gaze of the southern moon. For though Joseph had been born in London, that did not alter the facts, nor did his impeccable accent and manner, nor his scientific employ in the center of English medicine, nor his service in the queen's army, nor his English mother. He was Italian, and his father had been named Bartone, no matter anything else.

As with Angelica and this sailor, the Italian element had formed no small part of Joseph's power over Constance, even at the beginning, before she knew what he was. When he did reveal the truth, prior to his offer of marriage, she understood the sway he had held over her from the moment he walked into Pendleton's and caught her eye. And here she saw the effects of that hot blood on cool even in the sailor's chubby face: the gradual weakening, the curiosity, the slightly frightened wonder to be near something unnamable but spiced and taunting in its certainty. Yes, Angelica had all of that already, from the blood in her veins to her nearly black hair. The desire in the sailor's eyes was unmistakable. Angelica was desirable—Constance saw it reflected in the eyes of nearly anyone who spoke to the girl. Joseph should have been satisfied: Constance could give him no son, but there blazed as stirring consolation this most perfect daughter, growing more perfect and more like her father every day, less like the mother who had nearly died to create her.

Constance bridled: need her guilt extend forever into the future? Surely Joseph, even in his disappointment, could not conceive that she had done this to him with intent. She had not accepted his proposal of marriage aware of her physical limitations—how could she have known? Did other women know before they had been tested that they would emerge successful? Did their bodies whisper promises that a proper woman could hear, while Constance had taken her own body's silence for consent? She had asked the midwife, the first time, as the old woman returned to the room with more rags, "Why didn't I know?"

In fairness, Constance was not, after all, *barren*. She had been, if anything, altogether too rich a soil. And she had, when all was accounted, produced for him this wondrous girl, growing so brutally fast, already rid of her babyish plumpness, already resistant now and then to Constance's kisses, washing herself, feeding herself, in love with the hairbrushes and combs Constance had eagerly given her, and then at once regretted as Angelica insisted upon combing her hair by herself. It was almost unbearable (the sailor hung from a low branch, and Angelica pointedly ignored him even as he shouted for her attention), unbearable to know that she would never again squeeze the dimpled bottom of a baby, spread powder on smooth fat legs and kiss the tiny drop of a navel. Once and once only was to be her reward and purpose in this life. She could have wept, if she allowed herself, like this boy, fighting tears, having fallen from his branch and bloodied his nose, thus winning at once Angelica's keen interest.

"I am sorry to interrupt your conversation," she said to the interlocutors, "but I must remind Angelica that dinner awaits us. We ought not disappoint Nora. And surely you are expected at the Admiralty, my very handsome sir."

"Good-bye, Angelica," said the sailor, moving without a thought to embrace her but deftly intercepted by a governess and mocked by Angelica.

"Are you hungry, my love? Nora has promised us a fine fish." The girl did not reply. Yet another injury, the very first day after sleeping apart from her: she had somewhere learnt the skill of ignoring her mother. They walked in silence. Angelica's face was blank. Once, any change in Constance's voice could produce a corresponding shift on the girl's face. But now the child was learning to control her expressions, guard her treasures even from her mother. "Answer when I speak to you, you disobedient child." Angelica's face at once collapsed, too terribly readable, and Constance pulled the weeping girl to her in hot regret.

IV

Angelica was nearly asleep. Unwilling to let her mother leave the bedside, she strained for conversation. "Is Papa a sailor?" she asked, her new friend's image strong in her memory.

"No, darling. He was a soldier once, but now he works."

"What is work?"

"Work is what every man must do."

"What must Papa do?"

"I do not know, my angel. He must care for us and protect us. He must cure disease. And *you* must close your eyes."

She did, she nearly slept, exhausted by her day, but still she struggled back. "Where is Papa?" Constance thought she asked.

"He is at his work. You will see him at breakfast."

"No, *there* is Papa."

Constance turned with a start, for he had appeared, behind her in the doorframe. He dismissed her: "I will see the girl off to sleep."

"You need not trouble yourself," she began, but he only restated his intentions. She withdrew, granting him this role he had never before desired, and she could feel, almost smell his continuing and constant anger. He was man enough to pretend otherwise, perhaps even believe otherwise, but was not clever enough to hide it from her. He had been angry since long before he banished Angelica downstairs, angry at Constance, at the doctors' strict and drastic abolition, at the compromises life demanded of him. Constance did not blame him for despising her. He had sacrificed so very much to make her his wife, but never would have done so had he known what more would still be required of him when no chance of escape remained. A proper Englishman might possibly have accustomed himself to these constricting circumstances, but not an Italian, constituted to bear no such deprivation and discontent. Well he should despise her.

When he descended, Nora laid their meal before them. "Was the girl resistant again to her new arrangements?" he asked, but without true concern.

"As you say, there is no choice in the matter."

He chewed and nodded, long after the sound of her reply had faded. "How did you occupy yourselves today?"

"You are kind to ask. It rained ceaselessly this morning, and so, after her first piano study, Angelica was most diverted by your book of plates. It was very kind of you. 'Papa's book,' she calls it. I read her the name of each animal in English and Latin, and showed her the skeletons and the drawings of the muscles. Some of it is rather, I would think, ill-suited for her, but if you think it wise, I certainly do not object. She worked quite studiously at the piano and makes fine progress. If you would be so good as to listen to her, I should think you would be most impressed. I will tell her we must prepare a recital for you. She will have an ambition then, and that will inspire her. Then we had a bit of sunshine, so we took some air in the park, and she played with a young fellow who was most enchanted by her company, but she is amusingly discreet about him, will reveal neither name nor details of their private interview. We stopped at Miriam Brothers for the tea, but I find their counter boy to be unacceptably forward, and I am rather of the mind we should take our custom elsewhere."

She would gladly have prattled on until, numbed by details real and imaginary, he fell asleep at the table. The approach of night was of deep concern. Retiring with Angelica so far away rendered nightfall painful enough, let alone the other lurking worry: Constance could no longer rely on the girl's proximity and light slumber as a precaution to fend off the forbidden. A second night without incident would be a miraculous reprieve, but only for a day. If not tonight, then soon, the question would sharpen to a point of terrible contention, and her fear blended with pity for his equally difficult but inverted predicament.

It was neither her choice nor her will to disappoint him, but this had proven incommunicable for years. Even after the first poor soul, seven months after their wedding, the doctors had voiced doubts. "God does not intend all women to be mothers," murmured one shaking ancient, kindly despite his hateful words. Six months later she failed Joseph a second time, and the new doctor was more coldly candid. But they were wrong—she could still stimulate a flush of pride at their error—for ten months later she had given him Angelica, though the child was most vicious in her arrival, endangering her mother's life even after she had been safely delivered. Constance could take no nourishment, nor stand. She could not, at first, even feed her child without fainting away. When Nora brought a wet nurse for her approval, the meeting so saddened her, she did not speak, so Nora took the leading role, questioned the girl, had her undress to display her nipples to Constance. "Madam? Will she do, madam?"

Does your assignment to me allow for an observation? Then, please understand that you—like all men, with your collegial Cavendish Square consultations, mild spa waters, or bitter tonic—could never be expected to feel the lasting pain of Constance's medical history, a history with which your wife and sisters, mother and daughters would sympathize. Constance's heart was broken by clumsy doctors for women and never properly set, those *specialists* who in their ambition to be unquestioned masters barred the door to wiser midwives, then examined their patient with icy hands and untrustworthy eyes. In her own home she bled for them, shrieked, called out for children who would not be born or would not breathe, then reached for the daughter who nearly murdered her with her rough arrival onstage, while the doctors spoke openly of the child's imminent death and the mother's evident delusion, as if she were deaf as well as despondent. Even when both mother and child survived, sharp lectures continued, delivered too close in frosty surgeries while her husband was always far away.

For three years after Angelica's birth—undeniably an inhuman burden to place on Joseph—the doctors' strict prohibition did not lose its cooling, astringent power. But at last, eleven months earlier, Angelica asleep at their feet, neither of them had restrained their worse instincts. Constance had woken in the darkness, startled and drowning, enveloped. She cried out, "The baby," still not clear where she was or with what many-limbed force, so deeply and recklessly had she been asleep, but he paid her no heed, and in truth Angelica slept easily at their feet, never woke to defend her mamma who, half-wrapped in dreams still, was by then embracing the body that embraced her. "The doctors told us not to," she whispered in his ear over and over, but without conviction, in tones increasingly belying her true desires. She would pay a bloody price for her insincerity.

The next day they walked past each other silent and ashamed, and fear began even then to seize her, and he had no words or gesture to disperse it. Five months later she failed him again, again unable to hold tight to his child, likely his most precious son, speculated the midwife. Again the price was paid by a lost soul, falling from her with such clawing agony that Constance suffered the inescapable vision that it was covered with spines, as if children softened inside a proper womb as they grew, but they began their time there as a lump of jagged iron. At the final moment she called out to the old midwife to take care of her hands, for the monster's blades would surely slice the flesh of her palms.

That failure—Constance's third—was now six months gone in memory, and Joseph was forgetting. But Constance would never forget Dr. Willette scolding her while she wept at his words, though she merited his chastisement. "Mrs. Barton, do you wish your daughter to be motherless? Do you? What I said at her birth, when you were restored to your family only by the grace of a most merciful God, I now see I must repeat in even stronger terms." That latest loss was most of all a punishment for having dared defy the doctors. Dr. Willette had berated her without cease, even as she held her face in her hands and her belly twisted in pain. A more fitting punishment could not be conceived: "Mrs. Barton, you are not qualified to take exception to the teachings of medicine. You pursue your own desire at your family's expense."

"What would you have me do?" she asked her judge. He only busied himself with his painful, cold inspection. "Please. Tell me. What must I do?"

"Madam." He rose and looked down upon her in exasperation, wiped his hands fastidiously on a rag as she lay there still splayed. "Would you have me paint you a picture? Very well. You are to desist entirely. To practice *pudicitia pervigilans.* Make of yourself a *hortus conclusus,* madam. If you find this too great a strain upon a lascivious and intemperate will, then you shall perform a rigorous and unremitting *ratio menstrua* and prepare for the worst should you make even the slightest mathematical error. No other technique will do. One cannot rely upon the gentleman's precision in the practice of terminal cessation. And even if one could be certain of his performance of his duties, I could not promise you anything resembling safety. Of course there are charlatans—London will vomit them forth, be assured—who with neither qualification nor science will offer you wicked solutions devised by mechanics of limited skill but unlimited depravity. I advise you in no uncertain terms, madam, that they will prove themselves both immoral and ineffective. God and science are in perfect union on this point."

Constance passed weeks in bed, convalescing with halting slowness, the thought of her child without a mother haunting her gray, melancholic days and black nights. Angelica daily visited her, but at Nora's side. Each day Constance saw the girl more firmly attached to her Irish minder, and she knew that the longer she lay there in her weakness, the more certainly she would lose her one living child to a fat freckled Irishwoman hired by advertisement, housed below stairs, paid by the month. "Nora, leave Angelica be. You neglect your duties pretending to be her mother."

And now Joseph had ordered Angelica removed from the room. A reasonable fear of waking the child would no longer protect Constance, and though he would not admit it even to himself, despise her he most certainly did. Were she he, she would never have so patiently accepted this frigid sentence. She would have forced the issue by now, the devil take the consequences.

Now, this second night undefended, she lay in the dark that came so blessedly late in June. She prepared her seawall against the tidal onslaught to come: "They said we must not take such a risk, my love," she would say in soothing, cooling tones. "Sure as they could be about anything, my love, they were certain of that. We were fortunate in our last mistake." She could not say that—*fortunate* was a cruel joke after her most recent failure. But it did not signify, not this evening, for after only a few minutes lying in queasy readiness, she heard his breath and then soon after, the deep accompanying undertone. A miracle with the life span of a butterfly: the dangerous, hot moment passed. He had not demanded what he was most certainly owed and could never be paid.

A quarter past three. She crept downstairs to look at Angelica, whose face, unguarded in sleep, still mirrored her soul. She owed him another child, as many as she could bear. It was all she existed to achieve. Her body was in every fold and from every angle made for children. What was to become of her and her poor, betrayed Joseph if the doctors were to be treated as deities, insisting for their tribute on her cloistered desiccation and total uselessness? Tomorrow night she would defy them. I am not afraid, she thought. But that, of course, was a lie. Afraid to leave Angelica and, most selfish, afraid to suffer again.

She watched the candle's flame dance in the grease and fling its trim teardrop shape in all directions at once until it covered the pool with its blue skirts and two moments later with a soft spurting sound exhausted itself, sighing to match the breath of the sleeping girl and Constance's own consonant breath. She must at last return upstairs and *consent*. He would think she believed herself too fine for him. She dishonored their bed, not with any living man, but with fear, the doctors' servant. Constance could not float away, far above the house like this, her breath consonant with the sleeping girl's, constant only to her fear, denying her consent to the one who had saved her. In her dream, her own hunger overwhelmed her floating body, and she knew that only Joseph could feed this ravenous hunger. She wished to be gentle with him, deny herself her meal despite the ache of appetite, and so she restrained herself and ate only handfuls of his hair, but that did not begin to stanch this constant hunger, and she was forced to remove from his sleeping, malleable form all the easily detached parts, devouring his fingers, ears, nose. Still she burned from this acid hunger, and she knew at once that she would be more quickly satisfied if she were to use her other, more efficient mouth. "Whatever am I thinking?" she corrected herself. "I have no second mouth." But no sooner had she thought this than she was short-breathed with fear, and she looked away to escape the sight. She must never look at it, be constant in her vigilance. She pleaded with herself not to look, but to no avail: there it lay, the second, more vicious mouth, bloodied. She turned, weeping with pity, to Joseph's sleeping form, wishing that this mouth did not require her to destroy him.

"Come along. Up to bed now," he said, waking her. He stood above her, a new candle in his hand, and she nearly shouted *No* in her desire to protect him from the threat she still dreamt, her body wet and trembling.

V

The next morning, she rose early to bring him tea and buns upon a tray. Angelica played on the floor, and Constance served her lord in his curtained bed, brushed crumbs from his beard, and spoke words of love. She meant him to see that she would render him all the warmth and dutiful love she safely could.

He was at first dazed, softened by sleep, and he looked upon her with gentle wonder, as if only a part of him—a sweetly childish part—had yet woken to this idyll, this clearing in their forest of misunderstandings.

But how easily he then destroyed it all, how swift his anger, for the only pretense he required was the slightest noise from Angelica across the room, not possibly enough to disturb him, but since he could not otherwise justify his continual fury at the woman who at that moment was stroking his cheek and feeding him marmalade, he could only divert the exhaust from his inexhaustible furnace of rage by blaming a blameless child.

When he left, she read last evening's newspaper, open upon the table, speckled with brown drops of his tea. The paper (like all the others, nothing more than a detailed bill of mortality) cackled of London's latest blood-splashed villain. Two more assaults, bearing all the grotesque hallmarks of the first, had taken place the night before between the hours of midnight and four o'clock. The officials charged with public safety opened themselves to questions of competence when they admitted to being "puzzled" by what they had found at the two murders. How, for example, had the two women—married, respectable—been removed from their homes at that black hour, with no one to witness the abductions? And what was the meaning of the atrocity visited upon their hands? Surely if these had been robberies or only more wicked violations of the person (only!—she noted the word), there was no need for such savagery, identically performed on both victims. It was not out of the question that the markings pointed to a foreigner, perhaps a heathen, and the inspectors allowed that they had consulted experts in the British Museum with some knowledge of tribal rituals in Africa and Asia. The newspaper scoffed at the constabulary's "expert puzzlement": surely a maniacal black-skinned barbarian with the need to practice his sorcery would be remarked in the streets of London.

This, then, was London, men mocking men hunting men who in dark corners preyed with incomprehensible rituals upon women. But not in daylight: it was her London, too, and she would not be frightened indoors. With Angelica asleep, she set off into the afternoon rain. She would have paid calls, had she any to pay, but she had no one remaining to her. So she wandered and gave money to the widows she had come to know in these many lonely walks.

Once she had scarcely remarked her lack of society, desiring no company but Joseph's. From the day he walked into Pendleton's, her expectations of his companionship had been high, though she could today barely recall why she had nurtured such hopes. "Joseph will be my life's adventure," she had told Mary Deene. She could recall the certainty of that emotion. "My life's adventure."

"He's a man," Mary replied, in no way agreeing with Constance's assertion, and not without a certain tone of envy, the plain girl's plain bitterness.

"To learn all there is to learn of a single man will take at least a lifetime, if not two," Constance argued. "That is a marriage."

"He's a man, Con. Most hide no more mystery in them than that chair."

Constance remembered the flood of pity she had felt for Mary. She had found the end of loneliness in this stranger who had walked into the stationer's, and she wished Mary and all the other girls might find an end to theirs, too.

She had been a fool to pity Mary Deene, she knew now, standing across the road from the building that had sheltered her for eleven years, the iron gate, the oaken door, the vast and windowless façade.

The contemplation of Joseph had demanded rather less than a lifetime, and for this she had left behind those who had sustained her. She had dismissed them coldly, though at the time she absolved herself as realistic, making the sacrifices her new husband deserved. She meant to enter his world cleanly and would make no mistake. Constance Douglas carefully kept her admirer from the Refuge and would never allow Sarah Close or Jenny Harris to meet him or know where he lived. When the day came, she bid them a polite good-bye. "Shall we not see—" Jenny began, quite slow to understand what Sarah had anticipated. Sarah interrupted the ridiculous question, "Good-bye to you, too, Con. Best luck. Come along, Jen." In other cases she intended or pretended that friendship would survive change. Mary Deene had been too important to give up. There would be a way, they promised with clasped hands and wet eyes. But after just a single visit to the Barton home, Mary kept herself away, and Constance did not write. What had become of her? Constance did not know—to her shame. She, too, had perhaps found a hero-prince or gone abroad, been one of the fifty-six unfortunates slaughtered far away in their beds. She had been ashamed of all those fine girls who had befriended her when she was alone. Ashamed of them.

In the weeks leading to her marriage, she imagined her new people, hers and Joseph's. Mr. Pendleton, her former employer, kind as he had been, was going to be quite suddenly beneath her station as the wife of a medical scientist. He would have her generous and kindly custom, and she would never behave as so many wives and daughters had behaved towards her. She would enter with a smile and hold out her hand as if to a friend or an equal—or not precisely an equal, though she would not conduct herself as if they were *not* equal. It was difficult to picture precisely how she *would* act when the moment came. When Mrs. Joseph Barton finally did require stationery, well, the Bartons lived nowhere near Pendleton's. Constance's custom went to McCafferty.

Amazingly, though they lived too far from Pendleton's for purchases, they did not live so far that the district did not know, as if from magic, that Constance had "come" from there, as if she had been born there, or been purchased from the gray velvet case in the street-side vitrine. Three days after their return from their wedding trip, a woman on the pavement noticed Constance stepping out of her new home. "But, but you are not—of course you are! You are the girl from Pendleton's. You are *exquisite*. But I will never forgive James Pendleton if he has reduced you to making deliveries."

All at once and by mechanisms too discreet for her to follow, everyone knew that she had risen from depths vulgar or simply amusing. Evidence reached her with something less than certainty, as if she were hearing voices far away. Had those two women passed and turned to remark on her? No—they had laughed, but not at her. Someone said "counter-jumper" quite clearly. But that could not be in reference to her, since she was no longer a counter-jumper. She was the wife of a gentleman of the district; esteemed by other men of science, he would likely bear an FRS after his name someday, or—"jumped the counter so far she landed in an Italian bordello."

Constance absorbed the blow. She chose to absorb it, realizing that she had long known it was coming. She even accepted that there were those who viewed Joseph as unacceptable. Her ears were open for any slight now, and she heard plenty: this man of southern climes was dark, immoderate. She was a schemer and he her victim. He was a corrupter and she his victim. Some voices behind fences, governesses in the park, took him for a Jew. That he was not a Jew did not refute the charge, nor could Constance fully rid herself of the notion that the accusation was to some degree just, pointing to a certain essential component common to Italian and Jew. He had, after all, denied her a church wedding, and many of the Popes had been Jews.

Returning home from her aimless walk, she found Angelica on Nora's knee. "Is your work complete, then, that you can amuse yourself thus?"

"Yes, madam. And Mr. Barton has been, madam, and asked me to inform you that him and Dr. Delacorte will be at an exhibition, madam, and Mr. Barton will be late returning."

"Dr. Delacorte taught me a piano song, Mamma."

"Did he? How kind of him." Harry Delacorte was a hateful fellow, Joseph's constant companion. The cheek of him, lurking in her parlor, speaking to Angelica in her absence! He had behaved unspeakably, criminally, to Constance some months before, though she had of course dutifully kept the fact from Joseph. And now he entertained Angelica.

When Joseph's long evening with his friend extended itself mercifully on, Constance lay in bed enjoying the sleepy peace of a female home. She had for so long expected to come upon peace as one turns a corner and finds a flower girl. Such a persistent hope was a weighty expectation to haul through one's life, slowing the step and dulling the wits, so much time spent in futile anticipation. She had expected Joseph to end loneliness, but she carried loneliness in her as a growth or an abscess. Even in company people remarked it. Isolation was as much a part of Constance and as little her choice as her eye color or the silver lightning bolts scratched by dead children along her hips and belly. She had once imagined Angelica would cure it forever. How quickly a little sailor proved the foolishness of such hopes, even if Joseph were not threatening to send her away to school.

He would be home soon. She would leap from the bed if his restraint faltered, or hers. Or she would struggle, sleepless again, and tomorrow her temper would be short and her strength sapped, the pull of sofas overwhelming.

But Constance was asleep when Joseph returned from his boxing exhibition. She sensed rather than heard his arrival. Later she struggled back through the halls of sleep and heard him climbing the stairs, opening Angelica's door. An instant later he was at the top, nearly in their room, and some smell preceded him, sped through the air, and scratched at Constance's nose and throat, wafted in and out of her uneasy slumber, announced an impossible number of Joseph's exits from and reentries to the room. A harsh smell, though not unpleasant, and familiar, but not upon him. Then he was in bed beside her, and she hovered at the point where pretending to sleep and willing to sleep were indistinguishable. He seemed bathed in the fiery aroma, his hairy skin pressed against her, and she kicked her legs as if to ward off a nightmare assailant.

She awoke with a metallic taste on her tongue, cold air on her face, the bedclothes tossed away. Joseph lay as if running, naked in midstride. The clock's hands strained to the right, and a childhood rhyme returned: "Quarter past three, look to the right of me. Quarter till nine, to the left all is fine."

The bed's hangings closed behind her, and she walked into the corridor. She struck a match and lit a candle. Only there at the glass did she see the nosebleed, still bubbling, that had chilled her face and stained her dress. And that smell again. It had entered with Joseph, clinging to him, and now it clung to her, that fume stronger than the horse waste from the road, than the flowers in the vase on the bedside table, strong enough to penetrate the blood in her nose. She walked downstairs, the blood on her hand lit by the candle.

Angelica's door handle was icy to the touch and resisted Constance's efforts to turn it. The smell was stronger still, great clouds of nearly visible golden fumes rising from the slim space between the bottom of Angelica's closed door and the floor, where Joseph's boots stood guard. The odor stung Constance's eyes, and her tears melted the dried blood on her face. She struggled with the door; then suddenly it turned easily, as if a hand on its opposite side had yielded. As it swung open, the smell struck her with force, and she leaned against the doorframe to dispel her dizziness, and her nose began to weep in a vain effort to expel the intrusion. With her free hand she covered her mouth. The smell was sourceless, yet strangely contained. Despite Angelica's open window it filled every corner of the room but scarcely crossed the threshold into the hall. By the ragged candlelight, she saw Angelica asleep on top of the bedclothes, her dress askew, her legs crooked and odd. Constance crossed the room and closed the partially open window. Low in the sky a parenthetical moon rested nearly on its back. She turned to the bed, and Angelica was sitting up, blinking.

"Mamma. Is it morning?"

"No. Lie back."

"What has happened? Who bit your face?"

"Just a nosebleed. Quiet, love, quiet. Lie back."

"Will he bite my face?"

"Quiet, love."

"The piano is too loud."

"No one is playing the piano."

"Yes. Every night the little Princess of the Tulips plays it. She is nervously constituted. She sleeps poorly."

Constance petted Angelica, who rapidly fell back asleep. She smoothed the bedclothes and with a wet red thumb wiped a drop of her own blood off the girl's cheek, stranded there with a maternal kiss. Only then did she notice the wooden-framed, glass-enclosed butterfly next to the bed, an ugly gift for a child, left in darkest night for her discovery, pinned and splayed, revealed in its most unbecoming details. Having come upon such a sight in such circumstances, Constance, of course, dreamt of them not long after, asleep in the blue silk chair:

The beasts dragged their slick and dripping hooves over her dried, open lips, and she felt her throat close. They stepped on her open eyes. She knew she would never forget the sound of it, if anyone should ever rescue her. The butterflies spoke, an inhuman noise rising from all of them at once. Their wings trembled to the piercing drone, and she understood the oscillating sound: she was to blame. "Such is how God treats the wicked, Constance," they said. "Just so. And so. Cry all you like, my girl."

VI

Nora, can you not smell it? It pervades everything. It is feculent and sets the skin quite to creeping." The maid nodded. "I could scarcely sleep from the fumes. Open the house and wash it away." Nora set off to find the source of the odor, but Constance stopped her. "Wait. I saw the cracks in the good service saucer, Nora. Please simply admit to me when such damage occurs. You know I will never chastise accidents, only deceit."

"Begging pardon, madam, I don't know nothing about cracked dishes."

"Enough. Go air the house."

Constance went upstairs and stopped in her doorway, astounded at the sight: Joseph had shaved precisely half his face. The left side was still her husband's, her betrothed's, her suitor's. But the right! He had not trimmed or shaped his beard; he had mown it entirely away, and there was half a face she had literally never seen before, speckled here and there with blood. He was stropping his razor and examining his work in the glass. "Time for a change," he said to her small, distant reflection.

She drew slowly closer. "Is it? I am so . . . you did not speak of this . . . drastic intention. It is quite . . . Are other men shaving themselves bare this season?" The white basin was growing a black beard in opposition to his loss.

"There comes time for old arrangements to be swept away. Forgiveness, one could say."

"Whom are you forgiving, my love?"

He only set more soap upon his cheek. "As a boy, I would stand where you are standing now and watch him shaved. By a valet or even by my governess. It seemed a sacrament. He was always bare-faced."

"But that was the fashion then. You hardly ever speak of him."

Seven years she had known Joseph's face, unchanging, unaging. Now, at once (or rather in two halves) he was presenting her with a vast and profound alteration. He was no older, no less handsome, only new, newly made with different expressions to learn, and unquestionably, too, more Italian.

When Constance returned to the room twenty minutes later to collect the bedclothes and Joseph's shirts, she found Angelica upon his knee. They were whispering to each other. He was dressed for his day, and the child was caressing his newly naked cheek, first with her own hand and then with the wooden fingers of her doll. "Does it please you?" Angelica asked him.

Constance announced her presence, and Joseph turned, revealing his other cheek, still bright red from a diagonal cut. She brought him a towel. "How old are you now, child?" he very seriously inquired of the girl on his knee as Constance dabbed at his blood.

"Four!"

He looked at Constance, as if the answer illustrated something he had intended. "Do you remember yourself at that age?"

"I scarcely do. I think of it very little, given the sorrows of the time."

"I should think you were a most beautiful little child—the picture of the woman you became," he said with this other, newer beautiful child on his lap, and both mother and daughter attending to his face.

They saw him off together, Angelica holding her mother's hand. Inside, all doors and windows thrown open, June air entered their home, and Constance reclined onto a sofa, pulled her daughter into her arms.

She stroked the hair of the girl, who stroked her doll's hair in turn. "I knew your papa by that beard," she said, marveling at all the shared history he had shaven away on a whim.

"You are new here," the bearded man had said to her, presenting payment for his two leather-bound ledgers, India ink, and castle-top card case.

"I am, sir. Mr. Pendleton has only recently taken me into his employ."

"Well, then, congratulations from one of Mr. Pendleton's customers. You are a most welcome presence. The shop is livelier for it." His accent revealed him as a gentleman of quality. Some filament—was it mockery?—silvered his voice. He passed her the coins, one at a time, exceedingly slowly, it seemed to her now, seven years later, standing in the kitchen, watching Nora black the stove, scarcely listening to Angelica babble of the exploits of Princess Elizabeth. In memory, his actions slowed to near stillness, impossible slowness: the customer pressed each coin flat in her palm, slightly imprinting it into the soft flesh of her hand, and, with each coin, retotaled the sum, never looking away from her eyes. The memory accelerated to its correct speed: she handed him two coins in return, wrapped his purchases in thin paper, sealed the packet with the fanciful avian seal of *Pendleton, Stationer,* thanked him, and bade him good day. "I am certain now to pass an exquisite day."

Mr. Pendleton had prepared her for precisely this, of course—placed her in her position to provoke just so. "Our gentlemen pay a premium to feel that their time spent in our house is exalted, from the moment they enter. The smell of leather that greets them, the sight of the cases, well-polished, and, not the least by any means," Mr. Pendleton had said without any trace of appreciation of, or desire for, what he was describing, "are the lovely young ladies who shall answer our gentleman's questions, compliment his taste in fine *objets,* and guide him to the purchases that *she* would find most apt as accoutrements in a man of her intimate acquaintance." Only then came tutorials in wafers, seals, almanacs, card cases, shades and grades of paper, the proper method of wrapping a gentleman's purchase of a box meant to hold paper for wrapping boxes.

Mary Deene sneered. "You'll be well advised to show your pretty face the next time he comes sniffing around. Ask him polite as you can what ink he likes for dipping his quill in. And make certain your Mr. Pendleton knows the local gentlemen come to refill their ink pots all the more often since you've been at the counter. I wager our old men will start pouring their ink onto the street so to come back sooner and press their coins into the pretty white hands of Connie Douglas. The streets will be stained all black as a Bombay baby, and us plain girls will have to buy ourselves new pattens just to walk through the rivers of ink." Constance offered that the stranger had perhaps been kindhearted. Spotty Mary laughed and carried on, "Oh, yes, lining up, they'll be, gently sliding their hard coins into your soft fist, spilling their ink, while Pendleton rubs his hands."

She could recall (ignoring Angelica's imperious complaint about this or that) her heartbeat of fright when he appeared the very next day, claiming to have forgotten to buy a desk calendar the day before and to have suffered, as a result, the annoyance of the colleague who had requested it. He wished "to redress the omissions" of the day previous. He stared at her, unblinking, like a snake. Unblinking? Certainly not, though she recalled not knowing where she ought to look. Her certainty of his innocent kindness fled, replaced by a feeling (not entirely unwelcome) that—

"Mamma, you are spilling, Mamma!"

"There's no call to berate me, Angelica. I can see perfectly well." Nora rose from her knees to push a rag through the white pool, and the memory of her feeling shimmered away. She could recall the event, of course, but the underlying meaning, which she had nearly grasped, now eluded her.

Sometime later, after more purchases, each less necessary than the last, she saw him not far from Pendleton's, a chance meeting, and, properly, he did not attempt to greet her until she had acknowledged him and stopped. He asked how Pendleton could afford to permit her off the premises. Might she at some later time be available to walk with him in the spring air? She could, of course, invite a friend or her mother to accompany them. She did not know how to accept without revealing her situation. "You would be doing me a great honor," he pressed, as if her silence signaled coquettish resistance.

"Do you ever think of the day we met?" On three occasions in their marriage Joseph had asked that question, always alone in their room, as evening lowered. Each time they had then proceeded to his pleasure.

"Mamma, you are not looking at the Princess of the Tulips. Look at—"

Three times he had grasped the nape of her neck with a firm paw. "The day we met is as clear to me as if it were yesterday, Con."

"Mamma! Look! Look at the princess!"

"Angelica! Stop shrieking at me for one moment, can't you?"

The child's tears rent Constance's heart less roughly than the tiny face, stunned by her mother. Constance, too, ached from the injustice, as if it had been she pleading for a scrap of attention, all while she had selfishly indulged her own games of memory, fondling dusty, unreflective old baubles. "There, there, poor child, sweet angel-girl, Mamma's sorry. Let's you and I be off to the park. When you are ready, my tiny love. There now."

Outside, Angelica's eyes dried in the June sunlight, and she munched the lavender sweets Constance bought her in apology. The girl was worth everything. She was living proof, her eyes bright from the confection, that Constance had made no error of judgment that day at Pendleton's, no matter the bare-faced man who had now replaced the bearded one.

VII

id you have no fear at all? All those years at war? To be decorated for *courage*." They had lain next to each other, the first morning of their wedding trip. She was amazed at his myriad gentle kindnesses, his slow disclosures of his life before her. "I should have been too fearful to fire my rifle."

"As it should be. The British woman is of too high a value as a mother and protectress of the home to send her off to foreign conquest." She lay, after her life of trial and poverty, in an unaccustomed, almost inconceivable calm. She savored in small sips the first taste of her new, unimaginable wealth. He had lifted her into another world, in which one roamed Italian villages, then loafed in bed long after the sun had risen, while outside the window mountains rose and frosted themselves in the clouds. "Do you know, though, there *are* some nations where the women are the warriors and the men the emblems of peace. There exists a kingdom in black Africa where—queendom, I should say—where everything is quite topsy-turvy. The queen reigns not as our gentle Victoria reigns, but with an iron fist. Her army is all women. Fierce devils, too."

"You are telling stories to your new wife."

"Not a bit. True as this bed. I have had it from the mouths of men who have seen it with their own eyes. The women rule everything, make all decisions, while the men cook and see to the children when they are young. But when the girls reach a certain age, the mothers take them in hand, take them from their playmate brothers and gentle papas who weep at the loss of their brave, unruly girls. The mothers pack the girls off to schools where, from women, they learn their figures and letters, the history of their strange people, and they learn to fight, in the manner of this army of Venus.

"I cannot recall the name, something like Torrorarina. And the women woo the men, you see, pursue the shy males, make promises of marriage. And the women wander the roads after dark, scoured inside by surging appetite. It is immoral *she*-wolves who lure young *men* into dishonorable actions, and if the couple's sin is brought to light, it is the man who is chased from proper society, while she simply gains notoriety as a bit of a rascal. The dishonored men, and many of the sons of the poor, often fall into further dishonor. They ply a disreputable trade, just as some unfortunate women do in London. These men survive from the fees they can wring from their hungry female customers."

"Men? Doing that for women's payment? It cannot be."

"Absolute truth," he insisted. "Some don't fall quite so far but end instead in their queer, barbarian theater, where they are at least accepted in some quarters." The story was now certain nonsense, if it had not always been, but he had been solicitous of her pleasure, had exerted himself to entertain her.

"It cannot be," Constance repeated. "Men are men and women women. They are different and desire differently." She laid her head upon his lap.

"How far have you traveled in this wide world, my bride?"

"No farther than this bed. But the book you made me read, the naturalist fellow, the *Beagle* fellow—he said as much, and he has traveled even more widely than you. We are just well-behaved apes. It is you who believe this, and now you say the opposite."

"Not the opposite, only to point out the limits of it. Just as we eat more than bananas, in other ways clearly we are *not* apes. And in this, this—how to call it?—this *distribution of desire,* we British are unlike the French, who so resemble us outwardly, and from these she-Casanovas of Madagascar we are quite perfectly the opposite, from which we can conclude that *desire,* as you say, is a matter of culture, not evolution. Desires acceptable and encouraged among one people are discouraged among another, and we sign on His behalf the name of God at the bottom of our catalog of proscriptions and customs. We British have our approved behavior, and we shun those who would stray."

"But you are Italian," she teased.

"British, my girl, as much as you. We are British *because* of how we act, the precise manner with which we temper our apish appetites. If you knew a Briton who behaved in every way like a jungle savage, in what way would he still be British?"

She could recall—separate from the words he spoke—the *feeling* of him; he was light and gentle and entertaining. Amusing her was of importance to him. Having won her hand, he would strive to win it again and again. But the words—his easy talk of Britons behaving like animals, the acceptable variation of men's appetites from country to country—tonight, on her sofa, as she watched the light fade, the words would no longer easily separate from the recollection.

VIII

Though the windows had remained open all day, still that burning aroma lingered. Nora closed the downstairs, and Constance shut the child's room herself, worried the window's loose fittings.

Upstairs, she came upon Joseph disrobing. The transformation that had overcome his mood was extreme, simply from shaving his face. She stared openly at those new contours, and he, too, gazed at the glass. "Identical twins, it would appear," he said too loudly. Rarely had she seen such enthusiasm in him. He stated again how much he resembled his father. He stepped behind her, laid his hands on her shoulders, pushed his fingers under her nightdress to touch her bare skin, and spoke in riddles: "He was not a wicked man, my father. I have judged him too harshly. If he seeks my forgiveness, even now, it would be churlish to refuse, would it not? Forgiveness, Constance—you know all about that. Womanly nature and prerogative. Still, such an extraordinary sensation."

His hands were upon her. He was avid. She had not prepared him properly this evening. Her thoughts had been elsewhere. From behind her he brought his smooth cheek close to hers, and she spoke without thinking: "I am not fit this evening for your affection, my darling."

"I would not presume," he responded, too readily, and withdrew. Her imbecilic error was plain to them both: in a matter of days he would return, and she would be indefensible, for this lie required a month to regain its efficacy and would be true sooner than that.

He slept. She stared at the ceiling. Constance had none but herself to blame for her isolation. She drifted through her days on cushions and linens. She had all the money she could desire. The bed lifted her higher, and her eyes shut. She would have spent freely for a few moments of Mary Deene's shocking conversation, but Mary Deene and the other girls had dispersed. She fell asleep and there Joseph smiled upon her in Pendleton's, sliding the hard coin into her soft fist. "Have you no one to whom I should apply, then, for the honor and pleasure of your company? Have you no protector at all? You may in time consider me a friend." Coin after hard coin, an ominous inquiry, his delight at her lack of a guardian. "Have you no protector, then?" Coin after hard coin into her swollen, yielding flesh, her hands aching from their burden, then the doctor holding her down and reminding her she has no business, Mrs. Barton, in disobeying. Another coin and still another pressed into her throbbing, bleeding hands, and Angelica was screaming most terribly. Constance opened her eyes. No nightmare: the child was screaming. With shaking, still aching hands, Constance ran down the stairs, down the hall, and burst into Angelica's room. "What is it? Are you hurt?" She swept the girl into her arms, pressed her awkwardly against her, difficult to hold the weight and sprawling limbs.

"Mamma," murmured the blinking girl. "My hand."

"Your hand?" Constance pulled the child's contorted hand from between their tightly pressed bodies. "Are you hurt?"

The girl's face changed, and she sobbed slightly, repeated her pathetic plea, "My hand," before closing her eyes. Constance set the child back on the bed, where she at once rolled away, her hands pressed under her cheek. Only with difficulty could Constance pull them free and examine them. She fetched a candle and returned, held the light to her daughter's unmarked hands. To have dreamt uneasily of aching hands and to be woken by the girl screaming, complaining of aching hands? An idea both sweet and horrid: they shared nightmares. Hard coins had pressed into those tiny soft dream hands, too, and the dream pain tore forth waking screams.

She snuffed the candle out. When her eyes had adjusted, and a gray shadow of a sleeping girl had formed, she climbed the stairs in the dark. She recalled Sarah Close whispering to her in the black of one long Refuge night that dreams were restless and scattery and sometimes seeped from one sleeper to another in close proximity, or to one whose heart was tied to yours by God. Quiet tendrils sped from her to grasp Angelica even in sleep.

She lay down, and Joseph at once complained. "Whatever is it now?" He held his watch at an angle until he could read it by the ceiling lantern's dim gray. "Damn it all, half past three. Whatever's the matter with you, Con?"

IX

In daylight the notion withered, both as a plausibility and, even if true, as a matter of pride, since Angelica had apparently suffered fear and pain born in her mother's soul. Were Constance constituted less melancholically, she could dream of sweeter things, and her child would—far below, or far away in another man's home—sigh and absorb from the humid night air her mother's contentment. Nevertheless, the sight of Angelica playing by herself and, unknowingly observed, rubbing her hand as if it pained her, brought Constance a moment of potent, swift feeling, tears welling above pursed lips.

She left the girl at play with Joseph's jolly assertion that, despite this being Nora's monthly day at liberty, he could safely pass an hour alone with his own child, thank you. Bowing her head before his routine mockery of her "superstitions" and his routine refusal to allow Angelica to accompany her, Constance took her leave and departed for church alone.

She sat far in the back, this married widow, this childless mother. She arrived last and departed first. When she had truly been unmarried and childless she had sat only at the front, early to come, late to leave. Such was her compromise with Joseph's thoroughgoing rejectionism, and with the visible disapproval of the warden and the women. She walked home quickly, fleeing the scorn she felt massing behind her.

And she returned home to chaos: Angelica lay facedown on the parlor floor, and her shrieks drew sympathetic overtones from the piano's strings. The resulting unearthly wail ground Constance's teeth against each other. Across the room, Joseph, in a burnished attitude of boredom, leaned against the doorframe, unaffected by his child's distress. "Is she hurt?" Constance called over the noise.

"Not a bit of it," he drawled. "She has apparently lost her mind."

The girl kicked the floor until she spun onto her back and then kicked the air. Her face was swollen, red, wet. Her voice was hoarse: "He is *not* my papa! Not my papa, not my papa, not my papa, *not.*"

"As I said," he muttered.

It was with great difficulty that Constance restored the child to herself, while Joseph looked on, here and there troubling himself to inquire after Constance's methods, but otherwise helping not at all and reigniting the child's fit by sighing loudly or calling her a "troubling specimen of a girl."

"What began this?"

"Ask the vicious little dervish yourself."

"He," Angelica moaned, shaking in Constance's arms like a feverish newborn. "He wants me to eat a deer."

"Oh, it is too absurd." He abandoned her with the flailing child.

The event would not have been so disturbing—Angelica did from time to time collapse into fits of anger for no reason that would impress an adult, and if he had insisted she eat venison (if Constance understood correctly), it was no great surprise that events quickly outpaced Joseph's skill to control them—but later that same Sunday afternoon, when he approached Angelica with an offer to read her a book, she fled his advance and hid behind Constance's legs, crying. He shrugged and retreated upstairs while Constance attempted to maintain an expression that would not imply she thought Angelica the slightest bit justified.

"Why are you behaving like this towards your papa?" she whispered.

Angelica became younger with each phrase, thinking to make herself more loved and thus better protected: "I prefer you. I prefer Mamma. Angelica loves Mamma. Me love Mamma."

"And I you, angel-girl. But we must behave for Papa. We must not trouble him. We must do whatever he asks. He is our protector. Do you see?"

"Does he protect Mamma, too?"

"Of course, my child."

X

An accusatory crescent moon peered through the parlor window, examining Constance as she read. London's murderers inactive, the newspapers necessarily trumpeted details of the slaughter farther away. Although the name of the place and of the native perpetrators fell away from Constance nearly as soon as she had read the words, the image of the events had not released her since she first learnt the news. The fifty-six murdered British women and children had been surprised from the very first instant. Constance felt this unreported, unreportable detail in a deep and certain place: the mothers had been paralyzed (and thus rendered even easier victims) by believing, even as the knives sliced, that the horror could not be happening, because the women had seen no signs of its approach. They had never imagined that these brown men hated them so. Lulled, they had lived free of any doubt of their safety. They had thrived under some scorching foreign sun and watched their children chase exotic animals over sand. They had felt no concern even as their own men appeared, too early in the day, shouting instructions, encouraging calm. The next moments, horrible in their own right, must have been worsened by their illogic. Who are these infuriated men? Are they strangers or men we have seen and not noticed, who gladly brought us tea only yesterday? They could not possibly hate us so much that they would harm a child.

The full truth, when it presented itself, must have dazzled like direct sunlight. How long could the women bear to stare at it? Those who were not killed at once must have gone mad: this is what men will do when unleashed. We were never safe but only dreamt we were. We were never loved or sufficiently feared. They will hurt even my sweet child, my Meg, my fine Tom.

The newspaper pronounced the retributions to come, the severe correction Her Majesty's army would deliver the murderous brown devils. General Mackey-Wylde would be unforgiving in his chastisement. But Constance knew the wrong people would be punished. And these new mistreated souls would then nurse blisters of grievance. And those grievances would burst and weep and sting until the newly vengeful would set out to slash their enemies, and the nearest at hand would be more women and children. And a new general would have to administer new corrections.

Constance and Joseph sat before the hearth, inhospitably cold, though midsummer was only a fortnight hence. "Do you think he will find the guilty parties?" she asked.

"They are all guilty: those who did it, those who hide them now, those who encouraged them, those who silently approve. The problem is a surfeit of guilty parties. We are asking too much of Mackey-Wylde to sniff them all out."

"But what enraged these men so? Why do something so unimaginable?"

"There is no reason. They are only barely men. Cowards, animals, ruled by fleeting appetites or grievance."

Cowards, then, though one could rightly ask if all cowards knew they were cowards, as she knew that she herself was one. Perhaps these men thought themselves courageous. Perhaps they *were,* in their manner, for surely they understood they could not drive us away by murdering a few innocents, and yet murder they did, struck down those whom their better selves must have known were worthy of their gentleness.

Surely they grasped that murdering British innocents would only bring down upon their heads the wrath of the Empire, and yet they slaughtered. Was this not a horrible and backwards courage?

Joseph had told her so little of the war he had fought, and she could not just then recall the unpronounceable name of the place where his heroics had earned him letters of praise and a medal kept out of view. "Have British troops ever done anything like this?"

"Have you gone mad?" She had not meant to anger him, had only allowed feeling to follow feeling until words left her mouth. "Do you imagine all men are such beasts?" No, only that these brown beasts were also men, and must have thought themselves soldiers, too. "My Lord, woman. The British fighting man . . ." and she smelled his pride in being taken for one, though he was in fact that halfway man between British and brown. She imagined him in army uniform (as she used often to do), but this time, he was not in taut braces and gleaming white trousers. She saw him wet, frightened, and enraged, his face muddied brown, and under his hands writhed women and children.

She remained by the coals, her apologies for her foolish chatter not nearly sufficient to calm his temper. Alone in the darkening parlor, she heard his steps upstairs. She would go up at once if she heard him approach Angelica's room—she stopped herself mid-thought: Whatever is the matter with me? He is right, I am not thinking clearly, and shall muddle myself irreparably if I do not take firmer hold of myself. Why ever should I fear him going to kiss his girl good night? I should rather fear a man who did not.

How little of him there was to be found here, amidst the furnishings, in the objects of memory. When he brought her there as his wife, the house had been nearly empty. And now, alone, she felt it empty again, despite all her efforts. A new detail she had heard during her errands: the dark men had cut the children's heads from their bodies. The blacks had, under full morning sun, when no horror should be conceivable, hacked the weeping heads from the thrashing bodies and displayed them to the mothers.

The floor creaked behind her. "I am sorry," she said without turning, but no reply came from the dark. "Please do not be angry with me. I was confused by the newspapers."

The coals broke and settled in the ash. She saw reflected in the windowpane a man's face behind her own, but, turning, found no one, only the dark room and doorway to the dark kitchen. The floor creaked again, but now she also heard Joseph's step high above. She bit her tongue and ran to the stairs. She tripped on her skirts, of course, and struck her knee against the edge of the wooden stair and cried out, but was up again, just ahead of whoever was grasping for her skirt, had it now and tore away a strip with a sound like ripping flesh. She ran up both flights and into her room, and in the time it took her to cross these last steps, to close the door behind her and call Joseph's name, as he was pressing smooth tomorrow's trousers on a table, two thoughts struck her at once: that she had imagined all this, and, in her fear and moment of danger—false though it was—she had run for the help of her husband, rather than running to offer help to her child, and she was ashamed of her doubly proven weakness.

She stumbled into her husband's arms. "I am so bad a wife to you. Small and stupid and frightened by shadows."

He insisted on showing her that all was well, brought her down the stairs, lit for her the bit of skirt caught on a stair wire and the carpet that had come up, lit the empty and again homey parlor, his arm around her shoulder. He led her back upstairs. "We have been tested, both of us," he said, folding her in his arms and pressing her head to his chest. "I am aware of this, Con. Sorely tested. When we are apart from each other in our hearts, the space is filled with dark, cold thoughts." His mouth was at her ear. He kissed her neck. "There is nothing to fear. I will never allow harm to come to you." He kissed her cheeks and her ear, kissed her neck with his lips and teeth. "Do you think, ever, of the day we met, Con?"

"My love, I must look in upon Angelica." His teeth pressed against the throbbing soft skin of her neck.

He seemed not to have heard her, but then all at once he released her. "Of course." He turned away. "Of course."

When she unwillingly returned, he was asleep. This fifth night with Angelica sequestered far beneath them, he had demanded none of his rights, and she silently thanked him for his restraint or his exhaustion. She lay on her side and watched him until she could discern a feature or two. She saw at last the outline of his closed eyes. His eyes dashed back and forth under their lids, and his lips parted, and he breathed rapidly, wheezing a little. "Lem, hold her down, damn you," he said at once, clear through his sleep. His expression was one of unrestrained sensuality. "Hold her down, can't you?"

XI

She resisted, but sleep took her nonetheless, and when her eyes opened at quarter past three, she could not recall succumbing. Five nights of this had smudged her ivory features. Five nights she had awoken at precisely this same watchful hour, to peer through the murk with dry eyes at the shadowed and distant clock. The same minute each night, the sleeping mind's virtuoso conjurer's trick, her body alert, as if ready to receive a message of the highest importance, but finding only the messenger's riderless horse.

Angelica slept soundly. Constance sat in the blue chair, only for a moment, to rest her eyes and listen to her sweet girl's sounds, but then she woke in daylight, cramped, her feet on Angelica's bed and the girl herself awake in Constance's lap. "How long have you been on top of me?"

"A week," Angelica replied thoughtfully. "And hours."

Joseph still dallied upstairs. "May your papa savor the sloth he so desired," she whispered to Angelica and carried the girl down to breakfast. "He deserves his rest," she rephrased, more kindly, as they reached the front hall.

"Do I?" Joseph appeared at the bottom of the stairs.

"You startled me, my love. I did not hear you descend."

"Shall we institute a system by which I alert you when I change floors? Perhaps bells? I should try not to move so lightly about my own home, but when well rested I am quite nimble."

"Nimble, nimble, nimble." Angelica liked the sound of the word, and she repeated it mindlessly as Nora served her and Constance inspected the stove-fire. "Nimble, numble, bimble, thumble, thimble, thimbit, bit, bite." Constance had worked on the Refuge stoves and still took pride in her ability, even years later, to find flaws in Nora's maintenance.

"I had a dream!" said Angelica.

"Did you, my dear?"

The Irish girl was, unsurprisingly, given to sloppiness and temperamental resistance to her tasks—ingratitude to Joseph as her generous employer and to Constance (now applying some blacking to the side of a flame cover) who was responsible to that same employer for the quality of Nora's work. It constituted ingratitude, too, to God, who had seen that Nora Keneally was taken in and expected, in exchange, to return His kindness in the form of work.

"Did you hear me, Mamma? They bited me."

"Not 'bited,' dearest. 'Bit.' Bit you? What bit you?"

"What I said. In the dream. Mamma, what's warm under my neck?"

"I cannot understand you, Angelica. What bit you?"

"All over my neck and ears, they were rabbits and mices and butterflies."

"Butterflies have no teeth."

"But I *feeled* them on me."

"What are you saying? Come here, let me look at you."

Constance pushed the girl's collar down and her hair aside. "Mamma, you are hurting me. Mamma! Stop now!"

"Hush, hush, it is all right." Her neck was red. "What is this? You are scratched here." Constance touched the red line down the girl's nape, slightly raised into a ridge. "How did you come to acquire this?"

"From Nora."

"Really?" Constance nearly laughed aloud. "Nora, how is this?"

The Irish girl smirked as she looked up, flushed from the open oven. "Madam, I'm sure I don't know what the child means."

"No, it was *nice* of Nora, Mamma. The flying man and his butter-flies were going to bite me, and Nora cut him with her gleaming, big kitchen blade, but she cut my neck, too. It does not hurt because of the magic oyment."

"Angelica. You must never tell untruths. Your lies hurt God. They make His wounds bleed and His angels weep."

"Yes, Mamma."

However Angelica had received the very slight cut, surely it was re-markable, at the very least, that the girl had dreamt of being bitten, teeth gently pressing her ears and neck just as Joseph's lips and teeth had in fact pressed against Constance's neck. No, not remarkable: absurd. He would explain logically. She met him as he descended the stair. "You are hurried. I am sorry to delay you."

His irritation shone. "What then?"

"I cannot quite say."

"Well, then perhaps I shan't tarry."

"No, please. Angelica is beset with some, some pain. Not pain—"

"Some pain not pain. Excuse me."

"Discomfort. She has felt it these past two nights and mornings."

"Send Nora to fetch a doctor."

"I cannot say if I should. Your patient guidance would be welcome."

"Why can you not say? Does she need attention or no? You are a better judge than I, my dear." His tone was mocking, perhaps referring to their holiday when Angelica fell ill, due to him and despite his asser-tions of her sturdy health.

"The pains are very curious."

"Con, will you not speak plainly? Is it a feminine question?"

"Her discomfort is—the word eludes me—it is coincidental with— that is it: *coincidental.* Her complaints are coincidental with pains she—I do not know what I am saying. Her hand and neck. I suffered identically, you see—"

"Are *you* quite yourself? Are you feverish? Does she require a doctor's attention or no? Can you and Nora not see to this matter in my absence?"

"Of course. I apologize."

"But do not fill the child's head with nonsense. She repeats whatever you say, you know." He took his hat from the mahogany half-moon table at the entry and clucked his tongue at her as at an uncooperative piece of laboratory equipment. "Come to me, my dear. There is no need for apology. We vowed to each other last night that we would close this gap that has troubled us. So, look to the child's well-being, and tell me of it this evening. And have the doctor fix you a sleeping draught. You have become quite an owl in my bed. Give us a kiss. Excellent. Until tonight."

"Who is Lem?" she remembered to ask as he reached for the door. He turned slowly back to her, expressionless.

"Say that again."

"Lem. Who is Lem?"

"How could you have—has he come to annoy us even here?"

"You dreamt of him and spoke his name," she said, smiling and straining to soothe his rising temper.

"He is no one of interest. A beggar who waylaid me on the street. Fetch the doctor. And do not parrot any absurdities to him. The girl will have nightmares. Do not dramatize. She will settle in no time— mark that."

She marked it, and his tone, as he left. How easily he elided the distance between real complaints and nightmares.

She did not fetch the doctor, as the child made no further complaint, and the mark on her neck certainly required no attention. But, that very evening, Angelica mounted her first real resistance to her bedroom, to her bed, to sleep—a vast emotional display that struck Constance as far too complex to be the manipulations of a willful child. "I feel queer," she said at the end, shaking her head to hold her eyes open. Her legs struggled against the tightly tucked bedclothes.

"Queer, my love?"

"I do not wish to sleep."

"But you are tired."

"Please do not let me sleep."

"Why ever not? Everyone sleeps."

"I wish I didn't. I don't wish to sleep. I feel queer. When I sleep."

"I will watch over you. I will not leave this chair. Would that suit?"

"Promise me. You shall not sleep. Swear it, Mamma."

"I do." Constance laughed lightly. "I will remain vigilant." Almost with that smiling word Angelica slept. And almost immediately thereafter, Joseph entered, coming up from the parlor to fetch his wife. He asked if the child was not yet asleep. "Nearly so," Constance replied. Very soon after, he descended from their bedroom for her, and she said, "I shall be only a moment more," and pretended to busy herself arranging Angelica's clothing in the wardrobe. He left again. A large new crack ran the length of the wardrobe's back panel, and she felt the piece vibrate under her touch.

She could hear him pacing upstairs, and the wardrobe rattled, and she knew that if he came to fetch her a third time, it could only mean that his eleven months of patience had come to an end, and the time she had borrowed with her lie nights earlier had come due. He would risk her life for his desire.

She heard his step descending and absurdly felt like a little girl about to be scolded. She could not muster an excuse: the clothes arranged, the windows shut, the bedsheets tidy, the books away, the girl snoring, his step in the corridor . . . "When will you do me the kindness of returning to your proper place?"

She was wrong to resist him. She could say nothing in her own defense, with the child's bed between them, but cite yet again the doctors' warnings. "I promised her," she began foolishly instead.

She sat in the blue silk Edwards chair until his tread above her fell silent. Pleasing no one, she tried to resist sleep. When she could no longer resist sleep, she instead dreamt of resisting sleep. She squatted in a rough garden behind a house. The tall grass crept up her night-skirts and tickled her legs, drew red bumps upon her skin. She vowed to stay in the grass and never to sleep as adults do and demand of children. She was cold and the last of the sun was melting away. I never sleep, she told herself, for I would feel queer. I blink at times, but only that. And then came that scorching smell.

Angelica perched on the edge of the bed. "You see," she accused, her face still puffy from her nocturnal travels. "You see? You were asleep. You promised me. You lied. A good mamma would not leave me alone."

With the Princess Elizabeth in her fist, Angelica ran past her dazed mother to find Nora and demand her morning milk and bun. Her temper did not soon recede, and Constance faced over breakfast the child's anger and Joseph's alike.

XII

He left far earlier than necessary, manifestly unable to tolerate another moment of this life forced upon him. She had betrayed him last night, and this morning, with Angelica angry at her, she felt the loss of his love keenly.

Faced with a deprivation most unnatural, he had displayed a heroic restraint, and she had responded with fear. If she were in his place, she would never have been so kind, would hardly consider her health at all when evening fell, but simply take his pleasure and let the risks see to themselves. If the worst should come to pass, one could simply begin again, or enjoy life without the burden and expense of an unconjugal wife. Constance had not merited his generosity these many years, had demanded only to know why it did not stretch on endlessly forward while she denied him his rights.

Therefore, within the jagged limitations of her health, she would now set things right. This bright morning she understood her power to make him a gift he would cherish. She could scarcely contain herself when she saw she could, in one gesture, make him happy again, make him know that her heart was his and that her thoughts turned naturally to his contentment, despite circumstances. Yes, this gift also and coincidentally served her purposes, but that was not why she had conceived of it.

I can easily imagine her self-deception at this point in her desperate and frightened struggles, and the fleeting but disordered relief she must have felt at her ludicrous solution, like an opium-fiend or a woman in a dream: she would restore his home laboratory to him, and all would be well. How cruel she had been, all those years before, mercilessly wielding her little-girl voice, tuned precisely to charm her wishes out of her new husband: "This smelly little room, of course, shall have to be a nursery, shall it not, Papa?" And he had drawn her close, kissed her, and whispered, "I suppose it shall." He had pressed his hands upon her and the next day begun packing his work away.

She would surprise him with her ingenuity, and at least *sympathy* might spark to life between them. With a laboratory in the house, he could give Angelica, if he so insisted, some lesson in his malodorous chemistry. Or—if he truly meant to pursue the notion—a schoolmaster could come some hour or two and administer instruction in this room. Still finer, Joseph would feel that he held sway over some discrete and sacrosanct space, and might therefore not feel that need in other chambers.

She could not wait until evening to present him this gift, to see the bloom of his satisfaction with her. She would render him this pleasure at once, return, and have Nora replacing Angelica's possessions upstairs this very day. She left Angelica—still petulant towards her mother—in Nora's care and set off, aboard the omnibus he likely rode, walking the streets he likely walked.

She noted what he must see every morning and imagined turning her step towards the daily toil of science to earn the family's keep. The sight of a horse drinking water might remind one of something and something else and then something else, and at the end of this woven rope of wisdom, one is swung to a clearing, and there one realizes a cure for some illness. The smell of a flower girl's basket quickly overpowered by the stink of rubbish in small mountains, or the pyramid of oranges in the vendor's tray that rotted from the bottom first: the city seen from

Joseph's eyes was a web of disease and health entwined, to be teased apart by clever scientists.

She had never seen his laboratory. She prepared herself for vats of fire, monastic scientists peering through delicate microscopes in silence, a forest of great metallic spheres and blown-glass towers. In paintings, she had seen laboratories depicted as a sort of busy smithy, but in the novel by Mrs. Terrell, the hero toiled alone, deep in the bowels of the Alpine castle, in an underground chamber cold as winter even on a July morning, from which icy depths he produced an elixir to save the royal heir, pouring the starkly blue potion onto the child's lips, a single azure drop into the dry scarlet mouth enough to restore the boy and the dynasty.

She could not for some long period find Dr. Rowan's laboratory, and she had several times to request assistance, contradictory, first from an aproned boy running between buildings with a large parcel nearly too heavy for him, and then from an old man on a cane, who answered her with evident suspicion in his eyes. She passed but a single tree in the vast complex of buildings, next to which three male pigeons alternated distending themselves for an uninterested female, content to shrug her wings into the form of a heart. Through another gate, she entered a maze of arcades and doors opening upon doors, entering a building only to leave it quickly by the rear, amidst a constant flow of men pouring from one structure to the next. Finally, she came upon her goal, sheltered in a small courtyard, as if swallowed entirely by another building, a single storey of brick without windows and, standing before it, in the shade of its overhanging blue-green roof, was her own Joseph, smoking and taking his ease in conversation with a younger man. She watched him a moment before he saw her, and she watched his face change when he noticed her. His colleague stepped away and entered the building. "Whatever has brought you here?" His face registered a boy's confusion; perhaps he remarked her heightened state.

"I have a surprise for you. I could not wait another moment to see your pleasure at it."

"Your presence is a surprise in itself."

"May I see the interior? The good work you do for us all every day?"

The outside tips of Joseph's eyebrows sank lower than usual, and he pressed his frown more tightly. "Visitors are generally not—"

"But *you* are a senior man, and *I* have a marvelous gift for you. Come, show me your work, and I shall tell you of my most happy inspiration, how you can advance your standing with the doctors at any hour of the day or night." She stepped behind him to open the exterior door.

"You may not at first understand the—" But Constance placed a finger upon his lips and whispered in her little girl's voice, so long unpracticed: "I am so terribly proud of our papa." She found the interior door locked. Joseph hesitated, would perhaps have still forbidden it, but a man exited at that moment, and Constance stepped through.

The room was dark, of course, without windows, but larger than its exterior suggested, and she felt that its total silence was in response to her entrance. The smell, too, startled her, and as her eyes adjusted she was unpleasantly aware of her stomach and other intimate aspects of her person. Her vision returned. She saw Joseph's colleagues, unmoving and silent at their worktables, staring at her. An excruciating noise then burst and spread like a fire taking hold, slowly in places, then evenly throughout the room in a strange and fluid unison, waves of noise, now from close at hand, now from far across the shadowed hall. She wished to retreat, but pushed forward down an aisle between tables and metal enclosures. "I don't understand," she said softly. Joseph slid his hand around her arm, but she pulled it free. "I don't understand," she repeated. "All this time? You kept this?" She could not help herself: so keen was her desire to express her innocence in what she saw that she reached out to open one of the barred enclosures. "Why are they—"

But he seized her hand. "You must not touch. It can affect the purity of the results."

"I feel quite the same," she said and again shook his hand away. She felt his colleagues' eyes on her. They all wanted her to vanish, imagined their own women in this dark, reeking world. The men stared at Joseph, too, demanding in still silence that he repair this breach in their black secret.

"Let us go back out to the air, my dear."

Watched by all the men, she penetrated farther into the room, the echoes of the caged animals' pleading. "They are suffering terribly," she said.

"Most likely not. They are not capable. And, of course, such things cannot be measured."

"Measured? Can you not see with your own eyes? Perhaps that is why you keep the lights so low."

"Enough. Enough."

"Barton, who is our lovely guest today?" someone called. She eluded Joseph's diffident grasp and walked away from the unnaturally cheerful voice.

Along one wall, diagrams hung. Skeletons of humans and animals, like those in the book Joseph had been so eager for Angelica to see, shivered side by side in the breeze she produced as she passed them. Those blades laid out in sparkling precision on leather strips: men must have their tools in order. She would have thrown open the locked gates, freed all the beasts, but to what end? She had not the courage to kill them, and surely death was the only desire they still possessed.

He reached her at a trot, held her arms tightly. "I warned you this might confuse you. These are no one's house pets, you know. There are pox today that no longer threaten Angelica, thanks to work like this."

The breath left her, and the flesh of her stomach pressed against its stays. "Do not mention her name in this room, do not even think it."

"You shall lower your voice. Come along." And with a grip of steel around her arm, the soldier walked his woman back the way she had come, all eyes upon her, the door held by a fat and foul old man who said in a filthy, menacing voice: "In other circumstances, madam, in other circumstances."

Outside in the bright court she breathed deeply to flush the smell and the sensation. He still clutched her arm, and her stomach seized her: *his* hands had done all that, the blades and the blood. "You cannot be expected to understand, but you shall obey and respect."

"Oh, how do you bear it?" she pleaded before this absurd hardness.

"It is no burden to produce the benefits of science."

Only last evening those hands had touched her bare neck and shoulders, her face. "You talk like a corner preacher. And that smell! I smell it on you at nights, though I suppose you must scrub yourself bloody to be rid of it. Do you know, I once thought it the wretched perfume of some other. I should have preferred that. I should have. Better that than—"

"Why did you come here? To interrogate me?"

"I have been so blind."

"I do not know what you are saying, nor, I suspect, do you. Go home, Constance. Go home."

"Does your heart not break? Not at all?"

"Now. Go home."

She stumbled from building to building, court to alley, in and out, stench and blood and men of science and young boys running their errands. The tips of his fingers had placed food in her mouth.

He had kept this from her. It was no wonder, but that he had done it so efficiently cast light into him, revealed a character distorted by deceit. They had discussed his work the very day he had asked for her hand as his wife. The very day. He had taken her to Hampstead, and in the Heath he had described his work as heroic, and he had said, "Is there truly no one to whom I must apply, were I to ask for your hand as my wife?" and her heart had stopped in order to gather strength for its gallop to come, and she had begun to cry. He had brought her that joy minutes after diverting her attention from what he did every day to living flesh. He took her as his wife with that laboratory in his mind. He took her and created those failed and twisted children, all while thinking of these other monstrosities in that hall of agonies.

She found at last the final gate and nearly ran into the street. The omnibus waited. He had passed by Pendleton's just here, had seen her through the glass, had entered to press coins into her hand with those same bloodied fingers. He had stroked her cheeks, pressed her breasts, caressed her belly, had—Constance stepped off the omnibus before it had stopped, and she stumbled to the side of the road where the smell of the horses' waste was welcome. The rain stopped.

Pavers were at work. The sound of their rammers echoed off a narrow court with pools and rivulets of mud and sewage at its center, and the echoes of the rammers and then the echoes' echoes off the closed buildings on the other side produced the tantivy of a horse, galloping but unmoving, straddling the earth with its enormous hooves, clopping without end. Only then did she hear the other hooves, a real horse moving too quickly through the street, its eyes like polished globes, its hansom listing, moving on only two wheels, and from its box the driver jumping clear. The hansom fell, the harnesses twisted, and then the horse, too, fell, and took such a strangely long, long time to fall, but not, strangely, long enough for a young girl who stood as if unaware, moving not at all, wasting that strangely long, long moment by merely standing up from the muddy road with a scrap of something white she had just collected there.

The child's pleasure at retrieving that bit of white did not fade, even as it was falling under the twisting black animal's spattered, muscled flank. Her hair was flung over her face, and Constance even had time to thank God for sparing her the sight of the child's round eyes as she was pushed to the ground, and then that awful mass rolled and thrashed atop her. The child could not scream but others did on her behalf, though they were at first audible only in the rare spaces between the dozen pavers' ringing rammers, that larger horse still galloping over the contorted form of the smaller.

The black horse's black eye spun in its socket and crusted lashes. It futilely shifted its legs trying to haul itself to its feet, but succeeded only in grinding its haunch against the muck, and under that writhing sleekness of muscle lay the still child, facedown, driven into the slimy pools and sharp edges of unfinished paving.

The pavers and the driver ran to the horse, and a woman at Constance's side cried out, "He done it! I saw him! He pushed her under!" and waved a finger and a fist at an ancient man leaning against the wooden fence closest to where the child fell. One of the pavers heard the words and ran after the old man who had, at the accusation, begun to lope feebly away. The paver drove his head into the old man's back and brought him to the ground. Constance could bear no more and fled, her speed only slackening when the accident and its attendant cries were streets away.

XIII

She returned home far later than she had intended, but she had required hours to calm herself, and the thought of her home, even after all she had seen, did not soothe her. She called for Nora, "Has Angelica supped? Where are you, please?"

The piano was closed, and Constance knew that Nora had disobeyed her, had not enforced Angelica's session of study. How quickly the dull administration of her empire replaced the darker stuff of the day! She must remind Nora not to make of herself a ridiculous playmate to the child but to enact the will of the mother.

The kitchen and the dining room were likewise abandoned. She reached the stairs and only then heard Angelica's muffled laughter. She followed the sound up to the door of the bath. She heard Angelica tell Nora, "You made a perfect tub. Mamma cannot cook it half so well. I freeze or I boil." Another of the tiny daggers daily hurled at her.

She reached for the door handle and then heard the impossible sound: "Well, perhaps I have only been fortunate in my first effort." Joseph's voice? "Now, show us how you clean yourself." She opened the door to a spectacle absolutely beyond all experience: her naked Angelica, half-submerged in the small round tub, and Joseph, kneeling on the floor in rolled shirtsleeves, offering her a cake of soap, a world turned upon its head.

"Here is your mother, then," he said, unashamed of his adventure. Faced with Constance's undisguised wonder, he talked on and on, a blur of early departures from the laboratory, of postponements with Harry Delacorte, and a desire to assist Constance, to make more pleasant this new order in the household. "I thought to make Angelica understand she is not isolated by our rearrangements," he said. "And to prove it to you as well, my dear."

He was peculiarly adamant. He performed this charade of domestic duty, this clumsy inversion of Constance's world, solely to demonstrate that he was capable of dismissing her, that she did nothing of value that could not easily be performed by another, by even a man, that the care of her child—her only function—did not require her in the slightest. He certainly proved that Angelica would yield to him at once with coos of "Papa!"

She brought towels and Angelica's sleeping dress, and her offerings were accepted with his thanks, but never his surrender, this man who only today had engaged in his ghoulish, bloody wizardry. Constance could hardly bear the sight of it, Angelica amused to have her hair brushed by her father's stained hands. "You are going to cause her pain, twisting the brush like that," said Constance, seizing it and working Angelica's hair herself. But it was Angelica who protested, "Oh, Mamma, he does it nicely. Please, Papa, come back."

How easily he could snatch from her all that she loved. She surrendered the silver-backed brush to his nasty, veiled amusement. She retreated from the unnatural couple, a step at a time, waiting for sense to be restored, for Angelica to request a return to the pleasures that bound them to each other. Constance leaned in the doorway, busied herself in the hall, walked to the stairs, still hoping to be recalled, then descended, but not a word of protest pursued her. Instead, until she feared she would sob or scream if she heard it again, the songs of "Papa bed!" and "Papa book!" bubbled out of Angelica in a voice ever younger, an intentional rendition of herself as a smaller, newer child. "Papa kiss!"

She played the piano carelessly. She began "Ice Music," but after a few minutes, she was playing "The Wild Woods," and she could not recall having stopped the first or started the second. She sat in the restored silence. Four years and some months, after all her suffering, was to be the brief flickering span of her life's joy. Off the child would now go to his teachers. Home she would fly to discuss science with him.

He had led her to this very piano, when it had been his. Constance had been his guest for supper, and she had confessed she could play. "Please do," he requested, almost a boy's voice, arising of a sudden from the man's broad body. "It was my mother's, and hardly a soul touches it anymore." She did not enjoy playing for others, and when he sat behind her, it required quite some time before she could forget his presence. Finally she played as if alone, until, the final note ringing, he seized her around the waist and the neck, pulled her face to his, and lost himself in repetitions of her name.

Tonight her arms hung down in silence, and she touched the legs of the piano bench, and splinters bit at her. She knelt on the floor to examine them. New cracks ran the length of three of the turned-wood legs.

She walked upstairs, listened outside Angelica's half-closed door. She recalled her own mother peering around corners to look at little Constance, alone or with her father. Joseph sat on Angelica's bed with his back to the door, leaning over her as he read to her of a fox conniving for a treasure of some sort.

He had once read to Constance like this. Early in their marriage, the same low tone murmuring close to her own ear, Joseph had been a potent blend of husband, lover, and restored father. He had recited from a book with a leather cover dyed the color of fire. She recalled the poem: a demon inserted itself entirely inside the body of the damned by its navel and transformed its victim into a lizard. The invading devil distorted the very flesh of the unfortunate's face. "Hair sprouted upon one / As it shed from the other" was all she could bring to mind now of the Italian poem, though the image had not left her: a being entering your very body and changing you, seizing control of your parts but leaving your thoughts and horror unlimited, imprisonment all the worse for its intimate closeness, as nothing remains your own but fear and disgust and shame. "But it would be lovely," she had said. "It may tickle, I suppose, but one would be free of all worry. Let the demon concern himself with all your decisions and toil!" He laughed with her, kissed her brow and the lids of her eyes, called her his enchantress. Tonight he inclined over Angelica in her stead. Angelica could likely feel his breath on her face.

He had characterized this evening as a gift to her. He had canceled his plans to watch yet more boxing with unsavory Harry Delacorte as a gift, to ease the strain of her nightly tasks, to do her some service by shouldering her soft work. Nonsense. Neither was it an apology for what she had seen today. No, this was a lesson. He meant to teach her how a wife should behave. There were other lessons a wife would be reminded of tonight. There would be no refusals.

So she dithered in the kitchen, returned to the piano, listened to the darkening house's creaking, unsteady silence. The gray June gloam thickened until it revealed itself as blackness, and Constance awaited his inevitable call. He was not asleep. He was waiting for her. He had finally forgotten whatever fear or sympathy had once restrained his nature. A scientific measure of his love: the fear of her dying could restrain his self-interest for eleven months. How much did he love her? Eleven months' worth.

She returned to Angelica, asleep and at peace. She adjusted the Princess Elizabeth's position, as Joseph had placed her incorrectly. There was no use sleeping in the blue chair; he would descend for her. Perhaps, in his overdelayed, straining appetites, he would think nothing of staking his claim right there in the child's room, would seize his prize on her very bed.

She reached the top, set one foot in front of the other until she stood before her closed bedroom door. No light showed beneath. She had offered him hours in which to fall asleep. She entered for her condemnation.

She heard little of what the waiting man said in the dark room. "I think it time we overcame our understandable fears. There are solutions to our predicament, other solutions," he leered. Her life in the balance, she mutely nodded, sat on the bed, removed her dress without assistance or prompting. Her hands and will were his. She did not repeat the doctors' orders. She even foolishly smiled in defeated agreement. She tried and failed not to think of his hands on those poor beasts, their pleading expressions as he hovered over them with his knives and explanations. He touched her with those wet hands, and her eyes rolled behind their lids. Her stomach rebelled. "We have been torn asunder by doctors and infectious fear, and that is no way for us to live," trilled the bronzed Italian with boiling blood, the son of ancient Romans, soldiers carved in the statue she saw on their wedding trip: three of the Romans seizing the maiden who had resisted one of them. "I will not allow any harm to come to you, you know. There are other ways man and wife can repair this breach."

"Fear paralyzed her": an empty phrase from her favorite books, in which women were struck dumb and motionless by drooling ghouls and suave vampires. The source of her tingling paralysis was not simply fear but dual and contradictory desire: she wished to flee, and she wished to embrace him. And so she did nothing. "You are my only Con, nothing to fear, my only Con." The low drone of a mesmerist. That part of her that would have run for the door, for the street, leaving even Angelica behind, was now falling asleep, and this toneless voice called forth her own, perhaps suicidal, appetites. The pushing hands, the single-mindedness of the male, and her own desires pouring past self-protection. "There is, for example, this. There is no danger to us in this," said the man who reigned over that hellish laboratory, and she complied with his compromise for a moment, a moment more, his hands tightening on her head, pulling her hair.

She sat up. "Do you hear?" she gasped. She seized her dressing gown. "Did you not hear?"

"Of course, but she'll fall back asleep, damn you."

His protests were drowned out as Constance ran down the stairs towards the gathering screams. She swept Angelica—sitting, eyes closed, that hoarse shriek flowing out of her body in a knotted stream—into her arms, and the girl beat her mother and the surrounding air with her fists, and then the shrieking was chopped into the most vicious coughing and desperate gasping for air. Her eyes opened, and tears poured forth. Her body jerked against her mother, who struggled to hold her tight.

He appeared. *"Choking,"* Constance spit at him, unable to calm the wild, sobbing girl. "She was *choking.* I tried to tell you."

"Choking? Were you?" he asked Angelica, who was at once petrified at the sight of her nude father. She nodded shyly at the unprecedented spectacle, pressed her face into her mother's shoulder. "On what?" he demanded.

"Choking," Angelica murmured in the smallest of voices, burrowing more tightly against her mother's neck and already fighting her way back to sleep.

"Put on a gown, won't you?" Constance whispered harshly, rocking her daughter in a wide, swinging arc, and the naked man retreated upstairs.

She breathed rapidly and felt her chest would burst. Her fear that Angelica was at risk for some disease of the lungs quickly passed, for soon the girl was asleep. It had only been a nightmare. Choking. A thought skimmed across the surface of Constance's mind, too ugly to examine directly, and she shivered to shake it from her. Imagining herself cold, she turned to the window, but found it secure, and then that evil thought returned, stronger, as when one's eyes adjust to the dark, and all at once clear forms appear where before only blurred shadows had floated. Choking. Choking, as Constance herself had been—Angelica had been choking at the moment when—and then Constance's entire body was seized by a strange ache or nausea, as if her arms could grow nauseated, and she would have thought of anything else, but the effort failed: Angelica had been choking, just then, precisely then, choking as Constance had been, the girl's terror palpable even before Constance had opened the door. The aching hand, the bitten neck and ears, and now—and Constance fled the room, left her sleeping girl, for she herself needed to hear someone say she was not mad. She stepped into her own room. "She is asleep," she said. "But I have the sensation of something most horrible. You must tell me I am not . . ." and Constance saw him standing, still nude, half-lit by the gray from the window, and he was—she sought in vain for the word, but she had none, only images of zoo animals or mythical beasts, paintings of devils or the damned drowning in their own vices "—but I have forgotten, I should be certain she sleeps and—" She retreated at the same speed that he hunched backwards into the shadows, and she ignored his rasping call, blamed herself for leaving Angelica's side at all, the lunatic notion that *he* would be able to explain this horror. Him! He was drunk, had nearly made her drunk while their child had been—what?

She flung Angelica's door shut behind her, threw its flimsy, childish bolt. The twitching candlelight she had with unsteady hands at last ignited emitted a string of stinging smoke, and Constance squeezed shut her eyes, and there the white-skinned, dark-haired Joseph became a dark-skinned, white-haired fiend, his black teeth bared in his passion.

XIV

In morning, night fears will vanish as shapes bathe themselves in light, reveal themselves to be not devils but desks. Else one would have to accept that Angelica felt pain inflicted upon her mother's body. There was not even a word for such a delusion. Nora had left a knife on the block, and Constance—very slightly and without considering the experiment overly—slit the flesh of her thumb and at once dropped the knife, plunged her wound into her mouth. Cursing herself for an imbecile, she went in search of Angelica, found her atop the stairs—painless, bloodless—pouring invisible tea for the Princess Elizabeth. "Papa says you tell lies, Mamma."

"He said I—?"

"And God does not pay attention."

"Your papa said this? To you?"

"Mamma, what is 'gregious'?"

"I do not understand what you are saying, Angelica."

" 'Gregious.' A gregious of the first most."

Constance wrapped a cloth around her thumb, and Joseph passed through the hall, fierce and silent. His presence today excited an opposite influence on Angelica, brought forth fearful whispers of "Mamma, lap." His departure inspired her to troubling confidences: "He is not like you," she purred to her mother's mingled pleasure and worry. "He is different. He does not like the Princess Elizabeth." That claim—childish nonsense—hid something Constance struggled to understand. "He *hates* the Princess Elizabeth," Angelica reiterated.

Of equal worry, evening fell, and at his return he displayed a restored mesmeric power over the child, despite the girl's morning fears and midnight complaints. Father and daughter had shown each other for four years nothing but indifference, but now Angelica insisted upon his company, delighted in his talentless reading of stories. Now she sought out his scientific texts filled with grotesques. Now she found the piano a torment unless preparing a recital for him. The child was being led away, and Constance could only see her receding back, as through thickening branches.

Nora was winding the eight-day clock at the bottom of the stairs, Constance was cutting the stems of the peonies Joseph had presented her with a chaste kiss to her brow, and Angelica was bowing before the piano to her father's applause. But how poorly Angelica then played! Pieces she could execute without trouble in daytime collapsed near his influence, and when, as a result, she collapsed in tears, he simply said, "Very well. Up to your bed then." Far stranger still, the child stopped her wailing at once and without a word of complaint obeyed. "You see how order restores itself," he pronounced. Constance in turn came to bed when instructed and was, as a reward or inducement for future compliance, allowed to sleep untroubled and untouched.

But twenty-four hours later the three positions in the parlor rotated slightly, and his temper was as unsteady as the gas under the streets. "Play the piano," he demanded after supper.

"She has been preparing all day. She will be so pleased to try again."

"No, damnation, not her tinkling. You, Con, you! Like you used to play for me." He waved the frightened child off to bed.

She played. He sat behind her, out of view, and when she finished, he seized her before she could turn. He held her face from behind her and said, "Do you never think warmly of me?" He led her to the stairs, and when she began to say she would take a moment to look in upon Angelica, he held his finger to her lips and shook his head.

"But the doctors," she remembered to say tonight.

"There is no risk," he replied, precisely as he might have claimed there was no floor beneath their feet.

Flight was impossible. He touched her, and then her own body, too, was one of her enemies, and one opponent too many. She would stop thinking. She would allow him to do what was best, as a man should, taking her welfare and Angelica's into his accounts, and only then satisfying his unremarkable appetites. Or if this was to be the end, so be it and let it all end.

He spoke with difficulty, and Constance longed most of all for him to be quiet. He had a device, he was saying, still talking, that would protect her from any ill effects. She would be entirely safe, his gift to her. She covered her eyes to shut out the sight of him and wished above all that he would just stop talking and be done with it, quiet and quick, kill her, then, if that was his desire's dictate. Men and their routine, impossible promises of safety. "A gentleman's coin purse?" Mary Deene scoffed in memory. "A gentleman's coin toss, I say. It'll catch his conscience, but not much else."

She bit her lips, willed herself to say nothing as he marched her towards an inevitable horror, some weeks or months ahead. She gave herself to this rough soldier, and she clung to him, as perhaps the animals clung to him, as the women and children had clung to the knife arms of the black devils. Soon she learnt how weak she was: she would not have stopped and turned back even if Joseph allowed her. He had ignited some suicidal fuse in her that would not be extinguished. Constance would die and could not tolerate the pleasure her body offered her now in feeble recompense, a venomous serpent's trick, poison that warms the body and infuses the victim with the desire for yet more poison.

When he had fallen into a stupor, he whispered, "My lovely, lovely stationer's girl. We are well. You are well. All is well." Promises of safety.

Her body shocked her awake, and the clock claimed quarter past three. Perhaps all was well. Perhaps his device had saved her life, preserved a mother for Angelica. Of course, if he had murdered her tonight, they would not learn for weeks if the arrow had struck, and more months would pass before she at last died of the wound.

She gathered candle and matches, crept from the room. She had heard nothing from Angelica tonight of all nights, so it was proven now that the other coincidences had been merely her own foul fancy. Down the hall, the shadows preceded her glowing hands and closed again behind her. She felt herself swallowed by the black, in her sphere of light, passed along through the night's dark innards.

A voice whispered behind Angelica's door, and she entered, her body at once cold and wet. It was there. She saw it plain: floating inches above Angelica, its face the color of tongue and contorted just as Joseph's had been. It was descending upon the sleeping girl, like an angel of death or ancient god of love, intent on breaking the tiny body to its desire. But Constance had interrupted. It stopped short, acknowledged her, and relented. It held its mannish form, wore Joseph's face, then became first blue fibers then blue light and as light alone streamed away, into the girl's wardrobe, penetrating the narrow aperture of the two doors.

Angelica slept still and soundly. Constance—her breath shallow, her eyes stinging—opened the wardrobe. On its back panel a dark stain had spread across the surface of the cracked wood, damp to the touch. For three hours she burned candles, and at every sound she held the light high, and the wind and the street noise and the brush of tree branches and the sighs and creaks of an old house asleep mocked her, the terrified mother prepared to do battle with a rattling windowpane. At times she came quite dangerously near to convincing herself that it had not happened, that it could not have happened, and she had therefore seen nothing, but she failed. Her fear of the truth was not as strong as her pride, and she refused to shirk and blame some mythical womanly tendency to fantasize. Daylight would bring doubt, but if doubt served only to excuse one from bravery, then doubt was cowardice in disguise. She would sit awake all night, every night, rest only in daylight. And? Distill motherhood into nothing more than the guardianship of her child's sleep?

The stars weakened and fled. Angelica's eyes opened as the morning star slunk away, then closed again for a full minute. When they re-opened, she leapt upon her mother's lap.

"Mamma, you are here! Sometimes you are not here."

"I am sorry for those times, my angel."

"What will we do today?" she asked her mother and her doll both.

"That depends. Are you feeling quite well?"

"Might we walk in the park? Will there be a sun?"

"I think there will. Are you certain you wish it? The park, I mean? It is a long walk if you do not feel yourself."

"The park! Please, Mamma. We can run there. I will show you!"

"Of course, my angel, of course. You are quite yourself after all."

"Why are you crying? Mamma, don't be sad."

"Not sad, angel. I am so pleased you will run in the park today." It was over. She stood with Angelica in her arms, and she would stop, would never mention any of this, would take a draught and sleep as soon as Joseph had left for the laboratory, would willingly and obedi-ently gulp a draught every night and stop her ears. She was done with it all, would be a better wife and mother.

"Mamma, did you see the flying man?" the girl asked, and Con-stance had the sensation that her legs would not bear the weight of her and this child even long enough to step back to the bed.

She set Angelica down, kneeled before her, pursed her lips to smooth the coming tremors in her voice. "I think I did. Tell me about him."

"He comes often. Sometimes he is pink and sometimes blue. Did you see him, really? Truly?"

"I did. Does he hurt you?"

"Do you think he will?"

"No, my love. He will never hurt you, because I will protect you."

"You are upstairs! If he hurts me, I should have to run to you! You won't protect me!"

"I will, my love. I swear I will."

"Can we go down now? The princess finds this upsetting."

XV

Whatever is the matter now? One can scarcely catch one's breath in this house. You seem bent on maintaining chaos."

"I saw—have you seen nothing? Does nothing feel out of balance?"

"I hesitate to answer. I suspect you will not appreciate my words or tone. I think you might learn to govern yourself rather—"

"I saw, last night, hovering, something, over her. She has seen it, too."

"Hovering? Over whom?"

"Angelica. Floating. An apparition, a stream of blue light. It resembled—it meant to do her a specific, masculine harm. Visibly."

"My God." He peered at the ceiling. "You put in her head this notion—"

"No! I have done nothing of that sort," she interrupted, to the amazement of them both. "I was silent and *she,* she said it to me. She had seen plainly and precisely what I had seen."

"So you confirmed her infantile fancy."

"What fancy, when both of us have seen it? Have you truly not?"

"Seen blue lights? Hovering masculine dangers? Are you such a ninny as this? You indulge her and yourself. You question me and show insufficient regard. You spout nonsense, and she mimics you, and you take her mimicry for wisdom. For God's sake, have Willette give you a sleeping draught."

She had expected doubt, hoped for it. But this anger, as if she accused him! He wanted her silent regard. He wanted her asleep, by a doctor's hand.

Constance was rendered immobile for the day. Back and forth, round and round, the possibilities pursued each other's tails, while she tried futilely to sleep: she had unleashed this horror upon her child; no, she had imagined all of it, evidence of a repellent soul, worthy of her husband's bile.

The day sped by, and Constance watched the sun's retreat as if she were a shipwrecked Antarctic explorer. Night crept from the east of the city, and signs of its approach gathered everywhere: the shifting hues of the ceilings, the haze that collected at the end of the hall until the tree-tops visible through the entry transom blended into each other and then vanished. Constance sat, bent forward, in her own house, in the small morning room off her own parlor, on her own long chair of scarlet and black, and she wept as if she were still a filthy, friendless girl of eleven, alone in the coach office with no one to collect her.

"I'm sorry, madam, to startle you. I didn't mean . . . Please, would you need a kerchief?" Constance, humiliated, took Nora's rag. "If I might be of any—I do hate to see you unhappy is all. Not my place, I know. Should leave you be."

"No, please, not just yet, Nora. Come sit. Here is fine, next to me." Nora sat at her mistress's side, obviously wary of this perishable companionship. "You must not worry, Nora. I am sorry. I have been visited with such misfortune."

"You might feel freer for the talking, madam. You must know, if it's in my power, madam, to, not to presume."

No one had offered in so long a time. "Something has hurt Angelica."

"Our sweet girl?" Nora stood, crossed herself, knelt at Constance's feet.

"I saw it last night, as plain as I see you now. It is unspeakable, what it wants. She is in danger, every night, each night worse than the last, whenever she closes her eyes."

"What of Mr. Barton? Has he not seen? How could he doubt you?"

Nora knew that Joseph had doubted her or would. She knew so much, of course, walking in their home, silently and invisibly. "I have so little strength left. Every night I die of fear. Where is Angelica now?"

"Above. Please, madam, I know someone. I can fetch her. She understands all them dark things, but she's fearless as any man."

The promise of help seemed like a dream. It was impossible that someone should exist who could help her, impossible that Nora should know her, impossible that she could simply go fetch such a person now. Nora said, "She has helped in the finest houses, madam."

Hope, possibility rushed into her leaden legs, and she stood. "Please, yes. Go at once, tell her I am in desperate need. Bring her at once. If Mr. Barton should inquire, say—I do not know. Not a word to him. Go now, please."

Constance donned Nora's apron and took her place in the kitchen, an unaccustomed position she had not held with any frequency for many years. She had without hesitation instructed Nora to be dishonest to Joseph. Her heart had spoken: at the first gust of fear her faith in him had been snuffed. She only feared that the Irish girl could not be trusted to hold her tongue, and with a hard, masculine calculation, she weighed the girl's loyalty.

She prepared for his return. At the slightest noise, she inhaled and readied herself to lie, but when he did in fact stand at the kitchen door, it was in total silence, and she turned unprepared, starting at the sight of his rain-dripping form. He placed his hands on her haunches. "Oh, is it *you* at the stove? Where's Nora?" Constance's lie hooked its barbed limbs inside her mouth. "She had, I sent her to find . . . She was feeling poorly, her health of a sudden." Constance realized with satisfaction that to a man, even a medical man, the declaration of feminine indisposition was a potent talisman of repulsion, a mystery beyond inspection, an invitation for the male to gratefully retreat.

He spoke hardly at all to her, ate without complaint the food she had prepared so badly. Angelica, delighted with the novelty of supping with her parents, posed question after question to him, her unstable mixture of childish blather and eccentric adult chatter: "Papa, why do crocodiles weep?" He pretended to take pleasure in her conversation, asking his own questions in return, explaining the preservation of ice throughout the summer, leading the child through a series of examples to guide her to his favorite topic: how beasts transform into other beasts over hundreds of years.

He did not inquire after "the flying man" or Constance's concerns of that morning or Angelica's health. He did not ask if Constance felt unwell or worried after last evening's terrible mistake. He noted only that which pleased him and discarded the rest.

At every noise, she looked for Nora and her rescuer, but they did not appear throughout the meal or when Constance cleared it away and tamped the coals in the stove and the last of the June gray had left the sky, hurried off by green clouds and spasms of rain flailing the windows in nervous bursts.

Upstairs, she slowly drew a brush through Angelica's hair, and the girl gripped her mother's leg; the child's nightly fears were forcing her back under her mother's protection. But then Joseph entered. "Shall I read to you? We can allow your mother to rest."

"You must be tired, my love. You need not entertain her."

"Will you stay with me as well?" Angelica asked her mother.

"That is hardly necessary," he ruled. "Let your mother go."

Angelica leapt from the bed and lit upon all fours like a cat, turned her head sideways to examine her small collection of books. "Mamma, you are hardly necessary," she sang. "Papa will read."

Dismissed, she waited on the stairs. Still Nora did not return.

She could risk no action that might summon it forth tonight, for her role was beyond question: the evil was plainly invoked by Constance's weakness, materialized as an expression of that weakness, and tormented the child precisely in proportion to the mother's fault. She could not for a moment place herself in any position that might inflame Joseph.

Some minutes later she heard the minor melody of Angelica complaining and then the sliding note of her cajoling charms. In reply

Joseph spoke too low to be heard, and some time after, Angelica's soft sobbing was followed by Joseph's appearance in the doorway. The hall fixture lit half his face, and he extinguished it. "Come along upstairs," he chided Constance and stepped past her. Angelica called, "Papa! Come back!"

"What is it?" he demanded from the stair.

"I'm frightened."

Joseph shook his head and continued on his way.

"The sudden darkness, Joseph. One cannot fault her."

"I do not. She is a child. But neither will I encourage her." At the sound of his receding steps, Angelica began audibly to weep and called for her mother. He spoke without looking down behind him. "I suppose you will indulge her."

Angelica cried out, "What if devils injure me while I sleep?" Joseph puffed out a burst of amused air, laughed at the child's plea for help from her protectors. Abandoned by the adult to the nightmares of existence, children are expected not to mind. "I WILL NOT STAY ALONE!" she shouted.

"Perhaps I can, for only a few minutes, calm her," Constance offered.

"It is nonsense. And you have caused it."

"Please, please, please, please come, Mamma."

"I shall be only a moment, my love," she said to Joseph's back.

His reply floated down the black staircase: "This is all your doing."

The two faces—Angelica's and the Princess Elizabeth's—cowered together, pressed against each other in the silver light cast by the ripening moon. "Please, Mamma." Angelica was sobbing. When some time later Joseph descended with an icy "Are you truly not coming?" she replied, "I fear Angelica is a bit overwrought, my love, from whatever you read her. I may sit with her, only a bit longer." He relented, enraged and wordless.

"Did you see the flying man, Mamma?" Angelica asked when morning came.

Constance offered half the truth, to reassure them both. "No, my love. I think he will not come if I stay and watch you."

XVI

ny blue spectres, my dear?" Joseph raised to his lips the tea she
had made in Nora's continued absence this morning. He had
not touched Constance, and Angelica had therefore not been disturbed. He knew as much. "Any vampires? Any cause to sleep another
night away from your proper place?"

"I apologize," she answered. "I intended to be at your side, of
course, but she was terribly taken with her fears. Groundless, I know."

"All of this behavior, yours as well as hers, redoubles my concerns about
her education." Show her your fine laboratory then, Constance thought.
That would educate her about you most eloquently. "You will do well to
watch your tongue," he continued, "as this is not your affair to decide. She
begins at Mr. Dawson's Monday week. I have seen to the details myself."

"Of course. As you see fit."

"And you shall not wander the house another night. That ends
now."

She had scarcely time to consider his threats, hidden or plain, for,
within minutes of his strutting departure, Nora at last appeared at the
door, followed by a woman of striking proportions. "Madam, Mrs.
Anne Montague, as I described. We waited for sir's departing."

The visitor entered gracefully, despite her dimensions, but then stopped in the vestibule, though Nora continued into the house and Constance held the door for her. "And you are Mrs. Barton. Of course you are, you poor, lovely creature." The taller woman interrupted Constance's effort to muster phrases of hospitality, saying, "You are not sleeping well, my dear," as if she were not a stranger, but some friend of long standing, summoned in times of crisis.

"I am sorry. I must appear dreadful." Constance's hands rose futilely to touch her hair.

"The contrary. A beauty, only fatigued. You must excuse my making a personal remark. I find it difficult to hide my feelings from people I like."

"Do you know me so soon?"

"I know people very quickly, Mrs. Barton, and I do very much like what I have so far observed." Still Constance's marvelous guest remained in the vestibule, staring down over her broad, long nose, seeing nothing and no one but Constance, ignoring Nora's passing to and fro, the framed mirrors and etched-glass panels and dark wood Constance had arranged with such cost and care. "Such a fine, womanly courage you have, Mrs. Barton. Come, give us your hand." Mrs. Montague reached out to Constance, who still waited inside the second door, worrying with her fingers a fold of her skirts behind her.

"Please come in, Mrs. Montague."

But the woman repeated, "Come take my hand and *lead* me in, Mrs. Barton. The evil that troubles your home must see that I am your invited guest."

She spoke of Constance's troubles as facts, the first voice to do so, and Constance felt herself drawn up to shore from raging waves. She extended her small, damp hand and took—or, more truly, was taken by—the other's strong grasp. "I am so relieved to have your counsel," she confessed softly.

"Precisely! Two women together can withstand quite anything." Mrs. Montague laid an arm around her hostess's shoulder, walked her to the parlor sofa. "Nora, I think your mistress would benefit from a spot of strong tea. Milk in mine, if you please."

At length, Constance regained her balance and constructed a rickety conversation. She displayed the portrait of Joseph in the locket round her neck, and Mrs. Montague politely acknowledged his attractions, but, the tea finally in place, the older woman sent curious Nora away and waved her hand to dismiss Constance's ritual chatter. "Mrs. Barton, let us speak please only of vital matters. Nothing else interests me. Our Nora Keneally tells me you have need of help. I felt it the moment I touched the handle of your front door. Your walls sing with the unseen. I am at your service, though your need may be less than you think, for you are obviously a strong woman."

"Mrs. Montague, do not mock me, I beg you."

"Courage now, Mrs. Barton. Whatever is here has seen me enter by the gentle touch of your soft hand. No harm will come of speaking your troubles. Your husband is away? Excellent."

Her husband *was* away, and Constance felt a fool. She had through uncommon and disloyal subtlety infiltrated this woman into his home. She felt the dry ache of sleeplessness. "I have perhaps committed an error, Mrs. Montague. I will recompense you for your trouble, and I hope you will stay for tea, but I suspect I—I misspoke to Nora, who may have misunderstood."

"Do you doubt then what you have seen and felt? Have I come to this house to coddle a ninny? I have far too many occupations to trouble myself with that, Mrs. Barton, and I do not in your case believe it. Listen to me for a spell. Do you know the history of this house?"

"It was my husband's father's."

"Before him, Mrs. Barton. No? I knew the house at once when Nora came to me. I am surprised you do not know its long history of darkness. I suspect your husband knows it, but has kept it from you, likely to protect what he mistakenly believes to be your weakness. You look quite alarmed, my dear, but there is nothing to fear, now that you and I confront your troubles together." She stood and with closed eyes touched the wall above the hearth. "Your husband's family came here when? And has he never spoken of Eliza Laight? The Burnham family? The Davenport girl? The ghastly prison that occupied this street in medieval days?" She opened her eyes. "Have you truly never heard of the tragedies that have beset this house again and again? Let us put those aside for now and address certain practical matters, so that I might better understand your troubles and prescribe a course of treatment." She removed a paper from her cracked black leather satchel, smoothed it on her lap, and read from a long list of questions written in a thick hand. "Have you seen furniture in motion? No? Candle flames extinguished? Cutlery frosted and ice-cold to the touch? Snuffers that burn the hand? Ceiling moldings melting and congealing in turns? Whistling winds or small clouds? Paint chipped in patterns—faces, animals, body parts? Food containers upended? Bedsheets stained without having been used? Shadows moving independently of their subjects? Carpets fraying before your eyes? Have you heard the bellowing of unseen animals? Milk curdling too soon? Stove fires unable to catch or burning without fuel? Dust collecting in places where Nora has only recently cleaned? Conversely, dust never collecting where it ought? On a particular step or newel or knob? Casements that will not open or will not seal no matter the effort made?" Anne Montague continued her list of mild horrors, and, at first, Constance in increasing puzzlement and even amusement answered no and no again to this catalog of pale frights. Mrs. Montague turned over her sheet of paper and recited from the equally long list on its reverse: "Have you had a sense of general unease? Have you suffered interference with your sleep?"

"Yes, without question, but it is far worse than any of these," and Constance felt a small thrill to realize that the world of spectres had chosen her for something more vile than their usual violations of housekeeping. "I feel that my child is in danger."

"You are her mother. If you feel it, then it is a fact."

"Something has—I do not know how to explain. If I were not weak, she would be invulnerable. I have allowed it to harm her, but you must believe that I did not know. I see you think me very foolish."

Mrs. Montague set aside her notes to take her client's trembling hands. "There is no danger of that, Mrs. Barton. I think you the least foolish person I have known in some very long time."

"I find myself requiring just such kindness. My child suffers—I cannot bring myself to say it."

"Mrs. Barton, I have heard all manner of horror in my years helping ladies such as yourself. I cannot be shocked. I do not pass judgment. I am also—I wish to make it clear in every way to you—not a man. I do not think like a man, and I do not wish to. You may be troubled by reporting something that—in what they so glibly call 'the cold light of day'—you think I shall find impossible. Trust: do not tell me what you know or what you can prove. Tell me what you *feel*. Then we two *helpless* women will see what we can see!"

It was a staggering sensation, how quickly this lady understood. Constance felt her words restored to her after having been for so long imprisoned, and precisely by what Mrs. Montague described: the iron, incomprehensible constraints of men's habits and laws. She had been held to false standards, ever trying to please the male mind. And yet, Mrs. Montague was at first glance almost too mannish for her own philosophy. Constance would have preferred a mother made entirely of clouds, not all this heavy, perfumed flesh and hands so hard.

Mrs. Montague held her ear to the walls, closed her eyes to sniff the air. "Odd. I can almost smell something unnatural?" She opened her eyes. "From the beginning now, my dear."

But the beginning skittered backwards away from Constance. The first dream transmission to the child's hand? Or the doctors' dark warnings? Angelica's birth, the first dead child, the day Joseph appeared in Pendleton's and chose her? It was a knot of knots. Her efforts to describe life in her home were, as quickly as she spoke, superseded by the lives that were being lived there. She was describing an inconceivably intricate tapestry, and no sooner had she succeeded in pointing out some fleetingly significant corner of it—Joseph's plans to school the girl—than the whole shape had unwoven and reconstructed itself, leaving only that corner in place, but now—by her very act of selecting it for special attention—rendered irrelevant. Speech was too slow to capture the lightning of his words and her sorrows and his behavior and the mysteries of nighttime and his face in certain light when seen in conjunction to the sleeping girl's or the girl on his lap stroking his newly naked cheek and the comparison of his behavior at that wretched laboratory and at Pendleton's years earlier when he performed that "science" in the morning and paid court to her in the evening. "I feel as if I am gliding above an ocean of darkness, as if the world were held up on molten rock. I see a glimmer of it and then it flees. I feel very foolish."

"Because you are trying to explain as a man would demand. I am not a magistrate. That is *their* way. Gavels and microscopes and ledger books, all the lenses they use to make themselves feel better, as if they can control or account for that mass of motion you describe so eloquently. The truth is not in the small details, Mrs. Barton. It is in the *whole,* which is perceptible by only one organ: the heart, seat of intuition. The man who tells you he knows why something happens, from its root to its effect—that man is lying, certainly to you, and perhaps also to his childish, quaking self. And the man who says a woman's feeling about something is less valid than the ever-holy 'facts of the matter'—well, I ask you: do you think if women were ministers and viceroys, that there would be wars? Do you suppose, Mrs. Barton, that London's prisons are teeming with murderesses? Do you suppose that the monster so lovingly depicted in the newspapers this morning, with a fourth female victim laid torn and dead upon a rooftop, do you suppose that this villain is a female?"

"Can it be that I see things, and Joseph cannot, and they are truly there? Or am I mad if only I see them?"

"Or does he dissemble when he says he does not see them? Your daughter speaks of them? Then the possible combinations of perception multiply quite rapidly. Who is seeing what is there, who is denying what they see, who is feigning ignorance or knowledge, who chooses to misunderstand, who would in all honest good nature wish everything meant something else? The only answer is to have perfect faith in your own perceptions." They sat hand in hand, silent. "So you fear," Mrs. Montague prompted, "that your child suffers pains caused by inhuman forces."

"There is more. My husband is unwell. He appears almost to have been replaced by another man. Or something in him has broken. I do not know when. I fear this fracture in him was always there, even when he first spoke words of love to me. Or only recently has life snapped his restraints. I was not strong enough, you see, to be a proper wife to him, as he deserved."

"I beg you, leave the recrimination to men, my dear. If you are guilty of something, your testimony will not be required. We have no dearth of hanging judges in this country."

"Mr. Barton's desires," Constance tried again, "his appetites are too strong to be contained in him. They are taking form outside his body." Constance led her adviser from one piece of inexplicably damaged furniture to another. "There are cracks everywhere, sofa legs, these dishes, and the largest is up in my child's wardrobe, into which that unholy thing fled. I can feel something cracking in him, and then I see objects cracking, all over the house, as in sympathy."

"For him or for you?"

"And I am the bridge these overflowing desires have used to escape him. I tried to please him, as he insisted, at costs I cannot ever forgive."

"Of course you will forgive. You cannot do otherwise. You are a woman and a wife. You are trespassed against, over and over, and you forgive. In some languages, it is the very definition of their word for *woman:* she who forgives trespasses against her."

"It is too horrible to forgive if he knows, or refuses to see. I—*she* suffers—I should close my mouth, go blind. I should almost prefer I were dead." She was nearly whispering, and Anne Montague brought her ear quite close to her client's mouth. "My child suffers pains, which locate precisely to my own points of, of conjugal submission. She suffers those pains at precisely the instant of my submission to my husband's will. Do you see? It is my fault. You must relieve me of this. She suffers commensurately with my willingness to submit to him."

"Willingness. He does not compel you?"

"Not precisely. Yes. He compels me to compel myself, or I compel him to compel me, and this pleases some part of me beyond my control, which disguises itself as something fine, but when I at last see its true nature, I am powerless to resist, and my child is screaming."

"The danger is inhuman but motivated by human appetite. And you have seen it." Mrs. Montague considered. "Whose likeness did it bear?"

"Joseph's," Constance said at once. "Among many others."

She shut her eyes, saw it hovering over her sleeping child, and, precisely as in one of her recurring dreams of restoration of all she had lost in her life, Constance's head was cradled, her tears encouraged, and her hair stroked by a wave of mothering kindness. "That's a fine, brave girl," came the deep and soothing voice. "We will cleanse the noxious airs of your beautiful home. All will be well, I promise you."

"No!" Constance sat up straight in refusal of that most wondrous promise. "I may be dying."

"You seem the picture of beauty and health. A rose."

"I am going to die in childbirth. I almost believe he intends me to. That is madness, is it not?"

"Either madness or horribly true. Are you certainly with child?"

"I feel it."

Mrs. Montague refilled their cups. "There is much we do not know. We must temper the masculine urge to *conclude* with female tolerance for lingering uncertainty. Your husband is likely entirely blameless in this horror."

"Then why did it wear Joseph's face?"

"Four possibilities. One, you are suffering from a *spectre.* The presence of a dead person determined to torment you, disguising itself as your innocent husband to sow confusion and fear. They do this. Or, you have seen a *wraith,* the image of a living person soon to die, which news I hesitate to give you. Third, a *fetch,* that is, a slave-spirit, in thrall to some living master."

Anne Montague's words settled into the thick carpet like dust. "I have not the strength for this," Constance moaned.

"Twaddle! Do not despair. Nothing you have said leads me to suspect him of engagement with the other side. Does he frequent séances?"

Constance laughed outright, despite her tears and the contraction of her flesh she had felt only a moment before. "Then far the likeliest, and the least troubling, is that you suffer from a *projected manifestation,* the physical embodiment of a living person's overpotent emotions. The damage to the wardrobe and such lends credence to this possibility, as you naturally suspected because of your husband's uncomfortably constrained position. In this sense, as your husband's discomfort eases, so shall the manifestation be flushed from your house."

With Angelica still in the kitchen at Nora's feet, Constance led her adviser on a tour. Mrs. Montague laid her hands upon the child's bed and wardrobe, sniffed the areas Constance had identified as the sources of the nocturnal aroma. "Dreadful," she agreed. Then, sitting on Angelica's bed, she asked how the Bartons had met, how he had courted her, declared his love, how he behaved in their hours alone. "And his profession? Your home is elegant and enviable."

"He is a scientist. He seeks the cause of disease in animals."

"A veterinarian?"

"No. I mean that he looks inside animals for the cause of all disease. Dogs. He does such things to dogs."

Mrs. Montague was silent, and across her face passed an expression of deepest sorrow. "A vivisectionist."

"He has arguments. To defend his actions. He says it is noble work."

"Men will confuse blood and nobility. I have heard those arguments. I recited them in other days. 'No truer glory has man than this / That for his king his blood has spilled / And the blood of his king's enemies / And in his enemy's rivers of crimson he has thrilled.' Men cannot help what they are, Mrs. Barton. We must not fault them."

The wise lady scattered powders and rubbed herbs against the casements, threshold, and wardrobe, tied threads of different colors to the bedposts. She instructed Constance to maintain and refresh these preparations and to recite certain incantations of protection and expulsion. She examined each garment in Angelica's wardrobe, setting some aside for closer treatment.

"I wish I could return to life before I had seen all of this."

"But do you not long to be the hero of an adventure, Mrs. Barton?" The question was extraordinary, and Constance hardly knew what to say, began even to laugh. "Have I amused you? Excellent. From our earliest girlhoods, we are taught to look to others to secure our happiness and to define our duty. But even the smallest boy knows that *he* is the master of his own destiny and that he may rely on none but himself and nothing but his own heart and wit to be the hero of a grand adventure. Do you not wish this for yourself, Mrs. Barton?"

"And put my Angelica at risk? Certainly not."

"She is already at risk, through no fault of your own. Your adventure has begun despite your inclinations."

"No fault of my own? I wish I could pardon myself with equal certainty."

Mrs. Montague clasped her hands around Constance's and leaned close enough that Constance could see the disparate colors of her face, which, at a distance, combined to produce the impression of a single hue. "Mrs. Barton, of this I am quite certain. You are innocent because you cannot by nature be anything else, and if you allow yourself to doubt it now, of all times, you will be placing yourself and your child at even greater risk. Promise me you will follow my instructions, rely on my experience, and above all, have faith in your pure innocence. I ask, further, until we have learned more, that you do not reveal your fears or my counsel to Mr. Barton. Allow him to believe all is well, that you have noticed nothing. As we learn more, we may well find he should be in our confidence, but until then, we must act with circumspection."

Constance's education demanded the entire morning. After the treatment of the rooms, Mrs. Montague guided her client through methods of containing manifestations through words, gestures, subtleties even of the kitchen stove to be shared with Nora, detailed advice on how to evade any risk of serving as a conduit to the ectoplasm. Throughout this introduction to what Anne termed "women's science," Constance felt her strength grow, not simply from the amassing of knowledge, but from Anne's conversation and care.

However, the remedies would not necessarily be immediately and completely effective. As the progression of disturbances had become more severe each night, Constance should brace herself for worse that very evening and worse still to come. "I do not mean to alarm you, my child," Mrs. Montague said as they sat again in the parlor, Constance's new tasks and recipes dancing in her head, "but the waxing of the moon can affect such horrors. Both its proven influence on ghostly activity and the sway it holds over the behavior of men of a certain constitution. If your Italian husband is such a man—your descriptions leave little doubt—then we may expect his internal fires to burn more brightly as heavenly Diana swells. Do you, by and by, know her story? It is not inapt, given your sufferings, so if I may steal a moment more of your time . . ." Constance took pleasure in the modesty of the request and was touched that Mrs. Montague might think she would prefer to be with anyone else. She called Nora to bring them dinner in the parlor and keep Angelica at her side in the kitchen.

"Diana, goddess of the moon and the hunt, disdainful of the perpetual, dreary discord among the male gods, scorned them and descended to earth to cavort with her ladies-in-waiting, her loyal and lovely nymphs, to gather their counsel and take comfort from their soft, unargumentative company, to bathe together under the cool wash of her attendant moon, secluded, she and her ladies, within branch-woven groves obediently risen from the soil to shield them from eyes that would be scorched by the sight of their recreations. But some men will not accept the protections we offer them and will instead probe, against their better interests, until they have squirmed themselves into mortal risk. So it came to pass here. A hunter, Actaeon, a slaughterer of animals and a destroyer of peace, penetrated these tender barriers and inserted himself where he was not welcome. He spied what he ought not have: the alabaster skin so slightly silvered by Luna's expansive gestures, the plash of cinnamon water scooped by small hands and sluiced with sweet laughter over gleaming strands of blackest hair, smoothed and cleansed by patient gentle fingers. Did he gasp or cough? Did this brute hunter bumble on hands and knees, scraping through dry brush and crackling twig to advance or retreat?

However he alerted them, the puny intrusion left them unimpressed. They did not dash to garb themselves. No, they only all at once fell grass-silent, disappointed and annoyed, then clucked, first in pity at him and all like him, then in louder protest, and Diana, monarch of this idyll, turned her head slowly to scowl at the panting vandal. He fumbled for his weapon! He would have slashed at all this beauty! Instead he felt his head burn as if his very hair were the fires of hell, and moon-blackened blood poured down his brow and blinded him. And the sound! The sound, most horrible of all: the moist crunch of those stag's antlers sprouting through his skull and flesh, quick as a serpent gliding through the damp leaves of a forest floor. He would have wiped away the flowing blood that clotted his thickening eyelashes, but as he raised his hands, his fingers fused into useless hooves. The last human cry he was able to push through his closing throat was for his men and dogs to rescue him. He stumbled out the way he had come, pushing his long, slender forelimbs through the spines and snap of the pleached woods only to find his snarling, spittle-muzzled hounds awaiting the master whose voice they had only just heard, a master who must have flushed for their execution this magnificent, meaty, weeping stag thundering towards them through breaking branch and falling grass, hot blood coursing beneath its soft, earth-brown hide. The dogs leapt upon their prize, drilled and tore with their curved white and black teeth, recognized no scent but the intoxicating musk Diana had injected into the warm night.

"And from the grove, the gentle laughter resumed, the soft fall of water, the pool smoothed again to calm, opaque black, a perfect, unrippled restoration."

Considering her girth, Anne Montague showed a surprising lightness on her feet, rising to enact Diana's petulant offhand flick of her magic, and even dropping to the floor to reproduce Actaeon's haunch-swinging backwards crawl of panic. Constance spoke over her own loud applause, "I should think you could grace any stage in London! You are far more wonderful than anything I have ever seen at the Pantomimes."

"You are very kind. I did, in another time, almost another life, it feels now, make my way upon the stage. But the hour! I must take my leave, dear."

"Must you? I feel such a lifting of my burdens in your company."

"Courage, my dear Constance. May I call you Constance? While you face the night bravely here, I will be at work on your behalf, studying and preparing. With time we shall scrub away your troubles. See to your protections, and all will be well."

With an appointment to meet in subtlety the following day, Anne Montague was gone, and Constance stood with her cheek to the drapery and watched from the window until a cab had carried her guest from view. Constance had so long suffered without the pleasant decompression of sympathetic conversation, and her home was now terribly bare after Anne's departure. She worried that the house had seemed unwelcoming and inhumane to that wondrous woman. For every curtain and carpet, every hanging and armoire, still Constance felt as if she had done nothing but arrange a few sticks inside a vast hall. She had tried to make the house mirror herself, but it would only ever be a mirror of its master, though she might tinker.

Now she worked diligently to prepare the house according to Mrs. Montague's instructions instead. She sprinkled salt at Angelica's threshold, at the front of the house, on the windowsills, and told Nora not to sweep it clear. She instructed Nora how to prepare suppers and breakfasts according to new knowledge. She told her what drinks to serve, in what quantities and combinations, told her to cut up old rags precisely to the size of all the looking glasses in the house. Nora's tasks now included covering them each night (after Mr. Barton had retired) and uncovering them every morning (before he descended). Other, more intimate prescriptions Constance would apply herself to Angelica's person and her own. The activity, the decisive progress against her troubles brought her a generous measure of relief, perhaps even joy, and now she craved Angelica's company. She carried the girl to the piano, and Constance's relaxed facility at the keyboard lifted upon its smooth wings Angelica's fledgling fumblings.

XVII

The child is named Angelica? Not Angela? Intriguing, to use the Italian," Mrs. Montague had noted in the first minutes of their meeting. For so long the child's naming had pleased Constance, as evidence of Joseph's husbandly love and forgiving nature. But now, in the harsh light of the past week and Anne Montague's fresh examination, the history suggested something else.

Constance had awoken on that vicious, miraculous morning of Angelica's birth, the tenth or hundredth time, with the sensation of emerging through thick warm fluid, her senseless dreams indistinguishable from what she saw when conscious. At last, she knew she was truly awake, for a new strand of silver encircled her neck. A locket nestled against her throat, though she could not pry it open with her shaking fingers and broken nails. "Where is my child? Is it dead?" she asked the empty room, and the empty room replied, "No, no, quiet, dear, quiet." The midwife, banished by Willette and Joseph hours before, was then at her side, taking the room's voice into herself as her own. "Shall I bring you your Angelica?" Was it neither son nor daughter then, but some monstrous third thing? The midwife returned and laid upon Constance's rattling, damp chest a wrinkled oddity. Constance could not recognize what it was meant to be, never having been presented with a live newborn before. "Is she not a gift from God?" asked the midwife. "Angelica. God's small messenger, that means." And all at once the creature was just that, a small angel, her daughter. "How do we know her name?" Constance asked foolishly. "Sir told us it, while you slept." He had named the child when, said the midwife, they were all praying for Constance's recovery. "But you're a sturdy one, you are. Sir said so, and now we all seen it. You bled a good bit, you did, but you'll be fine as milk soon enough. And your Angelica, too." Such a beautiful name, his gift to her, Italian like him. The name helped her love the creature at her breast as her child. Her love crossed over the name to reach the child. Had the midwife placed the distorted, sickly animal nameless as well as naked upon her, she fancied she might not have loved it at all.

They had never discussed names, while she was carrying, not once. The thought of its likely death had been so strong in her mind, and probably in his, too, that names seemed an unlucky topic. The prospect of half-baptizing another dead or nearly dead child was more than she could bear, though when she allowed herself to float, untethered, into sweet currents, she always presented him with Alfred George Joseph Barton. She awoke from her imaginings with a live child, a messenger of God, the loveliest gift from Joseph and God both.

But now. This name, this Italian name, this name he produced with no explanation then stuck upon the child while Constance lay unconscious, nearly dead. A memory of someone from another life? An earlier wife? As Constance would someday be an earlier wife. And a younger child would bear Constance's name. Ever younger wives and children in alternation.

"Where is my she-messenger?" he lately asked upon entering the house, a lightly tossed bit of blasphemy and a revelation that upon returning home he now sought the company of the child before that of his lawful wife. The child he had detested he now pursued. The wife he had once loved he now ignored. "They do not love as we do," Anne Montague had said today. "They do not love their wives as we would."

Anne's voice persisted in Constance, even these many hours later, and she faced the approaching night unalone, for, whatever the danger, she had in her ear Anne Montague's wisdom. When Joseph sat, brooding and silent at his supper, she could at least be certain that his wineglass was filled and that Nora was serving him more of the food prepared to Anne's specifications, with the correct proportion of "restraintive agents" and "integrative agents." When he asked how she passed her day, she easily produced an imagined itinerary to account for her hours spent in Anne's company, and she credited her adviser with guiding her tongue. He spoke, and she saw him through her friend's eyes.

Anne's influence in the household extended in other directions. Joseph climbed the stairs heavily and entered Angelica's room, only to exit a moment later with the words "She is already asleep" before sleepily trudging up to bed. But Constance found the girl wide awake. "I fooled him!" the child whispered, alert that something emanated from her father which she must resist at night.

Constance felt her guardian's protection lowering itself around her even here, as Joseph did not return.

She slept with the girl until just before dawn, then crept into her own bed scant minutes before Joseph awoke. She pretended to awake with him, and he kissed her. "This is fine, fine," he said, and did not grumble when she took Angelica to their secret engagement at the park, leaving him behind.

"The beloved Angelica," Anne said, rising to accept the tiny curtsey and watch the girl skip off into the square of green spread before the bench ringed by a semicircle of oaks. "She is true to her name." Sheltered from the morning sun by tree and parasol, they watched Angelica perform, mimicking others. She hopped with an idiotic expression like a passing boy, then promenaded behind a pair of great ladies after they had ignored her with simultaneous formality. She traveled in and out of Constance and Anne's view, near and far, between trees and topiary and the open green where other children played. "She is wonderful. A burst of life, a wood sprite."

Constance reported on her night, passed with neither conjugal ingress nor, as a result, any manifest transmission to the child.

"I am relieved beyond reckoning, especially after meeting your treasure," Anne said. "It is unbearable to think of harm befalling her."

"Might the danger be past? Might I continue to follow your good advice and—I would certainly pay your fee for all you have done—Joseph will relent, perhaps not send Angelica away? I might perhaps even escape the fate with which the doctors threatened me. I find myself courageous in daylight. The nights are far away and nothing I cannot defeat," she ventured. Darkness crossed Anne's face.

"Certainly. We must be pleased, of course, at last night's respite, but there is much we do not know, and much I have not yet told you. It may be that before our toil is complete, we shall need to cleanse your home of certain . . . previous infestations." The evening's victory might have been only a fortunate coincidence, Anne said apologetically. It was far too soon to congratulate their ingenuity, though she wished as keenly as Constance for a lasting triumph. "Four years old, you say?" Anne mused, as Angelica walked backwards across their field of vision. "That may be not insignificant, as we search for the source of your disturbance. I spent yesterday on your behalf engaged in various researches, refreshed my memory of the horror of the Burnhams. May I?"

"Please do," Constance replied softly, her eyes on her oblivious child.

"The Burnham family lived in your house prior to your husband. Mr. Barton's father may have purchased the home from Mrs. Burnham because, as you will soon understand, it would have been readily available, and it is possible—and more shame to the people of the district—that the only willing buyer of such a home would have been an uninformed foreigner. Either way, the facts are known: the Burnham girl, a child of *four*, was, beginning the very morning of her fourth birthday, so shaken by fits that her parents were forced to summon doctors, and upon their ineffectiveness, the vicar, then even a papist who promised to squeeze Satan from the child with his bare hands. These various consultations all foundered, and every few days, the child fell victim to worse and worse accesses of rage with no discernible cause. In these bursts of fury, she would recognize no one, heed no one, abide no boundary. Soon, the child was harming herself, cutting herself with any sharp object in reach, and it required several adults to restrain her. Later, she would rise from dead sleep, enraged, storm into her parents' room, and assault them in their bed. Understandably, the Burnhams began locking the girl in her room at night and barring their own door. Against their own child, their own sweet little girl."

A carpet of fast cloud unrolled across the sun, and its shadow sped over the green grass, overtaking Angelica, who was playing with another girl's hoop and stick, batting at it ineffectually. The children held hands in easy friendship.

"They loved their child, of course, but were helpless, and soon their home was thick with despair. The servants refused to sleep in the house—not so courageous as your plucky Nora—and after the girl had flung boiling water at a Scottish valet, the family found itself quite without allies. Mrs. Burnham was nearly mad with sorrow and extra household labor. She had no one to turn to, as the entire district had convicted them as the progenitors and keepers of 'the wicked girl of Hixton Street.' Then, one evening, the girl went, to her mother's keen surprise, sweetly and readily to bed. Mrs. Burnham regretfully locked the child's door nevertheless and then rose to her own room—the room you sleep in—to find her husband hanging from the beams of the ceiling. Are they covered now?"

"Yes." Constance's voice was scarcely audible.

"She took the letter he had left her, locked the door behind her, and descended, in terror and delirium. She sent a neighbor to fetch the beadle, and then, waiting all a-tremble, read the cowardly man's farewell, and she learned the cause of both his death and her child's torments these long months. She learned by his own written admission that Mr. Burnham had, years before he had known Mrs. Burnham, done something to a child. Something unspeakable."

"I do not understand your meaning, Mrs. Montague."

"Neither did Mrs. Burnham understand the hateful letter. He had done something unspeakable, the details of which were evidently unwritable as well. An act—he maintained, even at the moment of his terminal confession—that he had not wished to perform, which is not to say it had been an accident, or surely he would have written so. No, only something unspeakable *he had not wished to do.* The result, however, had been the death of that child so many years before, a death he had hidden, a horror known only to him, pricking his conscience for years, until, after a decade of decreasing dread, he imagined his guilt repaid, and he would now be left in peace by the memory of his crime. He married Mrs. Burnham. They were blessed with a girl of their own. He was free of his burden until the day when his daughter reached the very age of the unfortunate girl from his past. And that very day, her fourth birthday, the daughter's vicious tantrums began. Mr. Burnham apologized to his wife: these attacks, he wrote, flared not from their daughter's natural inclinations. Rather she suffered torments as the plaything of the slaughtered girl's spirit, only to punish Mr. Burnham. Mr. Burnham's vengeful victim controlled their daughter's limbs and mad moods. He hoped with his self-eradication to end the pain of his wife and child alike. May God have mercy on his soul."

These events had occurred in Constance's home, a corpse hanging above her own marriage bed. "What had he done? Surely you know."

"I can speculate, but speculation will never bring me closer to the truth. Do you see? It is essential, my dear. Men, as a race, are capable of actions and thoughts that women are not. That is any nation's strength. That is how nations are built and great works produced. But this simple truth often begets tragedy. Let us simply agree that there exist in the hearts of men such urges and capabilities as the female will never grasp, never perform, never—and this is our blessing and our curse, Constance, as women—never even *conceive.* We are simply, constitutionally incapable of thinking these thoughts. When Mr. Burnham wrote that he did something *unspeakable,* it is to us as women quite literally *unthinkable,* too. Oh, dearest, you need not shake at this. Calm yourself.

I do not for a moment imply that we are without defenses, only that we must rely on our intuition, rather than on plots or dark intrigues. Perhaps it is no wonder that horror is again taking root in a home that has seen such unfortunate evil and never been cleansed of its spectral residue. We know nothing yet. Last night's respite may mean we are on the correct path, or it may mean nothing at all. We have only just begun! Come, give me your hand. Take hold of yourself. You do not wish to alarm our Angelica there. She sees you. Wave and smile at her! She captivates, the miniature of her kind and lovely mother."

Anne, too, was a kind and lovely mother. Each time Constance pleaded, "What is to be done?," there sat Anne, smiling and calm. It amazed Constance that Anne was childless, for she was the very essence of *maternal*. She breathed wisdom and forgiveness, explained and excused at once, just as Joseph, inversely, muddied and cast blame. When Constance said, "It has been immensely painful to Joseph that I cannot perform all the functions of a wife," Anne snorted with laughter.

" 'The functions of a wife'! You were denied a mother on this critical point, so please allow me to pay you the honor, my sweet. First, the sole purpose of all those unbecoming instincts, as even men of science like your fellow must acknowledge, is for the creation of children. In this role, you have proven yourself more dedicated than the queen's fiercest soldier or any damp and stumbling pugilist your husband too warmly admires. You have given him, with nearly fatal consequences, a beautiful girl, whom any childless woman would envy as I do, and, by your own description, you have entered thrice more into a condition proving your willingness to abide by the laws of wifely behavior, and you may be in such a perilous state even now. You have even done so when medical men—with more credentials and wisdom than your husband—have instructed that such behavior bore likely mortal risk. And yet he was all too hungrily content to permit you to endanger yourself. Second, you do bear a responsibility to your husband, but it is *not*—as he would have you believe in his panting lectures to you on 'the functions of a wife'—to respond to his every hourly whim like some poor slave girl in a sheik's harem. No, despite his stated wishes and for his better interest, your *function* is to civilize and cool him. We ask our women to marry a man of fiery youth and then as soon as possible help him extinguish those urges so that he may comfortably become a dignified man of middle age. Husbands are not meant to burn like youths or defile their surroundings with their bottomless thirsts, each vile satisfaction stoking a renewed appetite for satisfactions, ad infinitum. No, we mean for our men to unleash, with haste and as much modesty and shame as they can muster, those inclinations—a few times—for the multiplication of our race, and then tame them, never to feel them again. Else, no society could function. All those boiling males bumping each other, brawling, murdering? His science knows this: for any man, even a married man in conspiracy with his wife, an excessive depletion of seminal liquor is typically fatal. Really, to have you submitted to that French canard that a wife's function is to serve as a husband's regularly submissive victim upon whom he may commit the savagery as often as his boiling blood demands it—it shocks one that such tales are still foisted upon the unknowing in this day."

She had made Constance laugh yet again, the hundredth time in two days, after two hundred days without laughter. Feeling freer than she had felt in so very long a time, she noticed that the girl with whom Angelica had just been whispering was now lying alone upon the grass, kicking her legs in the air. A governess soon appeared to scold her and replace her upon her feet. "The girl at this tender, blossoming age," Anne was saying as Constance craned her neck to search for Angelica behind them, "is by nature nearly complete in her perceptions and intuitions, but unable yet to formulate in plain words all her wisdom. We silence her at our own peril." Angelica had quite disappeared. Constance rose, shielding her eyes from the sun's glare. She called quietly, hesitating to disturb the park or irritate her child likely nearby, but then she shouted in increasing alarm as she received no reply. Anne, too, rose in concern.

Anne called out loudly, and at once—her voice maternally magnetic—Angelica was flushed from the wood to their left and, holding high her skirts, ran to them. "The flying man was in the forest! He chased me!" Through her short breath, she laughed triumphantly. "But he got stuck in the tree branches! Now he shall leave us in peace."

"You must never tell lies, child," said Constance, holding the girl.

"Quite so," Anne interrupted, "but you must never fear telling the truth." She lifted Angelica and placed her on the green metal bench between them. "Now, dear, sit with us, please, and let us discuss this as three ladies. What do *you* think we should do to keep the flying man out of your house?"

"Will you protect Mamma and me?"

"I will indeed."

"I do not like when Mamma is frightened."

"I do not suppose you do. But now it is a lovely, hot Sunday. We are in the shade of this park, just us three ladies. We shall solve this problem together. What suggestions can you offer me in my task?"

Constance watched Angelica concentrate all of her powers of thought, rise to the challenge set to her. Anne drew forth from the child the finest aspects of personality, shaped her into a woman with a simple request for help, and Constance admired them both. "It is best," Angelica said seriously, "when Mamma sleeps in the blue chair. That keeps him outside or hiding away."

XVIII

The moon thickened, its swelling nearly complete, and here and there threads of cloud drew faces across its surface, scowls turned slightly away, significant glances withheld in shadows.

Sunday supper began early and finished late, Nora's extra labor well worth the effort and expense. As they sat upon the edge of the bed, Joseph reached for Constance tenderly, and she, as Anne had taught her, smiled warmly, took his hand, lifted his legs up and onto the bed, adjusted his pillow, kissed his brow, stroked his face, waited—not long—for sleep to take him. "It is difficult to resist," he murmured at the end. Anne was protecting her. Somewhere in London, she was seeing to Constance's safety, or simply going about her evening. The thought of it must have pleased Constance.

She lay beside him, atop the bedsheets. She would rest before going down to her blue chair. An evening's peace, the second in a row, seemed likely, but there, above her, starkly white in the window-borne moonlight, loomed the ceiling, and behind its blandly posed smooth surface hid the beam from which had dangled the broken form of Mr. Burnham. This evening's victory had been won under his pendulum shadow.

Mr. Burnham had invited evil into this house, where now flourished another wraith, fetch, spectre, manifestation. If this phantom acted out Joseph's most hidden desires, desires so shrouded in manners and gentility that he himself did not recognize them, what then *was* he? He desired Angelica as his bride and would replace Constance with her? He had said Angelica resembled a younger, healthier, happier Constance. What then would become of the superseded bride? No role remained for the enemy, for Constance must become precisely that in such a scheme. The enemy must be dispatched, of course: the black, the Frog, the Irishman—that was what men did. They identified their enemy (from signs and emanations no woman could intuit), and they dispatched it. These two easy nights marked, perhaps, only Joseph's patient triumph. He could stand aside and allow events to proceed, while keeping the female calm and stupid. Three, four nights ago now, she had made her fatal error, so why should he not yield to the walking dead woman who, for a short time still, would roam amongst the living, plumper and fainter every day, until with a scream and a gush she would pass entirely from the stage?

She felt she had failed as a wife, whose duty was to cool a husband's appetites. She had not led him to calm, and now she was paying for her tardiness, her pride in her beauty's power over him, her own lusts. The food and drink, the salt and herbs, would not suffice forever. They offered only temporary security, a wall of paper painted to resemble brick. A pyramid of bricks in a yard, awaiting laborers. Laborers stinking of whiskey. A grozing iron. A doctor saying "Dropsy" and a little girl laughing at the sound—

She woke. The room was lit nearly to daylight by the moon. She was alone; Joseph had vanished in the blue light. She must descend at once, at once. She closed her eyes and heard in her tugging semisleep the muffled beating of the wardrobe warping and popping. Then, in a dream, she pressed the side of her face hard against its vibrating doors, her nose bent against the rattling wood. Again and again she flew through the air, threw herself against the wardrobe until her face bruised and its wood cracked.

She awoke again, fully, a quarter past three, the moon melted away, but still she heard that thumping from downstairs. Joseph had returned, if he had ever truly left, and he slept deeply despite the pounding noise. She stood, her eyes hot and her legs uncertain. Her steps were too loud on the stairs. She fell against Angelica's door and flung it open. The wardrobe was agape, Angelica's clothing vomited forth from the shelves and rods. Her small dressing table was askew; the items on it had been shifted into grotesque patterns, and the Princess Elizabeth was splayed on the ground. Angelica slept, but her body was twisted precisely to match the doll's. The wardrobe glowed blue, then faded.

So. Even if Joseph did not touch Constance, still her dreams placed the child at risk. She had released this horror, and it no longer required her unwilling consent to roam.

She set everything to rights in the darkness: the doll, the table, the brushes, the clothing in the battered wardrobe. She sat on the floor, saw the room and its infinite menace from Angelica's low point of view.

She fell asleep there, on the floor at the foot of her child's bed, and awoke at the sound of rustling above her. She rose to her feet in time to see Angelica's eyes fluttering open. She carried the girl downstairs, only to witness Joseph's angry departure for his day and night away on laboratory affairs, dispatched by his employers to York. "You are now free in my absence to clean the child's room by moonlight, Mrs. Barton," he said in parting.

"I love Papa," Angelica declared soon after, over her milk.

"Yes, my darling. And he loves you as well, I do not doubt."

"He does. And so we shall marry someday."

"Will you?"

"I do not love you," Angelica continued brightly, untroubled. "I am *fond* of you, Mamma, but love is what a man feels for his wives, and a wife for men." Angelica accepted her mother's gentle corrective explanations with keen interest, perhaps some doubt, and concluded by refining her views: "Very well, then, I love you as well, but only as a child ought to love its mother."

"Who has taught you to speak like this?"

"Must I keep *that* a secret as well?"

"As well as what, Angelica? What secret are you keeping from me?"

Angelica laughed wildly, her mouth open and spittled. "It's a *secret!*"

XIX

With Joseph in York, Anne arrived that evening for their work together, but Constance surprised her by turning her round only a moment after she entered: "Gather your wrap again or we shall be late. First we amuse ourselves, and *then* we shall face our dangers." With Angelica in Nora's care, she led Anne to the theater where she had taken a box that afternoon. A week earlier she would never have dreamt of attending a play with a friend, without Joseph, without even telling him. But now the very word *theater* carried new meaning.

She chose a theater Anne had mentioned in passing as one where she had once performed, and her friend was clearly touched by the gift. But the spectacle was rather ridiculous. It opened with a ghost, a player painted a ludicrous white with black rings about his eyes, a most unalarming spirit, though his living son threw himself to the ground in a frenzy. "Did the performance please you?" Constance asked as they walked through the dark and the thinning crowds, certain she had selected a frivolous entertainment that had bored Anne.

"Kate Millais stomping about as Gertrude cannot please anyone. I wore that gown when she used to stomp about as Ophelia, and she is unchanged except fatter and louder, if possible. And you? Did it please you, dear friend?"

"I scarcely saw it. My mind was awhirl with thoughts of you. 'This was once Anne's home. Here are the lights that lit her comings and goings. Those are the high boxes from which it was most costly to watch our dear Anne perform.' Are you blushing? Very well, we shall discuss the play. Answer me this: the ghost is meant to be a friend bringing warnings, demanding vengeance. Does this strike you as true? Or is such a spirit more likely a deceiver?" They strolled, arms linked, alongside the park. Constance absentmindedly tapped the black spears of the fence, then said, "I am certain he is aware of what is afoot."

"You are not speaking of the play now. Patience," Anne counseled. "Resist condemning awhile longer."

Constance was disappointed not to be congratulated for her courage of conviction. "He means to replace me in her affections," she pressed.

"He said this?"

"I hear his influence in her words when she speaks."

"He is laying siege to your relations with the child?"

"He is making intrigues, as you said. I cannot peer in and understand his schemes, but something is queer. He speaks of educating her as a companion, and he savors this separation he has engineered. It begins only a week from today."

"Take heed of me a little longer: there is much we do not yet know. Tonight we observe and explore at our leisure."

"Well, then, I shall obey, but I have another surprise for you first," she said eagerly, only to be annoyed to find Angelica awaiting their return, awake.

The girl had resisted sleep and Nora's discipline and now stood, her feet bare, upon the sofa. "I don't like to be left alone," she said with swollen eyes, and Nora only shrugged in exasperation.

Before Constance could begin scolding, Anne replied lovingly to the girl, "Of course you don't," and lifted the uncomplaining child easily, carried her towards the stairs. The sight of them together dissolved Constance's irritation. "Your sweet mother will be up presently," Anne said. "But I have a secret to tell you first, and for this we must speak in your room."

Her enthusiasm restored, Constance turned to the dining room. She had instructed Nora closely over the menu, and had done the marketing herself, visiting the Miriams for tea and Villiers and Green for the wine. Twice that afternoon she had corrected Nora about the settings and experimented with the location of candles and lamps on various side tables. Now, with Anne abovestairs, she assured herself of Nora's work, resalted the soup, lit the candles, lowered the gas.

"She is quite asleep," Anne descended to report. "And she will keep my visit a secret." She stopped, stood in admiration of the table laid sumptuously for two. "Whatever is this vision? My dear, your kindness is boundless."

"Having you here, my friend, is a solace I feared I would never enjoy again." She took Anne's hand and led her to her place. "I am not alone, and I cannot say how long it has been since I have felt that."

They shared a gigot of lamb, a purée of turnip, a tart, and cheese from Ruhemann's, a meal of such luxury that Constance had made purchases on credit, a vice she had never before indulged. At the end, Nora served Joseph's port wine, and when Anne asked if he would not remark its depletion, Nora replied to their delight, "He never has before, madam."

Constance sipped the ruby syrup squeezed from sun-browned southern hills. "If the night should pass without incident, does that not prove his role?"

"Perhaps not. He may carry the evil in him against his will or without his knowledge. He may only be a necessary element to its appearance. You are too eager to locate and limit your adversary, while the truth is likely more complex."

Constance, rather to her own surprise, was vehement: "And *you* are too giving, Anne. I can no longer manufacture explanations to excuse him from what he has become, what he perhaps always was. He would corrupt her. His true nature is nearly always visible to me now. My vision has become more acute under your tutelage, or he is less able to shroud himself. When he does disguise himself and attempts to appear as he used always to do, it is grotesque, a monster dressing as a man. He loathes her for not being a son, loathes me for no longer being a girl. He would have her resemble him, engage in all the cruelty he dresses up in the name of science. He brought her to the park the other day to play with another child, the son of his friend Harry, who has made the most unacceptable conversation with me, and Angelica tells me the boy speaks of nothing but killing and mayhem."

"You are more angry than frightened now."

"He would make her into a boy, you see, to be a 'scientist' like him. And into his wife—he would make her his wife. To replace me." Constance blushed. "A boy and a wife? I am not making sense. That is what comes from port and trying to impress you with matters you understand better than I, my friend."

"But you do impress me. Every time we speak I am more impressed. You intuit knowledge I have acquired only with years of study."

On this occasion, wax candles in hand, Anne led Constance from room to room, touched the small cabinets Joseph kept padlocked in his dressing room, the spring-locked presses in the cellar. "He has never once opened them in my presence," Constance said. "When I ask what they contain, he refuses to reply."

"Well, then, here is something to hide from his prying eyes in return," Anne replied, presenting Constance with a box of scientific paraphernalia. She explained the herbs, crucifixes, sacred water, the use of lamp oil.

Constance sat watch over Angelica while Anne reexamined the house, read each room for signs of infection. An hour or more later, she returned and led Constance upstairs to her own bed. "I have cleansed your room, as a beginning. Now I shall take watch downstairs while you sleep. You are in terrible need of it, without question. I cannot imagine what rest you have had these past weeks." Constance accepted the kindness, allowed herself to be cajoled into bed like a child, her objections swept aside. The physical pleasure in simply closing her eyes astonished her.

She did not know how long she slept before Anne was urgently shaking her awake. "Open your eyes, my friend, and tell me now, quickly, did you dream? Now?"

"Not a flicker."

"Then we have a thorough acquittal! You are no bridge to this thing, for it has been, and not in response to your dreams. We have a game now, oh yes!"

"You saw it?" Constance sat up, alert. "What face did it wear?"

"I weakened it," the huntress excitedly reported.

"It retreated into the wardrobe? Blue light?"

"Precisely."

"And my angel?"

"Slept soundly throughout and does still. It could not penetrate our defenses, and I believe I gravely wounded it as it fled. The holy water sizzled its edges, and it gave off that stink. Ah, your heart should lift, my friend, for it is weakened, without question. We will conquer it soon."

"But is it Joseph's?"

"We have made progress. You must continue your labors, human and spiritual. Your safety depends upon it. Not only Angelica is at risk."

"But is it Joseph's?"

She followed Anne's speedy descent to the kitchen and prepared coffee by the faintest intimations of dawn. For all the talk of progress and conquest, so many obscurities lingered. Anne, too excited to sit, would speak only of work still ahead, dangers and tests. Constance had hoped that somehow everything would have been clarified and resolved by this long night's adventure, and yet now Anne drank her coffee, consulted the sky, and hurriedly said she must, for the best, depart before sunrise. "We are nearer a solution than ever, my dear friend. Proceed with caution, and I will continue my work. I mean to do nothing but see to solving your troubles." With a warm embrace, she charged away and left Constance standing alone.

"Bless you," Constance called after her, more polite than confident. She longed for Anne to dispense with the melodrama and ghost-story ambiguities, to put an end to it all there and then, or take her and Angelica away, as a reward for the theater, the stroll through the night, the meal, the trust, the payments.

XX

As Constance returned to the kitchen, the first sounds of Nora just audible beyond, nausea gripped her, and in countless other ways she heard her body sing of its changing condition. She retched, again and again, and collapsed, feverish and foul, against the walls of the closet.

Was ever murder disguised thus? How crafted by a demon mind to cloak hatred in love and dress death as birth! He had murdered her that night with her own sighing consent, with sweet caresses and whispered vows, and he could with most perfect alibi now recline in his ease and patiently play the loving husband, until he would simply change his mask and play the mourning husband, and no weapon would be found, and no inspector called to investigate.

He returned from York late in the evening, by his own description terribly fatigued and "strangely weakened." He turned down the light immediately upon entering the house and would not look directly at her. He said in a constricted voice that he wished to be left to himself, to sort his baggage and wash. He meant to retreat at once to bed. "But was your voyage a success?" she asked as he fled before her up the stairs. His replies were hurried, uncertain. He nearly ran from her into his dressing room, hiding his face.

The thought was seductive: Anne had "weakened" the spectre, and Joseph was retreating from her, claiming vague weakness. "What happened in York?" she asked through the closed door. "Will the doctors reward you?"

"Leave me in peace." His voice was peculiar.

Tonight she would press her advantage. She lay atop the bedsheets and watched him sleep. It was past one o'clock. She slept as well, dreamt of an aroma with will and a body. It pursued her, stifled her breath, pried at her closed fist. She awoke, and the seeds of that dream were revealed: Joseph, wide awake, held her tightly by her upper arm and wrist, and her flesh burnt under his prying, twisting grasp. His mouth was upon her hand. He saw her open eyes and at once released her. "You were dreaming," he said and turned away. "Your thrashing awoke me."

When his wheezing again rasped the air, she descended. Tonight she would fight, if only to prove to Anne that she could. She discovered new strength. She could for the first time contain her fear, see its jagged boundaries from all sides, a monstrous but not quite unmanageable weight, around which she could throw her arms and lift. Her heart pounded, but it did not deafen her. "Action brings courage," Anne promised. "A simple trick men use all the time."

In the corridor she opened a small drawer in the walnut chest, and from under extra pillow dressing and frippery of no conceivable accidental interest to Joseph, she withdrew the box of Anne Montague's professional oddities. In her oil lamp's steadying light, the man on the paperboard box's lid resembled Joseph, when he was still bearded and himself. "The crucifix is too readily trusted," Anne had lectured in her confidential stage whisper. "It is frequently useless, but in your case unique circumstances may prevail. Your husband was born a papist. For such a man at the precipice of disintegration, the sight of it may cast the projected manifestation back into him." Constance draped one of the cheap tin crucifixes (forbidden in his irreligious domain) around her neck, and took the other to place around Angelica's. "The bouquet of rosemary and basilicum—the marriage of devotion and memory—is, I

confess, similarly uncertain. It has proven itself in countless cases a potent repellent, for memory itself can sicken a spirit contorted into evil.
One occasion, the smallest sprig of the stuff sufficed to dissolve a ghoul
into a fine malodorous ash, which we swept up—tittering like young
girls—and poured into the street where one dog and another and then
another promptly relieved itself upon the filthy remains." With stead-
ier hands Constance collected the damp bundle of leaves and needles.
"Your most potent weapon by far is simple prayer. A child's rote recitation will not serve but to provoke your adversary. You must feel every
word forged in a pure heart." Constance despaired: to make pure a
heart such as hers? When fear and anger filled her? "Fire—a simple, old
oil lamp's flame—is to the material of a spirit an impenetrable shield.
Thus protected, you will need a means of dispersal, to drive the force
from the child's bed, then from her bedroom, and finally from your
home. Holy water will work upon the infestation as lye upon a rat."
Constance lifted two blue glass vials. "This"—the blade with the bone-
white handle Anne had added to the box only at her departure—"I
would feel well knowing you have this, though I doubt you will have
any need of it."

She stood, and at once the air in the hall began to move, breezes assaulting her in layers and patterns, almost visible piping of rolling air
along the walls and at eye level. It meant to extinguish her lamp, to defeat her shielding fire from a distance. Blue light poured from under
Angelica's door.

She entered, raised high her flame, but found only Angelica asleep.
No blue or ghastly forms, only the tiny white foot exploring the edge of
the bedding. Angelica breathed steadily. She was untouched and safe.

Constance's relief was mingled with discomforts: an ache in her legs,
a pain in her jaw, and then she saw the glowing eyes peering from the
black corner beside the wardrobe and heard its whispered voice: *Girl.*
She flung a vial of holy water where the eyes had been. The phantom,
as fibers lined with short fine hairs, attempted to flow past her to Angelica's bed. Waving her crucifix, Constance placed herself in its path,
then pulled the chimney from her lamp. Kneeling, she opened the

lamp's font and dribbled a line of oil on the floor around the bed. She lit it and at once the beast recoiled, as Anne had promised, probing the perimeter of the fire, sniffing for a gap in the flickering defense.

Angelica had not woken. Constance, her hand complaining of some injury, stepped over the flame and laid the second crucifix on Angelica's chest, then turned back, holding the herbs and lamp before her. "Our father, our father, our father . . ."

The spectre was nowhere to be seen, neither the blue light nor the glowing eyes. The far window was open. She crossed to it and leaned out, but saw nothing between her and the next house. Behind her the erratic ring of flames sputtered on the wooden floor around the bed, and she was ashamed of how ineffectual her inspiration appeared now; the demon could breach it easily. She reached for Angelica's wardrobe, prepared to thrust the herbs at whatever emerged. She put her finger through the iron ring and in one motion threw open the door. Nothing.

"Mamma?" Angelica was sitting up. The feeble flame, pushed by the breeze from the open window, had sidled up and like a kitten rubbed itself against the bed's hanging muslin ruffle. Angelica stumbled to her feet atop her pillow as a few flames began to peer over the end of the bed. "Mamma!"

Constance swung the girl into her arms. "We frightened him off, my love."

Intending to smother the small fire, she set the child down next to the door, which at once flew open, revealing Joseph, enraged and wild-eyed, half-dressed, black blood streaming down his face from precisely the same spot where Constance's holy water had struck the demon-face only moments before. His jaw muscles beat like a heart, and Constance saw the fury in his shoulders and the pumping fists at his side. She looked at her own feet: stillness and unaccusing quiet might defuse the maddened anger at work under his tensed skin. Anne had taught her to behave just so when faced with a physical display such as this. With a curse he pushed Constance aside, lifted Angelica away and placed her at the far side of the room, where she at once began to shriek. He ig-

nored her and threw himself into the minor work of extinguishing the
failing fire, issuing military commands, making a display of his small
tasks.

By the time this martial performance was over, Angelica's cries had
grown more desperate. She howled and writhed and bled in her
mother's arms, for Joseph had set her down directly atop the broken
glass of the holy-water vial, scattered below the uncovered looking glass
by which the ghost had likely arrived and escaped.

Joseph meant to seize the bleeding child from Constance. "Surely
she needs her mother," Constance attempted, but he tore Angelica
from her arms and commanded Constance to light the gas, fetch water
and bandages. The glistening moon lit his face and bare torso unnaturally white and his blood glossy jet. "Do as you are told, damn you."
Her carefully marshaled courage fell away.

She had failed Angelica. She had not destroyed the spirit, only
driven it away, temporarily, and at a terrible cost, for if Joseph was now
proven to be her enemy (his face bloodied by the transmission working
in the opposite direction), then he was also likely aware of her knowledge. She hurried to cache her weapons back in the McMichael's Herring box, back in the drawer, under the camouflage of womanly linen.
She stuttered to herself trying to compose a lie that could distract his
notice, make commonplace the broken glass, shrieks, flaming bedsheets, scorched floorboards, and whatever Angelica might even then
be revealing in the interim.

She returned with the items he had demanded. Joseph had laid Angelica on the cleared bed, her nightclothes pushed far back from her
smooth leg. Her sobs alternated with laughter already, as he stamped
her tiny bloody footprints upon his naked chest and cheeks, his own
blood from his injured face mingling with his daughter's. "Wait for me
above. I shall tend your wound in due time," he said without looking
at his wife. "Shut the door."

She could not leave him alone with Angelica, so she sat on the bottom step. She had accomplished nothing. Some immeasurable time
passed, as she rehearsed her calibrated explanations, before he emerged,

leaving the room behind him dark and silent. "She has the idea that when she sleeps fire can leap from the floor and attack her," he said, a veneer of sarcasm coating the hard wood of his earlier ferocity. "Your turn for attention. Come." She heeled.

Upstairs by brighter light he washed himself, melted the girl's brown footprints from his torso and face. Only then did he examine Constance's cut hand. He handled it roughly, did not apologize for the water's sting. He practiced every day on mute beasts and treated her no differently. He squeezed her wrist until her skin blanched, and she wished to cry out. He offered her a drop of rum, but she shook her head, feigned a courage that had long since abandoned her. He bandaged the cuts she had accidentally inflicted upon herself with Anne Montague's small blade. "What is this?" He produced a shard of jagged, fluted blue glass. "It was in Angelica's foot."

The truth pricked her cheeks, sought to melt her lips. "Likely something of Nora's," she managed. "Careless cow."

"Why do you skulk through the shadows of my house in darkest night?"

"It was nothing, my love. I awoke for no reason, my old habit. I thought to peek at her asleep. I found the room a little close, so I meant to lift the sash. It stuck. I should have put the lamp down. I struggled with the window. At once it opened. I fell backwards a step, the lamp fell, and the chimney shattered. The font was loose, my hand lit upon the glass, cutting it, and in my pain I pushed it away, and that spread the oil on the floor. I was only just realizing the danger when, to our good fortune, you appeared."

Anne would have been impressed by her confident actress's demeanor. She recalled, before she had finished speaking, her other model for such performances: her own mother used to tell stories, too, to steal enough time for her children to hide themselves when Constance's father came home increased by gin. When had Joseph come so closely to resemble Giles Douglas? How long it had taken her to see it plain! It was testament to the potency of Joseph's surface charms that he could deflect her notice from such profound resonances. All men resemble each other, Anne said, not far beneath their masks, and in certain moments of revelation they cannot disguise themselves and all look alike: atop a woman or an enemy, when hatred or desire burns through restraint, when they kill or merely play at it in boxing rings and fencing salles.

"Your worry now causes me worry." He stood behind her. "I can scarcely recognize you of late." He sighed like a play-actor. "Where will this all end?" he demanded, his fingers moving on her shoulders. "You have imagined something. You have allowed yourself to be confused. There is nothing to fear."

He was no fool. She was no actress, nor even a crafty and resourceful mother. He knew all. He placed his hands on her cheeks, held her face, spoke false words to lull her into a child's or new bride's faith in him. He meant certainly to proceed to his southern pleasures, even as she and her daughter still bled, or because they still bled. "You are most understanding and forgiving," she said. "You are right. I have been like a woman in a cloud of late, and dropping that lamp—well, it should not surprise me if you forbid me from touching anything in the house. But you rescued us, bless you."

His lips glided across her brow. "You must be more careful," he whispered into her hair. "You and the girl are too precious."

"May I kiss her good night?" Joseph escorted her, two unfailing paces behind. He stood, hunched in the doorframe, and she kissed the child's eyelids, which fluttered like a kitten's. She whispered, "I saw the flying man, Mamma. He rode a pink and blue beast with terrible teeth."

"I sent him away, my great love," Constance replied, hidden from Joseph's view. "Sleep, sleep."

Her guard led Constance back to his bed, cradling her bandaged hand with excessive, ironic care, a threat of violence disguised as an act of tenderness, and the household's new roles were all terribly clear.

XXI

She awoke all at once to that voice whispering *Girl,* and her eyes met this newest spectacle of corruption: he sat at the far end of the room, already dressed, cheek shaven clean again, hair sleek, plaster on his cut face, and Angelica upon his lap, her mismatched feet emerging from under her nightdress, a parody of a painted mother and child. They snickered at her blinking confusion. She had slept too terribly late, had to reach Nora before he did. "Have you been below? Does Nora have breakfast prepared? You should have woken me. Angelica, come down with me and let your papa alone."

"No," he replied with an icy smile. "I am susceptible to Angelica's charms at the moment." She heard his insinuating voice as she fled to the kitchen, her blood thrumming the side of her neck: "Your mother, Angelica, you see, is . . ."

"Your hand, madam," Nora began, but Constance stopped her with urgent instructions, begged the Irish girl to feign joy at the blue bottle's discovery, sorrow at its destruction, shame at having caused sir any trouble and having hurt the girl. "I can't, madam," Nora hesitated, but Joseph was already descending the stairs carrying Angelica's laughter.

"Rickeliss!" Angelica exclaimed. "Quite ribicaliss!"

Nora kissed Angelica as Joseph looked on, unreadable. "Your mother told me. Are you hurt, girl?"

"No!" said Angelica. "But a pink tiger bit my toes!"

"Angelica, that will do," Constance said. "Nora, she injured herself on something of yours."

"Madam?"

"You shall attend to your work more carefully, if you value it."

"Yes, madam."

"Nora." Joseph spoke slowly, triumphantly. "Your mistress is not well. She needs her rest. You shall provide her peace and solitude today. No visitors, if you please, and keep Angelica well occupied so she does not trouble her mother. Am I clearly understood?"

"Yes, sir."

"I expect my instructions to be followed precisely."

"Of course, sir," the servant replied with downcast eyes.

He rose. "Come, give us a kiss, Angelica," he said, a new manner of morning departure. All had shifted. The child placed her small wet lips against her father's cheek. The corners of their mouths touched. "Good-bye, Constance." He left, and neither child nor maid would meet her eye.

"Nora," she began, "we are not to take him too literally. He is over-solicitous of—"

"Madam, I would never contradict Mr. Barton's commands. I know you wouldn't want me disobedient."

"What are you saying?"

"I can't be a trouble to him, madam. And you, too, you should—"

"I should what, you wretch? You would advise me in my troubles? You?"

"Please, madam, I should be at my work, and you should sleep, rest, as sir advised. I'll bring something to help. Angelica, run and play piano like your mother would wish." Would? Was she not standing before them?

Her imprisonment was enforced by Nora and accompanied by Angelica's strangely skilled piano playing. She retreated upstairs to consider, but was met by Nora and a glass of water with a bright, flocculent cloud at its center. "Please, madam, this will calm your nerves, as sir requested."

"Am I permitted out of my home, dearest Nora?"

"Sir was plain, madam, about your need for peace and rest today."

"Can you fetch Mrs. Montague for me?"

"Please don't ask me to do what I can't."

"I could do your work while you brought her. He need never know."

"Please, madam."

"I see. You may go, Nora."

She poured Joseph's silver opiate away. She turned the pages of the book at her bedside, but saw no words. She closed her eyes but did not sleep, below Mr. Burnham's shadow. Her door was not locked against her, but she did not open it. She listened for Anne, but no bell rang. Late in the afternoon the door opened quietly, and Angelica pushed the bed's hangings to one side and climbed up next to her mother. "Mamma, I want to go to the park."

"I cannot today, my goose."

"Will you not tell him you are sorry?"

"Whom? Your father?"

"Say sorry!" Angelica was angry. "I want to go to the park, not to school!"

Later he appeared in the doorway. "Are you feeling better, my love?" he asked brightly. She stood with her back to the window, as far as she could retreat from him. "Quite what you wanted, a little rest for the day."

"Yes, prison is delightfully restful."

His face darkened. "I see."

"I am not such a fool as you think me," she said.

"I have never until now taken you for a fool."

"I may die, but I will not allow harm to come to Angelica even so."

"You are being childish."

"I could imagine nothing worse than being a child in this house."

"What are you saying?"

"I *saw* you," she hissed. "You."

"And precisely what did you see?" he sneered.

"I will not permit it. I will not sit idly by, will not abandon her. My end is decided, but hers is not. Do you hear me?"

"Excellently, as you are screaming. A day's rest and you are only more disordered than I left you." He stepped towards her, and she grasped the sill behind her. "Come. Sup. You are likely bored after your convalescence. We shall take some air together."

They ate in silence. Nora brought Angelica from the nursery to wish her parents good night. "Don't worry, Mamma," Angelica said over Nora's shoulder as she was carried off. "Papa has made everything safe now. He is very clever!"

Joseph indulged Constance's requests with magisterial nods. She was permitted outdoors in his company. She was allowed to look upon her own sleeping child while he watched. She was allowed to undress and wash herself under his inflamed eye. She was permitted to lie in her bed, to drink a little water with a powder he administered. She was allowed to cry briefly and quietly before he ruled, "Enough now." She was allowed to close her eyes when he kissed her lips and when he promised that all would be well again. She was allowed to know that he ached to seize her. And when, quite precisely the moment he pressed his hands upon her, Angelica cried out for her mother most pitifully, once, twice, again still louder, Constance was forbidden in cool tones from investigating the "child's manipulations." She was allowed instead to feign sleep at his side and periodically to open one eye only to see by the intruding full moon that he wordlessly watched her without cease. At last she was allowed, without his interference, to dream of whatever happiness she could.

Quarter past three and the words *You are expected* roused her to silence and stillness. She peered through a screen of lashes: he slept. She wished she could simply trust, obey, close her eyes, somehow un-know what she knew, as her own mother had seemed never to know.

She opened the drawer in the walnut chest, but her apparatus was gone. So. In Angelica's room the beast waited for her, high in the shadows of the ceiling, for all the world a spider until its eyes betrayed it, and when it saw her recognition, it no longer hid but was all at once near Constance's face, breathing that golden aroma upon her in the overheated air.

Tonight, aware of her defeat at Joseph's hands, her enemy displayed its nature and urgings without restraint. Its noise was new, worse than laughter, wetter than breath. It did not flee to the wardrobe or slide through the gaps in the window, and when Constance stood her ground and held its awful gaze, its face ran through its repertoire of masks. It donned Joseph's attributes: the angle of his brows, the heaviness of the lids hanging over the outer corners of his eyes, though these burned yellow and red. The demon was floating above the ground—ragged and moist, lit an uncanny blue—and it sprouted Joseph's dense limbs, grew thick hair upon them.

It transformed for a moment into a fascinated butterfly and then a most hideous man and, as that man, with rough knuckles stroked her cheek, pressed his hand over her mouth, and it felt not like flesh but something hotter and harder. She knew that if she wept, her nose would fill, and breathing would become impossible, but its smell against her was yet more obscene than before. She would end by suffocating, the meaty edge of its hand pressing harder and higher against her nose, the whistling wind of her breath forcing its way through an ever narrowing gap. Its voice was in her ear—not a voice, less than a voice, a flow of breath, a braid of barbed oaths and tender avowals: "Who's a darling, darling girl?" It coiled around her waist.

It melted and reformed into Harry Delacorte, and, as Harry once had done, it looked her up and down, slowly and vulgarly. With a grimy caress it brushed her hair off her face. She squeezed herself to make a noise, but none emerged. It lifted her—this beast she had conjured—and dropped her in the blue chair. Its audience installed, it flew to its stage. It petted Angelica's hair, pulled loose strands away from her eyes, all the time looking only at Constance. It allowed Constance, butterfly-pinned to her seat, to hear its thoughts.

It pulled Angelica's bedding away. Her body was curled into a tight ball. Still asleep, she muttered, "I don't like being tickled, Papa." In reply it cast its face as Joseph's again, but with skin black as a native murderer gripping a child in blood-spattered fists. It lowered itself over Angelica, excruciating in its slow deliberation, until it floated horizontally above her by the narrowest of margins. Its long hair streamed behind it, and its mouth gaped. "No," Constance moaned, or thought she did, and its face slid closer to the child, leering, and it licked the girl's cheek. The devil melted into the form of Dr. Willette, who, after Angelica's birth, kept examining Constance long after she wished to be left in peace, spoke of the mortal risks of even the briefest conjugal contacts, insisted upon a course of pelvic manipulation and release. The beast became the doctor to the last detail, pulled its mustache, consoled too close, reenacted that censorious speech, but now to the little girl.

"And me?" Constance croaked. "Am I not to your liking?" In reply it left Angelica and slithered around and along Constance, spread itself over her, in front and behind, its fingertips moving over the back of her neck to the first down-covered ball of spine. "There now," she attempted a tone that might allure, a little girl's voice. "Surely I am your true heart." She caught sight of her face in the glass and felt at once an idiot, a parody of a woman of pleasure, a feeble and elderly parody— most of all—of the sleeping girl.

Yet it accepted her offerings, in exchange for the child.

She could not say for how long this assault raged. She did not resist, but wished she might die. When she knew that she would not die, the knowledge purified her despair. She commanded herself to keep silent, this could be no worse than any man's work upon her. But it was. The pain was more vicious and less local, and there was no approaching end, no promise of release, no warmth at all. Rather, the savagery accelerated with insistent and unending increase. Its words of love, their meanings inverted, came in the voices of Joseph and Harry and Pendleton, the doctors, merchants of the district, her own brothers, the men who spoke to her in the park despite her efforts to repel them.

The pain expanded, as if she were being impregnated with pain. She wept, and its dry tongue ran the length of her cheek, swallowed her tears as she had once been promised a lover would. "He'll drink away your tears and keep you forever safe," sang the ghoul in a low voice, mimicking the girls from the Refuge who had warmed themselves against that promised man. "A prince for you, Con," it sizzled. "Here I am, a prince for sweet Con, come at last." Its nails cut her skin, and she bled. It ran its fingers over her blood and licked them clean. "You're our girl, ain't you?" It wore a new face, though it was blurry, and that scent choked her. "You've the devil in you, don't you?"

And the irresistible thought came to her: Take Angelica instead—you may have her. But she did not speak, and it did not hear, and nothing ended until, high in the air, she was turned roughly, and she felt the spectre melt out of her, off her, away from her, and she dropped to the floor, her head striking the bed's runner. She opened her eyes with difficulty and found the room emptied of the evil. Blood ran from her lip, her eye was swelling, but Angelica lay still, curled tight, untouched.

She hoisted her sleeping child into her arms, carried her down the stairs, leaning against the wall whenever her legs trembled. She placed her on the parlor sofa and crossed through the kitchen, opened Nora's door, coughed her name in the darkness, but the servant did not move. She sat on Nora's bed and seized her shoulders, pleaded for Anne Montague's address, pleaded that Nora not reveal her destination to him. "Whatever's happened? Your face, madam!"

Nora's mistress with shaking fingers and hurried promises of repayment took Nora's money from Nora's purse. In the vestibule she saw herself in the glass, but would not clean away the blood or filth, for vanity, too, drew the demon. She stepped into the cold rain and rippling black pools of lamplight.

She ran awkwardly with the girl in her arms, then walked several quiet streets more, unable at this drunk and desperate hour to find a cab. At moments she thought the creature still attended her. She could feel its voice, insinuations still steaming in her ears, tongue against her neck. A man approached, and she nearly fell to her knees to beg his assistance. As he passed, the smell of the beast was lifted away into the mist. The evil could not exist in the sight of others—Anne had said so: "The eyes of crowds protect us. The weight of living eyes is too much for the dead to bear." Anne's voice, only Anne's.

She could not possibly walk much farther carrying the girl. Twice she thought she would drop her. She wished to drop her for her own escape, and she detested her cowardice. The rain stopped. She could not take another step. The rain had only paused for breath and now thrashed her in earnest.

A black horse drew a black hansom from the end of the black street and stopped in front of her. She was soaked, sobbing, shaking, unable to walk, her child awkwardly under her coat. The hooded cabman's black boots struck the black walk, and a black glove opened the door. She felt the cold and wet even more acutely when she sat sheltered against the seat's stiff, cracked black leather.

Delivered into more darkness and rain, she beat the iron thistle against the door and cried out Anne's name, and no one replied. She wished to awaken in Anne's arms. She feebly kicked the door and whimpered, until at last Anne, lamp in hand, appeared, took Angelica from her mother, led the way into a dark corridor and up and up, up six pair, the child in her unfailing arms the entire way, while behind her Constance moved slowly upon aching legs and blistered feet. Not a word was spoken until Angelica murmured on Anne's low bed from under a green knit blanket, "Animals are eating the princess. Her forces blew the wind away. The smells smell smelly." She opened her eyes in the new room, saw her mother and Anne by low light. "He wants to finish this business at once," she said and fell back again.

Anne slid shut the wooden screen that separated her bed from the tiny front room. She held a glass of sherry to Constance's lips. Despite her exhaustion, Constance could not stop moving, paced the room, threw herself down on the chair or sofa only to rise again in fevered recitation. "I am defeated. This adventure you—I am powerless. Tell me what to do. If I murder myself, will it end? It will be back, no matter how I yield to him. I will die from it. I am with child. Is this not a cause for joy in happy homes? It is my death sentence, and still the thing comes for Angelica. Am I not—is there nothing—will you not tell me?" She fell to her knees before her seated friend and lost the use of words, had only a coughing cry, a howl like a rising "no," and Anne, her own hands shaking, took Constance's head into her lap. "This must end," Constance choked out her one conviction. "This must end."

"Yes, my sweet friend, yes."

"I am beaten. He has beaten me. Let me stay here. We will live here with you, and he will never find us."

"I will end this. Quiet, my dear, I will end this. You will be free, and Angelica, too." Anne descended to her knees, kissed the top of the sobbing woman's head, kissed her wet hands, her slicked cheeks, held her tightly to her chest, rocked her until Constance let herself go down into sleep.

XXII

Constance awoke to her friend dabbing the blood from her swollen face. Above the local roofs, a single wandering fragment of day streaked the black sky.

"We have only a few minutes. A cab is waiting below," Anne said.

"Where are we going? No—you are not—please. How can you ask this?"

"You know you must. What else do you propose? Shall you become a stationer's girl again?"

"Stop."

"Constance, hear me. I promise you this will pass. You will be released. But if he wakes to find you have fled, do you think that will be the end?"

"Stop, please."

"The demon is not impressed by the distance from your home to this one. It will not be deterred by such contrivance. And the man? Do you imagine he will allow you to depart? To install yourselves elsewhere?"

"Please stop."

"Shall he have your pin money sent to your new apartments? Or do you prefer to report each morning to the mercer for your assignment of tambour-stitching paid by the penny?"

"Anne, I beg you. Do you require more money? I can find it for you." She would shame her friend if necessary.

"The devil take your money! If the solution were flight, do you not believe I would have suggested it long ago? Do you imagine I am not constantly considering your best interests?"

"Then what remains to me? Tell me, please, if I cannot flee with her. There is no law to keep her bound to me, only to bind me to him? I am alone."

"You are not."

"Can I not somehow surrender? Return to a time when I did not *know*?"

"When evil rends the protection God has extended over us, it is our duty to stitch it together. Women's work, stitching. Were you the only victim, it would still be a sin to drop your stitching, but you are not alone, are you?"

Constance asked without hope of an answer, "Will nothing end this?"

But Anne rescued her: "I will end this. Tonight. It is the last night of the full moon. You must return and play your part boldly. Draw your enemy close and douse it with holy water." Anne filled Constance's pockets with blue vials and another small blade. "Draw the ghoul to you, so that it has no escape. I will do my part elsewhere, but you will not be alone."

Her friend sat beside her as the cab pushed forward, dispersing the night as they drove through it. "I swear to end this for you. Do you trust me?"

"I do."

"And you do wish me to end it, no matter the cost?"

"I do."

"Then I will weaken your enemy first with my works, and you will confront it in a greatly reduced condition, and you will defeat it."

XXIII

You have again exhausted yourself. Asleep in a chair."

"Angelica called for me in the night. I should have returned upstairs to you, I know."

"You should have done. But, as you say, the child needed you."

"She did, my love."

"And so this is where you comforted her and where you fell back asleep."

"Yes."

"All night in this blue chair."

"Yes."

"Here."

"Yes yes yes! Where is she?"

"She is having her milk with Nora. She had very odd dreams."

"She shall adjust in time, as you say."

"You want another day's rest, at least. I shall instruct Nora to see to you."

She accepted her imprisonment, for Anne had promised. She gulped his prescribed powder and awoke seven hours later, well after noon, not only rested and content, but with mounting excitement.

Anne had promised. She washed slowly, luxuriously, touched perfumes to her naked flesh, brushed and set her hair, tinted her face, the violet skin around her damaged eye, dressed with care and uncommon elegance. Anne had promised.

She descended the stair with a sensation of arrival from a long and arduous journey. The house smelled fresh. Anne's work was already taking hold. Nora was arranging new-cut flowers upon the lacquered-walnut console table in the parlor's corner. "Madam, you startled—you look so lovely. Is there company tonight?"

"Mamma!" shouted Angelica at Nora's feet, her doll lying facedown on one of Joseph's books, upon a plate of a skinless man. The child ran to her mother, smothered herself in the cone of her skirts.

"Dearest, did you comport yourself like a lady while I rested?"

They shared tea with the Princess Elizabeth and then went to the piano. "I want to play the man keys," Angelica insisted, climbing upon the bench to her mother's left. They played a slow piece to train the hand in crotchets and quavers, "Four Little Maids Go Walking in the Woods." Their four hands, larger and smaller sisters, moved slowly in parallel, the little left hand leaping over its mirror image to occupy the space just vacated by the large left hand. Angelica stopped playing to ask, "How many of my hands do you have?" She grasped her mother's left hand, held her own right against it, palm to palm. Constance's fingers folded over and perched upon the tips of Angelica's. "I mean to say, how many hands, how many of my hands—how many of my hands are *in* your hands?" Constance laughed. "No, the *bigness*," the girl elaborated to no avail, and Constance held her to her breast.

At that moment of slow happiness she saw Joseph rapidly pass the front window, approaching the door in conversation with an invisible other. She sent Angelica to her room. "I want us to play more," the child protested, but obeyed, took herself upstairs, singing an unsteady variation of the recent melody to words of her own composition: "Two maids walking, walking in the woods / One falls asleep, much too asleep, and then there was one / One maid weeping, weeping in the woods . . ."

The cherry-wood eight-day clock showed only half past three— Joseph was home very early and now held the door for a stranger, an old man of fine dress and manner, but with a face hanging low and heavy, thick flesh draped from old and yielding bones. "Constance, here is a colleague I have long intended you to meet." But as Joseph spoke he was examining his own face in the vestibule glass, and Constance knew, like a match catching, that he was lying and that all to follow would be lies as well.

"Dr. Douglas Miles," she repeated, her hand against his old lips. She expressed her delight at meeting him, this guest infiltrated on false pretenses, willingly cloaked in her husband's transparent lies. She would draw him close, this newest conspirator. Anne had promised the end tonight, but only if Constance were bold. "And you, my dearest, I am so pleased to have you home early." She kissed the cheek Joseph lowered without looking at her.

Dr. Miles gave a stage performance of his own, praised the loveliness of Mrs. Barton's home and the tea and cake she speedily produced (sending Nora upstairs to sit with Angelica). The doctor circled her, watching her from sidelong, feline angles. He desired something of her, was impatient for something from Joseph, though the men did not look at or speak to each other, and Joseph lingered mutely in the corners, or soundlessly touched the piano's keys.

The old doctor's face drooped towards his teacup as if its rising steam were melting his cheeks. "I must compliment you, Mrs. Barton"—his jowls swung—"on your sense in decoration. Your home is a regular advertisement for that Peter Vicks fellow. I know several women who admire his designs."

She did not need to feign her pleasure at the remark. It was alarming, how precisely and easily Joseph's agent had touched upon her pride. She had indeed, when transforming Joseph's scantily outfitted bachelor's palace to a family home, relied on Peter Vicks's Galleries and his *Magazine of the English Domicile*. "Joseph quite needed a feminine eye. The old soldier's home lacked, he would be the first to concur, a certain softness." She turned to Joseph, who leaned against the door, as far from her as the room permitted. "Will you not join us, my dear?" she asked, and her voice wavered at even this mild untruth (that she wished his company, that this was a social occasion), but the old doctor seemed not to notice her nerves, and merely waved a forkful of lemon cake under the knobbed pink tip of his irregular nose. "A fine piece of work," he said, and his dry, uneven lips formed an unpleasant, crooked smile. "A tender crumb and a subtle flavor." He prodded his mouth with a napkin. "You are a queen of the domestic arts, Mrs. Barton." When he rubbed his face or hands, for a long moment his skin held the position into which he had pushed it, valleys and ridges carved in soft, speckled flesh. As he lifted his tea, under his shirt cuff she saw a growth on the ball of his wrist, a smooth dome of distended skin, pink from its contents and the strain of stretching, at once magnetic and repellent to the eye.

Joseph at last found his voice: "Constance, please make Dr. Miles comfortable. I, unfortunately, have forgotten—" The rest of his lie escaped her attention, for in those first few words she had already heard the smooth rhythm of untruth, knew he had meant from his arrival to leave her alone with Dr. Miles and had only now ripened his excuses. His apologies and departure (and her smiling regret, kiss, and display of gentle forgiveness) passed in an instant, all performed for Miles's watchful eye. She stood at the rain-streaked window, observing her husband's flight into the wind and damp. "A pity, my poor dear in this weather." With her back to the room, she examined the reflected doctor in the pane, where she saw him examining her in turn.

"You have a daughter, do you not? Mr. Barton speaks of her with such pride and affection." And so it would begin at once, before she had even turned to him. She composed her face as his questions slithered out of their cave. Is the child well-behaved? Does she take after her mother's beauty, her father's demeanor? The girl must certainly please her mother. The mother *is* content, is she not? Or . . . ? Is there, perhaps, any more of the lemon cake to be had? Is anything troubling Constance? Really? Is life as easy as all that for her? She will excuse an old man's intrusive curiosity, a *friend's* curiosity, for he hopes she might see him as a friend. She does? Excellent. Has she then, for this discreet friend's ear, any honest complaint to make, as most wives quite permissibly do? This is a lovely district to raise the girl, do they take fresh air together often? And who plays the piano? Will you play for me?

Tonight of all nights, when Anne's promised conclusion twinkled just some hours ahead, this man had been sent to gauge her suspicions and assess her plans. Joseph had dispatched a spy to flatter Constance in a manner Joseph no longer plausibly could and to extract her knowledge of what was loose in the house. She was being probed by yet another doctor, selected and discreetly paid by her husband, the shiny sovereign set by the door. And this one, feigning kindness, would pry and sniff until he could satisfy Joseph that she was placid, ignorant, his obtuse victim still.

Constance studied her guest's false face and thought of the child's rhyme about the Catholic conspirators against Queen Elizabeth, a faint signal of helpful memory flashed from the Refuge: "The pacts were made, the parts were played / The wicked left the good dismayed, but good Queen Bess was ne'er afraid."

A loving wife would answer all questions, carefree. A loving wife would appear joyful if expectant, hopeful if not, might even blush here and there, call the old man "wicked" with a gleam in her eye and more cake on offer. Tonight all of this would end. Anne had promised. "Would you not play something?" Dr. Miles insisted. She chose the lightest music she could think of, a gavotte, to the slapping old flesh of his applause.

"Mr. Barton told me you saw his work," he said, the final chord still hanging. "Was that upsetting? The sudden sight in the flesh of what has only been intellectual conversation, well, it can disorient one."

How cleverly worded his shrouded meanings, for that was precisely the issue in this house: the flesh reality of intellectual conversation. "Do you find me disoriented, Dr. Miles?" she teased. "Joseph's work is of vital import, but you cannot ask me to explain it well. I only know how proud I am of his efforts."

Lemon crumbs adhered to the ancient mouth's webbed corners.

"Mrs. Barton, you are a lovely woman, and a very fortunate wife. You have a husband who concerns himself with your health in a manner very few men do." She heartily concurred. "Have you any worries, any fear of him?"

"What an amusing question. Why ever would I have any fear of—well, yes, fear *for*. Since you would inquire, I shall be bold: the sad truth is that Joseph does work himself too hard. He is, I *fear*, rather too solicitous of his family's welfare, when he has so many other, more important concerns." She felt his eyes upon her. She was not convincing him. She poured more tea.

"I mean to say, Mrs. Barton—thank you—I mean to say that often the wives of men of science, or men who have seen war, feel their husbands rather colder than the dashing young fellows they wed in churchy white."

"Oh, then you do not know Mr. Barton very well, Doctor. Cold? He is *Italian*. A hot-blooded southerner!"

"Marvelous!" The old man chuckled indulgently. "Hot-blooded! And if there were a bite more of this tender concoction."

"For a man with such passion, I could bake all day and night."

He had sent her into the kitchen with intent, and now she returned to a renewed attack. "You were educated at a charity school, Mr. Barton tells me. A painful adjustment, I should think."

"His unstinting generosity," she replied, betraying none of her astonishment that her husband had revealed her origins, "is without peer."

She would be spurred to produce no complaint, as that was Dr. Miles's evident goal: provoke her to grumble and then, slowly intoxicated on the liquor of his false sympathy, reveal her knowledge and her weakness.

"Monday your child begins school. Does it annoy you?"

"Annoy? I confess, Dr. Miles, it is difficult for a mother to see her child grow, so much daily evidence of passing time, the approaching end of my life's task. But annoy? Certainly not. I expect the child to learn as rapidly as her father would wish." This leering stranger was conversant with her life's every detail: the Refuge, her visit to the laboratory, Angelica's schooling four days on. She could deny nothing, could only deny that she had noticed the true meaning of anything.

"There are times," he continued, and a tic developed over his eyelid, pushing the thin yellowed skin over the edge of his black iris, "when one may be excused for requiring a rest. I am quite aware—as is your devoted husband—that our women toil on our behalf, under emotional burdens unknown to us. A time away, to refresh one's spirits, could be arranged in a trice, for the asking."

A "restful" separation from her home and child could be diverted only by total obtuseness. "What Englishwoman would accept such unmerited charity? When our husbands have withstood sufferings we soft women never have? A woman's work is a tribute to our men. To crave rest! I should find it a disgrace, if I may speak plainly to you, as a friend, Dr. Miles."

He considered her over the rim of his cup. "Might I meet your daughter?"

There was no certainty what the girl might say, and if he demanded to speak with her outside her mother's presence, all could be lost. "You are very kind to ask. It would be an honor to display her conversation, sir." She rose to the girl's room. There Nora sat on the blue chair, a newspaper crown on her head and Angelica pretending to be bound hand and foot to the bedpost. "Come, angel. Nora, fetch her to her bath in two minutes, not a second longer."

Downstairs Angelica curtsied and said she was delighted to know Dr. Miles. His gaze upon the child was unnerving in its singularity. A contradiction or revelation and Constance's future would be black. "Angelica Barton," he said. "Angelica Barton. Miss Barton, you are quite the small duplicate of your lovely mother."

"Thank you, sir. Mamma is very lovely."

"She is indeed. I think"—he continued and, tilting to his left, dug with strumming fingers in his right waistcoat pocket—"I do. Here is a tasty licorice"—he held his closed fist under Angelica's nose—"for the girl who can tell me"—her eyes slightly crossed towards the sweet floating within range of smell—"how your bedroom came to have that"—Angelica bit her lip—"fire."

Everything. He knew everything, and with this word would take everything from her—the child, her limited freedom—and would send her to "rest." She looked to Angelica, upon whose wisdom everything now depended.

"When we cause accidents, we confess promptly," Angelica recited and reached into the opening, dry palm, and Dr. Miles began to laugh. "Mamma tripped upon my doll, and I truly am sorry, sir."

"A wise child! And you, Mrs. Barton," he turned to her, "you are a delightful hostess. And I have taken far too much of your time."

"I quite enjoyed our conversation, Doctor. But I cannot imagine what is keeping Joseph. He will be terribly disappointed."

"No matter. Tell him, if you would, that I will speak to him another day. Tell him I said gentleness will be its own reward. And, if I may be bold, may I say to you, Mrs. Barton, that your husband understandably values you so very highly that he may be guilty of superfluous concern for you. It is not by any means a dreadful crime, is it, Mrs. Barton? I do hope you will absolve him."

"You are an excellent friend to us both, Dr. Miles." She waved as he climbed into a standing carriage, joining there two men who had sat within it, apparently awaiting him throughout this mad interview.

Absolve him. She shut the door, Anne Montague's promise wrestling with this Dr. Miles's request: Shut your eyes, Mrs. Barton, shut your eyes, there is nothing to alarm you here, only a husband too solicitous of you. Absolve him.

XXIV

Joseph's comings and goings in past days had become so obscure as to be sinister in themselves. Tonight he had not even attempted to advise her of, or explain, his absence. He did not return for supper, nor when Angelica went to sleep, nor when Nora lowered the gas and retired, leaving the prisoner without a guard. Constance remained alone in the darkened parlor, and still Joseph did not return. Night uncoiled. Anne had promised the last full moon, and there it rose. She had promised the culmination of the evil, an enemy softened to receive the mortal blow. Tonight Constance would be prepared. Anne had promised.

At quarter past three she stood, lovely and ecstatic, in full moonlight in the parlor, and still he had not returned. She did not doubt the manifestation would appear despite Joseph's absence. Perhaps he kept himself away so *she* might rescue *him,* as he had once rescued her, and he would return only when she had finished this, driven away his torments.

She climbed the stairs with grace. She could see approaching events before they occurred. They even began to move according to her desires. She needed only to glide forward, to concentrate upon her deepest knowledge, unmediated by masculine thought, for to stop and think would be to press her foot through the ice beneath her. Aware of everything, she felt no fear. She even felt—in a moment as elastic as a chord held floating over the piano—its absence, the void fear had left behind, a discrete and shaped coolness, as when alcohol evaporates from one's skin.

Outside Angelica's room, she knew precisely, could almost see, where it would be waiting, descending to prey upon her daughter's flesh. She entered, met its eye, and without a word invited it away. How simple it was to create a surface for it—for him, more accurately—and to gaze with quite precisely the expression of desire she knew it craved. Constance looked upon his changing forms and faces, his meager menaces, as upon a boy striving to impress her, as Angelica had encouraged that capering boy-sailor in the park. She smiled as the women in Finnery Square smiled at the men who circled them in shadowed cabs. She found it entertaining, this play, for she could shift her surfaces as easily as he, could change her shape and face, spin a kaleidoscope for him, too swift for her dazzled adversary. She appeared to yield only when it suited her, and all the while underneath was herself only to herself.

She knew he would leave Angelica untouched in her bed, knew she was more alluring than even the fresh child, and without looking back to confirm it, she climbed the stairs to her own room. She smelled him in pursuit.

She disrobed for him. She lay upon her bed for him. He was ridiculous. He croaked words in a grotesque imitation of human seduction. She laughed at him, but modulated her laughter as it left her mouth, so that its true meaning was known only to her. Was this all the beast required? For this she had quaked? He was only a domestic nuisance to be sorted at her leisure; no cat trembled at the arrival of mice. She had spent so much of her life in pointless fear. A mother managed such matters with little fuss.

He approached at her invitation, hovered above her in his blue light. She placed her hands behind her head, beneath her pillow, to her preparations. Gentleness would be its own reward.

The simultaneity amused her most of all. She had conceived it while she slept that afternoon, its beauty and balance: they penetrated each other at the same instant. She found his suddenly frozen mask almost pitiful, as he—it—realized what she had done, the blade wet with holy water entering him as he entered her. The creature lost its ability to change form, and she examined its paralyzed features with an interest slightly scientific, but as a woman, not cold or distant, but sympathetic to the pain of the subject. With her free hand, she touched the blue light of his fading cheek as he produced sounds she recognized but with their meaning quite altered now.

She waited and watched. By the round moon, her wrist was as black as one of those native slaughterer's. One does not claim that she watched from far away or saw her own body as if she were floating above it—no, that is the language of dreams or of the novels at her bedside. Rather, she observed herself from the past and from the future. She was her own mother so long ago, and she was her daughter some distant day to come. She was Esther Douglas behaving at last as she ought to have; she was her own Angelica learning of all that Constance had done for her.

Vanishing, it rushed now through its repertoire of masks, face after face in pain: Joseph, Dr. Willette, Dr. Douglas Miles, Dr. Harry Delacorte, Pendleton, Giles Douglas. She held her right hand firm, pushed the blade back and forth, into and out of him in a gentle rhythm until he—it—dissolved into wisps of drifting smoke, winking lights, smoldering fibers.

At any moment, Joseph would return, her love, calmed, older, drained of urges and violent heat, restored as the husband and father they longed for.

She slept deeply, dreamlessly.

PART TWO

Anne Montague

I

I cannot imagine that Anne Montague was ever a beauty of any sort. She had been on the stage, true, but never in roles that demanded great physical grace: the confidante, the woman spurned, the less favored sister. No pictorial evidence of her youth survives, or none that she ever showed to me, but there must once have been, somewhere, sketches, at least, if not paintings or a photograph, commissioned by *some* admirer, a man of lesser wealth, I must suppose, who could not afford to keep a leading lady and so instead, after a swift and frank stage-door negotiation, armed only with sparse bouquets and tables at lesser restaurants, won Anne Montague, equine and loud, a nymph of no conceivable water, but still an actress, still he was keeping an actress, and he could boast over a chop, "She'll bankrupt me, she will, but she's worth every penny," and he would incline his head and accept toasts to the health of a devilish fine fellow.

Anne was a specific and acquired taste, to be sure, and it would have been the rare gentleman indeed who was so taken with her that she ever woke for a few days, perhaps a few weeks, in a private flat, surrounded by pale luxuries. These were few and brief, these stagy interludes, for the spirit that haunted such select men was weak and easily exorcised (by Anne herself, inadvertently).

But at last her career upon the boards arrived at its intended, happy conclusion. Wealthy James Montague asked for her hand and, with it in his, led her from the stage. Anne was intemperately proud in her departure, offending many who would a year later recall the snub and gladly deny her roles or even friendly assistance. That single year later, her stage career scuppered, her spendthrift (and by no measure wealthy) husband dead, and bleak financial waters roiling about her, she set herself uneasily afloat using such skills as she had acquired in her previous profession.

Her subsequent record of success as a consulting spiritualist, as with all of those compassionate listeners who minister to invisible troubles and complaints, eluded flawless quantitative measurement. She certainly captained unequivocal triumphs, where explicit spectral visitors were shown the door thanks solely to her intercession and practical guidance (the use of roots, holy symbols, incantations of expulsion, et cetera). Conversely, many ladies wished, of course, to hear from those they had lost. In truth, Anne scarcely knew a woman who did not, especially those stranded in marriage, particularly if marriage had required the removal of a young girl from an Irish or country family to a new home and life in faraway London. Who did not long to gaze upon a dead parent, sibling, child, friend, animal? And so, she summoned the sorely missed dead, drew forth their faces from within looking glasses and upon clouds of smoke. She loaned her mouth to their voices, her writing hand took their dictation, and their survivors wept and paid with satisfaction.

And there were also failures, no good denying it. She was clumsy at times and was shown out of homes where her work was lacking. And she was pursued—once, perhaps twice, one forgets—by angry husbands who would have reclaimed their wives' pin money, disbursed to this neighborhood "witch," "charlatan," "thief," actress. How could Mrs. Montague have known that one lady received so little allowance that she paid her fee from sums removed from her sleeping husband's pocket, blaming that wandering, ghostly money (when roughly interrogated) on *his* forgetfulness, the short-changing iceman, their long-fingered children, and finally on Anne Montague.

She learnt that husbands were capable of deluding themselves, to fine detail, denying phantasms they had certainly seen, describing a world more suited to their philosophies, rather than amending their philosophies to allow for the world, preferring to treat any evidence to the contrary as the superstitions of "old wives," a phrase of which Mrs. Montague, widowed and childless, grew terribly tired in her years serving her clients. She therefore always discouraged her ladies from sharing their investigations with the gentleman, unless he was forcefully interested in spiritualism. Else, negotiating with enraged husbands set too much strain upon the vital work Anne and the wife were undertaking.

She would admit, too, in some tragic cases, when she was first learning the nuances of her second trade, that her science simply failed against the superior strength of massed darkness. The old woman who lived for too long alone under the eaves of an ancient house in Wallis Road, for example, hanged herself, but not before she had written a long, long letter. It was not soon read because, having no one to call on her or to note her absence from anything or anywhere, she had hung from her ceiling beam for a long stretch of winter cold before a turn of the weather prompted complaints of leaking from the ceiling below, which led in turn to a forced entry. The letter, left beneath her feet for easy discovery, was rendered illegible in many places by the same natural outpouring of life that had so inconvenienced her neighbors downstairs. What could be read, however, complained bitterly of Anne Montague's failings—as a friend, as a protector, as illegible. The deceased also wrote with equal venom of the sneering local children, the conspiracy of dogs and cats, the fairies and air-pixies, the long-toothed spiders in her walls and ears. All of these she blamed more than Anne Montague for giving her "a life no person could bear, as God is my witness." But she flung curses at Anne's head, for Anne had not "dispatched them to the other world like as she had promised and what been paid for." The demons seemed to be harassing her even as she wrote that very letter: "No you'll not have my pen, you devils, I'll tell the truth before you chase me out, now off me, stinking biters! Off me!"

Like all those who fill professional ears with emotional trouble or anxiety over events still to come or events long ago, Anne's clients either told her the truth, sincerely told falsehoods, or knowingly lied. She adjusted her treatment accordingly, of course, though it was necessarily difficult to establish which condition pertained, and, if at times her ladies saw things that she could not, Anne was faithfully catholic enough to admit that she may have been blind and they wise.

Usually, or perhaps only often, her customers spoke the plain, occult truth, just as a man who complains of being followed may not be "paranoiac," sir, but pursued, and Anne's science in this field grew rich from experience. She conducted séances and expulsions, dispatched the unwelcome dead or taught the living to coexist with them when necessary.

But she would not have been able to survive (not to say *thrive*, because she never did thrive until she met Constance Barton), she could not have survived solely by ridding homes of objective supernatural disturbance or summoning for conversation the promptly loquacious departed.

For example, at times people very much wished to see ghosts, but the ghosts would not appear on demand. In such a stalemate, it was certainly best to provide the bereaved with the simulation and stagecraft that satisfied their needs, rather than to deny them this simple kindness, only because the petulant residents of the other side could not be troubled to respect the wishes of those they left behind.

And, in some cases, many, Anne discovered she could succeed merely by listening well to the living, to the wife who at last spoke freely to Mrs. Montague of her loneliness, or her distaste for her husband's manner, or her pain over children lost in war or factory work. After a few such candid chats over weak tea, the air in the house stopped heating and chilling in turn, the water flowed without moaning or bleeding, dishes no longer leapt from hands to smash against the walls, beds ceased to shake in intimidation, and Mrs. Montague received lavish thanks, her small, discreet payment, and invitations to come now and again, as a treasured friend.

She explicated for a certain type of haunted customer—young, lonely mothers and brides aching for numbness in the third or fourth bitter flush of marriage—the nature of the world, teaching them how to adapt to conditions beyond their escape. She taught from her own experience how they might more comfortably manage their lot, their husband's demands, their isolation. If this conversation was conducted entirely as a discussion of, and treatment for, phantoms, then so be it. I can see your smirk from my writing-table, sir. No, that does not mean ghosts did not exist; it means simply that they were not the only problem a young woman might face when placed in daily proximity to a man, wretched with appetite and corrupted by his new position of unchecked tyranny.

Those condemned to such lives often preferred to blame the dead for their suffering—for who would defend the unjustly accused?—and that was much for the best, for Anne very early learned that there could be too much knowledge. Too complete a cure could provoke as much pain as the original complaint. What good came in opening the eyes of a tormented lady if she could not manage the inescapable situation she then saw? Had Anne brought such a patient any benefit? Early in her second career, she successfully transmuted a poor woman's horrors from the spiritual to the human—no ghost caused those bruises, the girl at last admitted. But still the bruises did not stop. Doctors of your ilk would be pleased to "cure" as many as Anne did, but to what end? There was nowhere for such a cured woman to turn for further assistance. In those cases where ghosts were blackening the lady's eye and loosening her teeth for her, Anne sometimes recommended a talk with a sympathetic brother or a trusted policeman or a liberal vicar, but then she was rarely paid for her work.

Excepting those occasions when she led séances and required extra hands to effect details of the event while she was indisposed, serving as thrashing, bleating, immoderate medium, Anne Montague did not employ assistants. She did however cultivate maids of wardrobe and hall maids and sub-footmen and even a few valets, freely offering commissions, questioning them cannily and subtly, never forgetting to inquire after their own children, whose names she never bobbled after hearing them only once, before probing the spectral hygiene of their masters' homes. For all this effort, however, information that led to work on behalf of wealthy clientele was scarce, and rarely did she enter a home that much impressed her. Money was a cunning prey, wilier than ghosts.

II

The door creaked below, late in the night, followed by squawks of conversation, heavy steps on the stair, the expressively disapproving knock against Anne's door, and the exaggerated blowing of a nose, crafted to signify interrupted sleep. "Mrs. Montague!" Mrs. Crellagh wailed. "This is not the hour for proper visits, and well you know it." Anne's landlady would certainly complain of the disturbance again in the morning, even more bitterly.

Meanwhile, Anne's visitor, being for once the caller rather than the doorkeeper, had not the meekest interest in imitating the threshold ceremonials of the home where she worked, and so had pushed her way past not only the hunched landlady ("Send her down to bed, can't you? I climbed your six pair myself, not like I had her carry me up") but past Anne as well. Anne produced her compelled apology, being at the demon Crellagh's mercy, fortunate to have the rooms for the little she had to pay. "Never again, Mrs. Montague, the last, the very final time, mark me."

Her guest was already at the fire. "Annie, you recall your dealings with Michael Callaghan? Because I've got a fine one for you, if you're still paying for ghosts." Her shawl was off, and she was settling onto

Anne's sofa, unlacing her boots, all before Anne had placed her as a maid-of-all-work come from the same Irish village as that Callaghan, a subfootman who had once arranged for Anne's contract to sweep clean the ghost of a dead horse from a Stygian stable. "A little something to drink would not be unwelcome, Annie, my dear." Anne thought the girl's name might be Moira or Brenda, but no, Brenda was that unfortunate governess who had been cashiered when discovered choking one of her young wards in a fit of pique. Moira? Charlotte? Alice?

At the end of her second yellow sherry, with her chilblained toes steaming before the fire, the girl agreed to a slightly improved version of Anne's usual terms (a coin now and a percentage of Anne's fee later, if an arrangement was reached with the suffering employer). She described the victim as having very generous pin money and being notably free with it. "She gave me too much for the cab, and I've had a fine evening, I have. She sent her precious Nora off early, and so I've naturally enough taken a bit of a holiday before calling on you, so tomorrow we'll need you to say you was out when I came, and I waited. Clear? I've a night ahead of me still, so I'll collect you at seven tomorrow morning?"

The maid, like nearly all household staff and the Irish girls in particular, displayed immeasurable, laughing pride in knowing all there was to know of her lady, seeing more than her lady meant her to, understanding the lady's workings better than the lady herself, turning the lady, in a pinch, whichever way around her finger she needed. While these reports were more reliable than not, truth and lies were delivered with a consistent tone, and the monologue wanted filtration for backstairs braggadocio, envy, blindness to nuance or manipulative false compliments, excessive pride in milady's confidences to her maid. Anne pitied Nora, taking such pleasure in her merciless portraiture, being able to say whatever she wished against the goddess of her daily existence. Because even here (at a distance, loosened by sherry, talking for money), the Irish girl still twitched with the same ineradicable reflexes of daily circumspection. That circumspection was literal: she looked around her as she spoke, as if her lady might somehow be here or crouching near a communicating fireplace elsewhere, as if all London's hearths were interconnected to spy upon domestics. At least Anne had never fallen as low as service. Whatever the wage, one developed a slave's lumpy soul.

As a habit, milady wept oceans, even on fine days, but this past evening, it was worse. It was children's hour, time for Nora to be at the kitchen work. "I wasn't trying to shirk, I wasn't, fair and square, madam was meant to be with the child." But tonight the lady was hidden away. Nora came upon her in a dark corner, no fire, no gas, no lamp, sitting in the shadows, howling. She talked a horror, evil in the house, ghosts roaming the upstairs at night. The Irish girl had not seen anything of the sort but, then again, was never upstairs at night, so couldn't say. Still, she had to note, "Madam keeps ghost tales at her bedside, stacks. I think she's seeing things what probably—well, that's your affair."

The lady in question had been married now for some six years to a cold and hard man, older than she by fifteen or twenty years. Nora was brought into the house directly after the wedding trip, and they kept no other servant, though in Nora's opinion the means certainly existed to do so. Sir was a doctor of some sort, but kept no surgery in the house. Sir was most generous with pin money, and milady was generous, too, in her turn, right kind, in fact, always making gifts to the tradesmen, and to Nora, too, at Christmas and her anniversary of service, and Nora was allowed one day a month to herself, and it never occurred to madam to withdraw that, and she had given Nora dresses, not that Nora could wear them, of course, as she was larger than madam, "as larger than her as you are to me, Annie," but the fabrics were good. The woman could go too far, sometimes, with her generous side, and Nora had heard sir scold her spending.

"How does she take his correction?"

Meek as mice, never answered back, but didn't change much, either, at least not for long. She liked to spend on herself and her little girl, and if there was any extra she'd give it away in alms. He *was* plenty cold and hard, now that they mentioned him. "I wouldn't want to go to him with ghosty stories, all frightened of the dark. He's not going to make it better." He didn't say much to the little girl, or to Nora or in Nora's hearing. Slow-moving fellow, near as anything to a tortoise. Big, droopy eyebrows, eyes half-closed, never smiled, bow-legged and boxy. "Never could have won a lady like that, a beauty really, excepting for his money, and . . ." Nora had it from other maids in the district that he lifted her to his station. Married her for love, fairy-story love, "but my lady is nothing more than you or me" (an elision that Anne faintly smiled upon). She was a country mouse and didn't want anyone to know it, so there was always plenty of fine-lady drama, *I won't be spoken to in this manner, That's the final time she can expect,* and the like. She was a counter-jumper, you could see it plain once you knew. She gave herself away all the time, but was as bad a snob as a duchess. Nora had seen her shout down her dressmaker's little delivery girl with poison she could scarcely credit, *You little thief, you thieving little slut,* but it never lasted. As soon as the girl agreed to change the dress for nothing, madam was back to her old self with her child at the piano or off to give food to a stranger or a lady who once was kind to her.

"Is the husband never soft with her?"

"I change the bed linen on the third day, but I can't say there's any cause. He leaves her be, who's to be surprised? After so many years, she's just a shopgirl, not worth his fine conversation, can't entertain none because new people make her jumpy, that's plain, can't hardly take her out because she don't like to leave her girl, or she thinks people are laughing at her."

"Does he beat her?"

"Ought to," Nora cackled. "Lord, your fine sherry is going right to me. See, she never talks to tradesmen like she talks to their girls. Always forward with the men, and when they do entertain, now and again, she talks to the gentlemen in a way that would get a girl taught a lesson back home, laughing and blinking wide at them, even his colleagues. But he don't notice."

Likely a minor haunting, but perhaps not. Either way, Anne meant to determine precisely what the lady could pay before she met her, and here Nora's expertise was worth her commission, as the maid could tell Anne in detail about the family diet, cleanliness, economies. How much wine is in the house? Good wine? Does she keep horses? How do they keep their linens and underthings? How often do they bathe? Do they replace things at the sign of wear? Who does the stitching, you or her? Does she use lavender water or French perfumes?

"What's all this stuff to you? If she's got banshees, you'll wave your parsley all about, and that's it then, isn't it?"

"How much precisely is her pin money?"

"Medium. Not like some ladies. Mary Kennedy's been a maid of wardrobe to a lady ten years now, and she says, just for her dresses now, nothing else, you understand, the lady takes from her sir—" The holes of Nora's knowledge were packaged in blankets of excess detail, and Anne had no choice but to listen until the Irish girl took a breath or a drink. Was it a God-fearing home? Sir would have none of it. Doctors, you know. It was all fairy stories to him, and madam just bowed her head when he started with that. "Has the husband ever looked at you in a way? Said anything of that nature?"

"Listen to you."

"Well, Nora, you're an attractive young thing."

"Now you're the one seeing spirits."

"Has he? Has he looked at you like that? Like this?"

"Ha! You could give a girl a chill like that. No, he don't look at me at all. Probably don't know my name. I think I'd like him more if he looked me over like you just done. No, he's cold as fish eyes."

He had been a soldier, and Nora had heard this and that, of course. A fellow Nora knew from back home had been out there with him, with Mr. Barton, in war, and he won medals, honors, Mr. Barton did, "but he never mentions them. Keeps them in the bottom of a drawer, the middle drawer of the writing-desk in the little room next to the parlor. I've seen them in there, true as anything. But my friend, he says Joseph Barton was a nasty one, a tough devil, black in his heart, did things over there."

"Meaning?"

"I wouldn't know, would I? Tea, is that all you have to drink now? Where's the nice Spanish we opened our talk with?"

III

Nora returned next morning with tales of her stolen night and, talking without pause, lazily led Anne to an omnibus, for which she made it clear Anne should pay, and then to another and then a third. They finally established themselves in a small green square opposite Hixton Street, side by side on a bench partially screened by hedges, from where they could watch a fine, narrow, three-story house of painted brick with a pretty court enclosed by a fence of recently cleaned black iron. The shutters and windows were all open to the day.

"There. That's him there," said Nora, hiding herself. Anne, eager to examine the husband incognito, crossed the road to absorb his approach, his gait, how he moved his eyes, the revelatory first impressions. There was something unpleasant specifically about his mouth and heavy-lidded eyes, the movement of his stiff limbs. His legs were thick, hardly legs at all, hinged pillars or logs. He was heavily built and short (shorter by far than Anne), tilted slightly forward onto his toes, as if he were in search of food or battle. Anne saw simmering violence in him, and in his density she noted an analogous mental slowness, perhaps even dimness. Surely he was an educated gentleman, a medical man, but bland, unimaginative. He was of the type that squinted hard at one, as if penetrating with his glance, but in fact to disguise his inability to see.

The wife, though, was of an entirely different world. Distraught and exhausted, as Anne's clients never failed to be, she was also lovely. Well-favored and fashionably dressed, she wore her straight chestnut hair loose to her shoulders, and it framed a fine, oval face with scarcely a line or a blemish marking its even, pale complexion. Her sea-blue eyes sat deep and shy behind long lashes and above a sculptor's ideal of cheeks—Anne could almost see the shape of the head under the beautiful skin. Her brightness and wit may have been buried below her sorrows, but not beyond the range of Anne's senses. The lady moved with grace, an unsurprising sadness and slowness to her, but underneath, the struggle of joy and childlike sprightliness strained to emerge through her pain, a subdued illumination from within. Anne was reminded of the plates in her Shakespeare: not the crafty Portia, nor playful Viola, but one of the simpler heroines, Juliet, perhaps, or Cordelia. Fine eyebrows and the small mouth turned faintly into the slightest tragic smile, with no consciousness of the tragedy to come: yes, an actress if she ever wished to be. If she could speak properly she would have made a fine Eugénie and left them weeping, even in a matinée, with her every gasp for air down in Dumont's dungeon. Kindness and generosity were plainly her foundation stones, but, equally evident, they were at risk. That barbarous type who had just passed Anne outside was squeezing far too tightly the beauty in his clutches, and she was fading.

Constance Barton struck Anne as more girl than woman in these first minutes, struggling to stand tall as hostess while any number of hesitations played upon her face. Anne held her small hands, examined her palm's omens and promises. Mrs. Barton's efforts to entertain, disrupted by the trembling threat of tears and an unsteady voice, enchanted Anne, and she swept forward to assist the failing hostess, for even Constance's feeble politesse revealed the fineness of the home. How often had Anne's usual fishwives bothered to offer tea before coughing up their petty complaints? Proceeding by her usual methods, Anne walked the downstairs, remarking the luxury of the home as she went: she interpreted the scatter patterns of salt and flour for her new client, but noted at the same moment the quality of the floors upon which they scattered.

She asked to see the locket Mrs. Barton wore about her marble neck. Within it nestled the husband in daguerreotype, repellent in his silver frame, pressed against the soft skin of his prisoner's throat, clinging in his tiny form, claiming ownership. His whiskers would scrape grooves of paler white when he rooted there, as his miniature double did now.

Anne was delighted to see how quickly the lady took to her, gathered strength and confidence, even developed the ability to speak plainly from Anne's support and from the questions she always asked to prompt a new client past fumblings and hesitations. This one began with predictable embarrassment, claiming there had been a mistake, politely insisting that what she had seen "could not be" (as her husband had no doubt lectured her). But Anne easily set her straight, deflected Mrs. Barton's efforts to escape her discomfiting position, and soon enough the lady grew quieter, more visibly unhappy, and Anne knew that they were now close, until all that was necessary was to take the small hand, push the strand of chestnut from the smooth cheek, and whisper, "Speak."

During the earliest remarks that followed, Anne suspected the young wife needed a sympathetic ear more than anything else, even to the exclusion of everything else. As she spoke, Constance Barton blossomed at the slightest sympathy, the most mild touch or encouragement, as if she had been starved of it for years, as if she were not the lovely wife of a doctor, but an outcast or a drunken smith's bruised woman. So perhaps there was no large fee waiting here.

Constance spoke first not of haunting, but only of her district, her child, her husband, her courtship and wedding and life since, her suffering in childbirth, the demands of her physicians. She was overdue, it was plain. She had no one to speak to (she said as much, catching herself after minutes of talking without a pause), had no one off whom she could hear the echo of her thoughts, sift the foolish from the fine, and Anne began to hope there might indeed be a longer engagement here, if only to discuss prosaic troubles.

The lady's horrors, when she finally elaborated upon them, were difficult to interpret, perhaps from her modesty or uncertainty as to what she was expected to say. In conflict with herself, Constance Barton was unable to arrive at her best judgment on nearly *any* point, and in the matter of her infestation she was least certain of all. No sooner had she attempted to describe the vision than it was impossible, she must have dreamt it or, if it were truly there, it peculiarly proved *her* culpability; she must somehow have invoked this horror.

She stumbled in her tale and would stare at her hands or the floor as she struggled to explain the chaos of her home. When her story choked itself off completely, Anne prompted her with a history of the house, reports of previous hauntings on the site. That these may or may not have been precise actualities was neither fraudulent nor relevant in Anne's technique, for the poor woman found her voice again, freed to push her way towards her truth. You, sir, rely on similar methods, do you not? And with far less efficacy, I might add.

Constance's missteps and hesitancy surprised Anne not at all. Her clients often began in inarticulate confusion and after some time thinking in her company were able to explain with increasing eloquence and detail the spectral shocks that had only a few minutes earlier defied expression, hid "beyond words." True to this pattern, Constance Barton would seize upon a phrase—"his restless spirit," for example—and, intuiting that it was explanatory of *something*, would be able to look Anne in the eye and discourse upon the theme: "His restless, untamable spirit. He is Italian, you see. His desires are stronger than—I hope you do not think me vulgar. You see, the doctors have placed strict . . ."

The husband was a foreigner! Nora had not mentioned such a thing. This explained a great deal: foreign and a soldier. In life and onstage, she had known soldiers to be either diffident to the point of invisibility or men who took such pleasure in slaughter that their natures, once rewarded for fully expressing themselves, could never be contained in civilian life, and heroes in peacetime contorted into thoroughgoing domestic tyrants.

Whatever the troubles disrupting this fine and well-furnished home, Anne was moved to a depth of pity uncommon and surprising to her. Here was this slight, perishing beauty, tucked amongst the plush pillows of the gargantuan sofa, this girl who had aspired above her station and found her new altitude to be no more hospitable than the climes she had left below. Motherless before, she was every bit as motherless now, but in infinitely more need. Still, Anne was careful with her words, for the lady likely had a temper, could transform in a blink into the snob she had long studied to become. The descent from trusted adviser to subservient tradeswoman to dismissal could progress rapidly with a client whose sensitivity to her station was so evident.

Granted time and patience for her circular tale, young Mrs. Barton finally produced a report, in increasing detail, and Anne was torn. As with many other lonely women, the story had only appeared with encouragement and only after a catalog of more earthly complaints: isolation, boredom, medical worry, fears of her sporadically attentive husband's rushing musts. But her occult complaint was unlike anything Anne had ever heard, certainly not pilfered in hacked pieces from novels or the stage and then monstrously reassembled, as was so often the case. The lady whispered her strange report: her husband's touch upon her flesh transmitted itself to the flesh of their child. Whatever the truth, what an actress this one could have made! "If I resist him, she will be safe, but I am too weak to resist. I have caused this. I opened a gate to it. What sort of mother would allow this?" Constance began to bounce, unable either to sit or to stand in her rage turned upon herself. "I am beyond forgiveness, I am the most vile of women."

"Quiet yourself, my dear. You must not even think such things."

And as quickly as Constance had lost control of herself, she regained it, restored herself to her pathetic matronage: "Would you have more tea?"

Some women, starved for attention, fabricated. Some spoke honestly of imagined visions. Some had truly seen inarguable ghostly activity. In all these cases, however, once the client had spoken, she would cling tightly to Anne's presence and her own rigidifying tale. But Constance Barton began to waver as soon as she had described her infestation, as if she felt it incumbent upon herself to distract her guest from the slick and stinking evil now heaving and bubbling between them. Her conviction of her husband's role would vacillate, too, and she plodded through muddy uncertainty, qualifications, redoublements, then splashed hurriedly to his guilt, only to curl of a sudden back to where she had begun: "I believe it is not him, unless it is his hidden will, he may know of it, even will it, or perhaps cannot resist it, for it is him, his doing, his fault, it *must* be, I can feel this much, I know it, though I do not think what I have said is possible, I am wrong or, at least, certainly Joseph is entirely unaware of it. It is inconceivable that he is aware. Perhaps if I tell him what I know, as clearly as I have told you, he will help me." Constance fell back from these exertions to gaze at her tea, the wavering willowy limbs of steam, sudden sharp cusps rising and falling back onto the silvering surface where faces leered just beyond recognition. The lady was wishing her troubles away even before Anne had been able to determine what those troubles were and whence they hailed.

Yet worse, Mrs. Barton then *raged* at her husband, blamed him for the disturbance, and finally placed his face on the grotesque, perverse manifestation she had seen. This would not do either, and Anne attempted to divert her client from rash conclusions. Absolutely no good could come of such confusion. First, Anne's fee would certainly be lost. Second, such an accusation could only produce a conflict that the wife could not hope to win. Most important, Mrs. Barton was simply, in all probability, wrong, confounding the fish of the ghostly problem with the fowl of her distaste (not unjustified) for her Roman master and the imprisonment that was every English wife's lot. But it did no good to call the fowl a fish when for years to come the wife would have no choice but to make do with that fowl. Accusing the man of satanic practice was not the route to a marital truce, invariably Anne's goal. He was not a sorcerer or a warlock. He was just a man, bad enough to be sure, and likely cruel to her in countless ways both petty and extreme (with his affection for violence, boxing, warfare, and the sexual mistreatment of his wife). Anne therefore quickly offered several explanations for seeing his face on the spirit. That said, it would do no harm to understand his nature: "Has he ever laid a violent hand upon you?"

"Who?" An absurd question, a fan to cover a pretty blush and forge a lie. "Certainly not. Joseph is very gentle."

"A gentle soldier."

"He was mostly a medical man."

"Cited for his courage, I believe you said. And the medicine he practices now, is it gentle?" An inspired question, and Anne saw its effects at once. Mrs. Barton's assumed pose fell away, leaving her nude and ashamed: "It is unspeakable." Slowly she described enough of his work for Anne to understand the type of man in question: not, despite outward appearance, a proper medical doctor at all, but a sadist, a servant in bloody matters, and his physical treatment of his wife followed suit. The husband had tired of her, Constance continued, and meant even to replace her with their child. "For her, I mean to say," she corrected herself. "He means to replace me as the girl's mother."

Replace the mother with himself, or replace the wife with the child? Her husband meant to send the child off to school, to force the child to spend less time (or none at all) in Constance's company. He had brought odd gifts, begun reading to the child, bizarrely intended to introduce the little girl to his cruel science, all in a rush of unprompted, uncommon activity. He pressed to replace the mother with himself.

But Mrs. Barton's description of the disturbance intimated a replacement of the wife with the child. She exhibited dishes hung in wooden frames, explained the fractures in them and in the wall behind: "It is as if he is trying not to do harm, and his effort is shown in the house. The strain tells everywhere. It appears in the dishes and in the gas. The supply is jittery and then roars into blue flame that Nora can scarcely temper."

"If you are in fact a bridge to the child's flesh," Anne said, "then presumably if you do not submit to your husband's demands, your child will be protected from the manifestation?" Constance's relief to hear precisely this solution was obvious, but then her face, briefly bright, fell again. "How can I resist him?" she asked weakly, and Anne, with a burst of warmth in her face and scalp that marked her finest moments of intuition, understood with certainty the nature of the troubles in this lovely, contorted home:

Here was a woman for whom her husband's conjugal attentions would likely be fatal, if they had not already been (for Constance suspected she was with child). That husband—a soldier and scientist of horrors who beat her, even in her possible condition—was not prone to excuse her from her obligation to be prone. (That he was not ashamed—at his advanced age—to risk his wife's life for his urges confirmed all Anne suspected of his character.) Worse, he—like nearly every husband honestly portrayed by a broken and haunted wife— compelled the wife with violence to do as he wished. ("He compels me to compel myself, or I compel him to compel me," Constance mumbled when Anne asked her directly, and Anne at once could see the nightly terror, the futile tears, the force, the blood and pulled hair.) Further, the victim was plainly of the self-sacrificing type and could not bring herself to refuse her lord something as small and worthless as her own life, such was her feminine selflessness and natural understanding of love.

Now, given this situation, a haunting materializes precisely and uniquely when the wife acquiesces to her husband's rank carnality, and this haunting threatens *not* the wife, only the child. ("She suffers commensurately with my own willingness to submit to his inclinations.") While an actual spiritual infestation was by no means impossible, Anne heard in this tale instead a plea for worldly assistance. This dear lady, motherless, thought it her duty to allow her master his savagery even if it killed her, but her secret heart offered her, in the form of this blue manifestation, an escape with honor instead: since surely the *child* was worth protecting, Mrs. Barton could no longer allow *herself* to be touched by the husband. She could, by her own standards of duty, insist on being left alone, not to save herself (as she ought to do) but to save her child (a "selfishness" tolerable even to her exaggerated sense of debt to her brute).

What expertise did Constance Barton therefore desire of Anne

Montague? Nothing more than the same service Anne had provided so many other unhappy wives: a lesson in how to contain the beast with whom she lived. "How can I resist him?" she asked meekly, and there lay Anne's task. This case was more urgent than usual, due to Constance's health, and the lessons would have to be couched in the language of the occult, otherwise the poor thing would reject all help, having decided that her own life was not worth protecting from a man, only her child's from a manifestation.

It was not that Constance was lying or playacting. Rather, she saw only what she needed to see in order to save her life, a perfectly sincere and justifiable auto-illusion, but one which would have to be maintained at all costs. That enchantment fell to Anne Montague to stage-manage, and rarely, perhaps never, had she felt so eager to perform well.

Among Anne's standard prescriptions, which offered the unhappy mind a sensation of progress—the scattered flour, the incantations and ribbons, the covered looking glasses—she devised a few suggestions quite precisely for Constance. When Anne recommended keeping spectres at bay by eliminating perfumes, avoiding excessive displays of the unclothed body, and by applying to the skin of the neck and arms raw garlic until a mildly foul scent resulted, she was protecting Constance doubly, from dangers inhuman and human.

"My poor, sweet child," she began with careful words to educate this orphan. "You confront one of nature's darkest forces, unconstrained, in your home, spilling over you and your darling daughter. There is in this world an excess of this toxicant, you see. It is quite exactly like a rush of sparks such as a scientist might harness. This lightning girds our earth, courses all over it with more force than can possibly be contained. Male desire far outstrips society's ability to inhibit it, and so we have large and horrible outbursts of it—war, as the most obvious example. War is a very simple phenomenon draped in the most complex frippery of dates and casus belli and insults and diplomatic efforts and imperial economics, but it is only the draining off of excess male desire. No woman has ever launched a war, and no woman ever could. Why would she? And on a far smaller scale, my dear, we see what is occurring in your home, for it is only in one well-managed household at a time that civilization tames this torrent, just as lightning is only useful when channeled into a single metal rod. We face, in this manifestation in your home, something like a burst gas pipe. We must repair the breach and then learn how to control that gas over time so that it never reaches the breaking point again."

"Does he know or not?" A question best left unanswered.

"I can hardly hear your little voice. Do they know? Is that what you ask? Some do. They relish it. Others, no. They speak of it all as if it were a grand mystery, or it required knowledge of the rights of succession to the Holy Roman Empire. You see, if you listen to their words, you learn very little. They seem like us when they speak of love, but they mean something very different than we do by these same words. They are not like us. Yet it is nature's cruel demand that we learn more about them than they know themselves."

The management of expectations fell within Anne's purview. That the wife would feel she could never forgive her husband was understandable, but her *intention* never to forgive must be purged. When she sobbed that she would never forgive him, Anne corrected her: "Of course you shall forgive. You cannot do otherwise. In some languages, it is the very definition of their word for *woman:* she who forgives trespasses against her."

Anne saw Constance's encouragement, for if this was all a natural outburst, it could be brought under control again. If there was precedent, there were methods to restore the proper order of things. "At the end of all this, I shall have my child and my prince of the stationer's again, drained of this fiery substance?" Anne smiled upon the tired woman. She need not yet explain the simple truth: the prince, if he ever existed, was long since dead.

She guided her client through a regimen of protections, marital advice disguised as spiritual advice: how to avoid physical engagement, how to cool him, how to encourage him to take his ease elsewhere and in other ways. "You must see to those of his comforts you can, wherever possible. As he is made content, so shall the manifestation recede from your house or be called back into him. One must not turn him out into the cold. Granted, there are modes in which he must be disappointed, but not in all questions. His other appetites may be indulged. In fact, they *should* be indulged, for the more fully he is sated by food and drink, by kindness and diversion, the less he will be troubled by appetites more dangerous and repellent to you, and the more forgiving he will be of his one, increasingly mild disappointment. Feed him, coddle him, evade him, calm him. This is within your power, is it not?" Anne instructed in the use of heavy food and wine, gave the poor, untutored lady powders, savorless but efficacious, when sprinkled over his food, in promoting relaxation and retarding the blood's superfluous excitation. "It is a question of integrating the wandering elements of his soul, restraining the passions, you see." How sad the things a motherless girl did not know! The pretty ones were always taught to attract, but surely the knowledge of how to repel was quite as important, as proven here by this case of literal life and death.

And she was an exceptionally pretty girl. It was no wonder her Italian husband felt keenly his long deprivations of her favors. He would not easily be weaned. Anne warned her, as clearly as she could: "I do not mean to alarm you, my child, but the waxing of the moon can affect such horrors."

When Constance smiled without worry, even briefly, Anne was so moved that she found herself performing for her, reciting old speeches from long-ago days on the stage, playing the clown, playing the poet, playing the enchantress, and cherishing the resulting applause as much as any ovation she had ever received. When the time came to discuss the details of payment, Anne hesitated, most uncharacteristically, nearly avoiding the topic, wishing she could, without petty concerns, simply help this woman, but even here her new client was a lady of unsurpassed charm and grace. "I quite understand," the sweet child hurried to interrupt Anne's stumbling words in turn and revealed without hesitation the details of her pin money, as well as the degree of her husband's flexibility in times of expanded household requirements.

"There are many things I can tell him we need, for the house or Angelica."

Anne bid farewell to a client in the best of all possible states: content and safely able to pay, calmer, equipped with tools and knowledge, prepared for her coming struggles, and, most wonderful of all, longing to see her adviser again.

IV

More often than not, the dead were frustrated or simply bored, and, in sinister vengeance, they often bored Anne Montague in turn. The wood of furniture imprisoned them, and their only solace was to make the sideboard groan in darkest night or throw open a cabinet door with a bang again and again, even when the living latched it securely. It fell to Anne to expel them, sometimes with the help of an actor-turned-carpenter posing as an expert of the occult and paid handsomely for all his skills.

Usually, when the dead were able to speak, they did not appear; when they did appear, smelling of lavender water, attar of rose, or mold, they were mute and then either desperate to communicate something they could not, or so serene as to be almost unrecognizable as loved ones once known for wit or nervous energy. Anne had seen countless ghosts of once wild people now grim-faced and slow, blurred at their edges, looking only for a place to sit but comfortable nowhere.

The dead had messages to transmit, with an urgency that made Anne's ears sting and her legs swell and her blood rush to her visibly pulsing temples, but when she offered them the opportunity to speak through her throat, when she had arranged every element of a parlor to

their known tastes in light and silence and closed eyes and hands gripping in a circle, what did the dead finally have to say for themselves?
"Where am I?" or "Remember me." Nothing more, and often much
less. "I do not like your bride." "Do not wear my dresses." "This is too
oily. Take it away." They were often rude. "I never liked you. Or you.
Or you. Or you," the skittering shade of a child told a circle of her
grieving survivors. The dead were often tired, confused, petulant, distractible. "That's not where I kept the sugar," said a baker dead from
syphilis, pointing to the ceiling. "I liked the sugar in my bed. It made
the feathers align."

Or they were pointlessly cryptic, knocking over the same candelabra
every eight minutes precisely for eighty-eight minutes on the eighth of
August beginning at eight o'clock, on the eighth anniversary of . . .
nothing that anyone could recall, no death, no carriage accident, no
fatal fire. At times their messages had no discernible meaning even to
their nearest family, unable to decipher pressing dispatches of gibber-
ish, as the dead wrote again and again with an invisible finger in the silver dust of a looking glass: "Remember to blaze!" and the family would
have been glad to do so, if they had known how.

But yes, very occasionally, the departed would glint with malice.
Death did not evaporate the anger or evil in some of them, only con-
densed it into a syrup that flowed in their translucent veins and seeped
onto the pillows and meals of the living. They approached the living,
leering and furious, until the living fell backwards down staircases.
They pointed at knives until the living cut their own throats for them.
They scared poor folk to death, from spite or to settle a score from life
that festered in them still. But they did not ever, ever *touch* the living.
They could lift items and with them strike the living—Anne had seen
the bodies for which no other explanation could suffice—but to *touch*
the living, as Constance believed a spirit now touched her child? This
had never been.

Anne sat on a bench, a foot or two inside the line of the shade, and
recalled her friend's first troubling, slightly unnatural moment in this
progression of infestation: a familiar but unidentifiable smell, out of

context, suddenly pervading her home, an odor that burnt the eyes and swirled most obscenely around the child's bed. The child's room itself had been resistant to the mother's entry, the door sticking as if held on its dark side, the handle cold to the touch. All of this was classically consistent with spectres and manifestations. With this, no sane person could quibble. And among the other early symptoms: the woman began to awaken at precisely the same hour every evening. After years of serving her as a palace decorated to her whim, all at once the house began to rouse and disturb her, leaving her unsafe at all hours. But no one had ever been touched before. That was a borderline that could not be crossed, and so for all of Constance's impressions, Anne could not doubt the diagnosis that had come to her the day before: self-preservation in spectral disguise.

These manifold symptoms did, however, offer the opportunity to provide her lovely client an extensive catalog of help. The lady's steadily flowing allowance would pay for ceremonies of eviction and various other activities to soothe the nerves and provide the pleasant sensation of forward progress, a necessary adjunct to the work of domestic education. The powders and recipes, one's bearing towards one's lord and master: all of this would have the more potent effect but would be in vain if not accompanied by scientific spiritualism. Throughout, they would pass hours together in activity and conversation, sampling Nora's cooking and the husband's cellar, long afternoons in that large, warm parlor hand in hand, Anne amusing her until the lady's laughter returned, and she had learned thoroughly how to calm her Italian tormentor. (He would still desire her, no matter the salts and spirits in his blood. It would be impossible to redirect all his thirst. Constance must learn to sate him with less than he sought. Anne would guide her here as well, though the thought of his hirsute paws on her smoothness lifted Anne's lip into a curl of disgust.)

"My dearest Constance," Anne said, rising to greet her friend and a positively ravishing little Spanish infanta. "The beloved Angelica, of course." Anne accepted the graceful curtsey and watched the girl skip into the square of green laid out before the bench ringed by a semicircle of oaks. "She is true to her name." She turned to her client, took her hand. "Now sit with me, for I have been awake nearly all night considering our best approach to your difficulties."

How disappointing, then, to discover Constance was as prone to fickleness as any petty clerk's dull wife, yet another foul-weather friend. She fidgeted and mumbled, all in preambling preoccupation, not at all the same sweet thing Anne had helped bring into clear focus only a day earlier, but unconvincingly posing again as a fine lady, already delivering herself of some prepared dismissal to her tradeswoman, and Anne scarcely needed to listen, so typical was the address: the night just passed had been a success, but instead of seeing in that a proof of Anne's efficacy, Constance concluded—perversely, predictably—that Anne's advice must never have been necessary in the first place. Next came the murmurs of termination, gracious offers to pay Anne's (implicitly unjustified) fee, hesitations and faint apologies. Anne had heard it all before, knew it was a request for *more* help disguised as a declaration of needing none. She was accustomed to deflecting and diverting these second-day second thoughts, using them to draw a client into a deeper understanding of her predicament and Anne's importance, but the backsliding had never so disappointed before.

Stung, Anne could also not recall ever pitying a stumbling client before, but here was sweet Constance pushing her face into a smile, and the bravery of her performance moved Anne. What energy she must have expended to arrive at this point, denying all she had seen, all the heartache of her haunted home, and now to sit, eyes on the ground, laughter pinched, a shrill and artificial titter marring her natural and lovely aura of tragically subdued liveliness.

Anne did not help her through her recitation. The waverer must struggle alone, the more clearly and quickly would she see the futility of the gesture. No doubt, after Anne's departure yesterday, she felt herself emptied of fear and pressure. Having spoken at last to someone, she mistook the resulting relief for an eradication of the original problem. She likely spent the evening thinking herself ridiculous, and when nothing happened last night (because Anne's treatment had been initially successful, or because her enemy had tactically retreated), she thought herself not partially cured but rather never troubled.

The ridiculous speech limped to its conclusion. "I wonder if I am not mad," she proposed as compromise, the common pitiable wish of the haunted.

"Do you jabber jumbled philosophies to cats perched on sills? Do you accost men in the street and warn them of their doom?" Anne sighed. "You are not mad, but you do risk being a fool. I did not take you for a fool yesterday."

Weak apologies emerged and withered in Anne's unreceptive silence. Of course, Constance would settle any expenses so far incurred. "I hope you understand my meaning," she attempted.

Anne turned to face her errant friend. "We must be pleased, of course, at last night's respite, but we cannot hurry ourselves to premature conclusions. There is much we do not know. I have learnt since yesterday something of the building, your home, refreshed my memory of the horror of the Burnhams." Anne improvised upon a familiar theme, the old Burnham story, adding—as an artist selects just those details most likely to affect a viewer—such extemporized elements as might aid Constance's understanding of her situation.

The effect of the tale of the four-year-old Burnham girl tormented by tantrums caused by the father's secrets was plain and rapid, far more rapid than in previous cases; Constance must have been hoping for precisely such a stimulant and corrective to her situation. "I am ready, quite ready, to leave you in peace if yesterday was all playacting between two girls. I will now play the dismissed tradeswoman for you. Pay my little fee and be done with me. But as your friend, I hesitate. Show me your face, dear." Mrs. Montague placed her large fingertips with their short-cut nails under Constance's chin and tilted the quietly crying face to her. Constance would have hidden in plain view, blinked and looked away. "Constance's futile flight from phantoms," Anne teased, holding each *ffff* sound until Constance smiled truly, in this grove surrounded by women and their small wards. Anne gently brushed the tears from her long lashes and kissed her forehead, erased with her index finger the

valley between her brows. "There now, the gates once opened cannot be
reclosed. You cannot un-see, though it burns you to look."

"Do you believe I am to blame? For the disturbance?"

"Take hold of yourself. You do not wish to alarm our Angelica there.
She sees you. Wave and smile at her!"

The variation on the Burnham theme spurred Constance to see her
own case more clearly, dislodged another detail from her memory. Angelica, too, suffered from tantrums, some more natural than others, but
one, most worrisome, had occurred when Constance had left the girl in
her father's care, a week earlier. Constance had returned from her hurried furlough to church and found the child in total disintegration at
her father's unmoving feet.

"More than a child's temper?"

"Far worse. And he simply stood, examining her suffering."

"Consistent with his scientific nature, perhaps?"

"Or with cruelty," Constance replied sharply. "He wished to let her
rage. And may have caused the fit intentionally. He was mocking her."

They took up their conversation from the day before. Constance
again spoke openly and honestly of her troubles, laughed at Anne's stories, absorbed Anne's teachings, and seized upon an opportunity: as laboratory affairs would take Joseph out of London the next evening,
Anne could come to the house for a longer visit to scrub away the rem-
nants of the Burnham tragedy. And to sup.

Throughout, Angelica—the picture of childish joy and freedom—
flitted near and far. When she stopped to listen to their conversation
from behind the bench, one hand on each of their inside shoulders, her
head peeking between them, Constance and Anne would do their best
to disguise the identities and horrors they were discussing, but still the
child felt the truth plainly enough that she would, unbidden, pet her
mother's cheek and urge her not to be sad. She promised she would
make her mother happy always and would always be good, before spinning off to charm a plainer child or distractible governess into playing
with her. She wandered off into the wood and returned with a garland
of tales: she had seen the blue manifestation in the branches. It was not

likely, to say the least, but was rather a request to participate in the discussion as an equal. When Anne gave her the opportunity to voice her thoughts, she quickly said, "I do not like it when Mamma is frightened." She felt her mother's pain and fear. "It is best when Mamma sleeps next to me," she said. "That keeps him outside, or hiding away. It does not dare touch me when she is watching." She had seen something, wished to say something, though teasing the testimony out of her would be difficult. Her visions closely matched her mother's, which supported a number of possible, and contradictory, explanations. She smelled strongly of garlic.

V

Angelica's soft cheeks and neck smelled of Anne's remedies even more strongly the next evening when Anne arrived to rinse the Burnham taint from the Barton home. Stronger, too, was Constance's conviction of her husband's guilt. The interval of a day had this time provoked an opposite effect: rather than convincing herself that nothing had happened, she had grown certain that her husband was to blame, and she was excitedly speaking of her theories from the moment she opened the door to Anne, even as the child listened from the piano bench or hung from her mother's skirts. Anne's efforts to cool her failed, and Constance's insistence on connecting her husband to her horror caused Anne her first hesitations about her diagnosis.

I do not mean that Constance's perseverance convinced Anne of what Constance was superficially saying; Anne still believed Joseph Barton—for all his sins—was not controlling a slave-spirit. Rather, Anne noted the perseverance itself as an "implication."

Moments of *implication*—where events slowed, and Anne discerned critical information hidden beneath words, within nonverbal sounds, behind facial expressions, even in attendant objects and scenery—were the most beautiful experiences in her life, even if they could also be painful or indicated the pain of others. Anne was not naïve; she knew better than most that the world was not by nature kindly or charitable. Neither, it should be noted, did she see a grand lattice of interconnection between all people, all events, all time; she easily confessed the plentiful existence of meaningless coincidence. She was not a fool who believed in anything one's whimsy could produce.

But the world was *built* along beautiful lines, in its general pattern and structure, even if in detail it was often brutal and ugly. And in her work, she had grown practiced and was made happy by seeing the faint connective tissue that did most certainly underlie daily life. For one who paid close attention, clues were there to be noticed. They did not demand attention, but they rewarded it. Certain moments, certain objects, certain words carried not a glow (that was a foolish term, meant to explain something of this sensation to dull men), but rather an innate but partial significance, a longing for completion. They were links in a chain, but the link to which they were meant to connect might not appear for days and then only far away, in an entirely different context. Yet these two links, in conjunction, when seen for what they were, could not be anything else, not coincidence, not wishful thinking. They reached across contexts to each other and then implied some next hint to come, or a conclusion only the attentive could reach.

Anne had been quite young when she first noticed her ability in perception and only slightly older when she realized that many people simply did not notice these waves of meaning which flowed by them every day. She noticed, too, that explaining what she could see to those who could not see it invariably resulted in their mockery of her. Most people relied entirely on words and waited to be told, to hear before they would listen. But Anne would not lie to herself in order to resemble them. Her observations were empirically proved right again and again. She knew friends were troubled before they knew it themselves, and she waited impatiently for them to reach the knowledge at last. She knew when a murderer would strike again or disappear. She knew from a sampling of a painter's work in the window of a gallery that the artist had been troubled by spiritual infestation, even though the displayed pictures showed nothing more than cows in sunlight.

Throughout the evening in Constance's company—at the theater, over supper, in every room of the house—she heard the arrival of these links of implication, rapidly, one after the other, even if their conjoined meaning was by no means immediately evident. To begin, as Anne was considering how she might, in the course of that evening's séance and cleansing, prove the husband's spiritual innocence, she was instead swept from the house, for Constance had taken a box at a theater, enjoying herself in her husband's absence. The first link: the theater was one where Anne had played, her last performance there having been as Gertrude in *Hamlet*. And again: tonight's play was none other than *Hamlet*. And again: Kate Millais, who had played Ophelia to Anne's Gertrude, now played Gertrude: a girl prematurely taking a mother's role.

Constance, further, spoke between acts and as they walked home, of her own mother, of the lack of maternal wisdom she had felt her entire life, and how she feared, as a result, that she had little to offer Angelica. She took Anne's arm, walking beside a green park enclosed by a fence of black iron tasseled spears, each with a black metal garland of roses winding down the spear shaft, each rose studded in turn with black metal thorns and between some of those thorns tiny black metal insects and caterpillars, an anonymous master ironworker's vanity, for even some of those caterpillars had been wrought down to the tiny hairs lining their segmented bodies. As they proceeded from lamp to lamp, Constance tapped her hand on these thorned spears and spoke of the coming removal of her daughter, a mere week away now, to be fed a diet of Latin and Darwin and who knew what else. The next moment, two young people came around a corner in fancy dress: a Catholic bishop and a nun, laughing, arms linked, singing a parodic Latin: "In cathedra ex cathedra ex officio rum pum pum . . ."

When they returned to the Barton home, the child in question was quite ready for them, standing as if she had known they were going to appear at that very instant. "I want *you* to take me to bed," she said to Anne and to Constance's surprise, yet Anne had expected just such a faintly glinting link. She lifted the child as Constance took Nora to the kitchen, and she knew that she had only to listen carefully to learn something of ringing significance.

"I have been waiting for you," Angelica said as Anne carried her up the stairs. "Such a long time. Turn left now," she commanded at the top, but as that instruction would have led them into a wall, Anne did the opposite, and the girl praised her obedience.

"You sleep here?" Anne asked, lowering the child onto its bed. "The royal chamber of a palace." The wardrobe, seat of such suspicion, supported more clothing than Anne herself possessed.

Angelica stroked her doll's stiff hair, black wire yanked from a doomed horse's tail. She moved her hands in a unique gesture, another link, quite precisely as Molly Turner had done night after night across from Anne in *The Dangerous Children; or, An Evening's Fright.* Anne had not thought of that play for years, until she recalled it only a few hours earlier, as she and Constance had come into sight of the theater. In that play, the seventeen-year-old Molly had played a girl of ten and had done it so well that some complained of a child appearing in an entertainment of such a nature. Molly Turner had also won her first admirer from that play, a man who had previously been paying vague court to Anne. He was the first of Moll's many conquests, Anne's last but one. "Might you tell me a story?" Anne asked, and lowered herself onto a richly covered blue armchair at the bedside.

"What stories do you like?"

"Anything you like. Tell me about your dolly. What is her name?"

"She was the Princess Elizabeth, and everyone knew her by that name, but now she is hiding her true self. She is now the little Princess of the Tulips."

"But why would such a lovely girl hide her name?"

"Pixies try to capture her. To teach her Latin. She escaped. But now they have sworn a vow of tears. When they find her she must sit atop a toadstool and enchant them, or the pixies will do something unspeedable."

"Unspeedable?"

"And everyone must be quiet when she tries to enchant them. They make her dance. And pixies are *exquisite* dancers, so they judge very harsh. And then the snow dances when the pixies command it, and she must not let any of the snowflakes touch the ground."

Anne considered. She asked very slowly, "If she makes a mistake, and she drops a snowflake, what is her punishment?"

"Hush! You must not ever say it," she whispered. "The pixies chastise mistakes with such grebious winds. Poor, sad Princess of the Tulips."

"Why is she sad, Angelica?"

"In the country of the tulips, she sleeps protected by brave angels with rose-thorn spears. If they touch you with them, you will die. *Forever.*"

"They protect the princess. Excellent. It is good to have someone to protect you. Are they protecting her from the pixies?"

"No. Something much worse."

"What is that?"

"Much worse."

"Does the princess's mother know what it is?" Anne asked, but the child only sighed and asked in turn, "Are you fat?"

"I suppose I am. I must seem very large to you. Am I frightening?"

"You are funny! Ladies cannot be frightening."

"Such a wise child. Where did you learn that?"

"Everybody knows that. That is how God made us."

"What frightens you, then? What is worse than the pixies?"

"You tell me a story now, please."

"Very well. Hold tight to the princess, and I will. Once upon a time, there was a queen, most beautiful, the sweetest of all ladies. But she was sorely troubled, for her king was not kind. Now their daughter, the princess, loved her mamma the queen with all her soul, and she did not want her mamma to suffer further torments, so the princess never told the queen of the cruelties that she, the princess, suffered as well. But the princess had to tell *someone,* and so she turned to the royal adviser. You see, the queen had one trusted friend."

"I know! I know him!"

"Him? Whom do you mean?"

"The Crystal Queen trusts only the Lord of Lights, and the Queen of Sweets looks upon Milord Licorice with glances of keen approval, and the Lady of the Trees will trust forever and only the good services of the Knight of the Waters. Every queen has a man like this."

"I see. It is interesting that you should mention licorice, for look what I have brought you. Is it good? Very well then, my dear girl, this queen trusted her wisest magician to protect her and her beloved little princess. And the princess knew she could tell the magician anything, and the magician would protect her. What do you suppose happens next? You may finish my story."

But the girl's mouth was busy with the sweets, and she could hardly close it, so swiftly did she push the handful of licorice past her lips. Anne waited, fearing the truth that was coming. At last the child swallowed dramatically. Anne wiped her little lips for her and listened with her ears and eyes and heart. The girl asked, "Do you eat sparrow-grass?"

"I do. I like it very much. With a sauce."

"P-p-p-p-pppppp"—she stuttered violently, turned red, and her eyes swung up and to the right as her face contorted to squeeze out the resistant word—"p-PAPA!!! says it is good for the kidneys."

"Likely so."

The child yawned. Her eyes closed then opened at once. "Who is in our ceiling? You said there is a man hanging in our ceiling. I heard you in the park."

Anne moved to the edge of Angelica's bed and said softly, "You will sleep now, and your mother and I shall see to your safety. And in the morning you will awaken and tell us of only the sweetest dreams."

"Where has my papa gone?" Her eyes were nearly shut.

"He will return tomorrow, and you shall not tell him I visited with you here, isn't that so?"

"I swear a vow," she whispered. Anne placed her large hand on the girl's head, swept it gently over her face, and she was asleep.

In this blue chair Constance spent her nights, watching her child, sorting through the girl's words, no clearer than the pronouncements of an oracle, or of the dead. But there was meaning in them tonight. The sensation of implication, of links joining to form an unbreakable chain, had rarely been so strong, and Anne felt herself nearly able to grasp its glinting end.

She left the sleeping girl but, instead of rejoining her hostess, walked upstairs and examined the lady and gentleman's suite. Rain tapped the windows; it had restrained itself long enough for Anne and Constance to walk home from the theater, but now the sky opened with terrible force. As the panes chattered and the light gasped, Anne examined the room where the Italian slept and shaved and fouled his surroundings. His influence was strong here, in the second, smaller wardrobe smelling of tobacco, the table with brushes, a silver bowl, a razor. She examined this last item, a souvenir of foreign war, a handle of soft gray stone, in-scribed with foreign words and symbols. One wall of his dressing room was covered by a hanging arras, a tapestry of a unicorn scene: the weep-ing virgin sat upon the chair, the unicorn had laid its head upon her lap, and she ran her ringed fingers through the white curls of its mane, and from the copse crept the hunter, curved blade in the right hand, silver bowl in the other.

She pulled back the drapery that enclosed the bed, pressed her hands on the pillows and coverings. *I cannot bear to sleep,* said Con-stance's body, the same hour every night. *But do not tread on me,* said the squeaking stairs. *But I must see to my child,* Constance pleaded. *Do not open me,* the child's door said. *What sort of mother would I be if I did not?*

Anne descended to a feast and lights spread before her, precisely the reception she had hoped to find in this house, more than she hoped, but now it disconcerted her. It was unmerited. She felt no ease, only uncertain what to say or where to place herself amidst such comfort, this madly luxurious meal that Constance took as her usual fare.

Constance seemed to feel no danger tonight, expected no assault. Instead, she presented a new side of herself, a gift of sorts to Anne. She was not pretending to be the hostess, nor was she unraveled from ter-ror. She was simply happy. "I have such a strange sensation when in your company," she said as they sat. "When I think for even a moment upon what is occurring in my home, what I am likely to face this very night, at the end of this lovely meal, I think I should go mad. And yet, simply to find you at my side, I am able to confront it."

"Women in your position often feel as you do."

"No. I mean to say more than that. More than they do. I do not wish you to think I am mouthing a commonplace. I am not speaking as one of the many 'distressed' who seek your counsel."

"I did not mean to accuse you of . . . mouthing commonplaces."

Constance signaled Nora to begin the service, the great lady at home and at ease. " 'Women in my position.' Are we always women, then? Have you never helped a man?"

"I have not."

"Are they not haunted?"

"I know that they are. I have read the words of haunted men, have heard their last tormented thoughts and confessions. But they do not come forward and seek help. I do not claim to understand them, my dear. Only the dead."

Constance considered, tasted and rejected words. Anne would allow her whatever time was necessary to formulate her thoughts, so strong was the sensation of mounting pressure, of another approaching link.

"Do you believe that peace is found in another's company or only in oneself?" her friend asked after a long silence.

"You are asking too much if you hope to find peace when your home is undergoing such a cataclysm."

"But this is what I mean to say! I feel it now, despite all of that. I feel it *now*. That is what I wished you to know." She spoke so unlike a man, and in words so distinct from what a man would wish her to say. Had Anne ever had a child, she could very easily be Constance's age.

"The sensation of peace and the act of marriage are presented to girls as equivalents, but rarely do they travel in each other's company," Anne replied. "I was married once, of course. He was a man of quite a bit less than one could reasonably have expected. Not long after I was delivered into his house, I was told that I would not have even a maid like your loyal Nora, and soon after, even that modest house slipped from his grasp. As did the small treasure I had brought with me into the marriage. And not long after, life itself was too heavy for his weak hands, and by the time I was your age, dear friend, I was a widow."

"It is my greatest fear, I must confess."

"Widowhood? Really? Hmph. My dear, you must learn to rank your fears correctly—that is one practice of the healthy mind. I have seen far worse to fear than a mild, mild bout of anuxoria. I felt quite liberated by my own case. The jointure was not large, of course. Do you know the terms of your own? No? Mine was not large, but I scarcely minded, as without his profligacy (which had been *mildly* charming when it was exercised on my behalf), my means felt greatly increased. But even finer was the pleasure of seeing to my own needs again, the liberty to be myself. The requirements of that role I had taken—devoted wife—weighed uncomfortably. I am quite fearfully selfish."

"You cannot convince me of it. You are like a medieval saint, putting yourself in harm's way again and again to help weaker souls."

"I work with great vigor because it leaves me contented. I am my own best protector."

"I have worked. Toil does not frighten me. Loneliness does."

"You prefer the company you find in this household to solitude?"

"I would wish for another solution, but of course there is none, is there? And so I am content for the peace I feel in temporary, select company." Constance reached across the table and pressed her friend's hand.

Nora brought port wine from Mr. Barton's cellar, and Constance again demanded Anne's agreement that her husband was to blame for the haunting. Anne defended him still, though she felt her strength for this battle failing. The renewal of these accusations troubled Anne further, as if, here and earlier in their talk, Constance circled a truth, drew as near to a flame as her courage would allow. "He would make her into a boy, you see," she said, "to be a 'scientist' like him. And into his wife—he would make her his wife. To replace me."

They sat before the fire with their port and shared one of Joseph

Barton's cigars. "Have you never wondered, dear, why it is we should appear to glide? Surely they have told you that in your life. 'Women should glide.' It is simple. If we glide, then we have no legs. And if we have no legs, men need not be tormented by the thought of our legs. But here, among only ourselves, we may have our legs restored to us." Anne pulled back her skirts so that her gigantic tree trunks, wrapped in white cotton and tipped in leather, were presented to the warmth of Constance's fire and Constance's laughter, and Constance followed her example. "Anywhere that women live free of men," Anne said, "they live with legs."

Anne left her friend sitting before the sleeping child and wandered the house alone, cleansing it of the Burnhams, in her way. Upstairs, she threw the bolt and lay upon Constance and Joseph's bed. Every night Constance awoke here, despite herself. Every touch from her husband was reproduced on her daughter. Constance Barton's soul wrestled with itself: something compelled her to awaken, even when something else tried to frighten her back to her bed. How wrong Anne had been—she felt it more each passing moment lying under the ceiling in which she had imagined the body of a wicked husband. Anne wished it were all true: far better that the spirit world had violated its usual principles and was assaulting the child.

The wife saw a manifestation because she could not bear to see the truth. All evidence of a real crime became distorted, transmuted into the spectral, because the human reality was unspeakable, even less imaginable than the ghostly. Anne had seen this natural contortion of the soul before. The sorely pressed, attacked mind will retreat within itself and create metaphors, which in turn become real. Constance saw blue demons, only to prevent herself from seeing her husband walk out of her daughter's room with his boots in his hands, close the door behind him, rise to their own bed on silent feet. She saw meanings in cracked dishes (or perhaps cracked them herself without noticing) rather than enter that room after him and find her daughter in the corner under the chipped and cloudy looking glass, her hands in her mouth to keep herself quiet. The mind created a spirit because Constance had at least a hope of exorcising a spirit, and for a spirit she could find an outsider to believe her and help her. She had Anne, as long as she had a manifestation. Otherwise, she had no recourse in law or society for the husband's evil.

Anne had been clairvoyant, only yesterday, in her variations upon the Burnham story. The tantrums, the wicked father engaged in unspeakable sin, the four-year-old child paying the price: in these improvised details she had received a message as a medium without even noticing it, thinking only that she was cleverly handling a troublesome client. The other side occasionally did seek to redress wrongs, and this time spoke through Anne without her knowing.

Lying there now upon that unclean conjugal bed, she could have beat the air with her fists or wept like Constance to have received this knowledge and be unable to tell and unable to act. She listened to pity's contradictory demands: open Constance's eyes to the evil under her roof and soothe her to live with averted eyes amidst evil's inevitability, to suffer, since nothing, not even lust, lasts forever? Advise her to run away with her girl into poverty and hiding? Or do nothing, quiet her with sleeping draughts, nurture her ignorance, distract her with séances, provide her legions of ghosts to chase away, to defeat in her imagination while imagining away her real horror? But what good was any of it if the husband meant to slaughter her, as she believed, this outlandish, smiling murder by birth?

Constance had tried to tell Anne, that first meeting, however many days ago, a lifetime ago: "It is too horrible to forgive. I should close my mouth, my eyes should turn away, fade to blindness. I should almost prefer it, or that I should be dead."

Constance Barton had risen to this wealth, the theater boxes and rich meals, and now each pillow that bore her form acted like the gum that fixes a struggling insect in place. She had been told cruelly late the price she was expected to pay and pay and pay for her sticky comforts. If she should choose to complain at the conduct of her master she could be returned to a harder world. That she only saw a ghost or two— ghosts whose behavior so closely hewed to that of their human inspiration—was a tribute to the lady's solid character.

The child below, in fear and pain, wept alone, lived with a growing belief that this was how it should be or that this was her fault, that these were the workings of adults who understood best how to use her. It was not the first time Anne had heard of such a thing, of course. London was sick with it, a conspiracy whose practitioners lurked and laughed in homes of every quality, but never had Anne met and so quickly loved the poor child as she did this unfeathered angel.

She fiddled with the padlocks of his cupboards, examined his writing-desk, the spring-locked cellar presses, not certain what she would find, but hoping, perhaps, to come upon some inspiration, a lever upon which to propel her friend and the child to safety. The police were unlikely to help. A wiser than average constable might consent to visit, have a word, nod understandingly at the gentleman's amused or offended denials, then leave behind him a villain now further humiliated and a wife and child in darker danger. The law had no interest. Nor would some kindly physician correct the distortions of health infecting the home.

She watched Constance in the blue chair, surrendering herself to sleep only with the most ferocious defense, her head snapping up and down. "Come, your bedroom awaits you, cleansed of everything," Anne said, sick at her own performance. She led her friend, more asleep than awake, to her proper place.

"I should help you," Constance murmured. "I should be at your side." But Anne lifted her into bed and with a touch put her to sleep as easily as she had the little girl below.

If nothing else, she had provided them some overdue comfort tonight. Constance had gone to the theater, enjoyed the air and conversation, spoken of feeling at her ease. She had eaten and drunk well, minutely revenged herself upon her husband's port. Anne had supplied a collection of spiritualist weapons, offering a sense of action and progress. Now Constance slept in her bed, safe, if only for one night. In a few hours Anne would wake her with a description of repelling the manifestation, wounding it, would prove to her, at least, that it was both defeatable and not her fault. No, it was not enough. She had done not nearly enough. If there were unlimited time, she could teach her to accommodate the swine, remove temptations, erect obstacles, redirect his furies and hungers, hide the child behind rituals and social engagements. But there may in fact have been no time remaining, and Anne had given the trusting soul a box of basil.

She determined, in this long night's meditation, that she would not ask Constance to see everything, but would do the seeing for her. She would look upon the most fearful things and cover Constance's eyes, for Anne was made of coarser stuff. Ugly, covered with life's scars, people like Anne should exist so that people like Constance could live finer lives. Constance felt peace in Anne's company precisely because Anne was willing to absorb and hide the vileness that made any sort of peace impossible. And then, the painful conclusion to this line of thought, the sacrificial compromise: if Constance could be kept blind, then the beast could force himself upon the child to his content, and the mother's life would be safe.

"Banished all the banshees?" Nora asked as Anne descended the stair. Anne left the house, ordered the maid not to wake her mistress.

She found her man in the second public house she tried. It was no great coincidence; he perpetually circled between three of them, and he always told the publican he was leaving behind which one could expect to see him next. He was regularly needed. Any who desired an audience knew to place themselves in his circular path. It did him no good to lie low unless lying low was required.

Both long since retired from the stage, he and Anne had an ancient history of shared scenes and late nights of drink, mutual help here and there with matters theatrical or practical, when neither had another to turn to for assistance. Since those days of comradely hardship, he had established himself in circles and trades as sporadically profitable as Anne's. They had always called each other only by their greatest roles: he called her Gert, she called him Third, though the playbills years earlier had listed him, in tiny print at the very bottom of the *dramatis personae,* as Michel Sylvain, Thomas Wallender, Diccon Knox, Abel Mason, and several others. None of these was his name, and he never felt the need to give Anne any other, and she never cared to force him.

"Majesty," he intoned this night and bowed low when she came to the dark end of the room, full to bursting at this late hour. "Your servant."

"I saw Katy Millais in my gown tonight. It did not please me."

"Usurpation and atrocity, Highness. Drink?"

"To your eternal health."

He never asked what kept her away, and she never asked how he had filled his time or his purse since last they met. If a service was needed, they spoke to the question at once. When the call was social, they spoke only of events and people long since past. Tonight, Anne said only, "I need an item of protection for a lady."

"How's her wrists, then?" said Third as he led her farther back to a locked door he kicked twice. "Dainty or more like your lovely branches?"

Nora allowed her back in the house, though complained of the time, and Anne was soon upstairs to watch the child's room at quarter past three, the hour that had so troubled Constance. The girl slept through, as did her mother.

Before dawn, Anne woke her client with her report: "You are no bridge to this thing, for it has been, and in no way was it in response to your dreams," she told Constance, still soft and blurred from sleep. "Your heart should lift, sweet girl, for it is weakened, without question." At once (and even when still drowsy!) Constance pressed again the possibility of her husband's guilt.

"Where have you hidden your weapons?" Anne replied instead.

Constance led her to the chest outside the sleeping girl's room, revealed the cached box. "Here's one more item." Anne placed the narrow bone handle of Third's blade in Constance's palm. "Hold it like this, my dear." She folded Constance's soft fingers into the proper position. What precisely was Constance believing, willing to believe, prepared to hear? She did not ask what the knife was for, and Anne made light instead: "All women should have one in their trousseau, but how rare the mother who thinks of it! Hold your arm tightly to your side. Just so. You'll have no need of it." Anne took it from her and placed it amidst the crucifixes and greens. Perhaps the knife would lead Constance to think of her threats as flesh. Constance must have already known that they were speaking in code, performing a charade, but she was intent on an unworldly explanation. "You have the courage of a lioness protecting her cubs," Anne said. "I proved this very night that your horror is vulnerable to these tools. You will rid yourself of it. And in time you may find that your Joseph is your pillar of support again." She closed the box, replaced it in its hole.

Anne hoped she was wrong. Perhaps the husband was innocent. Perhaps there was a lesser ghost, over which Constance would yet prevail. Her heart was most perfectly dedicated to kindness and purity; if any should deflect evil, it was this one. "I wish I had you at my side, defending me every night," Constance said as they descended the stair.

"How certainly and quickly you place your heart's trust, my Constance. It is sure evidence of your wisdom. I cannot be here for your next struggle, but you lack nothing that you need. I have made certain of it."

They shared coffee and parted before first light. "We are nearer a solution than ever, my dear friend," Anne said at the doorstep, and wished it were true. She could not have said what solution would suffice. She thought of that child asleep upstairs, of the food and wine and cushions and drapes, of the man due back in the house that day, of this gentle woman for whom ignorance was the only protection she could offer.

VI

He emerged and stood a possessive moment or two on his step, scanned the sky and street, dully pleased with himself. Anne's first thought—it was only natural—was her hope that his lusts had been diverted. Her second thought—no less natural, considering the circumstances seen from her perspective—was that if he *had* prevailed—she could not help herself—she prayed the mother had been left untouched, and the daughter had borne the assault. Some would say Angelica was merely learning sooner than most the ugliness of men. That knowledge was almost a gift when seen in a certain dim light. And she would be saving her mother's life, a praiseworthy accomplishment for a young woman. In a world of Anne's design, Angelica, the little heroine, would receive commendations, the newspapers would write of her, as they did, in this lesser world, of any second lieutenant who amorously presented his breast to an enemy ball speeding towards his commander and who, for his comparatively puny courage, suffered a moment's sting and then savored an eternity's fame.

As she had done the first morning while Nora hid her face, Anne crossed the road and approached him as he walked from his door. She scanned the parenthesis of his mouth and the angle of his glances as she drew close to him on the path. She hoped to extract from his face some clear knowledge of the events of the night before. He looked at her and stopped a moment, and she recognized the expression of so many previous husbands. Now would come the threats and demands for money to be returned. But no, Joseph Barton examined her frankly with his dull countenance, snorted, and walked on.

"He knows of me?" she asked Nora at the door, which opened before she had even rung. Nora blocked her entry and lowered her eyes, reply enough. "I am going up to your mistress."

But the fool would not let her pass. "She's resting. The doctor's orders." Anne forced the girl's hand out of her way, and she cried out in pain. "Please, miss, please," Nora protested. "If he finds you've been, I'll be set out. He struck me." Yet another scene Anne had played before, just as she had introduced herself to Constance Barton with words she had used before, and kept her early wavering attention with stories she had told before. And yet, as in a play, all at once those scripted words— this time, this one time—bore in their bellies profundities, unnoticed for a thousand rote recitations before.

"Tell her she must not—no, tell her that she should . . ."

"Please, miss," Nora whimpered, tears flowing.

"Nora, I am begging you. Tell her that I await her in our grove. All day."

Anne sat in that park until darkness fell, only three times leaving unwillingly for necessities and, upon hurriedly returning, examining every child in the hope that one might be heroic Angelica. Laughter behind her wrenched her head around. A far-off little girl batting at a hoop caused her to stand and give chase; she had nearly pursued the receding girl into a wood before she admitted to herself that it was not Angelica but some blander child, frightened by and fleeing from the large woman bearing down upon her. And so she sat, useless with worry. Her Constance was prisoner in her home, swelling with a fatal child, and her jailer knew all, knew she had nearly escaped his grasp. He would not err again. She made contracts with herself, if only Constance was safe and would come. She promised that this time, given another opportunity, she would tell Constance all she knew, suggest something useful, anything at all. She also cursed Constance for a fool and a coward and a liar: surely she could leave her own home and come put Anne's mind at ease if she truly wished to. She meant to avoid all payment and now was sleeping or gulping powders to forget what she had seen or refused to see. Perhaps she had taken from Anne all that she had wanted, a little expertise and amusement, a dinner companion, a mothering comfort. Anne was surely expendable. Perhaps the man had apologized or lied, and Constance embraced his better self with relief that she no longer had to spend an hour with that fat and ridiculous widow who forced herself into the home where she could never belong, spouting ghosty tales and her poor experience. It would not have been the first time, nor would it be the last, Anne supposed, alone within a circle of oaks, the top of a stained silver moon just peering over the far rim to cast Anne's swaying silhouette far behind her onto the gray grass.

She did not sleep and was not sleeping when she heard through the open window Constance crying far below, tapping at the door. She was down before Mrs. Crellagh stirred, and in minutes all her questions were answered, all worries soothed, and she was again performing her most comfortable role—not guardian, but guardian of Constance. She carried Angelica to bed, then helped Constance through the door and to a warming glass. "He has beaten me," her friend confessed the obvious, her face bruised, blood upon her skin and collar. He had locked her away, disarmed her. She was threatening to destroy herself to protect her Angelica. She was *in extremis,* and so no solution that could restore her would be too extreme. "My poor child, my poor little girl," Anne whispered, happy despite herself, lightly kissing the fragrant hair, the brow worn by tedious terror.

"Why me?" Constance moaned. "Why is this happening to me? If you would answer merely that, if I might but know the felonies I must have committed to have won the undying vengeance of such a pursuer, then I could bear these punishments. I do not for a moment doubt I deserve this, but I cannot remember why." A strange formulation, to be sure. "I sacrificed myself for her tonight. I gave myself to it, to keep it off her." This confession of maternal suicide was too appalling, and Anne stammered to find the correct combination of words, to beg her to say she had not done it, thrown herself upon her enemy's blade to protect a child in no mortal (at least) danger.

"Will you not make this stop?" Constance asked, anger suddenly obliterating her fear then in turn quickly subdued by an almost child-like wheedling: "Please, Annie, please. I will do anything. I will pay you anything, give you anything." The words and tone caught Anne un-awares, taunted her. For all her self-confessed venality and ceaseless worries about her financial troubles, for all her intentions from the very first scene of this adventure to profit from Constance Barton's pain, at this moment when the woman accused Anne of withholding some so-lution from her until a price could be met, Anne was ashamed and des-perate to correct her. She had none to blame but herself, of course; she had cast herself in this role of grubby servant, fingers always sidling towards the purse, but now she was offended, blistered that her audi-ence was taking her performance to heart. "The devil take your hus-band's riches! You think I could withhold comfort from you?"

"I want it to end, so terribly, only to end."

And Anne arrived, at last, at an act in the drama never before per-formed: "Then it shall. This haunting shall stop, and you and Angelica shall be safe forever. I will see to it. I swear it—do you hear me? I *swear* it. I will end this. Quiet, my dear. I will end this. You will be free." Anne descended to her knees and kissed the top of the sobbing woman's head, kissed her wet hands, kissed her shaking, slicked cheeks, held her tightly to her chest and rocked her until the sobbing receded, then held her still, rocked her until her breathing slowed and she fell into a dreadful, trembling, muttering sleep, but held her still, head on lap, kissed her again and again, soothed the rattling breath, kissed her still.

VII

I met Third, decades later, when he was an old man given to deep stage laughter and elliptical conversation, but no senile jabbering. Anne wished to introduce me to her old friend, she said as we walked to his usual haunt (a public house of sharply limited appeal), only to see if I might find my way to winning him a small role, or a job backstage assisting a dresser, or guarding possessions during performances, even cleaning. It was not until she had left me alone with this happy old man—with the words "My dear, ask him anything you like, and he will reply most truthfully"—that I understood I had been brought to him for some other purpose.

For when I told him that any friend of my aunt's was a friend of mine and assured him I would do my utmost to win him employment in the theater, his former home, he condescendingly thanked me for my condescension, but said he did not mean to try my patience by requesting favors of me, "of all people." Why of all people? He laughed. "I know who you are."

"From Anne or from the stage?"

He only said, "I haven't forgotten a line, you know. I don't want to walk onstage again, but I could do it. Give me a cue."

It was true. We verified it for a very entertaining conversation. I fed him the cues to every line he had ever recited, and he produced his speechlets without fail. There were not so many *words,* of course, though he had performed dozens of roles, since most of his burden had been the prose of soldiers and ruffians or, when verse, the chopped feet and cut meters, the stumps that prodded kings and dukes to warm the air with lengthy justifications and commands. (Far more often he had merely posed mute and menacing, bearing a sword, or drum and colors, or the pie in which were baked the ravishers of Titus's daughter.) But in our game, my memory faltered before his. He never hesitated and was able to produce from only the smallest cues ("Prithee, what news?" or *"Enter Messenger and Talbot"*), his few, difficult-to-distinguish lines as Watchman, Soldier, Goth Prisoner.

I had asked Anne, some days before, for the first time since I was a girl, what she supposed had ever become of Joseph Barton, and in that pub one bright morning I began to understand I was meant to find my answers from this ancient actor. Can you not see her generosity? In her love for me, Anne did not wish to be tempted to defend herself. She knew she could convince me of anything, paint the world for me as she saw it, and I would accept it, thank her, love her all the more. But no, she would let me judge her actions without hearing her plea, uninfluenced by my long love for her. And, too, in her honorable way, she would not admit to a shared guilt without her fellow conspirator's consent, and so she led me to him, under false pretenses, to allow him to confess or not, as he preferred, and to allow him to condemn her if he wished.

Third chose to confess only, with a non-sequiturial lightness, that "Your aunt and I have played this game for many years." And he looked at me as if that were all I needed to know. And I suppose he was right. He and Anne had likely conversed one morning thirty years earlier, perhaps just out of range of his clear memory by the time I met him. They would have spoken softly, playing with the texts by which they once had lived, instilling the old words with new meaning by a hard look or stress, dressing reality in plays.

"*Gloucester.* A silent corner now, a word."
"   *Cutthroat.* My lord?"
"*Gloucester.* I would be free of one whose wormy heart
Offends all those I love. A ravisher
Of innocence, a Satan guised as man."
"*Cutthroat.* A name, my lord, and lo! thy will is done.
I would through hell itself swim coolly if
It rid you of a rat, a mouse, a flea.
His name, his name! I hunger for it and
Your love."

When a text ran dry, Anne must simply have changed plays, knowing that Third would follow her across the gaping canon.

"*Lucian.* A man of vile mores."
"   *Second Servant.* A moor?"
"*Lucian.*   Or less.
A fouler villain thou canst scarce conceive."

She led him to understand her wishes, even as they were surrounded by other ears, who thought them only drunken actors.

"*Macbeth.* I will advise you where to plant yourselves;
Acquaint you with the perfect spy o' the time,
The moment on't; for't must be done tonight."
"*Third Murderer.* We are resolved, my lord."

PART THREE

Joseph Barton

I

The most rigid conformists flee eccentric parents, and so I imagine—for I see no other way to fulfill your assignment here, where I have the least material from which to work—that this one aspires to convention without always convincing himself of his success. He is not easily the master of his work, his home, his females. His wife disobeys, or claims to obey but only minds the letter of his law while the spirit of the thing flits away out of view, and he cannot say quite where their intentions parted ways. He exerts himself to please her, but can scarcely understand her, nor remember why he chose her so long ago, nor fathom why she accepted him. He suffers from that most modern disease infecting so many of our men: irresolution. He has abdicated his manhood. He has been lulled into allowing feminine impulses to overflow their appropriate canals and inundate his home. He never had anyone to teach him his role, and his instincts have failed him. Appetites trouble him that he believes spare others.

II

Harry Delacorte, my source for a few of my very few facts, shouted at Joseph Barton—to be heard over the massed partisans and so Harry could face the ring while he spoke, rather than turn and risk missing the damp impact of skinned knuckle against red flesh. "The midwife tells me I should have a third child before the night is through."

"Well! I had no idea she was so near. Are you pleased?"

"Do you know what that madwoman told me? 'It would be for the best'—in her wisdom—'that the child sleep at the mother's side, *for the first week or so.*' A week? My God, there wouldn't be any survivors. Have you ever heard such a thing? As if I were the leader of a band of Gypsies. I told her—Hallo! he'll feel that blow for a time. I asked her if we should all share rice from one big pot cooked over a fire in my bed-chamber."

"Sleep in your room?" Joseph marveled. "Madness. I wouldn't stand for even a single night of it."

"You know," mused Harry, curiously watching a fighter stumble backwards while his opponent continued to flail at his head, "these fellows are, above everything else, skilled at controlled fury. It's a sort of genius, I'd say."

"Their wives must be a canvas of bruises."

"Prejudice and slander! No, I rather doubt it. I should think these boys can afford to be lambs at home. Their quietest word should suffice to instill discipline." Joseph heard envy in this assessment, as Harry probably had to resort to other measures, though it would be hard to imagine much effect from them, no matter his fury. He stood well past six feet, but was slight as straw and always bent like a lakeside reed to hear others' words. He pinned his elbows to his sides and walked with small rapid steps giving him an air of fluttering, effeminate precision and the ability to approach in silence, even on the hard floors of the laboratory, speaking before one knew he was in the room, giving one the uneasy sensation that he had been perhaps observing one, unnoticed.

Harry Delacorte's aspect and high-pitched voice, however, reflected not at all his character: his appetite for female companionship, his vicious snobbery, his morbid humor. (Earlier that evening, he had laughed almost to coughing as he described to Joseph the game his two boys had recently invented in which they pretended to be soldiers coming upon the murdered bodies of their own parents—Harry and his wife—torn to pieces by blacks, and then set themselves upon a grand mission of revenge. "This is for my father!" Gus declared, slashing a wooden saber across Harry, playing the role of the African bandit chief.)

Joseph had befriended young Delacorte on the latter's first day in the laboratory as a medical student, a few weeks after Angelica's birth. Joseph watched Harry as Dr. Rowan instructed him in a series of quite basic surgical techniques on a specimen. When Rowan moved down the aisle to the next student, Harry, his face contorting, nervous from the sounds of the specimens, hesitated at the sight of actual trembling flesh and pink tissue. He was discovering, as everyone did, that the drawings in the anatomy text were useless simplifications, idealized sketches of a seabed, when before him squirmed only the waves of the opaque surface. Joseph, recently abandoned by his wife for an ungrateful baby, resolved (almost in imitation of her) to take the young man in hand. He watched as with shaking fingers Harry lifted a blade and held it above the specimen he could not keep still with his clumsy weak grip.

"If I might make a suggestion, sir"—Joseph abased himself, "sir" for these younger men about to accomplish what he fled from finishing sixteen years earlier—"one must simply trust one's hands to perform the task without consulting too closely with one's eyes." Joseph placed his hands atop the boy's and expertly guided the immobilizing grasp with the left and incision with the right.

"Yes, yes," Harry said, stepping back, rubbing his palms together. "I wonder if I haven't rather significantly misjudged my aptitudes."

"Oh, no, one persists, you see, and everything changes, sir. You will be a hand at all this in no time."

"Damn, it's nice to meet a good fellow here. You must be a prince working incognito. I'd shake your hand, but, well, obviously."

Harry, whom Joseph had protected from his evident incompetence and then befriended, was now Joseph's superior. After Harry took his degree, he had returned to the laboratory in the capacity of Dr. Rowan's chief assistant for the designing of the researches. It was a position that Joseph had thought he himself had perhaps earned, or could earn, despite not being a medical doctor. Harry had worn this laurel lightly, never mentioning the shift in relations between him and his former mentor. He continued to spend evenings with Joseph, frequented boxing exhibitions with him, wagered according to Joseph's advice, and won a fair amount as a result.

Lecrozier's fist cut below Monroe's defense and, like a cartographer, painted a newly discovered red archipelago across the bleached blue map of the canvas. Monroe descended to one knee, as if to examine its accuracy. "Well done." Harry applauded with elbows tight to his sides. "You know, I wonder if it's to be a daughter tonight. Which would you prefer, you were me? I suspect a third son would be quite amusing. One to inherit my estates, one an admiral, and this one tonight a bishop. Would be simpler. Boys are all quite the same. At two, they discover locomotives, and it is as if Jesus opened their eyes to the glories of heaven. A year later they are quite indifferent to engines but frothing for horses. At four, horses are suitable only for stupid children, and God's green earth exists solely to provide insects that must be captured, fed, and then crushed or set aflame. And now at five, Gus can speak of nothing but guns."

Monroe could stand no more, and cleaners converged to scrub the ring. Harry turned to examine the ladies moving in and out of the shadows at the back of the hall, their public's appetite heightened by the boxing (though their success here was proportionally less than what they used to achieve at hangings). "What do girls do?" Harry asked, lifting a finger to catch the eye of a red-haired specimen. "Yours, for example?"

"No idea. She is fond of her rag doll. Not indifferent to science. One does not spend hours discussing her pastimes."

When Joseph returned home, well past midnight, Constance did not stir, but the child did, sat straight up in her little bed pressed against the foot of his own. She would not go back to sleep, and, Constance snoring, Joseph spent two futile, infuriating hours cajoling, commanding, caressing until finally the girl closed her eyes, but by then he was too angry to do the same. A band of Gypsies.

III

At the start, Joseph could only have viewed my birth as a blow, a breath of destruction.

The destruction of his wife, most obviously. He had fallen in love with Constance's large, almost childlike eyes, which gave her an expression in repose that others would have had to expend muscular energy to achieve. But with each false birth, her eyes receded, encrusted with exhaustion. She looked more ill on each childbed, and he was ashamed that he often found her ugly during these crises, like the starving he had seen in war. She recovered after each effort, but only in part, never to the fresh beauty of their beginning, or even to the reduced state she had reclaimed after recovering from the prior loss.

Constance was dying in stages in these demibirths and then was struck hardest by Angelica. Even after surviving, she was tortured by the living child. Angelica's rhythmic wailing, for example, drove Constance to tears because she was still too weak to see to her assailant's needs. The cry was only a preliminary rebuke. A second stung when the din changed in tone, for that meant that Nora had taken the girl to the wet nurse who shared Nora's room. The third insult was the silence that the gleefully sated girl gave off, even more offensive to her victim, two stories up.

Joseph understood the newborn animal's requirements, but still this beast had nearly killed his wife and now proceeded to taunt its maimed victim, aggressive howls tuned to extract favors from the cowed and punish those powerless to please it. Its repetitive two-tone cry of victory came to remind Joseph of African war whoops surging sourcelessly from the dark bush, a rising wail intended to unbowel an enemy before battle.

His own mother had died in childbirth (in a manner of speaking). Her memory had haunted his father and his home, this same home where a baby now shrieked at all hours, as he had once shrieked for a mother who could not help him, until he fell in love with the breast of a wet nurse instead. His wife time and again threatened to leave him, as his mother had.

The destruction of his conjugal habits, of his comfort, of household routine. The emergence of Nora as a visible and audible resident in the house with her own voice and conversation to indulge. The slow and rapid destruction of principles and practices, as large as his sleeping arrangements and as small as this: the girl at six months took food into her mouth and promptly spat out the first bite, no matter if it was a favorite or novelty, vile or fine. The second bite would be taken greedily, but the first always emerged, as if she were a sommelier. He did not bridle at the costs of the child, clothing and feeding and paying its doctors, but food spilled, thrown, spat, while the adults in charge of her laughed at this wide-eyed biter of human flesh—he found it difficult to feign amusement. There was no space in the house where he could escape. If he could have soothed it himself, he would have done so, but there was no assistance he could provide. When he did attempt to treat the child as Nora and Constance did, apologizing to it for its rages, coddling it with warmer milk or cooler, exchanging (in the rare silence) assertions and counterassertions of resemblance between the child and Constance, even thus abasing himself to the mewling creature, still they smiled and pushed him out of the room, off to find some other space in which to listen, alone, to the hysterical hilarity.

This is but what every man experiences, you say. Yes, but some enjoy a spark of Darwinian self-love or godly affection. Should we then fault the man for whom there is so little charm in the event? Whose wife nearly died and then abandoned him to devote herself to her attacker? Did he give himself over to self-pity? Not all at once, but such traits require time to germinate.

He had once imagined children, he supposed, vague notions of sons, smaller versions of himself with scientific passions and a taste for English sporting life. When Constance was first with child, he had perhaps indulged in a bit of reverie here and there, walking to the Labyrinth or watching her uncomfortable sleep while he wiped her damp brow. He may have imagined a future professor of anatomy. He may have anticipated being the boy's first instructor, leading him one precisely calibrated step at a time into knowledge. He may have intended to present the child with a silver praxinoscope and enjoy his fascination as he peered through it. But these notions evaporated in Constance's first laboring fever.

"I want to give you a child," Constance had told him, soon after they were wed (though, at his quiet insistence, not churched). "I want to give you a child," she had said as they set off on their wedding trip. She said it again in the tower of their hotel in Florence. "I want to give you a child." A bride's gift.

"I want to give you a child," she had whispered, all of her strength necessary even for that thin, dry sound, less than an hour after the first loss, when he saw, as clear as knowledge, that she was about to die. He said, "Never again. You must never suffer like this again. I cannot see you like this." But his miserable words of love only saddened her more: "Yes, again. I want to give you . . ." And through his sorrow for her sufferings and the loss of her youth—all in a matter of moments—he felt a flash of wonder at her tenacity: she longed, even in this state, to give him a child? Even as the remains of her previous effort were being wrapped and hurried outside by the midwife, and lies about half-baptisms were titrated to anesthetize her? Only then, for the first time, did he wonder if she were truly speaking to him. She was delirious in many of her other pronouncements in these tenuous hours, and this familiar statement of devotion seemed distorted in context: "I want to give you a child," she said later, her eyes shut. He took her icy hand in his, blew warm air onto her blue fingers. "My Con, my only Con," he said, and her eyes opened. "Joseph? Are you here?" Had she not known that? Then to whom was she just offering a child?

"I want to give you a child," she had said after that, whenever he approached her with tenderness. She would chant this with such urgency that his mild refusals ("It hardly matters to me, my dear, considering your fragile health") served only to strengthen her resolve. "No! It is my duty to you. The most important thing, the gift I am here to bring you. All I have." This shocking declaration of faith had both pleased and distressed him. He did not care, not truly, if she gave him a child or a spaniel. He could not particularly imagine what he would do with such a gift, and his own family history, I strongly suspect, rather dissuaded him from the notion that the river of domestic contentment flows from the arrival of children.

"I want to give you a child," she had murmured, even as Angelica was alive and squalling in the room with her. And Joseph wept that his stationer's girl was going to die now, not even seeing that her useless gift to him was already delivered into his stiff and unwilling arms.

In retrospect, considering the role Angelica had come to play in her mother's life, his doubts about the purity of her ritual declaration were prescient. She had wanted a child for her own reasons, reasons so deeply ingrained in Constance or in all women that she would likely have been unable to say what they were, and she may very well have believed (he allowed his vanity and her sincerity) that producing a child *was* intended as a loving gift to him, that somehow *he* desperately desired progeny, all his words, inclinations, and history to the contrary.

But surely she could not believe it still. Constance's transformation from wife to mother was so thorough, so magically comprehensive, it was as if she were acting out some myth. She dedicated herself to the child to the detriment of all wifely responsibility, even of simple preference or affection for her husband. She, who had once so exerted herself to be charming and agreeable to him, now had no conversation that did not flutter about the child's latest squawk or sneeze. He lately had the impression, too, that she had learned to mock him in some subtle fashion, some intonation that made jibes at his uselessness, even at his intelligence, the meditative manner he knew others found slow. Even she, who once did not notice or mind, who once called him her wise tortoise and saw in his comportment the epitome of scientific perspicacity, even she puffed out her cheeks, tapped her foot, rolled her eyes just slightly when he replied too slowly and thought he was not watching her.

So in what possible manner could she still consider that the child had been "for" Joseph? The child had been from him, despite him, instead of him. Constance's withdrawal from him had been—if one looked from a position of high enough perspective—a nearly straight path from the moment of Angelica's birth. Mother and daughter were drifting farther and farther away, hand in hand, as if upon the back platform of a silently receding omnibus, "I want to give you a child" merely a misstated "I want a child."

Perhaps it had begun much earlier. Perhaps she had selected him as he frequented Pendleton's, and allowed him to think he selected her, had identified him as a man she could take from ("give to") and in turn discard, and he would never complain. She knew even then that he was a fool, a vessel of shameful appetites she could manage with ease. Now the two females would only grow closer and more similar, while Joseph stood aside, the eunuch-financier-protector of the sultanless harem. At times, when her singular attention was upon Angelica to the extent that she no longer even noticed if Joseph entered or left their presence, he would exaggerate his pain and allow her to see a portrayal of hurt upon his face, and would win as a result, sometimes, a sympathetically dispensed nurse's affection. Nearly as soon as he won it, though, he would wish to be done with it, the whole exercise humiliating him most of all.

The blame lay solely upon him, of course. He had allowed, one twig at a time, this nest of feminine tittering and silences to take shape in his home. When Angelica was a baby, with no language, Joseph could see no way at all to pass the long minutes of his stewardship over her, could not even find any scientific stimulation in her development, as the infant was far less interesting than the creatures he worked upon in the laboratory. He knew the baby wanted him to leave her and let the more expert coddler, player, singer, feeder return. "My dear, she's calling for you again," he would say in surrender. Even now, as Angelica became more recognizably human, when he attempted to inquire about her games, even to offer himself as a playfellow, the sheer repetitiveness of her conversation and fancies lulled him to sleep as she grew more excited.

I suppose you would diagnose his boredom as a sublimation of his own fear of impotence, or some such, would you not? That sounds quite like you. I am growing rather proficient at playing your role. And you would be correct, sir, but only in that he feared himself to be unnecessary to the child and, worse, perhaps even harmful. At the very least, I think he feared he bored the tiny creature as much as she bored him, that he lacked even spark enough to amuse this animal whose threshold of amusement must indeed have been very low, since the sight of her mother crossing her eyes or Nora pretending to fall down could induce such joy.

But, too, might not the term for this be *unrequited love*? The child's preference for Constance—*preference* hardly conveys the stark distinction the child made between Constance and the rest of creation, as if one could be said to *prefer* oxygen to noxious gas—was plain at every stage of its development, even in the scarcely human object a few weeks old. It was a preference that Joseph certainly shared and could even admire, but might Anne Montague's suspicions of him have been correct, unrequited love transformed into rage against its object? Admit it: you suspect he was guilty. Admit, too, that you look at me today, lying at your feet as I once lay at his, and you understand his crime.

He came to pass evenings alone in the park, pushing at the gravel under his boots, resistant to returning home, aware of all his prowling weaknesses, his ache of shame and resentment, his shiver of self-disgust. He watched the last children of the day overseen by seated mothers and standing governesses. A pretty little girl ran by, illustrating tangents with her hoop and stick. Two or three years older than Angelica, she would soon put away her toys, take up less childish exertions, fold away the sharp extensions of her personality into a tidier creation, compacted to play new roles. Angelica, so closely monitored and shaped by her mother, would be lost to him quite soon, even more unavailable than she was now. He would not have denied a mild envy of the sticky female ties, the shared laughter and tears between wife and daughter, between Constance and her gift to him.

IV

How low his expectations had fallen! All he craved now was a night's sleep. Four years he had tolerated the child's sleeping at their feet. Her midnight coughs and requests, even the merest bleats sufficed to rouse Constance to the child's side, smashing all normal life. This usurpation of logic, this parade of coddled fears and sicknesses real and imagined, had shoved the figmentary well-being of child and wife ahead of their true well-being. Joseph had, in brief, ceded control of the most central decisions of his domain. Constance had demanded it in her fashion. He could scarcely fault her for this, as it was her nature. He, however, should not have indulged her for so long, nor allowed her to imagine he was unaffected by her preference for the child.

He had recently detected faint signs in Angelica of a small person of substance, perhaps even intelligence, a fleeting interest in the natural world. He resolved, in a lightning burst of inspiration as Constance was resisting his decision to move the child downstairs, that Angelica be given an appropriate education in these matters, and in language as well. She would otherwise be too softened by her mother, who would never expose the child to anything but dolls and frills, moods and superstitions.

On this point and others he would clarify for Constance her correct role, and he would see her play it. The first night of his new administration he stayed away from the house until he was certain the child would be asleep. He returned to the satisfactory report that she slept in her own bed (though Constance complained the child had sobbed in resistance).

"She will adjust, I should imagine," he offered. He thought it likely that Constance would find this transition difficult, as well, but it would not do to surrender at the first sign of progress, and so he told her, kindly, of his intention to see to Angelica's education. He was not truly surprised by Constance's immediate opposition to his plans, her implication that he was not to make decisions about the child's formation. Her presumption of his irrelevance only confirmed how far from his control the house had slipped, and he responded sharply, "The day may yet come when she considers *me* a friend as well."

He regretted it at once. Surely the path he intended to pursue demanded from him an example of even temper, else Constance would have no model to emulate. He took her hand. She was cold, petulant. He felt in turn like a clumsy suitor, courting a woman whose true love had died days earlier, or languished in prison at his command.

"I must look in on Angelica," she said at once and fled to the child.

At the very barest minimum, he would now enjoy a full night abed, his first in four years. And yet, having instituted this most overdue reform, he found his nights were, if anything, more disrupted. This first night, when Constance returned, he was patient with her tears and melancholia as long as he could bear, three occasions or four—as many violations as he had usually suffered from Angelica's presence—but that fourth plaintive sob—with the sky still black and his head pounding and his eyes and gums dry—broke his best intentions. He simply said enough, enough, he could display no more enthusiasm for mourning a child's descent to its own bed.

The second evening, returning early enough to find the child still awake in its new bed, he asked for a moment alone with her, intending to calm her nocturnal fears. Constance surrendered this privileged in-

terview only with difficulty, but as soon as she left, the child took
Joseph quite by surprise: she threw her arms around his neck and kissed
him repeatedly. "Thank you, Papa!"

"Whatever for, child?"

"For this room! My tower room!"

"You are content here?"

Her gratitude was evident, and he saw no coincidence in this leap
forward in their relations and the reforms he had instituted. Leaving
the child happily in her bed, he descended to a meal with a sullen wife
who informed him, despite what he had just seen, of the child's miserable resistance to her bedroom again.

This need not prove perfidy; perhaps the child responded more fa-
vorably to him. Constance, expecting misery, saw misery, while he, expecting soft consent, was duly rewarded. Constance had, at least,
obeyed his instruction that, as a first step in the matter of education,
the child spend a few minutes perusing a book from his library, with
plates of anatomy and naturalist sketches, though his wife rebelled even
here: "I thought it ill-suited for her."

Constance now scarcely slept. They lay next to each other in silence.
He was ridiculously hesitant to touch even her hand, so skittering was
she, despite the superhuman patience he had shown towards her
fragility for nearly a year now, and three years prior to that. Within a
few minutes and without a word of apology, she rose, vanished from
the matrimonial bed for hours.

No, it was not as simple as he would have hoped; nothing in his experience had ever been. He allowed her to depart, to gaze upon the
child, and he waited in silence, until, still alone, he fell asleep. He
awoke, alone still, and rubbed his eyes until they would allow him to
read the clock. He descended and found the child asleep in her bed
and, across from her, Constance in a chair, in a posture of readiness, absolutely—but for her closed eyes—a sentinel, her fingers still clutching
an extinguished candlestick, held out before her to light the dark, a
sleeping woman watching over a sleeping child, the burnt black wick
casting no light. Her other hand dug into the arm of the chair until her

knuckles whitened and her nails had bent slightly backwards at their tips. Joseph stepped between the bed and the chair and caught his breath when he saw that Constance's eyes were not quite closed, only very nearly so. She had fallen asleep trying so desperately to remain awake that her eyes had remained slightly open, and in that narrow gap Joseph could see purest white, her eyes rolled up and away in the final defeat of her will.

He placed his hand lightly upon her shoulder, and she jolted to one side as if he had struck her. "Come along. Up to bed now," he whispered. She opened her eyes fully and saw him before her, and she cried out at once, screamed a single *no* so piercingly that he turned to see if it had roused the child. The force of the cry was enough to roll the girl slightly to one side.

Constance, trembling and perspiring, rose unsteadily to her feet, but refused his support, as if he were a hangman leading a martyr. "No," she repeated quietly and sat again, closed her eyes at once.

So she looked at him with starkest fear, recoiled from him, and would reject his company and his bed, after all that he had done for her, all that she took with her smiling daytime face. He considered locking the door against her.

But his anger dispersed with the gray morning. He awoke to her offering him tea and bread, and Angelica playing on their floor. "Mr. Barton." Constance smiled. "A morning of rest." "Good morning," he replied, trying to recall the events and anger of the night before. She gripped his hand, and he stopped searching for the justifying memory. "Are you well?" he asked. "Only," she said, "when you are content." She looked at him as she used to do, before the child and all her suffering and their separation. He recognized her expression's purity and simplicity and now its rarity, as if their years together had denied her the ability to respond to him openly. He was every day of less interest to her, but something in his new resolution had drawn her to him this morning. He longed, blinking in the new light, to say something that would recast him for her, that would render him less a mystery to her, or more of one. She sat at the edge of the bed and held his hand. It had been so long since she had shown him such attention. He felt both grateful and angry at the realization. He could almost separate the harsh words from the tender, could almost find the correct first word, and they would cleave to one another anew.

Instead, a scream burst from behind the footboard, and Constance at once dropped Joseph's hand and bounded to the girl's side, crying, "What is it, love?"

"Princess Elizabeth!" Angelica wailed. "She has hurt her hand terrible!"

"Oh, Princess," consoled Constance, disappearing behind the footboard. "Let us examine Her Highness's injury."

V

Harry would likely have some practiced quip or snippet of Shakespeare to bring to bear on the issue, but Joseph would not explain his domestic trials to his friend, now the father of three boys and the husband of a strong and loving wife. It was appalling enough that, between the Labyrinth and the boxing hall, he and Harry had stopped at the Barton home for tea only to discover his child very slightly under the maid's eye and his wife nowhere to be found.

Harry was predictably untroubled by what confounded Joseph. He at once folded himself onto the tiny piano bench alongside Angelica and set to teaching her a piece, complete with a story, voices, and jests. "Here is where the little Princess of the Tulips sets off to the magical garden," he said and placed the girl's hands on the correct keys. His tone both captivated Angelica and communicated to Joseph that Harry was by no means a fool. It was enviable, the ease of his manner, and all of a piece with Harry, his ability to enchant a female of any age. "The little Princess of the Tulips must evade the pixies," he said.

"Angelica will be starting her formal education soon," Joseph interrupted, stilted and absurd to adult or child's ears. "She will have some Latin in no time."

"Oh, your father is cruel!" Harry stopped playing and crossed his arms.

"Is he? Are you, Papa?"

"To make a sweet child like you toil in those fields of thorny declensions and bear all those heavy cases! The grievous wounds I still suffer, the abrasions of the ablative. It is no place to send a lovely girl to labor!"

"That will do, Harry. Dr. Delacorte is jesting, child." Harry's occasionally enviable levity was dispensed with indifference to context. "Nora, inform your mistress that we came and left, and felt sorely her unexplained absence."

"A marvelous girl, Joe," Harry said as they stepped back into the rain, brushing off his friend's temper. "The picture of her mother, ain't she?" She was without question a small duplicate of Constance's beauty—small and also undeniably fresher, the beauty Constance had boasted before she bruised it repeatedly against unforgiving maternity. The likeness was cruel: the child growing to resemble the prey from whom she had drained the life.

They walked, despite the rain and the gathering particular, and Joseph marveled at how easily Harry had won Angelica's attention, respect, laughter. Joseph could with effort perhaps recall three occasions when he had exercised a similar influence over his own child. "Let's stop here a moment," he said, inspired by the window front of a taxidermist. ("Excellent," Harry agreed. "I had meant to pick up a lion.") Joseph gravely bought a mounted and framed butterfly, a white-fringed blue marvel of design, a male *Polyommatus icarus,* certain to remind Angelica of one of those rare occasions, only last summer, when her father had seemed a most delightful companion. "I think Gus would quite enjoy setting that blue beauty on fire," Harry said.

Joseph's late father had had the same charms and swiftness. It surprised Joseph that he had only now noted the resemblance as they found a cab to take them to supper and then the boxing. They had nothing objective in common of course: Joseph's father had been a foreigner, an Italian still bearing the surname Bartone (shortened only for his English-born son), who had traveled to England as a young man representing his own father's affairs, fallen in love with an English rose, and never returned home, even after he was widowed.

"That first glimpse of your mother, Joe, was too enchanting for mortal eyes," Carlo Bartone told his eleven-year-old son in the room that was now thoroughly Constance's parlor. "She was a goddess, for whom my exile was not too dear a price. I was criminally, fatally enchanted." He lit a cigar, looked to the small painted portrait of Joseph's mother on the writing-desk, half-obscured by a red leather pen-cup. "She wore flowers in her hair and when she saw me, she widened her eyes and did not release me. I was expected back in Milan. I could not. You see, when men look at women, they stare deeply. At a soirée or theater, men's eyes hold their prey. But women's eyes *sweep* only, never stop. Except for prostitutes, of course, women's eyes sweep and wound us in passing. But your mother, her eyes stopped at mine and held me."

The realization of Harry's similarity to his father colored Joseph's entire meal. Harry's every comment was something his father could have said, each lightly tossed opinion, easy joke, assessment of a passing female form. Joseph seemed less his father's son than did his friend.

But then the strangest sensation seized him not two hours later. In the exhibition hall a hallucinatory silence swept past him: silence flung from the spectators' throats, silence ringing out from Crewe's left fist hooking and shattering Pickett's jaw, silence offered by the hawkers and the girls with the tobacco and the girls without the tobacco, silence blanketing everything for a long instant, timed precisely to permit Joseph to see himself as if from a distance, as if examining the work of a sculptor, and to register surprise at this sight of himself that had been awaiting his notice: he held his beer, stood in his usual posture, and inescapably resembled his father. He could have been the old man himself tilted slightly to the left, the elbow of his drinking arm propped on the wrist of his cigar arm. This was his father's manner to the last detail, the angle of his face to the object of his attention (not quite direct), the exaggerated X-spread of the legs. In his father's case that had been an aggressive statement of presence, but in Joseph's it was meaningless imitation become habit. Joseph had as a boy imitated this gestural suite of

Carlo Bartone's, but never remarked until now that he had never stopped, and now it was no imitation but sinewy fact. His father's ghost inhabited Joseph's limbs, for he was the same age now as his father had been when he died.

And then it was over: Pickett's legs refused to perform even the simplest task, and at that crucial moment the returned roar of the crowd seemed to cause his collapse rather than merely welcome it. Harry cheered, Joseph sipped his beer. They won two pounds.

Joe Barton's father never asked his son's forgiveness, never apologized for his failures, financial and moral. Joseph's most English inheritance, his mother's plainest gift to him, was his inability to live as his father had and as Harry did (his friend now turning to the back of the hall to select from the evening's buffet of companions). Joseph Barton would never possess that joyful lack of worry about consequence or cost, nor Harry's wit that so captivated even his own daughter. But, even if he did not resemble his father in manner or character, he was not without similarity, and that knowledge touched him strangely. His father had never asked his forgiveness, but Joseph resembled him nonetheless.

It is precisely what I do not know of Joseph Barton that is most important to our effort, is it not? What he thought in company, how he behaved when unobserved? The tenuous, fantastical nature of your assignment has never been clearer to me than in trying to paint, from a faded pencil sketch, this portrait in oils. He poses in near total darkness, lit by faint memory or the reflected stories of others, Harry Delacorte's polished and unlikely secondhand reminiscences.

"Enchantresses. Sorceresses, my boy." Father and son rode through the park in an open calèche. Joseph was perhaps eight, perhaps twelve, he could not recall with certainty. "This is how the English take the air," his father said, tipping his hat and smiling to passing women—riding or walking—with a theatrically accented but unembarrassed "How d'ye do, *signorina*?," indifferent to or unfamiliar with distinctions of rank, a radical distribution of his wealth of affection for this island nation of sorceresses. "That one there, Joe, look how she turns her head to the side. She is showing us her neck, she means for us to look at it and to become caught by it. Hold fast to the door handle! One must be strong." The boy did as he was told—he must have been only eight— and soon they were out of danger, for the present. "That one would have had us, to be sure. The spells they cast are manifold."

His father watched the world from odd angles, just over Joseph's head, just to the side when he was speaking to his son. The women in looking glasses and reflective windows intruded on their every conversation, even when his father did not mention them. He watched, unseen and breathing deeply, cigar smoke leaving his mouth in long, thin streams that pointed after their departures, like his hopes, not quite reaching them as they left a café or restaurant, left Carlo behind with a boy for company. His father would bite the tip of his tongue, his head tilted to watch their merciful, merciless flight, his cigar held off to the side, the boy's conversation nearly inaudible.

But within the house on Hixton Street, discussion was only of a single woman, the Calypso who had lured Carlo to this island and imprisoned him, the woman who had died bringing his only son into the world, his English son.

"I watch these Englishmen for years, Joe. I am not one, but you are. You talk like them. You go conquer something for England, that will settle the question for them. Listen." His father lifted a book from his writing-desk, open to the page he had just read and which so affected him that he had called his fourteen-year-old son to listen. " 'Englishmen ride out in the morning of their youth unto the furthest corners of the earth and then, pulled back as if by a spring clutching their heart, they are gathered up again, sped home, deeper into their home than they had ever known before they left it, drawn back into the arms of England, deeper still into a country house, and finally, deepest of all, into a corner of their study, with a globe on the desk, showing them everywhere they once had conquered.' You see, Joe?"

Motherless and usually fatherless, Joseph was raised by his Italian nurse, Angelica, whom Carlo entrusted with all decisions about the boy, submitting to her even when, on rare occasions, he held a parental opinion. Never silent and often insubordinate to her employer, it was Angelica who nursed the newborn Joseph, then fed him, washed him, dressed him, read to him, put him to bed. It was she who taught him his religion and took him to church. It was she who struck him, scolded him: "What does your poor mother think, up in heaven, when she sees you behave like that?" And it was she who would shake her head and hide none of her distaste whenever Carlo left the house alone. "Your father is a very great man," she taught him, sometimes with real enthusiasm. "Your father is a perfect monster," she would also say with more emotion.

He had posed before a looking glass! He had practiced standing as his father stood! The memory came to him now, and he closed his eyes to the boxing to recall the event more clearly. He stood before the looking glass in his father's dressing room (his own now), and he held one of his father's unlit cigars and turned his head to the glass in three-quarters, closed his eyes slightly and looked down his nose and to the side, as at a flower girl. "How d'ye do, *signorina*," he trilled.

He only noticed his keeper standing at the parted arras the moment she spoke: "You are a filthy wretch, and you will burn for a hellish eternity." He was strapped, denied supper, denied company, locked in his bedroom. He could not recall, opening his eyes to the boxing, what he had thought of this punishment at the time. The terror and isolation he certainly could recall, could recall weeping and worrying and crying out for Angelica to forgive him. But he could not recall if he had known what he had done to be separated from her, whose company at that age he still craved. Tonight, thinking upon the event, he quite comprehended her response. She could never have forgiven his father, nor any resemblance between father and son, and would have loathed the sight of him rehearsing a likeness. "That is not how Englishmen behave," she reminded Joseph repeatedly about his father's conduct, yet, were it not for his father's unforgivable behavior, he could never have been an Englishman. His father's lies protected Joseph, set him on a better path than he would otherwise have ever found. It was above all a question of forgiveness.

But then some overindulging fool spilt his whiskey down Joseph's shirtfront, and the brass and oil stink of it burnt Joseph's nose and scratched his throat. He had not drunk the stuff since the Army. Even the plentiful cigar smoke did not suffice to disperse the jagged golden clouds of it, and by the time he had covered the last distance home in Harry's cab, it was the only smell in all London, effacing gardens and standing sewage alike.

In the darkness between the vestibule and the stairs, he struck his hip against the corner of the massive end table Constance had insisted upon for this narrow space. An enormous volume of dark wood, crushing the rug, blocking the dark paneling behind it, it sheltered dishes in its dark gut and displayed more on its dark surface. And yet, rubbing his hip and cursing in the dark room, Joseph could almost see his father's light-wood standing writing-desk, which had once occupied this same spot. He could conjure that previous resident and its accessories—a dimpled pewter inkstand; pens in their cup; ebony-handled paper knife; a trapezoidal leather box for coins; and the portrait in its frame of tortoise. "Look at her, Joe. She would have thought you a prince beyond measure. She was an angel from heaven. I pray I am lucky enough to visit her once a century during my long residency elsewhere." Most likely true, but at the time, Joseph reassured his aging father that he would surely be at his lady's side, that she had doubtless by then charmed the recording angel to ignore this and that, and had commissioned from cherubic carpenters a pearly love seat for the two of them.

His noisy entry caused a lamp to light, and Nora appeared at the kitchen door, either off to bed or waking for her morning tasks. In either case, assured that the noise was only Mr. Barton, she turned away, and Joseph watched by the obscured light (dimming as she withdrew) as her apron strings untied behind her. The strings unknotted and slid apart from each other, a slow, intricate choreography, over and under, two serpents parting after the tangle of the vital embrace, going their own ways around Nora's wide hips as she disappeared into the kitchen, and Joseph felt a shiver of desire.

For her? For Nora? The fat Irish girl who billowed behind her the aroma of old butter whenever she passed? The similarities to his father had now crossed over from the evocative to the outlandish. These multiplying urges, leaving all sense behind, daily surprising him by their strength and illogic. It was biology, only to be expected, of course, independent of will or soul or (in this case) even beauty. Inhuman desire flowed freely around and between humans, forming lasting or fleeting currents between poles quite at random and for purposes unclear. His father had gladly submitted to these laws while Joseph tried to resist, with varying success. The absurdity of human flesh bubbled far beneath one's efforts to dress it in starched morals and silken ethics. Cloak it as one did, it still spoke and listened only to all the flesh around it, in a language indifferent and inaudible to human ears. To be shocked into sensitivity by Nora, of all the members of the species! If she could assault him, who could not?

"How like your father, how shameful," the first Angelica would have said. "Your mother is somewhere weeping to see how you carry yourself." She had in fact spoken those words to him, in his bedroom, he recalled, after father and son returned from an evening's adventures, including a visit, Joseph's first, to a house on Warren Street. Joseph, fifteen, had said not a word, but somehow Angelica knew all.

Tonight he stood in that same room and placed his gift for Angelica at her bedside, the blue and white butterfly in its frame. He sat awhile beside her. Her namesake had used to sit at his bedside in this room, lulled him to sleep with songs and petting when he feared this or that.

Upstairs he peeled off his whiskey-golden clothing. The room was black and silent but for breathing behind the bed's curtains. He pulled back the hangings, and the dim light from the ceiling lantern slowly painted Constance's silhouette against the pillow. She despised him. She was done with him. She lived for Angelica and nothing else, as his Angelica had once lived only for him.

He stood nude at the end of the bed. There she lay, the prize of his peace, his beauty, there she lay. So that, then, was that: from dreaming of possessing a woman to remembering that possession with ardor, and between these two vast expanses of desire and reminiscence, the eye-blink of possession itself. He lay next to her, but no sooner had he, from indistinguishable obligation and desire, touched her sleeping form than she let out a cry of distress or disgust, kicked away the bedclothes, and in her dreams ran from him.

VI

Joseph examined his half-shaven face in the glass. He had worn a stucco since his return to England from the Army, as if in England most of all he had wished to resemble his father as little as possible. No more: last night's epiphany blazed stronger still this morning, and the appeal of forgiveness thrilled him. He could, with each new region cleared by his razor, recognize so many similarities between himself and his late father that he could not believe they had never overwhelmed him before: gesture, facial details (long shrouded by whiskers), habits of speech, even a purring clearance of a throat or an exhalation of surprise. He had the impression of his father's actual presence. Not literal, of course, but a sensation of proximate sympathy, as if the old man had suddenly piped up years late and demanded a hearing, scattered apologies and extenuating explanations, read out the defense, pleading modestly for a reprieve from whatever gray, dank corridors his shade was condemned to roam. He understood his father as a man who had once been the same age as Joseph now was and had existed therefore with the same degree of partial wisdom, the same desires, the same incompatible requirements to himself and to others, the same constant demand to make decisions with limited information but to appear to act with perfect judgment. The old man presented his defense simply by appearing in Joseph's looking glass. Joseph had arrived at a meeting point where his father's ghost had been awaiting him for years, drinking at this boxing hall, shaving in this glass.

"As a boy, I would stand where you are standing now," he told Constance, who watched from the threshold as he wiped blood from his cheek, "and watch him shaved. By a valet or even by my governess."

"Are other men shaving off their beards this year? I cannot imagine how you will be. Will it not be difficult to accustom oneself to?" She would nervously question even this, his actions affecting no one but himself.

He had finished and was dressing when Angelica wandered in, searching for her mother. "Good morning, child," he said. "Did you like my gift to you?"

"What gift?" she asked, noticing him for the first time. He laughed at her obvious confusion at this man who had spoken to her with her father's voice. "Is it you? What has become of your head?" He took her into his arms and allowed her to touch his cheek, and her doll to do the same. "The princess is well pleased," she intoned. "But where is your face?"

"This is my face. Those were only whiskers. I did not always have them. When I was younger I did not have them."

"Then are you younger now?"

"No, I am getting older. That is the only way we go. We change and grow older."

"Shall I change?"

"Of course."

She touched the blood on his cheek and rubbed it between her fingers pensively. "Shall I look different when I am grown?"

"Of course."

"Do you know how I shall look?"

"Do you truly wish to know? Very well then, look to your mother. She is the likely projection of your future beauty."

"I shall look like Mamma?"

"I think it probable. Does that please you?"

"Does it please you?"

"It is time for your father to be off; leave him be, Angelica," interrupted Constance, entering on a pretense and swiftly ending any pleasant interchange between him and the child.

"How old are you now, my girl?"

"I am four," she replied urgently, and she held up for proof five widely stretched fingers.

He turned to Constance, who was dabbing the cut on his cheek. "Do you remember yourself at that age?"

"I scarcely do. I think of it very little, as you can imagine, given the sorrows of the time."

"I should think you were a most beautiful little child. The picture of the woman you became." She swept the girl from his lap and left him.

He noted himself in the occasional glass and passing window, including Pendleton's: there was his father's face suspended over leather folios, emblazoned over brass stamps. "I saw her through a window, a flower in her hair, Joe." And it was here that Joseph in turn had seen his wife through a window, and noted only now the parallel. At the Labyrinth, he welcomed his colleagues' comments, the various admixtures of surprise and amusement, the admiring, the scoffing, the clucking moral-tonsorial clairvoyance of both the clean-shaven ("I have always said a man with a beard is a man with something to hide") and the bearded ("Such a drastic change in appearance speaks of a conscience demanding attention"). Harry slightly lifted an eyebrow: "Something different about you today. Can't quite say what."

It had been difficult to win for long the love of the first Angelica. He recalled lying in her bed, unclothed. He had been ill, and she had seen to his every need, food and medicine, washing him. He recalled sitting up when he was on the way to recovery and loving the sight of her as she tickled with a feather the oval indentation at the round tip of his nose, his foolish nose. (He had it still—that round, round tip on a short angle, adding to his general air of idiot simplicity.) "That's my big strong healthy boy," she said, kissing him. "That's my fine young Englishman." But, hours or days later, in punishment of a sin Joseph did not know he had committed, she said, "I do not speak to boys like you." His father departed for a week's travel, and she did not say a single word to Joseph for three endless days, no matter how he pleaded, raged, or wept.

His father's business—the importation of tea—required frequent travel, and its trappings—reports of ships, bags stenciled with the names of Eastern ports—connoted great adventure. He would gladly have pursued his father into this work. "You shall be a doctor," his father insisted. "Your mother wished it, and she gave her life for you." She had been the daughter and sister of doctors, though Joseph never met them, as they never once paid a call.

Even when Joseph had the nerve to debate the point, Angelica would rebuke him: "Why do you wish to be like him?" The question was irrelevant, since his father's business faltered as Joseph approached his majority, then failed entirely in parallel with his father's health. As bits of furnishing and luxury vanished from the house, as the servants departed until only Angelica remained, seeing to father and son alike, Carlo Bartone would either set off with a bloom in his coat, preparing to roam the parks for serving girls and laundresses, or would lie at home, unable to rise or even speak, under the weight of sadness far larger than should have been caused by the mere collapse of his fortunes.

Joseph had only recently begun his medical studies when Carlo's misfortunes had nearly finished him, the march of solicitors and creditors and bearers of bad news a steady beat upon the front step. Facing ever stricter economies and expecting his father would lose the house, Joseph withdrew from the medical faculty and converted his limited medical knowledge into an enlistment in the hospital corps. His father was able neither to help him nor to hinder him, and the day came for the son to say his farewells. His father sat up in his bed. "Good of you to come, Joe. All of this will be cleared up when you come rushing back to England a conqueror."

"I shall be away for some time, Father."

"Yes, I suppose so." Carlo Bartone sat blinking in the morning light.

"I'm keeping that piano. And the house is protected, I should think," he added lightly. "I have signed it away so it cannot be seized."

"To whom? They can take it from me as easily, can they not?"

"Yes."

"So to whom then?"

"To your mother." So his wits had melted as far as this. "Where is she, by the by? I want my soup." These last words he spoke in Italian, irritated, pulling the bedclothes up to his unshaven chin. "Have you said your good-byes to her? Go do that, can't you?" These were the last words Joseph exchanged with his father, who was evidently out of his mind from difficulties and age.

Angelica was in the kitchen, sitting upon a high stool, a potato in her hand, but she was doing nothing with it, preparing no soup. "You are gone?" she asked Joseph.

"Carlo is not well. Do see to him. He called you my mother." Her face did not change, and precisely this reaction to the mad statement gave Joseph his first breath of pain. He had never been a swift thinker, he would always be the first to confess from this moment on, never having suspected what was in retrospect so patently obvious. "He is soft in the head."

"He wants you to know." Still her face did not change, though she stood and took a step towards him. "He must want you to know, finally." Joseph retreated from the pursuing old Italian woman as she raced to produce her long-rehearsed, long-withheld recitation before Joseph escaped. By the end she placed herself between him and the door to the dining room.

When Carlo Bartone's English wife was newly with child and unavailable for his pleasure, he had called instead on the maid Angelica in the downstairs room (where Nora now slept). She resisted his intentions, but insufficiently. She hid her condition until nearly the very end and gave birth, early, to a boy downstairs, less than a week after her mistress died upstairs delivering, late, a stillborn girl. The decision to arrange things more to conventional taste was quickly made.

"Listen to you!" Joseph raged. "He should have turned you and your bastard out of the house." It was a muddled reply, to be sure, combining snobbery, shame, and self-delusion in a single phrase. The contradiction only spurred him to further insults. "You should have had the decency to be ashamed. An English slut would have had more shame than you. A harlot staying in his house with your filthy child!" He said much else, left her sobbing, apologizing to him for the first time in his life.

He left England for ten years, fought and learned some of the trade stolen from him, learned it by sawing the legs off screaming bodies, by vainly bandaging wounds too broad and deep to stanch, by holding the heads of men thrashing and retching in their last moments, giant men of steel calling for comfort. He raged against his incompetence, against his father and his father's harlot. He saw mothers and children die in ruined villages.

Forgiveness was much on his mind, for his father and his mother, both dead when he returned to England, and for himself, too, heir to the nearly empty house left to him by "—by, well, really, how does one pronounce that?" The solicitor found her name amusing and intoned it with a thick and ironic accent.

VII

Joseph confirmed the logs were accurate to the final hour of the day. He initialed the remarks of the medical students, correcting here a term of anatomy or amending there an inexpressive description. He checked the security of the light hasps on the enclosures and the heavy locks on the windows and pulled twice against the chain on the main door. The noises of the laboratory quickly dissipated, replaced by the noises of the streets around the Labyrinth. One never grew fully accustomed to this transformation of the very world. Even Joseph, who spent more time in the laboratory than anyone else, found it disorienting still. Even Dr. Rowan himself said of the stark alteration of sounds, "Truth of the matter, I half expect the first person I meet on the sidewalk to cower pitifully and set to plaintive whimpering!" Joseph nodded and smiled each time the doctor brought out this jest.

He passed Pendleton's. Had he known, years before, that the beautiful rose behind Pendleton's counter would open as she had, would he have chosen differently? He had stood right here. He could so simply have surrendered to the wiser voice, the English voice that considered his station (already compromised), and treated a counter girl accordingly, but instead some other voice, dead and foreign, transformed him into an impassioned lover, his father's role.

He could have married higher. He was by no means wealthy, but was in better financial condition than his employment would normally allow and, in those heady days of being a returned "hero," could have wed the sisters of work colleagues, drawn to Joseph's prospects and edited history. Constance Douglas, on the other hand, labored in a stationer's, but her grasp on Joseph's imagination was both total and instantaneous. The moment they first spoke, he stumbled, fell, and broke his will. He told himself all sorts of mad tales: she looked like peace or England or love or a painted goddess in a temple. Her most obvious resemblance he did not note: that enchantress who had so altered his father's life, his stolen English mother.

A first impression is a promise of sorts, for one assumes that one meets someone in a representative temper. When instead we meet someone *in extremis,* they are in effect lying. And so it had been the day Joseph Barton entered Pendleton's in search of a castle-top, some pen nibs, and an English wife, the girl laughing gently behind the counter, pushing a strand of hair from her eyes and consciously "pulling herself together" to address her next customer, then smiling at Joseph. The mood she enjoyed that morning was rare, while to Joseph, it was a promise. Other moods, while not inconceivable, would necessarily be deviations from the probable dominance of her character set that destiny-drenched, sunny morning (as if the very weather were warning him that this could never be the norm).

For on most days, for some painfully long time now, Constance wore only an expression of sorrow or fear or worry or, on rare occasions, a conscientious smile, a faint echo of the joy that had captured Joseph on a morning constantly longer ago. He had once imagined his marriage to this woman. She would stand behind him and place a loving hand on his and together they would gaze at the hearth. She would ask after his researches with avid interest and even keen understanding, perhaps would use some homely metaphor, which in turn would inspire him to some new insight in his work. She would be something of a wit, amusing him in private at the expense of fools they tolerated in public. He might brush her hair as he had once brushed his governess's. His mother's.

He stopped to purchase a bountiful gathering of spring blooms for her, examined the flower girl as his father had always done, but could recall none of his charming phrases, their resemblance already faded. Constance would in turn likely praise the flowers, then hand them to Nora for trimming, soaking, and placement. He might as well give them directly to Nora himself. And so he bought a second bouquet; he would have his wife's attention in full.

The voice came from somewhere off to his side, and at first he could not see anyone in the crowd of traffic who could have produced it: "It's Italian Joe Barton, or it's Lucifer dressed as him." Joseph felt the eyes of passersby scraping over him, accusing him of responsibility for the words as yet without owner. "Why, you're unchanged, every hair on your head." And only then did he see a hunched and hatless figure separate itself from the shadows alongside a stationary carriage: an old vagrant, but one who knew Joseph's name and ancient sobriquet. His head tipped back and to the side in a strange and menacing motion. "Unchanged. I always said you'd stroll right through those murderous black bastards like they was fine ladies wishing you well." Joseph examined the eyes, screwed up and squinting, the chin now tucked low. "Well, what do you say to an old comrade-in-arms, Italian Joe?" The voice, inconsistent with the collegial words, was hoarse and unsteady, and Joseph did not recognize him, embarrassed not to know a man alongside whom he had evidently fought. "All these years, nothing comes to mind, eh? Speak up, I'm in a listening temper." Again his head jerked backwards and then to the side.

"What are you doing there?"

"I could ask you the very same, my fierce and bloody comrade. Let's you and me share a drink and some supper," the old man added in a hurry, then, leering, tombstone-toothed, said slowly, "and we will talk of the glorious things we saw under the Queen's colors."

Joseph would have declined, suspected the man of cadging, but to have called him by that name, to have referred to a shared past, and to have recognized Joseph precisely because he had shaved his beard that very morning in a mood of universal forgiveness—he could not fairly refuse a drink. He led them away from anywhere he might see people he knew, his forest of flowers tucked away under an arm, stems to the front, a blister of color swelling behind him. The old man favored one leg, and he made an obvious effort to draw himself up to his full height, which was only slightly superior to Joseph's.

"Italian Joe at last," he muttered in amazement. "I can scarcely credit it." His clothes were dirty, his boots old. Joseph felt that the admission must be made, but the old man already knew: "I never would have guessed you'd forget me. I never forgot Italian Joe Barton, nobody could. I won't. To the day I go to my reward, I won't."

"You must excuse my memory." But the old man did not set him at ease, nor for some time reveal his name, but continued to examine Joseph sideways and shake his head as if he were willing himself out of a dream. "You have me at a disadvantage. If we are to drink together, you must end my confusion."

"Watch your throats, boys, when Italian Joe says he's at a disadvantage."

A cannier man would have departed, left the beggar with his apologies and a coin, but today of all days, Joseph did not tear himself free. Perhaps there was no such day when his character would have allowed it. He found a discreet public house, and the old man's name emerged at last, in a slow, ironical, and unpleasant tone, as if the pronunciation of it would undam in Joseph a flood of bitter recollection: Lemuel Callender.

But the knowledge did nothing to ignite Joseph's memory, and he wished he had gone home, hoped to see Angelica—noted with some surprise that he actually hoped for it—for a few minutes before she slept. "Even my name don't make it clear? Are you playing at something deep with me?"

For all his desire to reminisce, Lem spoke little once they had sat, but ate and drank with undisguised urgency. His tic—for that was what it was—took him without mercy every thirty or forty seconds, but its complexity—two jerks backwards, eyes closed, tip to the left—seemed almost ritual, rather than a deformation of the nerves, as if it once had meaning, and having lodged itself in the body now echoed, meaningless, every few moments.

Several times Lem stopped as if he would soon raise a matter of some import, but each time simply returned to his food with another repetition of "Italian Joe don't even know me" until Joseph finally informed him that he did not answer to that epithet, had not heard it in years, since back there.

"Don't you? Not Italian anymore?"

"I never particularly was, sir. Just that fool Ingram's jape."

"You remember Ingram, do you? And now Ingram's dead one blue morning, torn up and splashed all about, and you have your ribbons and your medals and now you're as English as me. I follow. You have your fine honors, even if they were boned, eh?"

Joseph was idiotically wordless, insulted and slow to respond, of course, still thought perhaps he had misunderstood.

"Tell me, very English Joe, do you think of it much?"

"Of what?"

"There."

"I rarely give it a thought."

"A lucky man. Had a good time of it out there, didn't you? Made a name and your pile of loot." Lem wiped his cut face with the sleeve of his coat.

"Loot? You must be mistaken—I've no—"

"Because I do. All the time. Like they're still in front of me. Makes you not want to speak to anyone. And, Joe, I think of you all the time. I think of you every day, have done since the last time I saw you." He laid a leathery hand, every line traced and darkened with dirt, on Joseph's arm, pulled it to the bar. Joseph escaped his grasp to lift his beer. "Don't hear your old mates' voices now and again? Don't see them across busy streets? Don't lose a little of your fine English comfort, when you think what you did? The fellows who paid for your glory?"

It had not been so long as all that, hardly credible that one could forget a man such as this. Never terribly strong with names and faces, not a sociable man, still Joseph thought it nearly impossible he had known this Lem. Which was not to say the soldier had never seen Joseph or knew nothing of him, and perhaps this implied some malign intention. "You'll excuse me for asking, Lem. Where did we know each other?"

"Are you mocking me?"

"Certainly not, sir."

"Oh, you'll remember it soon enough. It will come back to you clear as June sunshine, my old comrade-in-arms."

Joseph was slow to perceive men's hidden meanings, was actually a little proud that he at least *knew* this about himself, knew that other men (Harry, for example, for whom he later sketched this disconcerting encounter as comedy) could read secrets in men's attitudes, make something of a parlor game of it. Yet, for once, Joseph could tell that this Lem meant him no good, was a menace of some sort from a past that Joseph could in no way recall. "I surely knew you, brave Joe, and saw your heroics." The old man returned to cutting his pie, more slowly now. "There was so much I was meaning to tell you," he said in a strange tone. He muttered something, then turned with an incongruous smile and politely inquired: "Married, are you, Joe? Found yourself a woman back here?"

"And we've a child."

"A child for Italian Joe! Nice for you, then. I'd love to meet them, Joe, tell your missus what a great fellow you were out there. Everything you did. She should know, and your little boy, too. A father like Italian Joe Barton—a young fellow should treat you like you merit." He swallowed and grinned, showed his graveyard mouth: "And your lady, a white woman, is she?" He delivered this coarseness with an implied shared taste in low humor, as if they were accustomed to spending long hours around a watch fire in each other's company. "Well, then, your appetites have changed, eh?" and the man guffawed. "A soft ear for you. Very nice. You fall asleep with your head on her soft English breast, and she makes it all peaceful like."

Joseph stood and left money enough to pay for the old beggar's meal. "I think we'll part company now, sir," he said, "and you'll do me the kindness of enjoying your pie with my compliments."

"I didn't ask for your charity." The old man's hatred was undisguised now. He pushed, one at a time, each coin from the bar onto the floor. "I'll die before I beg from you."

Joseph escaped, forgot his bouquet. Throughout the meal, his idea of home had sharpened in contrast to the old man's dull menace, and he arrived at Hixton Street strangely excited. He took the stairs nearly at a run in time to watch Angelica fall asleep without complaint, his butterfly nowhere in sight. He sat by her long enough to calm himself, then found Constance upstairs. He tried to explain the thoughts that had so filled his day. "Here I am at the age when my father—well, it scarcely signifies, but I see now that he was not a wicked man. He asks my forgiveness by resembling me, and I can scarcely refuse. It would be churlish." If Constance could know all he had felt today, then she would forgive him his failings, weaknesses, appetites, and she would behave as she ought. He crossed to her, simply to hold her in his arms. She fled him nearly at once.

VIII

Sunday, with its usual claims to Constance's superstition, coincided this morning with Nora's monthly idleness, and so Joseph and Angelica faced some hours in each other's company. Strangely, the prospect did not alarm Joseph. Amusing, how quickly a few nights of uninterrupted slumber and his wife's open hostility could recommend the child's conversation.

He read her a story, a little experiment in their new friendship: " '. . . more egregious than the first, the most wicked of all men. The baker would regret it, the old lady said. He would regret it most bitterly. And truly it was, for as soon as the crone departed the baker's shop, the wolf leapt in and licked his lips and growled from deep in his throat. His red eyes flashed like the eyes of a demon as he leaned back, preparing for his spring. The baker cried out, "I am sorrow! When I had the help of the townspeople, I turned them away with scorn in my voice. Now that I am in gravest peril, there is no one to come to my aid. I am lost!" The wolf leapt at the baker's throat, murder in its eyes and a thirst for blood on its lips. Its whiskers touched the baker's neck. Its jaws opened, and the baker felt its wet hot breath upon him, when from nowhere and all at once came the gleam of a blade. The wolf's fur was parted and its throat sliced. Searing blood sprayed and lit upon the baker's cheek where it mingled with his tears of fear and relief. The blood sprayed, too, upon the bread the baker had only just refused to share with the old woman. Whose blade had saved him? For at his feet the wolf shivered to its withers and breathed its least'—excuse me, my dear: 'breathed its *last*. Then the baker saw his rescuer: it was the tinker's boy. "You? You came to save me? And with my own knife? How is this?" The tinker's boy did not boast of his bravery, nor remind the baker of his un-Christian cruelty to the townspeople. Instead he spoke humbly: "Baker. This wolf's blood has made a stain upon your cheek, and you shall wear that stain forever. It shall never wash away, no matter how desperately you scrub. And the wolf's blood has stained your bread. Forever, every day, you shall set aside one loaf of bread, and that you shall give without complaint to whosoever claims it from you, and you shall ask for nothing in return, neither money nor favor. And you shall call this bread the Wolf's Loaf. If this you do faithfully, you will never have cause to fear the small cut on your neck, which I made when I did slay the wolf at your throat. You shall rub this magic ointment upon it every day. It will never trouble you. But if you are not faithful, if you do not unstintingly—" ' "

"What is stindingly?"

"Unstintingly. Without hesitation or complaint. ' "—unstintingly give the Wolf's Loaf, then that small cut will open wide, and it will pour forth in a red flood, and no doctor's wisdom will prevail to save you, and your head will never heal nor attach, and you will die most miserably." The baker nodded and looked in a glass and saw the red cut that ran across his throat. "I will do as you say, tinker's boy, and you may tell all the town what has happened here today and what I vowed." ' " Joseph closed the book. "What do you suppose happens?"

"He doesn't share. His cut opens again, and it runs all around his neck, and his head falls off! And those horrid poor people eat all his bread!"

"You have quite a thirst for this tale." As he and his child laughed together, he began to recognize his own home and his place in it. She in turn told him stories, of a flying man who came to her at night and upon whose back she flew high above the streets of London, from which great heights she saw the people and the buildings far below, strands of clouds tangled in her hair and the hook of the moon nearly catching her dress.

Angelica was, or could someday be, nearly an ideal companion. She could—it was not inconceivable—grow into a sort of friend, in a manner of speaking. She was not without the fundamental requirements of mind and temperament that her mother lacked.

"Are ghosts real?" she asked.

"They are not."

"Are angels real?"

"No, my dear."

"What of witches?"

"Figments, child. Figments."

"And Jews? Are they real or figments?"

He had traveled, two months earlier, for a flying visit to York to share Dr. Rowan's results with the "Sage of Sepsis" at the university there. Upon his return he was amazed to find that the girl had aged months in his two-day absence, and of course he must also have changed commensurately, and looking at Constance, after the realization had opened his eyes, he saw how much deeper those two parallel horizontal lines now furrowed the fat of her neck, rendering it tripartite, as sectional as an insect's. "What of dragons? Real?" In these first minutes of happiness since Angelica's removal to her own bedroom, in these few last days in which he paid her the closest attention of his entire life, he saw her aging at tremendous speed. Her vocabulary, her manner of addressing him, her ability to grasp his conversation: all of this was flying so fast into the future that he could not help but think of that future as a time in which they would be more closely tied to each other.

"You have never told me. Did you like your butterfly?" But the child had no knowledge of the butterfly, and a concerted hunt of her room produced none. "Are you teasing me?" she asked.

"Well, instead, let us look at the book I brought for you."

"What book?"

"The drawings of anatomy, the plates. 'Papa's book,' you called it, your mother showed it to you."

"Mamma showed me?"

No, she had not. She had kept it from the girl to spite him, to continue coddling the child, preparing her for a credulous future, and she had lied to him. Constance would seize even this most microscopic evidence of Angelica's similarity to or fondness for him, and crush it.

Not long after this infuriating discovery, the girl demanded a sweetcake. Joseph could find no such item. "I want Mamma!" the girl cried as it became clear that her wishes were not going to be met. How quickly those quaint little bridges he was constructing between himself and his child were burnt, and the girl transformed into a manipulative miniature of her mother. She wept like a spurned lover, her passing tolerance of him revealed for what it was, now that he had disappointed her. "Good lord, quiet yourself," he said. "Your precious mother will be back presently. It is not such a grave tragedy as all that. Quiet, can't you?" Nora, unbelievably, was still enjoying the morning's respite from her duties, and Constance dallied in her fool's worship.

The child shrieked for cake and would not accept his word that there was none. The child shrieked, and Joseph asked if she would prefer to be locked in her room. He offered an apple, but when that proposal was refused, and viciously, he withdrew from further negotiations, and her protests whirled beyond all control. She screamed, hurled herself at her father, and rebounded off his unyielding frame. She threw herself against the sofa, collapsed at once to the floor, kicked her legs. Joseph peered down at her from the doorframe, wondered how much longer Constance would tarry while this sorry storm raged. The girl rolled from side to side, wept without tears, gulped at the air as if choked by invisible assailants. "My dear girl," Joseph attempted, but that only further tormented her. "I'm not your dear girl, not your gear dirl, I'm not a deer, there are no deer here." Her grasp on reality seemed to quiver at this moment, and Joseph tried again to calm her: "No, Angelica, I only meant dear as in beloved, to denote affection." But she, standing now, leapt up and down; her fists pounded the sides of her own head. "I'm not a deer! Give cake!"

It was inarguably fascinating: this was the child Constance had created with such effort. Interesting, too, how completely she had turned her against her father; Angelica was driven mad at the prospect of his further companionship. "Girls don't eat deers, girls cake deers!" Her language was disintegrating and with it any recognizable "Angelica" as such. His daughter was vanishing before his eyes, collapsing backwards into some earlier stage of her growth. "Cakes! Deer! Father another deer! No! NO!" Her tears swelled her eyes nearly shut, and her nose ran. Still she leapt and bounded into the wall. Joseph attempted to prevent her from harming herself, of course, but surely he could not be expected to restrain her beyond that. Would her previous personality restore itself in a stroke? Perhaps he was meant to lead her through some exercise to rebuild her fractured little soul. "Angelica," he began, but this inflamed her further.

This raging beast was the same entity as the girl alongside whom he had walked the beach one evening last summer. "Papa, look, the butterfly breaked. Breaken." He had been walking a few steps ahead of her, next to a silent Constance. He turned back to where she squatted with her arms crossed, peering at something on the ground. "Broken," he said. "But butterflies don't break, they die." He joined her and saw the object of her scientific fascination, a *Polyommatus icarus,* still alive but unable to fly, as one of its blue and white wings had been half-consumed by ants, which still crawled along and chewed the wing's tattered edge. The prey staggered a step or two at a time, leapt towards remembered flight but then landed on its one intact wing, heavily by its own standards, as it had not experienced heaviness since it emerged blinking and damp from its cocoon. The ants merely adjusted and reinforced their long line of attack, carrying the colorful tissue of the still living creature along its very body, paraded back to their hills past hungry workers come to finish the job. The child's face thrilled Joseph: no horror, no fatuous moralizing, no fallacy of anthropomorphism. A child of three could show the purest fascination, exhibit the foundations of a scientific mind.

"Oh, it's horrid. Get away from it," squealed Constance, come to separate them. "Why would you want to poke at something so filthy, Angelica?"

"Leave her in peace, can't you? Would you crush everything of interest about her?" He stopped as soon as he saw Constance's penitent confusion, but should not have, for she was forming the child with such feckless emotion and unfettered nonsense. The girl was fascinated by Nature for a moment, well and good. The day might come when she would grow into a person of intelligence. She prodded the dying butterfly with a twig, and he felt an unfamiliar flush of tenderness for this person, developing adult interests, and also the same female prettiness and capacity for charm as her mother once boasted, that glowing promise of offering infinite prospects of pleasing him.

Angelica had caught an exceedingly mild, not to say imperceptible, cold that evening, and, of course, Constance, certain the child was sneezing towards the grave, insisted the local doctor be summoned. This fine old fellow, good enough to shatter his Sunday to calm a nervous mother, examined Angelica quite precisely as Joseph had, reached the identical diagnosis, prescribed the same treatment, and then, reading the situation expertly, raised an admonitory eyebrow at Joseph for allowing his wife to demand the consultation for a child who was not even febriculose. Angelica, meanwhile, kept telling her papa that she would not complain of her symptoms, so as to make him proud.

And yet now that person of interest, who had wished to make her father admire her courage ten months before, was being thrown onto its face, its fists beaten against the floor by some other animal sharing the same body, robbing her of intelligence, interest in Nature, intriguing sentences, physical charms, of all her appeal, except for that residual scientific interest Joseph took in the progression of her collapse. It—not even "Angelica" or "she"—it was still bleary with fury when Constance at last returned from her mythological studies.

"What did you do to her?" his wife demanded as she attempted to gather up the scattered girl in her arms.

"Do? Are you mad? I denied her her whim, as you should learn to do."

Constance, unable to talk the girl into reason, turned her over and struck her soundly. The shock of it stopped the child's raging, and, though she continued to weep after a second blow, her breath steadied. She flung her arms around her assailant, pressed her soaked face against the warm skin of her mother's pulsing neck.

"You strike her?"

"If she requires it. She must be restored to herself, not allowed to flail. The devil must be shown the door." She added, "No doubt you disapprove," not without a light rebelliousness.

"No, no, not at all. As you see fit." He remarked the child's obvious preference for her mother's company, even after she had struck her. He had seen the equivalent paradox displayed a thousand times in the laboratory, but to see it in humans, in the two females tied most closely to him, surprised him, despite himself, despite the pleasant shock he felt whenever Nature revealed her patterned secrets. He could not, even with effort, imagine himself striking the girl, could not conceive of the necessary circumstances, rage, passion, or hatred. Not even love would merit such an act.

Had he ever felt a desire so keen that its frustration would have shattered the container of personality? He had nearly lost his wife, pulling her back from death only to see her vanish into motherhood, and he was now of only financial concern to her. She exerted no effort to please him, was openly indifferent to his comings and goings. She was deaf to his words, blind to his regard, insensate to his gentle touch. If anyone deserved the right to spin and wail in hysterics, it was he.

Always nervous, prone to melancholy (quite understandable given her losses and her health), Constance now showed signs of something far more serious: frights in the night, sleeplessness, lurid fears for the child's safety. He found her asleep at strange hours and awake at strange hours. She slept in the parlor or at the girl's side, spouting mad and madder reasons to wander away from her husband. She flinched at his embraces (no matter how mildly he intended or executed them), spouting excuses plausible and imaginary. And today he had proof of her lying: the book of plates and the destruction or theft of his gift to the child, whom she had for years insisted was her gift to him.

That evening they sat before the fire. He watched her in silence. Her bare forearm pressed against the piping on the arm of the sofa. That stiff velvet cord imprinted her flesh, and when she moved he saw by the fire's light the soft impression it had left there, a reddened valley. He could almost feel it from this distance and longed to touch it before blood reinflated it, filled that ridge.

Instead, as if she could sense his silent intention to touch her, she at once provoked him with mad talk, spoke of English soldiers (in other words, of him) as if they were fiends, compared them to black murderers. He left her in frustration, but minutes later she ran to him, frightened by shadows. He calmed her as he used to do. "My love," he said tenderly and kissed her neck, but, having run to him, now she as desperately pulled away from him, bid him not to wait, as he needed his sleep, and she must see to the child. "Of course." It was some long time before she returned, or, more precisely, before he fell asleep alone again, imagining she might still come to him, rather than fleeing him, one floor at a time, shielding herself with the child, shielding the child with herself.

IX

He nearly convinced himself that Constance ought to sleep away
from him. If it calmed her, let her reside in the parlor or the cellar. But in practice, distance only magnified her peculiarities. In the
morning she stopped him on the stairs, barred his way until she had explained that Angelica suffered elusive pains no one else could see, but
which were in some mysterious fashion Joseph's fault. He maintained
his temper as best he could before this flowering derangement, even encouraged her to call a doctor. He attempted to escape, but not hastily
enough, for she would persist until she stung him: "Who is Lem?"

"Who is Lem?" she asked with no preface, so that he could almost
have thought she possessed magical gifts of perception. A man he could
in no way recall appeared out of the mist, tapped him for a meal, insulted him, implied dark knowledge, was left behind in a public house,
and the next day his wife asked after this shuffling apparition by name.
"Who is Lem?"

"A beggar who waylaid me."

"You dreamt of him last night."

"I did not."

"But how else could I know his name? You spoke it in your sleep."

"What do you believe I said?"

"Only his name, 'Lem, Lem,' several times. Only his name."

Rather than saying, "You spoke in your sleep, a nonsense word, half a lemon," she began with the name Lem, a person who must exist and whose identity she would startle out of him by using his own nocturnal murmurings to ensnare him into a confession, but of what? What game was this, indulging whimsies beyond all decency? Again he had the sensation that he was skulking from his own home as if he were a criminal or simply weak.

He opened the laboratory this Monday morning and welcomed the noise and the tasks ahead, their variety and their certainty: they had been here for him Monday last and would await him Monday next. Here was no frustration, no silent vague accusations, no childish intrusions.

He lit the gas, calmed those that could be calmed, distributed food and water, and began noting overnight changes. His pen needed a new nib. He turned towards the back of the hall and stopped short, felt his toes clench against the uppers of his boots. On the floor, in an aisle between two worktables—impossible. He raised a lamp. It was as he first thought: two human skeletons posed to simulate a certain act, the skinless grins almost appropriate. Their hollow sockets burned at each other in shared sensuality, but one of the lewd pair, propped on its stiff arms, seemed also to examine Joseph sideways, mocking, more indulged and engrossed by life's pleasures than he.

Obscenity here, of all rooms, this hall dedicated to human betterment. A low mind had been loose here, with what passed for wit in the Army among men of vulgar character and animal intelligence like Lem. Worse, the specimens had been at risk during the intrusion: there was no saying what such a person might have done to spoil the work undertaken here. For a moment, he imagined the impossibility that Lem himself had done this, knowing somehow that Joseph would discover them, read them as significant and—Nonsense. It was imperative to clear this away before the doctors arrived.

Closer inspection, however, proved that a hasty erasure would be difficult, as the vandals had run stiff wires over pipes and through drawer handles to secure the skeletons' position. He had succeeded only in moving a single cage and climbing atop the table to examine the knotted lines near the ceiling, which held the bottom figure's legs lifted skywards, when he heard the front door open, much too early, and the specimens were, for a moment, entirely silent. Dr. Rowan appeared, pale and ovine in the faint light, sneezing then bleating, as the animal noise resumed, "Barton? What are you doing up there?"

Joseph lowered himself to the floor and in desperation, before Rowan turned the corner, gave the dominant skeleton a kick, but he only produced a posture somehow even more offensive: the lower figure, obviously the female, flung its head to the side, as if further enraptured or tormented. Had he a metal rod, he would gladly have thrashed the lovers to ivory splinters.

"Barton? What is it?" Joseph could do no more. Rowan strode up.

"Sir, I have only just discovered this, this unpleasant—" but by then his employer was wheezing with laughter. "Did you do this, Barton? No, of course not," he corrected himself at once. "Oh, they have us, don't they? The devils! They do have us. Showing the old men a thing or two!" Exiting medical students had done this, Rowan guessed, not the first time he had seen it done, vandals stealing and depositing anatomy skeletons around the Labyrinth in such circumstances. "I once came upon one in my WC! At a moment of crisis, Barton! The demons had wired the bones onto the seat so tightly that I had no choice but to sit upon its lap to pursue matters." Joseph preferred not to look at the old doctor's red fat face. "Look at those two setting to their merry business! You can almost hear that one crying out! Still," Dr. Rowan blew his nose, "still, best to clear that out of here before the others arrive. Might want to have the locks changed when you can. Can't have students entering at will, troubling our friends here."

So Joseph was assumed to be one of the "old men," expected to indulge younger men's overflowing vitality, but to be wise enough to change the locks afterwards, one who would laugh with nostalgic affection for the outrages of youth, snickering with bone-dry envy at entwined bones.

She thought of him in quite the same light. No: rather, he was something else to her, something transforming, passing between youth's uncontrollable urges and senescence's dusty, grinning harmlessness. And in this middle stage, neither moist pupa nor desiccated, pinned moth, he was treated as some volatile substance to be handled with tongs until his inevitable decay was complete. She willed that decay. She longed for its acceleration. The delay bored her, and the risk that he might still have youth's appetites offended her. When she thought him lively, she feared him. When she smelled slowness in him, she was kind and encouraging.

The child, too, would have him old and uncomplaining. They were allied. *Allied.* The word rang in Joseph's head, a shimmering silver epiphany, long walled up but now revealed: each, for her own reason, wanted him old, and they conspired to make him old. Even her compliant, charmed doctors connived with her, issuing their idiotic decrees to her specifications.

An hour later, the skeletons slung over stools in the back, the oldest of the medical students, young Mr. Joshua, arrived quite late with a bandage across his brow, shy of it at first, slow to remove his hat, standing in shadows and turning his head at an awkward angle in conversation. But before long everyone had remarked upon the injury, and a few men had asked him outright; he simply muttered inaudible excuses. Several times the boy had to change the bandage as red and brown stars constellated themselves across its white sky. Towards dinnertime, Joseph, watching the fellow unstick the latest plaster with the help of a small looking glass, offered his services. Joshua sighed.

"Children, Barton?" the youngster asked as Joseph peeled the strips away from a seeping wound.

"I do, sir. A girl of four."

"Mind them, the devils." Joseph applied a damp cloth to the circular injury. "Everyone's seen it, I suppose there's no harm in telling you. A day or two ago, I have learnt, it seems the governess tried to tell my boy about medicine, about surgery and ether. You can imagine: 'A sleeping body feels no pain, so surgeons like your papa mercifully put the patient into a deep sleep before lifting the scalpel now, or removing a limb, et cetera.' Well, I awake in darkest night, last night, in sheerest agony, my eyes cloudy, my head blazing, the sounds of my own screams enough to wake me and the lady of the house. The first thing I am able to see when I wipe my eyes, and my wife has turned up the lamp, is Simon, the child, looking quite horrified, as you can imagine, when I tell you, Barton, that he had taken it upon himself to rise in the middle of the night and perform surgery on his sleeping father. He had decided to take a kitchen knife and remove the wart you will recall once graced my brow, a mild blemish, but Simon would have it off, and the governess had evidently neglected some details in her surgical seminar. The amount of blood! From what was, you will agree, not a bad incision for a novice surgeon the tender age of five. It poured off my head, a crimson torrent, blinding and choking me, my hands slick with it. A battle wound, you'd have recognized it, you're an old soldier. My wife has the maids scrubbing the day away, I should think. We will have to lock the nursery door when he sleeps now. A stiff precaution, but I cannot dally until he discovers ophthalmology."

Joseph took his dinner alone at an outdoor table a few streets from the Labyrinth. He reviewed a recent failed series of experiments, hoping to locate in the data a pattern to present to Dr. Rowan, even the slightest efficacy of the superficially disappointing counterinfectants they had applied to the wounds. Perhaps Joseph could discover one partially promising element to combine with other nearly effective constituents. He intended, here or by some other insight, to demonstrate his fitness for responsibility beyond his current station.

He wrote drafts of proposals and interpretations of overlooked results in a diary bound in leather and engraved on its cover with his name, purchased not long before from Pendleton's (another pretty girl standing in the usual place, the same tone of voice, the same look in her eye, these Pendleton girls so well manufactured, at least for a spell). This notebook now sat at the edge of the table, inadvertently turned outwards. He noticed passersby were reading his name, and he felt at once ashamed, as if he had been caught advertising himself (especially as he was in the midst of an effort to put himself forward to his superiors). His shame at making a display of himself (as he turned the book facedown) was the next instant titrated with resentment at the false accusations (now retrospectively visible) in those passing faces, since he had certainly *not* been trying to make a display of himself. Before he regained control of his rebellious thoughts, he silently berated those who had accused him of vanity with various sins of their own, evident in their dress, gait, expressions. It took some moments of accelerating rage before the illogic of his thinking fell back under the sway of the wiser components of his mind. Restored to himself, he tried to reconstruct how many minutes he had just sacrificed to such rubbish.

Just as one's mind could wander so that it was stripped of all belief or character (for he surely did *not* think anyone had wrongly judged him a narcissist, nor did he believe that the one woman with red hair who quite blankly happened to look at the betraying notebook was of loose morality), surely one could as easily *act* stripped of one's logic and morals. War was, if nothing else, a stage upon which the unwary were freed of their characters and forced to perform naked in a play of the most revealing action. He had seen the noble act cruelly, the meek fight like lions, the gruff reduced to girlish weeping over losses that were, at the most, symbolic. He had seen, after, when the guns were quiet but still warm, the looks of shock (and, in the case of the formerly meek, glee) to know that this then was who they were or could be: cruel, lions, girlish. "I was not meek, for all those years," they repainted themselves retroactively, redefining the time they had spent at home avoiding danger or disharmony. "I was quietly noble, and would not put my boldness on display." But this, too, was false, of course, as false as any other moment taken alone.

What of it? The better self could evaporate in an instant, not even in a moment of crisis or temptation, but in the most prosaic life: a notebook left facing outwards could make a man accuse an innocent woman of basest sluttery.

One heard stories of ordinary men committing dreadful crimes. Men who traveled in the best circles, who wanted for nothing, yet who stole. Men with neither fear nor worry, yet they murdered. Men adored by women, yet they raped. Either these men knew what they were doing (criminals), or they did not realize they committed such acts (lunatics). In such cases (perhaps the murderer so thoroughly described in the newspapers), one's watchful character simply went to sleep (as Angelica's had during her tantrum), and for the length of that slumber some other force took control of this flesh costume and went off to commit acts of its choice, criminally concealed them from everyone, including the man most likely to be a witness or obstruction, that usual manager of these muscles and eyes, and, once sated, skulked back to its shrouded hole as the unwary host woke from whatever reverie was necessary for his parasitical resident's seizure of power. Such a reverie, Joseph shuddered, would differ from his own (during the notebook episode) only in degree, not in kind. If he could lose himself long enough for some foreign voice inside him to accuse a passing innocent woman of being a harlot, was he criminal or mad? His transgression had been harmless, yet it demonstrated the paper thinness of the barriers holding one's better self in place.

Examine only normal sleep: for some hours, one's better self was lifted from its throne, and the rebels danced in the court until dawn. They spoke their darkest desires with the king's own lips and voice. The night before, Joseph had spoken of Lem. He had seen men in the hospital tents thrashing, whimpering in their sleep, confessing with equal shame to acts they had committed and those they only wished to. Some even walked, their eyes open and glazed. And if one fears that one's character is only loosely attached to its moorings, if one fears the parasites of one's nature, then sleep must loom quite terrible in its implications. So it must be for Constance, he concluded.

Constance fought sleep and scraped her way free of it as soon as she was refreshed enough to stumble through another day. She watched over Angelica's sleep, alarmed at all she saw, and in daytime dripped milky religion into the child's mouth.

"Papa, do lies hurt God and make Him bleed?" Angelica asked him that evening when he took her upon his lap.

"No, child."

"Lies don't hurt God? His angels don't cry?"

"You must not speak such foolishness. You shall be a good child be-cause it pleases your parents and you to behave properly. God pays no attention to such things, and we will return the favor by leaving him and his angels out of our discussions."

Such was what the child learned in the female house! Very well, he could not achieve a complete embargo of that, but surely the time had come to rescue Angelica from total idiocy, vaccinate her against her mother's excrescent charity-school fairy stories of angels and a weeping god, a milder version of the myths by which his own mother had once terrorized him.

Constance would expose the child to flagrant disobedience, too. That morning's tales of Angelica's mysterious symptoms clearly false, still Constance hid in the child's room. The girl fell asleep, and still Constance lingered, cleaning a spotless room rather than rising to her husband's side where she belonged. He rose from the parlor, requested her presence, and she refused. He descended from the bedroom, de-manded she return with him, and she refused. When he was forced to come to her a third time, she could fabricate no excuse, treated him with open disdain, would not even reply, but stood silent and scornful. "I see," he produced feebly, and retreated to his bed, bolting the door against her.

X

You've an even more morose expression than usual."

"I would not tire you with my domestic trials."

"Joe, Joe, stop," Harry commanded, and Joseph already regretted the little he had revealed. "A household runs to the man's will, see. He don't have to say a word. It's how he breathes. You don't need to hear the king's voice, even in our own kingdoms. If your domain is in disarray, look to your manner, sir."

"Britain is ruled by a queen."

"In name only. She's a king inside. But don't evade. Look at history books. I don't know about you Italians, but rebellions in England came under the weak kings, never under the strong ones. Fact of human psychology. I would add this," Harry said, dropping his cheroot on the ground and leaning in. "You seem to me a bit of an ascetic, and I can't fathom it. A man must lubricate himself against the frictions of life, especially marriage. You've dried yourself up into a rough surface. You scrape against things. Where's your pleasure, Joe? Are you mortifying yourself? Honestly, why the anguish? You're not headed to debtors' prison. You're not burying your children. You eat well. You're well-admired by Rowan. The secret is to remove yourself, not open yourself to annoyance. Let the governess have at the devils. You still have that giant Irish girl? Fine, have her bring the child around to you for inspection now and again, and then again when she turns sixteen, see what she's become. What she has *become*. Because you cannot fool about in the meantime trying to oversee her. Not your job at all, sir. You pay the tradesmen, make certain the governess has her head on straight. Use the rod or the strap on the child, entirely a matter of preference. Encourage virtue, haul it off to sing hymns on a Sunday or two. My God, Sundays. I do dread them. Chinaman's torture. Simply give your orders, then draw the curtain around yourself and try not to be noticed until the thing has grown and passed out of your home. If they resist your orders, have the good sense not to notice. And that is *all*. Of course, you don't have a son, do you? They can be quite amusing at times. Though this newest fellow—we have no more room, and I sometimes hear him shrieking in darkest night. He'll be lucky to survive a year with his brothers."

"She shuns me," he confessed quietly.

"Ah, then. How often are you calling on our tender friends?"

"I don't consort with them, and neither should you."

"Are you really a prig of this caliber? Come, you tell me your wife is refusing to participate up to one's reasonable contractual expectations—yes, I know, her health, all the more reason not to play Pope. You trudge around as dour as death, when there exists a vibrant garden in our kingdom dedicated to the preservation of your equanimity."

"An undignified, brutish pursuit of a very fleeting pleasure."

"Do you know other kinds? Is your life so full of lingering pleasures you begrudge your fellow man a fleeting one?"

Once, Joseph, newly returned from the Army, had taken pleasure in being told of his promise and the quality of his work. He had been pleased to find employment in a field so adjacent and relevant to medicine, to make use of the ad hoc training he had received abroad. His frustration at his aborted medical career, which had grated during his years overseas, could be held in check by an act of will, and he enjoyed hearing that if he continued to show such excellent handwork (for an untrained man) he could certainly expect to be senior man someday. But that day had come, and his expectations were fulfilled. His station was no longer elastic.

Medical students, younger each year, came for a day or a week or a month at a time and nominally worked beneath him, and they showed him a nominal respect. Harry represented probably the final instance in which a medical student considered him a senior colleague, rather than an old servant who cleaned apparatus, oversaw the mixing and application of pastes, the incisions, made records, kept the building's keys. He could see it in some of the younger students' expressions. He collected their bawdy skeletons. Some of them, he knew, thought him an oaf. There was little pleasure remaining here.

He stood in the fresh air of the laboratory's court, and Constance appeared, as if he were lost in convincing reverie, but the vision spoke. She was happy as she had not been for some very long time, and it lifted his spirits. She spoke of a gift for him, of her pride in him, of her desire to help him advance in his work, and he, fool of all fools, allowed her to pass into the hall.

Once, early, she had cared to ask after his work. He had been younger then, had likely boasted a bit of his importance to the research. He had likely feared a woman's response to a candid description of the process by which knowledge was gained, so had likely spoken careful words. He had described their processes in the most removed terms, to protect her and help her understand the value without the distraction of the cost, which would overwhelm a woman's emotional system. He had likely, he recalled now, spoken only of the work's results. She had been proud of him.

Her questions one dusk, years before, had enchanted him. "Might you discover an end to all sickness?" she had asked as they walked in a little wood of Hampstead, minutes before he asked her to consider becoming his wife.

"We might. We very well might."

"And then what will happen to us? Shall we all live forever? Or would new sicknesses not replace those you defeat?" He had laughed at her extraordinary notion. The womanly fear of unlimited illness and the womanly illogic of new infections taking the place of defeated ones charmed him.

Somehow he had never considered that today would ever come. He had been shortsighted, even willfully so, not to prepare her or more explicitly bar her. She entered the laboratory, repeating how much pride she felt for him. He then watched misunderstanding change her face with an unsurprising but disappointing speed. She took no breath to ask him what it meant, only accused him. She had never until this moment attached an image to his work. Now she forgot all he had ever explained to her, and instead interpreted what she saw according to her own womanly notions. She shook. She regarded him with iciest hatred. "This is for the welfare of mankind," he said, attempting to guide her back to what she knew, what he had taught her, but he loathed the weakness of his own voice.

Why had she come? Those murmured promises of a gift for him were but an excuse to see what she wished to see and now wished to hold against him as a black mark. She would not allow him to touch her or hasten her departure. "Imagine that Angelica fell ill, and a medicine could be extracted," he began. She interrupted with a vicious calm: "Do not speak her name in this room."

"It is not a simple straight line. You must imagine a vast web of knowledge still to be discovered. We fill the spaces slowly." He was a fool.

Rowan tried to speak kindly to her as she made her operatic exit. He even extended a social invitation, probably not sincere, but which of course she spurned, as she did all invitations.

Outside she turned upon him. "Does your heart not break? Not at all?"

"Now," he admitted. "Go home."

Dr. Rowan placed a hand upon his shoulder as she flapped from the court like a madwoman or a hawk, and Joseph flushed with shame. "Oh, you mustn't be too concerned, Barton. That is how they are, the vast majority of them. Here and there an exception; my Caroline has a stomach of Bessemer. But as a rule they've not the constitution. Shouldn't have invited her here, sir, bit of a misjudgment."

Joseph remained outside, perhaps too long, watched the rain spilling from the eaves. He had earned Rowan's rebuke. On several occasions he had lectured medical students and junior assistants on the importance of barring the door to those likely to misunderstand. Noises of protest had disturbed their work now and again, and Dr. Rowan's name—far more valuable than Joseph's uxorial pride—had suffered libel in a newspaper article written by a preening Irish playwright, known for his wit but without wit enough to understand what was at stake in Rowan's work, presuming to question a Fellow of the Royal College of Surgeons in order to sell tickets to a farce. Rowan, rarely angry, had called the writer "Lucifer of the stage." He waved the newspaper and shouted, "Satisfied to have people die as long as the survivors can enjoy his latest spectacle!"

He did not wish to return inside. The noise had bothered her. And the sight, of course. The aroma certainly affected the unaccustomed nose. He should pursue and comfort her. He should pursue and chastise her. He should treat her as always when he returned home that evening, not a minute early. He was still wearing his apron outside. He often scolded junior men for just that. They called him "the headmistress" behind his back. Harry once told him he meant to thrash the next fellow who said it, thus assuring that the original insult arrived at its intended target. Dawdling in the rain was unseemly and uncharacteristic. Rowan would soon send a boy to fetch him.

The rain suddenly stopped. A stunning silence replaced the snapping puddles and drumming roofs. Fat drops fell from the eaves, each more hesitant than the last, pricked by beams of new sun. The drops released and fell with such an appearance of slowness that, though he knew the physical equations that dictated the immutable rate of the falling water's acceleration, he wondered if there might not be a countervailing law of optics that caused this deceptive languor, some property of light or corneas or perspective that retarded not the speed, but only the perception of speed, as if a film of fancy might be laid over facts, a sheen of illusions, imaginative but irrelevant, of course, or relevant only in its power to soften—for the weak—the world's immutable hardness beneath.

One must accept them both, he supposed, truth and fantasy. One must not allow oneself to believe only in the illusions; that made one a fool or a woman. But, from time to time, perhaps it was not so dangerous a thing. His daughter still lived happily in the slow-falling rain, or even the *rising* rain, she had reported once. The dog-shaped cloud, the smiling dog with clouds in its eyes, the old beggar's gums speckled like a dog's: Angelica had described all these to Joseph at one time or another, this endless chain of comforts and entertainments drawn from the world's meaningless surfaces.

He had tried, at her insistence, to perceive pictures in clouds. A patterned series of ridges in a mackerel sky could almost resemble, he admitted (embarrassed even in front of this little girl full of such fancy), "the skeletal remains of the sea reptile brought out of the Dorset cliffs, by a girl, you know, not so very much older than you. She found something quite important, all by herself, simply by using her eyes and thinking."

"What was it? Did it truly look like those clouds?"

"Oh, I don't know. I suppose. It had been dead for countless centuries and had turned to stone, just like the stone around it."

"Perhaps someone made it out of the stone."

"No, it was once alive."

"Did you see it?"

"I read of it."

"Perhaps you are wrong. Perhaps God placed it there to fool you."

At the time he had laughed, admiring her little mind, the stories it produced, how nearly she could comprehend. But after her mother's performance today in the laboratory, after these past days residing with Constance's unalloyed fantasies, this memory's hue shifted. That day he had been charmed by a superficial illusion (that his daughter was a clever little storyteller), and he had not perceived the obscured, hard truth beneath: that she was parroting what she had heard elsewhere, from her mother or Nora or some chirruping church-mouse in a ragged coat, whom Constance had brought into the house for tea and biscuits while he was away. He would be confronted by his daughter someday in this identical situation, standing alone in a stained apron, pitifully pleading for her forgiveness for having helped to improve mankind's condition. He had done nothing to prevent it. It would happen. He would lose her, too.

For Constance's influence *was* strong. When he returned to the laboratory it was difficult not to perceive it through her eyes and ears. If one imagined oneself a woman without the ability to transcend immediate sensation and emotion, then this room could, he granted, have a disorienting, even painful effect. She did not possess a mind able to set aside the shock of a moment in favor of the delayed value of considered judgment, so she must have been seized quite powerfully by what she saw here. And the sound could be quite troubling. Joseph recalled that when he began his employment here, the noise had, for some days, disturbed even him (who had grown accustomed to the sounds of cannons, of men absorbing enemy fire, of the surgical tent).

The surgical tent. He could, without any difficulty, still recall the scratch of saw against bone. The first time he had wielded that blade, he feared he would retch or weep. Instead, despite every effort to hold himself impassive, he was grotesque: he sawed and laughed. A corporal was biting through the strap, and Joseph could not stop sniggering as his arm moved of its own accord. He had thought he would never accustom himself to those horrors, yet before long he was able to perform the most hideous tasks with his dinner within easy reach and his nervous laughter banished. Still, he had to confess, Constance had performed better than he at her first exposure.

XI

Joseph was meant to collect Harry from his home and from there proceed to supper and the boxing, but wisdom dictated he spend the evening with his wife and daughter, to repair breaches in discipline and in sympathy alike, to confront the results of his domestic negligence. Leaving the Labyrinth last, as was his habit, he stopped, therefore, at the Delacortes' to deliver his apologies.

Before the little bug-eyed maid could announce "Mr. Barton" in her faint Welsh voice, Harry had already shouted like a child, "Joe! Excellent! We need guidance in military matters." The family tableau on the parlor floor surprised Joseph, given Harry's stated indifference to his family, for there he lay on the rug, behind a troop of tin miniatures lined up against heavy horse under the command of a small boy. Two lemon beagles slept on the sofa, one's head on the other's belly. They were familiar, perhaps excused from service at the Labyrinth.

Joseph examined a painting to give Harry the opportunity to collect himself and restore order, but his friend remained prone, his chin in his hands, and the dogs did not stir from their absurd perch. "Sit down here and advise Gus, please, as to how you form up a phalanx, what have you." Joseph sat on the edge of the sofa.

"Please, sir," said the boy, "are they arranged properly?"

"I'm sorry. I was not in the cavalry."

"This fellow, Gus, this is the Mr. Barton I've told you about. He's not a doctor, but he learned to stitch on our wounded men in Africa. Well, one day, when the howling blacks break through our lines and come towards the hospital tent, our Mr. Barton here evacuates our wounded men to another location, all while organizing a few men to shoot, and he even led the guns from the front. Now, Gus, he put his few men in precisely the spot to protect the evacuation and give the impression to the nigs that we had reinforcements coming from the other side. The nigs thought they were going to find themselves trapped in a box and so scurried off. Of course there *were* no reinforcements. Mr. Barton saved the day. It was in all the newspapers."

"Is that true, sir?"

"In the main, I suppose. One does not give it much thought, you know."

"Not much thought? They pinned honors on him. Everything excellent that is English is in this fellow, Gus. You should be proud to shake his hand." While Harry lolled on the rug, the boy respectfully rose and presented his small hand to Joseph with great seriousness.

"Shall you be a doctor like your father, Augustus?"

"No, a soldier, sir. Like you, sir."

A child wishing to resemble him! The notion was so remarkable he nearly laughed aloud as he trudged home. He would never have such a child himself, and yet, if only Angelica were finished. That, precisely, was what he desired of her: that she, who every day more closely resembled the stationer's girl he had fallen in love with, would complete her infancy and become something else. He longed for her to exist in some purified and permanent state, without fits of temper, night fears, or an omnipresent doll, without contradictions and a slippery grasp on truth and a variable character. Glimmering through the dross of childhood he could make out a finer substance. It was a matter of patient extraction. Now she cried unnecessarily, but, when finished, she would be even-tempered. Someday she would come to exhibit the loveliness, the enchantress's beauty, he had first seen through the stationer's window. Now she was alternately engaging and childish in conversation, but, when finished, she would be well-educated, well-spoken, a suitable wife, or companion to her father, perhaps even a scientist, or at least scientifically minded. At meals, they would sit across from each other, and she would describe a discovery in a field he did not know well, chemistry or physics. She would ask after his work in turn and would not cry for dumb beasts; she would rejoice for people, children especially, whose suffering would be reduced. After the pudding she would fetch his tobacco, and, if by then his eyes had begun to fail, she would read to him by the fire. She would lean against the armrest of the sofa, its piping pressing into the soft white flesh of her forearm.

This vision came nearly immediately to life: he arrived home and found not Constance but Angelica, uncommonly happy to welcome him. At once she asked him to sit so she could play piano for him. He recalled, as she stumbled through her little pieces, Constance playing for him at these keys. In those days he had invariably been moved to seize her in his arms as she rose, watching her make music more than he could resist.

Still Constance did not return, and the child showed no signs of tantrums, nor did she wish her father to leave her in Nora's care. He therefore determined to be of assistance to Constance, for if her visit to the Labyrinth today had revealed anything, it was that she was overwhelmed by her responsibilities. And, if Angelica had indeed been resisting her new sleeping arrangements, he would teach her to conduct herself properly, as a service to his child and his wife alike. Leaving Nora in the kitchen, he led Angelica through her evening routine. The girl—thrilled at the novelty—did not complain but almost visibly matured to meet him. She declared it a delight to have her papa seeing to her.

He removed his jacket and collar, rolled his sleeves, and, feeling himself quite an amusing sight, knelt beside her tub. He helped her out of her clothes. He washed his hands next to her. She soaped herself and smelled of flowers.

His best intentions, however, were quickly met with suspicion and resistance when Constance at last arrived home from her mysterious evening's itinerary, a long truancy when she expected he would be away. "I wished for Angelica to see that she is not isolated in her new arrangements," he explained, and Constance at once offered with a strained kindness to resume the reins of the child's toilette. "I wished, also, to offer you a needed rest," he said by way of conciliation, but she would not retreat or apologize for her actions that afternoon, nor sit in pleasant conversation with them. She would only again and again attempt to dismiss him, first subtly (producing towels, combs, powders before he had realized what Angelica needed), and then explicitly, with offers to "release" him to his preferred evening amusements. Finally, the adamancy in her clenched requests became more than he wished to bear. "Very well, your mother shall finish with you."

"Papa stay!" Angelica cried at once.

Joseph did not lack for vanity. The sudden plea for his company appealed to him. Neither did he lack for vindictiveness. His anger at Constance's intrusion today and at her resistance to his olive branch tonight was strong. How presumptuously Constance had already installed herself in the spot he had just vacated, readjusting the bedclothes he had adjusted quite well. "Papa stay!" insisted Angelica. "I want Papa, too. Stay, Papa, stay!" Joseph hesitated, and Angelica's pleas redoubled in desperation. She shuddered and her face contorted until tears fell. "I don't want Mamma, *only* Papa!" she concluded, weeping freely and most movingly. A few days earlier, his company had been a matter of complete indifference to the girl, but was now one of pitiable urgency.

"What did you do to her?" Constance hissed.

"*Do?* That she should prefer my attentions for a moment? For once?" Joseph would have left the room, but the child loosed such a fearful cry that Constance called him back and without another word surrendered the field.

He read to Angelica and heard Constance lurking outside the door, then pounding her way downstairs to fidget at the piano. Angelica, sweetly obedient to her father, closed her eyes at his word, fell asleep. Her hair, soft and thick, felt against his palms as Constance's once had.

He climbed the stairs to his own room. Of course Constance was not there. He could sometimes see his frustrations and hers sprout simultaneously, their vines choke each other though they had been planted far apart, years ago, and now he and she were too tardy and overwhelmed to make the vast effort required to prune this knotted copse. He had meant tonight to be a reconciliation, a relaxant of inflamed tempers and tattered relations. He had meant to restore everyone to their proper positions.

He waited. She hid in the downstairs shadows. She feared him. He would show her that such fear was absurd. He would wait for her to appear. He would neither pursue her nor flush her from her post at Angelica's bedside. Such pursuit was undignified to him and likely unpleasant for her.

"I think it time we overcame our fears, our understandable fears," he explained when she appeared at last. He was surprised as much by his own words and actions as by her acquiescence. He had begun to believe that he had no more appetite for her, due perhaps to her age, health, moods, or simply as the result of his enforced starvation since the last calamity, as if her neglect had become comfortably habitual. Yet he desired her now, and now they drew together, in a fashion that could not conceivably alarm or pain her. He was considerate of her health, and his consideration was rewarded by her tender attentions, for a moment, perhaps two, until, of course, the child below called for her, and she fled him, cruelly, eagerly.

He pursued her, despite himself, dignity forgotten, and Angelica forced herself to produce a weak cough or two to justify her mother's attentions, and adopted her mother's words, claiming she had been choking, a dream or a tickle in the throat inflated to a tragedy by Constance's nerves and the half-awake child's susceptibility to her mother's influence. But by then Joseph's distasteful position—standing completely unclothed in the doorway before them—had driven him to retreat, ashamed and furious, his females' mutual preference exhibited in the most humiliating fashion.

Agitated, he waited for some time in the fading hope of Constance's return. But she would not. The room oppressed his spirit. He felt the urge to strike something. The room's darkness and heaviness suffocated. She had chosen all this stuff, precisely what would weigh on him, sap his nerves, erode the space in which he moved, compress the air available to his lungs. The entire house was uninhabitable. It stank of the feminine and repelled the male. He had tried to slow her pace of acquisition, when, not long after the wedding, it became clear that she had no sense of limitation, but would stack dark upon dark, thick in front of thick, blocking out the light according to her tastes and those of the latest "decorator" theory, as the house became a torment, room after room overcluttered, overpadded, overcurtained, the sun barred or absorbed.

He paced amidst the yards of encroaching scarlet and black, the curved console fronts in reflective lacquer, the line of the wardrobe like a woman in silhouette, the bed's canopies—the infuriating bed, where minutes before they had been so nearly able to close the abyss yawning between them. She preferred it thus. How close they had come, and she had flown off. He ached. At that unfortunate moment of mingled appetite and anger, desire crumbling discipline, she did in fact, unfortunately, return, catching him unawares. Her expression of disgust was unmistakable, and he became at once the boy chastened by his governess-mother in a comparable moment of discovery, a recollection he had not visited in decades. "In hell," Angelica had spoken terribly quietly, while she made him stand in precisely the shameful position in which she had discovered him, "onanists perpetually drown in a sea of seed, the seed of demons, black and oily, hot as pitch, filled with barbed needles. Onanists cough in this muck, always burning with an unappeasable desire and pain, as needles are driven just *there*," and she nearly touched with her glistening pearl of an index fingernail that spot where the barbs would be eternally lodged.

XII

Only Angelica spoke at breakfast. "Papa, are penguins flightful? Then are they chickens?" Normally he would have called for Nora to remove her to the nursery, and Constance would have looked stricken, but today he did not wish to be left alone with his mad and maddening wife. His stewardship continued to falter. These females intruded upon even the most personal corners of his domain, reducing him to a gawky boy where he should have been master. Before he left, he pushed aside his lingering embarrassment and attempted to soothe his flighty wife, took her hand, but its muscles withered at his touch. He told her she plainly had nothing to fear, for herself or for the child's obviously robust health. She nodded but would not meet his eye.

"Do not speak Angelica's name in this room," Constance had raved during her fit at the laboratory the day previous. The barb of that pointed remark lodged in his mind, a constant self-refreshing injury, and, as if his shame last night were a wound into which bacteria could seep, Constance's womanly horror infected him. He could only with difficulty perform his morning tasks without seeing them from her nervous point of view. At last, anger, a protective carapace, grew over the wound: he resented his absent wife's continuing intrusion, this assault by her willful misunderstanding and womanly sentiment, novel-fed and soft, stupid. He grew so enraged that, where only yesterday he had worked with purpose and aesthetic pleasure in the experiments and numeric satisfactions of measurement—febricitant response, reflexive posturing, the geographic progress of infection plotted on anatomical sketches—now he worked while silently rebuking his recalcitrant wife. "*This* is for the good of mankind. *This* will tell us how disease results from a wound. *This* is for your own good." Only after a passage of unnoticed and unrecoverable time did he remark the ferocity and imprecision of his work on the animal. He had again lost all sense of himself, for how long he could not gauge, just as he had with the diary and in his sleep, just as Lem's conversation implied he had once done for a much longer time. He hurriedly repaired his mistakes. The disorder of his home would pursue him even here, trample all before it if he did not regain control of it at once.

"Well, now Gus is all afire for *Dr.* Barton, hero of the Battle for the Hospital. He calls you *Dr.* Barton, no matter how I explain the distinctions. 'Papa, when can we meet *Dr.* Barton again? I have questions only a military man can answer.' Makes me feel rather small, actually," Harry added with an incongruous laugh.

The disproportionate pride Joseph felt at this offhand, and perhaps fictional, compliment only proved that he did indeed live a nearly pleasureless existence. Work (before Constance's destructive visit), the evenings spent with Harry, the moments in Angelica's company of late—though fleeting, these were the rare joys of a life increasingly without companionship or warmth. He resolved, again, to repair his home, and was immediately ashamed to realize how many times he had so resolved without solving anything.

He discreetly acquired from Harry a gentleman's item. For the remainder of his day, it sat in his pocket with the solidity of an engineering diagram or a bridge support. He carried home nearly as many blooms as he could hold, presented them to Constance, kissing her gently. His daughter uncharacteristically ran to his arms and begged him to come sit and talk with her. She asked if she might bring him tea.

Nora was winding the eight-day clock, and he sat, magically, as *paterfamilias,* as if the weight of all his failed resolutions had finally sufficed to restore the house's balance. His daughter strove to entertain him; his wife moved in and out arranging flowers and homely comforts to his tastes; the maid did her work in silence. In his pocket he felt the small square of oilskin in which rested the item Harry had given him without comment, jest, or question. It served as a talisman, his secret, for no sooner did he carry it on him than his home arranged itself.

He so heartily enjoyed this peace—it lasted through supper and the child's retiring to bed—that he did not dare request his rights that evening, did not wish to spend the potent coin he had guarded in his pocket all day. In truth, he had been fearful, he saw only the next day, not so much cared for as humbugged. He had hesitated because he did not wish to spoil the lovely, false veneer of the still life she had composed, only to face instead another evening's drama and disappointment. He had been beaten so thoroughly that the mere threat of more was enough to win his quiet acquiescence to her terms.

And so, twenty-four hours later, when she would have placed Angelica on the piano bench again in an effort to readminister the dose of domestic anesthesia, he sent Angelica away and spoke with a passion that surprised him most of all: "No, Con, *you.* Please. Do you remember the night you supped here, the very first time? You played for me. You do remember, don't you? I have almost never felt so fine as that night. I stood behind you. Play now."

She agreed. He sat off to her side, slightly behind her, and he ached to recover the feeling her music had inspired in him so many years before, a moment of perfection that he had never forgotten, a sensation of union with her and freedom from all cares, a pleasurable experience of losing himself (as he had so distressingly been doing in recent weeks). Instead, tonight, he felt only a weak dilution of that ecstasy. He had willed himself to believe that this repetition might restore them, refresh her youth and her warmth for him. He meant the music to carry him to the time when she not only had not aged, but *would* not age, when there was nothing in her vulnerable to change or time, her beauty, her love for him, his desire for her. He strained to achieve that state. She finished and rose, and, before his ears forgot the sounds, he took her in his arms, as he had done years before. "Do you never think warmly of me?" he pleaded.

She said only this: "But the doctors."

"There is no risk," he replied, upstairs.

He could not conceivably have acted more gently towards her. Considering the frustrations of the past days, not to mention the trials to which he had been submitted these past years, his kindly restraint merited a comment, a display of gratitude, an acknowledgment that in these difficult circumstances he was not monstrous, was not comporting himself like a Turk or a Frenchman. Instead what rewarded his civility? She wept throughout. He attempted to explain the device and her safety, but she was, in her mingled delicacy and anxiety, unable even to hear. His efforts to console her served only to worsen her anguish, and did little to stiffen his resolve. Her generous display of her emotions implied only that he was a brute or so unappealing that she would turn her head away, squeeze shut her eyes, chew her lip, sob like a child bracing herself for assault, rather than look him in the eye. When his behavior then altered itself to justify her reactions, it should not have surprised either party.

After, in the melancholic, angry silence, she made as if to skulk off, to haunt the child's bed. "Stay," he asked gently, and she complied, but too quickly, only from obvious fear. Whatever he had done in his life—and he would not deny his weaknesses and failings, sins of commission and thought—surely tonight he had done no wrong, nothing a man could not be expected to do. Still her fear and silent accusations would not cease.

XIII

I was reading something today quite to your tastes," Harry said. "A naturalist fellow, off describing the moist reptilia of Asia, found for our amusement a new species of toad, in China, perhaps India. Among this species, only the female's flesh is venomous to the likely local predators. You've heard of that sort of thing, but here is the odd bit: the mere touch of her flesh is poisonous to most of the males of *her* species, too. It does not kill them, as it does the predators, but her touch sickens the male, puts him in a temporary stupor. The fellows are drawn to her scent, of course, find her irresistible. Tastes vary, not for me to judge. Any rate, the males attempt to mount her, but not long after placing their little front feet on the alluring warts of her slick back, they fail to mate, fall backwards and simply droop there, quite literally stunned by her and now vulnerable to the same predators who shun the brightly colored females, knowing they are poisonous, but who think nothing of devouring a fine dun male, deliciously paralyzed like a *plat principal* at La Tourelle, courtesy of that same female. Stranger still to come, my friend. For, you shall recall, I said *most* of the males. Occasionally, a beau comes along, indistinguishable from his colleagues, and, transported like them by milady's divine aromas, he steps aboard. But this blessed boy shows no evidence of stupefaction. Rather, he extends his lengthy tongue in testimony of his amusement, stirrups the lady to completion, and hops happily away. Now note two things: first, his suitability to that particular female by no means proves his suitability to the next. It does not signify that *he* is immune to all females, neither does it imply that *she* is lacking in venom. Neither is true. He is only immune to *that* female, and she in turn is only powerless against *that* male, more or less. Second, before you begin to sing like a lady poet about Love's wisdom, finding for every she a he uniquely suited to her unique charms, know this: no sooner does our fellow unsaddle from the lady to whom he is immune and fated, then off he confidently canters to find a new one, who, as I said, is statistically nearly certain to defy him, leave him dazed and stupid for a descending owl or passing serpent or wandering peckish Chinaman with a taste for toadish thighs. Well, what do you make of that? God and His females will never cease to amuse and amaze, eh? I thought quite especially of you as I read that."

The hansom leaned to the left, turned too quickly, and Harry was pressed against Joseph's arm. "I think Constance may be ill," Joseph confessed quietly, as if the pressure had squeezed the admission from him.

"What's your diagnosis, Dr. Barton?"

"I mean to say troubled, rather than ill, if you see."

"Not entirely certain I do."

"Nor am I. She has been saying the most ludicrous things. I can scarcely understand what has come over her."

Harry recommended a former professor of his, a Dr. Douglas Miles of Cavendish Square, "something of a specialist on derangements major and minor." They descended at Harry's destination. "Are you certain I can't lure you along? An evening of fleeting pleasures?" he asked before the three-storey restaurant that served supper only on the ground floor. "Might be a less expensive cure than old Miles."

Joseph walked alone through the district and thought of Harry's evening ahead, his friend unknotting his cravat, then of the tangled skeletons, the female's head flung to the side when Joseph kicked the male. He had enough anatomy to know the muscles in the neck that would have flexed to make such a gesture in a living body, the muscular fiber, red and gray, the eyeballs rolling in their holes, the skinless sinews straining against each other, bone now cushioned from bone. And then the skin and the hair, the coloring, Constance's face, Constance flinging her head to the side, in no pleasure, but in fear or lunacy. Ghosts of blue light pursued her, and she frightened the girl with her tales.

The mist thickened, sour and stinging to the eyes. It glazed his face. Women appeared in doorways, one here, one there. He penetrated farther into their district, and they grouped in threes and fours on the edges of pools of gaslight. He was in a foreign country, amongst its citizens, in the interior, their language plainer and louder. They approached with offers and glided away again to recongregate in new formations. Among women like these, there was a calmness lacking elsewhere. In respectable London, women seemed to speed up when he glanced at them, scurried away though he meant nothing by his regard. Perhaps he inadvertently expressed some desire that startled them. Perhaps he exerted no more rigorous control over his expressions than he did over his thoughts. But he could look slowly at the residents of this quarter, savor the candid investigation of faces, which daily life forbade.

He pushed himself back to his repellent house, hoped against all experience and logic to find Constance asleep but Angelica awake, ready for conversation. Instead he arrived in a home on the verge of chaos. Nora had excused herself from her duties, and Constance had prepared a vile meal in her place. Angelica's company was the only pleasure, but after he sat with her in her bed, she ferociously protested his departure, haunted by Constance's tales of the supernatural. "I WILL NOT STAY ALONE!" she shouted, and her nervous mother, her eyes shadowed and red, leapt to her side and unsurprisingly indulged her whims.

Constance's disordered state proceeded into outlandish disobedience. She openly refused to come to bed and leave the child's side. The next morning, he informed her that Angelica would begin proper schooling at Mr. Dawson's in a week's time. "All this behavior, yours as well as hers, redoubles my earlier concerns about her education."

"Show her your fine laboratory, then," Constance replied icily. "That would educate her about you most eloquently."

XIV

He had at first been slow to remark the gradual degradation of Constance's person, the daily, infinitesimal accretion of change on her face and in her temper. But now in a single week a carnival of chaos had unfolded its tents and trumpets in his home. He could scarcely stand in the raging winds, felt he should bind everything in place lest it be swept away: memories, furniture, his child, his wife, himself. In the few days since he had sent Angelica out from the parental garden, the situation had come to feel irreparable and yet not a little risible. He was incapable of explaining it fully even to Harry. The topic loomed unapproachable for its very magnitude. To select and stress the single detail—Constance feared the dark, or awakened in the middle of every night, or imagined floating demons, or hysterically and viciously defied him—was both an overstatement and an understatement, even irrelevant, not to mention self-accusatory (for he had permitted this fear, wakefulness, disobedience).

He sat before Dr. Douglas Miles and lost the power of speech, would have exchanged the consulting room for a battlefield rather than say a word. He could not look the specialist in the eye, but allowed himself to become entranced instead by an enormous plant blocking the light from the French window, its green and yellow leaves thick and ridged, split ragged, unfolding from stalks as wide as his wrist, a swath of jungle trapped in this Cavendish Square second storey.

"Speak." Dr. Miles's ancient face hung heavily from his skull like a sack suspended from a stick. "Speak, speak. Time wasted will not be regained, sir."

Joseph cataloged her inability to accept the child's removal to its own nursery, her roaming of the halls at all hours of the night, her ceaseless fear for the child, her weeping without cause, her terror of her husband, her morbidity of thought—preoccupied with murderers and rebels abroad—her disgust at his work, her suspicious questioning of him, her talk of ghosts circling the child's bed. He lost track of how long he spoke and accepted Miles's offer of a sherry when he finished with a spell of coughing, astonished again at his own apparent escape from all decent self-regulation.

"A knife is required to cut a mind loose of its moorings," observed Dr. Miles, his jowls slung basset-low. "What infects her? The root of her behavior?"

"I have my own failings," Joseph admitted, stung to be so quickly recognized for what he was. "Perhaps my appetites—"

"Never mind your peccadilloes, sir," the physician scoffed. "You are not at issue here."

"I have determined to see our child educated to her station and talents."

"Nonsense. This hardly constitutes a cause of lunacy. Jealousy perhaps, in some women, resistance, disobedience. But you talk of low spirits, shattered nerves, ennui, neurasthenia, and hallucination." He counted the symptoms against his fragile fingers, and they bent nearly to snapping.

"She is unable to have another child, and she fears, unnaturally—she has taken too literally the admonitions of doctors. She fears, hysterically, you see."

"I do not. Speak plain, won't you?"

Joseph struggled to produce an appropriate description of their marital relations, but in embarrassment confessed instead, "I fear she is intriguing to turn the child against me. Though I may be at fault here, having been rash in my . . . My wife comes from a different—a charity-school education, you see."

"I do, sir. I do indeed. There are reasons—biological and necessary—for the manner in which a society organizes itself, as you may only now be learning rather to your cost and your disadvantage. Is she, in this recent crisis of character, less obedient?" Joseph confessed he was lately unable to exert much influence. " 'Exert much influence'? How often are you required to use physical chastisement?"

"I have never seen the need."

Dr. Miles was briefly astonished, then visibly irritated. "Your preferences may not be at issue, sir," he said at last. "You speak of a manifest psychic imbalance. I must make clear to you that you have encouraged that imbalance. Women's moods are madness in microcosm, Mr. Barton. This, science has demonstrated categorically. Conversely, madness in women is a magnification of the moods they normally carry in their repertoire, a magnification permitted by themselves and their feckless masters. They are, as a rule—and I do not purport to speak of your wife with complete authority yet—but as a rule they are a volatile substance requiring careful management in womanhood as much as in girlhood. Your child is a girl, you said? Well, damn it, if you can chastise the one, you can chastise the other, and your duty is to both equally."

Joseph could not confess he had never struck Angelica, felt lately more warmly towards her than to the mother.

"The loyalty and tenderness of women is a product of their glandular systems, Mr. Barton. Simple anatomy, you must surely know. You are a man of science, are you not? A lapse in accustomed loyalty and tenderness—which is a fair summation of your complaint—can arise from a depletion of that selfsame glandular system. I mean to say that science is extremely close to unlocking the very material nature of character, and I would submit to you that the troubles you now face are the result of your neglect in controlling earlier symptoms of your wife's glandular depletion. It is not an uncommon condition as the female ages. It may well be that this deterioration of female personality in the years between thirty-five and forty, after fifteen to twenty years of marriage, is an illustration of Darwin's model. It may be that this devenustation, the coarsening, both of physical beauty and of charm and character, is in place precisely to discourage late-life fecundity, which, selection has amply demonstrated, yields unfit offspring.

"As you have allowed this crisis to fester beyond all bounds, past the point of easy treatment, your reassertion of control will be rather more difficult. I am most concerned by her belief that spirits are wounding the child. She may pose a danger to herself or your child, perhaps also to you. You are laughing." Joseph had not at all been laughing, had not known that humor had entered the conversation. "I would discourage you from evading this question.

"You know, I am reminded," continued the old and yellowing doctor, and he rubbed vigorously the buttresses of his nose, as if to ensure their solidity, "of a fellow I knew, loved his wife beyond all measure. Couldn't do enough for her. Spent money on her like an Italian gigolo. Dressed her in the finest and the newest, filled the house in the afternoon with whatever gewgaws caught her eye in the morning. Every evening, another *festino* with the most glorious company. All to please and display her. Called her the greatest Helen of the day to anyone who would abide him.

"I supped at the fellow's home one night, met the lady in question. I, too, was dazzled, but only in that I had never seen such a startlingly unattractive woman. Hideous. And her conversation! A black shroud dropped over one's spirits. I certainly did not hold the minority view. It was written upon every face at the table. Except, of course, the husband's. He gazed upon her with an embarrassing fervor. Her dullest comment, her least graceful stumble—he warmed himself by it. He was mad. Or should we call it love, as the ladies like to do? Girls dream of a man who will smile upon their many failings as on the facets of a jewel. But how to explain the crowds at his many soirées, for his was the most sought-after table in London? It could not have been for the pleasure of peering at his dreary ladylove. Well, I understood with the first taste of the soup. I had never savored such genius in my life. What a chef that man had toiling in the back! The host imagines a table full of people admiring his bride, when all the while they yearn only for his table and her absence. I found my way into the kitchen and cornered the maestro. 'Just searching for the closet,' I said, only to learn a bit more about this Michelangelo. 'Exquisite victuals. Now what's your name, sir?' He was quite prepared to say nothing. Thought crossed my mind that the husband had cut the chef's tongue out. From behind me my host's voice rises, and his hand descends upon my shoulder: 'Dr. Miles! If you are so fuddled as to think this is the closet, then I wonder about the value of your medical counsel!' A jolly laugh, and my host steers me back to my ostensible goal, away from my secret desire. Do you see? He *knew* the appeal of his entertainment was the food, not his ghastly wife. Or he merely had the food serve as a magnet for his cold, metallic audience, to perform for them his love for the woman at his side. A strange display, you'll admit, especially when one learns that—the very night I was a guest there—she murdered him in his bed with a violence you would expect only from a rampaging Mongol of particularly irritable constitution. A horror, yes, after all he'd done for her, shown her, especially a woman of such low appeal. Your impatience is noted. Please attend to me a moment longer.

"She came before the law. Her defense, Barton? This fanatic husband, this devoted prince of the uxorial arts was—can you guess it? He was murdered in his bed by his charmless lady because he had been selling her to the Tsar's army night after night for years. You don't follow? She was mad, Barton, as mad as any case I had ever seen. She stood in open court and detailed the actions of Russian soldiers, whom she called by name after ludicrous name: Polawosky, Ivanovanovna, Belliniovitschskiovitch. She described what each soldier had done to her in the most repellent and perverse detail, until the judge cleared the court of all but the barristers and the consulting doctor, me. Her story was unshakable and consistent to the last detail. Each night, her husband would introduce one or more Russian soldiers into her bedchamber, leaving them to have their way with her in some horrifying manner unknown outside the Siberian steppe. The detail! Each soldier's history, preferences, manners, appearance—she never contradicted herself, and begged the court to protect her. Vladimirawiskypiskyovich, a Cossack, took her like a lion and demanded she purr for him and call him the Tsarina's favorite, and he wore his silver-white hair shorn close to his skull, because that is how his father had worn it, and because its color showed itself beautifully against the blue collar of his dragoon tunic (she had to agree), which tunic he kept in such fine condition thanks to a blind valet whom he had rescued from certain death at the hands of Magyar brigands. Wallamirsky would say nothing at all, but weep copiously during the act, which she could well understand, given his losses, but which did not by any measure soften her hatred of him, considering her position. And on and on. Well, the law is clear: she could not possibly be treated as a criminal. Even as one could pity the murdered man, off she went to Fairleigh."

Joseph, attempting to extract some parallel from this frothing story, or laugh if humor was in play, was attempting to ask a question, which, due to his physiognomy and Dr. Miles's excitement, was taken to be impatience, which trait Dr. Miles would not tolerate in those to whom he was good enough to consult. "Attend a moment yet, sir. You requested my expertise. Off she went, delighted at the court's decision, convinced she was being placed under royal protection. Only then did agents of the Crown uncover a wardrobe in the murdered man's chamber, cut into the wall, hidden behind his ordinary wardrobe. Mr. Barton, will you tell me what they found therein? No? Four uniforms of the Russian army, of different regiments, but all the same measurements—the murdered man's, naturally. He had been playing at some cruel game with his charmless and therefore placid wife, man's home is his castle, no harm done, but she had grown confused and evidently thought the game was real. Or perhaps she was a savvy murderess and was now using their harmless pastime as the grounds for feigning madness, saving herself from the gallows. I confess I wasn't certain myself. What, Barton! Are you blushing? Hemming and hawing about your own marital state I can understand, but, sir, we are only scratching the surface here. This tended garden we are pleased to call an English marriage is a subterranean jungle with a few dainty blooms on the surface. Surely you read more of the new science than I do, you must know what our ancestors were up to, up in the trees. More like Spaniards than Englishmen, but there it is. We were all up that tree once, and many still are.

"The jointure dictated that the house pass to the wife, but if she was to be remanded indefinitely, it would instead belong to the murdered man's maiden sister, and she was eager to collect her prize. In the deceased's writing-desk, the sister found a letter, signed by the murderess-wife and in her hand, dated some three years earlier and addressed to the Tsar of Russia. Our Mrs. X informs His Slavic Majesty, Tsar of All the Russias, that if his troops should ever be in London and in need of refreshment or feminine companionship, she was his devoted servant, as long as it was not in violation of the confidence placed in her by his cousin, Victoria. Had she written this for her husband as an element of their innocent conjugal theater? Or as a symptom of her lunacy, cruelly exploited by her satyric spouse?

"When I asked the unhappy woman to explain the document, she insisted she had never meant to commit treason, that I must explain this to the gentlemen from the Queen's secret service. She had not, in her weeks at Fairleigh, deteriorated in appearance or manner, as many do in those surroundings, but then again, as I mentioned, she had begun rather below the average. 'My husband forced me to make that invitation to the Tsar,' she insisted.

"We were strolling through the park surrounding the asylum, and I was certain she believed her story, certain she was mad. I left her in her pitiful state, returned to this very room and found awaiting me none other than that tragic household's most magical *chef de cuisine,* a Rumanian named Radulescu. It was as if an angel of heaven had descended into my life. I engaged him at once as the master of my kitchen, and he reigns there to this very day, in the same sequestered security he enjoyed in his previous employ. I do recall his miraculous appearance as one of the great days of my life." Dr. Miles lowered his bumpy yellow eyelids. "Last evening, he completed his performance with a tart of quince, a cloud of clotted cream out of which peered a crescent moon of such unsurpassed succulence that one could have wept, as Catholic pilgrims do before a renowned *pietà*.

"Yes, he had come to me looking for employment, as the dead man's sister was not to his taste, and he wished to escape that home, the memories of which troubled him. 'The wife is a beastly woman,' he said. She had frequently attempted to seduce my chef, often in full view of the husband, and was in many other ways exceedingly cruel. I asked Radulescu if he was certain, because, in all candor, he *is* a foreigner, who may have seen seduction where there was only kindness to servants, unknown in his land. 'Certain?' he replies, cool as you like. 'She was quite clear. The husband did not please her.' Radulescu described a home with a too-gentle husband who did nothing but cater to every whim of a woman of loose character and innate cruelty. Why murder him? Says chef, 'Because he came upon her with one of her Russians.' "

"I thought it precisely the *husband* dressing as the Russians . . ."

"As did I. My chef swears to me that the man of the house, despite the fullness of his heart for his lady, was banished from her bed, and even on those occasions when he gained access, it was to no avail, for one evening in the kitchen, under the influence of some ferocious Rumanian brandy, the husband admitted to the sympathetic Radulescu that he was unable to achieve 'even the potency of an elderly sheep.' A Rumanian proverb, apparently. And these Russians? They were young men recruited and delivered by the brother of milady's maid of wardrobe, for which both siblings were richly rewarded from the wife's excessive pin money, paid by the poor husband. So richly rewarded that they could not be found after the murder."

The tale did not stop here, but turned upon itself at least three more times before Joseph lost all track of who had been guilty, mad, or worthy of his sympathies. With the testimonies of each new character (a valet of Russian birth, the London tailor responsible for the Russian uniforms, a secretary to the Russian mission, a Scotsman impersonating a Japanese merchant), the meanings of both the murder and the marriage shifted, guilt fluttered from one shoulder to the next, taking wing again as soon as its claws had touched down.

When Miles seemed finally to have come to the end of his recital— Joseph held his tongue for a few moments to be sure no new witness was going to step forth and repaint all that had come before—Joseph admitted to total confusion.

"Now, I believe you are beginning to see the problem, sir," Miles replied. "I am rather of the opinion, based on your description of your wife, that she is approaching a crisis. A determination will need to be made, but I cannot, without speaking to her directly, order her remanding."

Remanding? This was suddenly far more than Joseph had intended to discuss. He had had no intention that he could recall of having her "remanded." He had come half in anger and wounded *amour-propre,* had not thought very clearly what his complaints of her behavior implied, or what responsibilities would ensue from mumbling them to a physician.

"At Fairleigh she might find some respite from her troubles and happily recover. But for now, do not indulge her fears. Reiterate your intent to educate the girl. Be kindly but firm, much firmer than has been your lackadaisical practice to date. And, by God, be watchful, sir. The instant you feel she may harm herself or the child, matters must be seen to."

It was difficult not to view his wife and his home (and himself) through Dr. Miles's eyes, and then impossible not to find the sight wretchedly shameful. That evening she fed and served him with a slavish and bizarre courtesy, as if she knew her behavior had come to the attention of expert authority, or perhaps Joseph, under Dr. Miles's influence, appeared more obviously a man not to disobey. She chattered of nothings, then studiously asked after his needs with an interest she had not displayed in months, perhaps longer. He told her he was being dispatched on an important mission to York on Monday, and she was keenly enthusiastic for him and the work that had so sickened her only days earlier. He was apparently perfect master of her and his home, precisely as he had wished, but, in this moment of triumph, he possessed barely the energy to reply, scarcely even the strength to rise from his chair. He was unsteady on his feet, the wine having affected him most powerfully, no doubt because his conference with Dr. Miles had so sapped him. He looked in upon the sleeping child, kissed her neck. He could have fallen asleep beside her on the tiny bed, but Angelica stank so profoundly of garlic that he recoiled, briefly awakened just enough to struggle to his own bedroom.

XV

"You shall marry me someday," knee-straddling Angelica purred, her nose nearly touching his. She saw her father's expression and hesitated. "Won't you? Mamma shall be your wife, too, of course," she offered by way of reassurance. "Until she dies." She could not help but stride to her joyful conclusion: "And then I shall be your only wife. Until *you* die."

How clearly the child saw the days remaining to him, his death an eagerly awaited event, even by her, distant only by as many years as she could count on her fingers. He recalled a conversation with Constance when she was nearly identical to this child and, like her, sitting upon his knee:

"You are so lovely," he had said, his hands in her hair.

"I shan't always be."

"I think you will."

"No! I won't." Her sudden adamancy, the shift of tone astounded him. He should have known even then. She wriggled free of his embrace and stood, as if making a logical demand. "Please agree now. Accept this. Tell me now that you know I shall not always be lovely." She had been quite serious. She refused to allow him to touch her again until he agreed that she would not always be lovely, though he had not believed it, in a tower room in Italy, and he assented only in such a way that she could never have believed him. "Yes, yes, no question, you will be most hideous!"

Today, with her daughter discussing his approaching death, the mother's obsession with mortality lost its charm in retrospect and now offended him, for *he* had been the older, was older still. *His* mortality had been far more the issue, while she insisted upon her beauty's transience, her life's fragility.

At Sunday supper he was plunged yet again into another semideath, his body stumbling from another suffocating meal and into another dreamless sleep. He could barely focus his vision on Constance lifting his legs upon the bed for him, unlacing his boots for him. He awoke Monday with his head pounding as if he had consumed bottles and bottles of wine. She was not beside him, of course, the exertion of seeing to his desires for two days running having overtaxed her. He found her asleep not even in the chair beside the child's bed, but upon the child's *floor,* clutching the girl's doll, surrounded by piles of the girl's clothing.

He rejoiced at his compulsory separation from her. On the train to York, London was stripped from him with the locomotive's lunatic speed. He was released from his worries and the refrain of what, in his position, Dr. Miles would do, Harry Delacorte would do, his own father would have done. He could feel the pressure inside him slowly abate, and in its place there rushed his pleasant hopes for his expedition. York would mark a transition, a change in all aspects of his life. He was shot free of his airless existence. Lincolnshire blurred by, and he studied again Dr. Rowan's notes and letter, and his own shorter report detailing certain patterns he had noticed. There was simply no overstating the responsibility of his assignment, and the value of exchanging some words with the genius of York. He slept at an inn and woke early, prepared to prove himself.

But the great man would not see him, kept him waiting hours on a cracked leather bench outside his offices, sent him his northern twin—

a slow-moving, sleepy-eyed "senior man" of middle years (likely with a mad, disobedient wife)—to collect his package, offer him tea, and bid him wait. Wait he did, for hours more, until a sealed parcel addressed to Dr. Rowan was given him to carry home on the next train. Joseph was an elderly messenger.

He stood before the door of his hateful home, as if only minutes had passed since his departure. The key weighed down his weak and shaking hand. He turned his back on his house and stared at the passing foot traffic, the black figures gliding by in the mist, leaning towards each other in murmuring pairs, secreting confidences beneath umbrellas, and beyond, the hacks, enclosing conversations, intimacies floating over the deep mud of the streets, behind drawn leather blinds.

He climbed the stairs with Constance in strange pursuit, as the symptoms that had clung to him the last two days now defeated him, the nausea and headaches. He had spoken rashly, even to her, of his "responsibilities," his hopes of garnering the praise of York's legendary scientist to carry home to Rowan, of winning his advancement in this research his wife so loathed. Now she chased him with questions, even to the threshold of his dressing room, suddenly and mockingly afire to discuss his work and humiliation. "What happened in York?" she baited him through the closed door. "Did you succeed as they wished of you? Will the doctors reward you for your work?" He stayed behind the door until she left him, and then he willed his feverish body across the room to bed.

She woke him, some few hours later. "What the devil is the matter now?" But Constance was asleep. But she had awoken him: the tumult of her mind at rest sufficed. She tossed her limbs, mumbled unintelligibly, whimpered like an animal cowering from a blade. He could see the disks of her eyes inscribing swift infinities against their lids. Her fears ate at her even in her sleep. Her face displayed the most extreme terror and sorrow mingled. The sight astounded him, dislodged something sweet and painful that had resisted flowing for some long time.

That pity, so long frozen, surprised him as it cracked and ran, so accustomed had he become to rage and stifled frustration and shameful secrets. So persistent was that rattle in his chest and thump in his skull that this new trilling warmth shocked him. He could almost have believed it was *he* who dreamt, so unreal was the sensation. A moment later he felt a splash of gratitude to Constance for presenting herself so unguardedly to him. His own appetites, failings, weaknesses were surely to blame for their predicament. How could she not be aware of them? His vision blurred, and he uttered nonsensical moans of sympathy for his wife's continued suffering, for which he was at fault. He groped in the dark and the bedclothes for her hands, found an elbow and a wrist. At once her sleeping protests increased: "I will change! Leave me to change! Look away!" He grasped her hand and pressed it to his wet lips. "My girl, don't fear." He nearly sobbed as he said these feeble words of comfort. Even as he whispered, her body shook, and her legs kicked. She rolled and writhed as if he and the parts of her he held constituted the only fixed points of a whirlwind churning ever outwards. "My girl, I am here." Her eyes opened with a start and she cried out: "No! Leave me!" but now she was plainly looking at him, not at some dream image. Her nightmare was not banished by the sight of her living husband; she had likely been dreaming of him. He dropped her hand, and still she stared at a terrible stranger. "You were dreaming," he said quietly, and the pity evaporated from within him with horrible speed, leaving him almost chilled. "You cried out. I took your hand." From what grave charge did he feel he must defend himself? She said, "I am sorry. It is my fault, Father." She closed her eyes and rolled away from his last effort to touch her. Father, she said, the only role she had ever meant for him.

They lay in silence, their backs to each other. Their feet, when they accidentally touched, shot away like startled prey. He felt the congealing bitter rage seep, viscous and cold, back into the spaces that only a moment ago were cleaned and warm with sympathy. He tried to stop it; he must not so easily retreat to anger. He had done nothing so terrible, not truly, nothing (at least) that Constance surely knew of. If he was treated by her as an enemy, it was because something was wrong with *her*, an imprecision, a soul sickness. His beloved girl was stricken, labored under horrible burdens. Miles had said as much.

After some time he heard her rise and in the hall strike a match against the murk and descend, of course, to her child.

He closed his eyes.

He awoke to screaming, though the noise did not reach him at once. He first had to struggle out of a dream prematurely hurled into its deafening finale: a crowd of women and girls screaming at him, frightened of him but demanding that he soothe those selfsame fears, that he be devil and doctor both, while he could only acknowledge the furniture, which was also screaming at him, denying what the women and girls were saying about it.

He rose from the bed and stumbled across the room, towards where, in his semiconsciousness, he recalled there having been a door. He was wrong by an inch or two and embraced the side of the doorframe, splitting his forehead against its corner. He ran into the hall, prepared to fend off the black attackers who had invaded his house, assaulted his screaming wife and child. His rage was more pure than it had been even in warfare. The blood ran down the sides of his nose. The spangled shock of his cut and his women's cries spurred him.

The waking tableau was scarcely as sensible as his dream or his intermediate state. His wife's hands shone with blood, and she knelt by a burning bed as a cold wind blew from an open window, and the child stood idly by, her nightclothes smeared red. He simply could not extract any meaning from the picture before him. He moved to the window, but Constance, doing evidently nothing in the face of whatever danger had bloodied her and set the room ablaze, rose, intent on blocking his way. He brushed past her, lifted the girl away from the spreading flame, and hurried to the far window to cut off the wind feeding the fire. He set Angelica down near the looking glass where she at once began to shriek, which renewed Constance's shrieking. In this howling Joseph set to restore order, bundling the bedclothes, smothering the flames on the bed and then the small cones of fire scattered around the floor like the encampments of a toy garrison. This battle won, he turned to the wailing females, Angelica now in her mother's grasp, but calling for him, "Papa, foot!" Her foot dripped blood.

He took Angelica from her mother's unwilling arms and laid her on the pillows, sent Constance for water and bandages. She resisted! She seemed not even to hear Joseph's words, had allowed her hysteria to reach such a pitch as to deafen her, and only after several requests did she appear to understand what was required. Her departure calmed the child almost at once. "Papa, foot," Angelica moaned again, but more quietly. "Papa Papa my papa."

"Quiet now, child, everything will be well," he whispered, and propped her feet on the singed and bundled bedclothes. "You're my fine, brave girl." The words themselves hardly mattered, as they did not with animals, for the tones that carried them could anesthetize as surely as alcohol. "We will have you hunting tigers again in no time." Her weeping became a weak laugh.

A curved triangle of fluted blue glass was wedged in the child's foot, and he began to perform the mild surgery required. "Here is a tale of a bandaged foot. Quiet now, listen to Papa. When I was in the Army, an old fellow I knew stepped outside his tent in bare feet. Very unwise, you'll agree, for he stepped quite precisely onto the open mouth of a sleeping ligerphant." He felt a fast pleasure, her willingness to listen, his ability to entertain, the smoothness of the small, white foot in his hand, his power to practice medicine at last on a person, on her, to comfort her, to be a gentle father, to forget his latest and countless failures. "As you know, ligerphants prefer to sleep with—what?" The girl repeated her natural question despite her plentiful tears and the blood staining her father's hands. "I assumed you knew. It is a beast with the teeth, whiskers, and mane of a lion, the trunk and legs of an elephant, and the stripes of a tiger, but of course pink on blue. The entire animal is no larger than a mouse, but it sleeps just as you do, Angelica, on its back, with its mouth gaping wide and its paws up by its chin. But unlike you, it has exceedingly sharp teeth, which are exposed in this sleeping posture. Well, this old fellow in my regiment—who could never sleep properly and was always up and about—out he tramped from his tent and stepped right onto those sharp ligerphant needles. He squeaked and hopped away, and the ligerphant awoke from a dream of hunting zebras to taste the soldier's blood on its tongue. It concluded, naturally enough, that it *had* slaughtered a zebra, so it let out its cry, to summon the other ligerphants to come share in the stripey feast. We all knew what would follow from *that*. Soon our camp would be overrun with ligerphants. They would eat all our food, poke holes in our clothing, leave pink fur all about, and that, my dear," he said to the little girl biting her lips as he wrapped her foot tightly, "would mean pink fur in our guns and our tea and all over our maps, meaning we would certainly lose our way, and we would not make it home to England, and I would not meet your mother, and we would not wed and then be blessed with the creation of you. And so—" He tied the last knot, pressed the foot here and there, pleased to see no spots of his subject's red blood seeping through. He laid a clean blanket over her. He closed her eyes by gliding the tip of his finger again and again down the bridge of her nose. "And so we ran about with our sleeping caps and a few lumps of sugar—to which the ligerphant is partial—and we swept them up. It was quite a game by the end. I, as the medical fellow, being the most adept with my hands, was the winner."

"You are a very excellent doctor."

He did not correct her usage. "I swept up into my large sleeping cap—"

"Four thousands?"

"Even more."

"Five hundred?"

"Precisely so. Now you shall sleep, child."

"Don't go. Please stay, Papa. Sleep here. What if my bed sets fire again?"

Angelica's fear, undammed by any sign that he might leave her side, rushed to fill all silences. She strained for conversation to keep him present and herself awake. "The fat lady said there is a man hanging in our ceiling," she said, her eyes closing even as she spoke.

"What fat lady?"

"No fat lady. I swore a vow of tears. She was not here in your absence."

When she slept, he watched her still, lovely and white and smooth in a bath of silver moon. She was Constance—not the spinning enigma, not the blood-splashed and ashen victim of childbed, nor the transformed mothering-beast that rose from that damp grave, but Constance of the shop counter, or nearly so. Angelica would soon be the very image of the girl selling Pendleton's goods, but a wavering reflection, as if cast on a black pool of moon-glazed water. She would, unsteadily and only at moments of repose, when one stopped one's breath, boast precisely her mother's lips and eyes, her very glances, the sincere and the contrived both.

In the child, manipulations and artifice were still transparent, and thus instructional. The open face taught him to read the closed, for there, as he emerged, huddled Constance on the floor of the corridor, and the array of her expressions and lies in the minutes that followed was explicated by the time he had just passed with the girl. Constance feigned first this then that, fear then worry, love then respect, and he saw the creaking cogs working beneath. He dressed her hand, cut from the lamp she claimed she had broken when trying to open a window. She claimed never to have seen the blue glass he had pulled from Angelica's foot, though several bits of it were scattered under the looking glass. Though he knew in the main that she was lying, he could not see precisely when or why or what truth she was burying. Any fragment of her explanation was plausible, but the totality of it was suspect. "What has come over you?" he allowed himself. "I scarcely recognize you anymore. You hide from me."

"I swear to you that I am hiding nothing. I have been nothing but candid in all matters to you. I owe my husband nothing less." He was looking away as she spoke, and he heard the same easy irony of Harry, even of his father. She wore a perfect mask of innocence, such as must require hours of careful preparation before a glass, or perfect innocence.

"Where will this all end?" he asked, behind her, his hands on her shoulders, and he felt her muscles contract under his touch as if to recede from him into the floor. Had he not woken, had he been out, her madness—or, to be generous, her mad carelessness—could well have taken Angelica's life, or her own, as Dr. Miles had foreseen. The thought that she could in some ricocheting lunacy actually do the child harm was no longer inconceivable, though it was also simultaneously impossible to reconcile with the memory of her gentleness at other times. He knew that the one need not exclude the other, yet he could not hold them both as true: if she were unwell now, she had not been lovable then, and if she had been lovable then, she was not unwell now, was not lying, was no menace to the child.

These two strangers had taken so much from him, and yet, at the thought of them coming to harm, tenderness rushed through him like a flame across paper, so painful that he held his wife's face and prayed silently to a nonexistent God that she not be unwell, not mad, not conjuring and fleeing oneiric phantoms, that she not hide her nature from him, that she be the same sweet creature from years ago, unchanged and unchangeable, as the child promised to be. He kissed her. "You must be more careful. You and the girl are too precious."

XVI

He awoke early. She slept. On the white inlaid surface of the armoire outside Angelica's room he noticed a shadow. He touched it, licked his finger. Constance had bled upon it last night. He opened a drawer for a cloth to wipe away the stain, and saw the brown tracks continue down, descending through levels of crisp whites to the bedrock of a paperboard box labeled McMichael's Herring, within which lay two small vials of the same blue fluted glass he had drawn gleaming from Angelica's slit flesh. The box also hid sprigs of greenery, tin crucifixes, small canisters of white and green powder, and a knife, unsheathed, its bone handle stained with the same brown that had led him to it. Here was the result of his womanly vacillations and delicate qualms.

He surprised Nora at the stove. "What fat lady visited the house in my absence?" She did not for long plead ignorance when the consequences of her lies were made painfully clear. He startled himself with the ferocity of his interrogation of the Irish girl and the keen pleasure it brought him. He enjoyed the speed with which he broke her and reestablished their roles. "Only nonsense, a lady with spiritualist knowledge," Nora began, but did not end until he learnt that his wife had been poisoning his food. "I tried to stop her, sir, but she said it was just salts," Nora wailed as he bent her wrist.

"Papa! You are first!" said Angelica when he came to collect his wounded child. She wrapped her arms about his neck and kissed his cheeks. "This is how we shall be when I am your wife." He carried her upstairs and with her on his lap watched Constance sleep.

When, soon after, her eyes opened, her placid expression of awakening was at once overcome by hatred and fear. She produced lies and sped away to consult with her broken confederate belowstairs. He gave her time, still hoped, despite all this, that she would not attempt to deceive him further, but would throw herself upon his mercy. His heavy eyes offered to close, to sleep it all away. Alas, when he followed her, he was treated to the hopeless performance: "The girl injured herself on something of yours, Nora," recited the angry mistress. "Attend to your work more carefully, if you value it."

"Nora," said her unimpressed audience, "your mistress is not well. She needs her rest. You shall provide her peace and solitude today. No visitors."

What would such a man be feeling, I wonder, as he walked or rode, eagerly or unwillingly, back to Dr. Miles's office? I suspect he suffered no further heartbreak for the loss of his wife. There was no more mourning to be done. He had been bidding her farewell for so many years already, had lost her long before, if he had ever possessed her at all. She had set this trap, wound the spring of its sharp teeth, ages ago, perhaps—most treacherous of all—before he had even known her.

No, I think my father felt no sorrow as he set foot in Cavendish Square, but a bracing anger carried him forward, rendered him decisive. I think it not impossible that he was relieved, even happy. There would be some local scandal, but he would be the indisputable master of his home, and free to be the father to his child. He would have the girl educated. They would dine side by side. She would, under his hand, become his most perfect companion. Perhaps Constance would return in some weeks or months, repaired and restored to an earlier form of herself. Or not.

Of course, he thought, as he stood before Miles's building, looking at the garden's life-sized bronze of Perseus grasping by her serpentine hair the ragged-necked head of Medusa, one could not manfully evade the shame that accrued to him in this affair. If she suffered from a softening of reason, a sickness of the soul, she could not, in the end, be blamed for what ensued. He had chosen her to be his bride. He had not noticed as her worse nature swelled grotesquely. It had been his duty to shape this woman, and he had shirked that responsibility. Her moods, like any woman's, were fierce and rapid, and he had for too long viewed them with an indulgent amusement—women would rage, it was their nature, it was why we took them to our bosom, to fire us up so we might draw heat from them, even as our steadiness cooled them. But this condescension only proved his failure, too, for their moods were trickles of madness. Unchecked by a wall of masculine strength, they would fill all available space. This was why widows and spinsters were universally peculiar; no one dammed their relentless, seeping expansion. And now Constance's tides lapped at the windows and stained the walls at waist level, and rose still.

Weak and unmanly, now he would plead for the intercession of a true physician, a proper father, a man. Miles would arrange everything. Joseph would at least protect his Angelica and never let her know the unnatural source of her danger.

But Dr. Miles was not to be found so easily, though Joseph returned at midday and again in late afternoon, stood in the evening gloam beside Perseus long after the doctor could conceivably still appear.

He returned home with no solution, forced to maintain the temporary limitations on her he had devised. He was not cruel, offered her fresh air, a meal, despite all she had done. He could almost fancy that his wife had been replaced, driven out by some other being now occupying her body, her fading beauty the precise gauge of how long she had been possessed by this rot. "I may die," she raved, "but I will not allow harm to come to Angelica even so. I could imagine nothing worse than being a child in this house."

"What are you saying?"

"I *saw* you," she spat. "You."

He was shaken by her words, despite the sureness of his position. "Precisely what did you see?" Or was even this an error of indulgence? Should he instead have forcefully instructed her that she had seen nothing?

"I will not permit it. I will not sit idly by, will not abandon her. My end is decided, but hers is not." And on and on, the vague accusations mixed with outright fantasy. Remanding her would prove him right. When Miles concurred, it would prove that none of this was his fault. His secret longings and lapses were not at issue here, nor his profession, his habits, his past, recollected or forgotten.

As with any animal or criminal, perfect and unceasing vigilance was an impossible ideal. He could not hope—even if pity so moved him—to keep Constance in his home, in her state, indefinitely. The proof of it came before dawn with the sound of the front door and with his groggy discovery that she had wandered the streets all night with Angelica then clandestinely replaced her.

He examined them by the rising light, the sleeping mother and child. If her changing appearance was a measure of her internal distress, then this morning brought a terrible and drastic decline. It made no sense even to call that woman his wife, or to use the name Constance anymore. She finally bore no relation at all to the stationer's girl. Her hair matted and filthy, her eyes ringed with darkest circles, her face bloodied and bruised, spattered with mud from her nocturnal lurking. This gutter crone was not Constance, but there, across from her, peacefully awaiting his rescue, lay the small original of Constance's beauty, patient and lovely, more Constance now than Constance herself.

XVII

M
r. Barton! Excellent! I have been hoping for someone to speak
to this morning. Did you? Why would you have done that—
I never consult on Wednesdays. Sit, sir, sit. Yes, yes, I do not doubt it,
but first, I had the most remarkable experience last evening, and I desire another's ear to make it real, if you see my meaning. While I am to
understand that you were haunting my garden, I was dining as a guest
of a fellow of the Royal Astronomical Society. We dined at the Society's
house, in a hall lit with moving stars on its ceiling. Barton, the Society
employs such a da Vinci in its kitchen that I can scarcely express my
wonder at his artistry. Each course, you see, represented a stage of
human knowledge of the universe. Soup—be patient with me, I am no
astronomer—soup was the universe as known to Aristotle: concentric
rings of a tomato and pepper cream laid over a black potage, and in the
center sat the Earth, depicted by a flat, round toast, colored blue and
supporting a very convincing map of Greece in a paste of sparrow-grass.
On each of those concentric circles, a floating item: a disk of tomato for
Mars, a lozenge of parsnip for Venus, a truffle of Moon, all of it speckled with a golden dust of stars—gold flake, excellent for the blood."

Joseph felt himself heavy in his chair, Miles's voice soothing.

"Next! The Persians, maybe the Hindus, I cannot recall, perhaps Chinamen—they believed the earth was a single, river-veined mountain balanced in the upturned jaws of a viper, and the sun, moon, and stars were supported respectively on the back of a turtle, on the upturned wings of an eagle, and in a basket held in the snout of a boar. Barton, it was a performance unequaled in my experience. Turtles, their shells removed and replaced with thin slices of beef sculpted as shell, under a bright yellow melon stuffed with a fiery pulp of oranges and radishes. The bird was enormous, a goose of such unprecedented mass and with its roast wings extended up and arched, like this, supported by piles of quails' eggs beneath, and balancing between the tips of its wings the moon: a surface of scalloped potatoes, seas of beans, volcanoes pouring forth molten cheese, forcefully extruded by some engine hidden beneath the table. And that Hindu boar! May Vishnu bless him, as large as you, this fellow was, but a sight more succulent, and in his jaws a basket, woven of noodles, holding a mountain of stars: the quail yolks floating in blancmange and—oh, I, yes, yes, recall: the viper and the mountain! Well, each of us had a jellied eel, coiled, mind you, jaws pried open, grasping in its maw a mountain of pork, streaming with a gravy somehow dyed blue for the rivers, you see. And now the pudding—I'm omitting a few courses, you know, I cannot say I recall the cosmologies of all those intertwined fish, the cheese carved as Copernicus's comets or somesuch. I have the booklet here, somewhere, explaining each dish.

"But at pudding, Barton, we arrived at last at the modern, scientific, and complete understanding of our universe. Five kitchen boys wheeled the display to us on a platform nearly as large as the table itself. The man was such a master—it would have been the easiest matter in the world to make eight orbs of chocolate and then ice them in the same sugar paste with slightly different colors. But no, he could not bear such pedestrian work. No, all eight planets orbited a lemon curd sun, each planet in turn surrounded by its appropriate satellites. The centerpiece for sheer spectacle was the Saturn, circled around with boiled sweets of every color pressed into floating rings the size of a brougham's wheel. And Jupiter! The Jovian Pudding! Apparently, Jupiter is orange and has an enormous red stain on it, though whether that stain is made of the sweetest currant and raspberry preserve, I suppose only our Creator will ever know. The icy poles of Earth? Meringue of vanilla. Venus? American oranges and beet sugar encasing a lemon cream and Genoa sponge."

Joseph now wished Miles's reminiscence might flow indefinitely on, freeing him from any thought of his own. He could have sat there until the sun fled and returned, gazed through the rubber plants at Cavendish Square beyond and absorbed at second hand the rivers of port, the forests of cigars, the conversation of the great scientific men gathered for an untroubled and all-male feast. Far too soon, though, with a handful of carved asteroidal nuts, the doctor came to the end of his recited joy and insisted upon hearing of Joseph's misery. "She set the room ablaze? Are you quite certain? So the hysteria has worsened, there can be no doubt. Derangement rooted in morbid fear of conjugal duty, cause irrelevant. You have attempted, in your manner, to exert your will over her, and she has resisted. She is determined to let herself go, it appears. She has chosen hysteria, and with that surrender of character, she has exposed your home to a grave infection.

"The child represents your wife's failures, thus her deranged self hates it and would, if her better nature is not restored, lash at it. None of this is terribly uncommon, Barton, in women of a certain class and constitution. Medical science proves every day what has been wisdom since man's Expulsion: they are *all* quite mad, to a greater or lesser degree, some of the time. They are ruled by the moon, as are tides. They are tidal creatures, sea goddesses. We love them for it, but they are prone to the same raging storms as the oceans. It is no wonder that the word *sea* is, without exception, a feminine noun in every single language that still wisely assigns gender to objects.

"She consulted a medium? Of course. The whimsies of spiritism boast their adherents in all ranks, including many eminent men who simply ought to know better, but credulity is one pox medicine is quite unable to eradicate. With women, the appeal of occult practices is quite deeply seated. I have looked into all these visions and visitations they so cherish, the vomiting ectoplasmic fabric, the talking tables, the automatic writing—it is womanly at its very essence, you see, and quite to the point in your own sorry case. At the root of all of this stuff festers an essentially sexual fear: the fear of transformation, or the desire for transformation accompanied by a fear of that selfsame desire. Examine, sir, the myth of lycanthropy—the monthly metamorphosis of man into wolf. Why does this frighten? Because there *are* creatures who, in reality, are unwillingly and horribly transformed monthly, with results sanguinous, painful, disorienting—a monthly eradication of character. And just as women fear this regular change, so do men, in their souls, fear being in any way like them. Hence, lycanthropy. Vampirism? Every carefully investigated case has turned out to be a madman, filing his teeth and attacking women to absorb their blood, in order to *become like them.* As you are a scientist, I can recommend some texts: Gellizinski, Kaspar, Ufford, Karl Knampa, even my own humble contribution can be had at Gower's in Old Compton. We are all circling the same truths, sir. Your wife fears her own wish to be transformed into a man. You frighten her because you represent that hidden wish in the flesh. And the spirits she believes haunt her—I wager you supper at La Tourelle—the spectres are attempting to frighten her *away* from her deepest desire, because her better self knows that this desire is corrupt. The spectres—though she could not possibly know it, or admit it if instructed—are there *at her bidding,* because she wishes to be frightened back to her proper place by an unquestionable authority—a role I begged *you* to play, sir, but which you abdicated, to your lasting detriment and hers."

Though some of Miles's philosophy escaped Joseph, one element struck him with force: to wish to change even as one fears change. This was beyond argument. He had fallen in love—if that was the term—with the girl in the stationer's shop, and as soon as he was able, he removed her and made of the girl a wife. He loved a slim, pretty girl and made her fat with child and tired from her trials. He had instigated a process that now careened, unstoppable.

He himself had been transformed as well, simply by being so closely linked to her and the child, had altered beyond the range of her love, altered as surely as Dante's damned: *A form perverted, not what it was / His every aspect changed.*

He had sat in front of the arched window, the tower apartment of a hotel five centuries old, the Duomo of Florence silver and black behind and beneath him, a full moon serving as a round reading lamp over his shoulder, and by its light alone he had read Dante to her. That moment, that peak of their happiness and perfect stillness together had already, even then—Joseph saw by the harsh white light of Dr. Miles's diagnosis—been corrupted by transformation, for not even an hour later she carried inside her the first seed of destruction, set to mar her beauty and youth and peace of mind seven months later. And though he had planted that seed himself with the kindest of intent, perhaps she had been wiser than he, right to fear him as the agent of transformation. On that moonlit night, in a fairy-tale castle, he had taken her with all the gentleness and restraint he possessed, but she had nonetheless cried out in pain and fear.

XVIII

No proper wife or mother, still she threw herself into hostessing. She entertained Dr. Miles—come to fetch her away—with the charm of her younger self. But she performed only as a gift to Joseph, of course, an apology of sorts, even an acknowledgment that she saw what was about to occur and wished him to see that she accepted it. Joseph was short of breath as he closed the front door against Miles's probing of her madness. Desperate for air, he inhaled only grassy horse dung and the roses of a passing flower girl. His eyes were wet! He wept for her, as she struggled now, too late, to hold herself intact, seeing only now, too late, the consequences of her weak will, sweetly presenting him a cameo of what she once had been, a memory for him to clasp in her long absence until she chose to regain her reason. Across the road the two men Miles had brought to subdue his wife watched him, but Joseph's tears would not be subdued.

And now night has fallen, and the particular gathers around, first the ankles, then the eyes. Does he tonight of all nights place a foot wrong, fall into the Thames or into the hands of cutthroats, cutpurses, kidney men? Not tonight; I never thought so, nor did Harry. Hired actors, then? Third denied it well.

Does he hurl himself from a bridge, into the muck of the embankment, into the lions' den at the zoo? Does he walk away from his family, tonight of all nights, await through darkest hours the first train, the boat for Calais? Unlikely. His wife has been remanded for a convalescent rest, his daughter and home are his own, tomorrow he cashiers disloyal Nora and begins his life anew as a man.

"Speculate, my dear lady!" you instructed me, so certain and so impatient, licking your lips for answers about me. "Even your speculation may reveal to us the shapes concealed beneath awareness." Always intent upon my concealed shapes. Very well, then, sir, here is my speculation, here where neither Nora nor Harry nor Miles nor Third nor Anne nor my mother could provide me any clue.

He tried to become lost, but failed, stared at the Thames and the Tower and the tarts, blocked his ears to the desperate cries he imagined rising from his home. He ached to rush back and save her from those strong men shoving her body into the waiting brougham. But he forced himself to stay away, fighting, with stinging eyes and useless fists, his desire to rescue her, until the tide of that desire abruptly shifted. When he knew Miles must finally have signaled his trusties and seen her bundled off, when he knew he would face a home without his wife, then suddenly he could not force himself to return, and he spent hours more in dazed wandering, resisting the lure of his new house, thinking aloud, kicking at rats, watching rain strike puddles with tiny white explosions, until, to his own astonishment, without any idea of the hour, he stood hunched before the door of his restored and cleansed household, and with rain-beaded fists sank his rough iron key home, and climbed the stairs to his cold bed.

PART FOUR

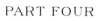

Angelica Barton

B ut when will he return?"
"Someday. Perhaps. After some time away. Papas do this. For now, I believe we should accustom ourselves to his absence. I do not think you will find that difficult. I will be your friend, if you shall have me. I can be an excellent companion in matters of the little Princess of the Tulips, in singing songs, and telling stories. Do you like these things?"

I very quickly came to love my Mrs. Montague, my auntie Anne, as a second and far more entertaining mother, especially in those first weeks when she taught us how to live without Papa, how to speak and behave without a thought for his mute disapproval or joyless praise. Of more pressing practicality, she prepared my mother and me for the curious world approaching our door. "His colleagues will call to see that you are well, to ask for explanations, which none of us have, and, most of all, to be *reassured* by your manifest concern for your er-rant husband." Anne laughed. "Yes, even in your hardship they will want *you* to provide *them* comfort, to prove to them that *their* wives would miss them if they should choose to vanish. Can you do that, dear?"

I felt very grand, in the weeks following Papa's departure, to have so many men wishing for a moment of my time and the charm of my conversation. Papa's disappearance had transformed and elevated me, and Mrs. Montague was my most helpful lady-in-waiting (if I was a princess still) or my dresser (if I was already becoming an actress). She helped me find my voice for these courtiers, these supernumeraries in our family's drama. "Where do you reckon your papa's gone to?" asked a very handsome man with a quiet voice and a vulgar accent, having already paid his tribute to me in the form of so many bright pink boiled sweets. "He flew off with the angels," I said, "sent for him by the Princess of the Tulips." This was the answer I had given Mrs. Montague when she had asked me the same question days before. She considered my response in silence for some time, then finally judged, "I think that a charming and quite perfect reply, my child." I recall the pleasure I felt in that delayed praise, her most adult approval of my conversation, and so of course I did not hesitate to provide that answer to every adult who asked me, most repetitively, that most frequent question. I varied only my tone, adding here or there a slight hesitation. "Did he really?" asked a pimply, red-haired man with more sweets. "Did you see him fly away with them?"

"Oh, no, sir. But he comes to me. The angels bring him to see me and to kiss me good night. It was he who told me it was so."

"Do you think your papa was very sad?" asked Dr. Miles, yet more sweets sticking to his thickened palm, lifting tiny mountains of his skin when I grasped them. His ancient flesh was translucent yellow, and beneath it blood trickled through blue canals. He resembled a picture I had seen in Papa's book of a skull with eyes and muscles but skin on only the left half of its face.

"He was only sad when I was wicked, sir. You think I made him go?" The thought that I had made him go made me sad. Making myself sad before these men produced a marvelous reaction in them.

I ate a great many sweets in the weeks after my father's departure. I felt that his absence and my growing cache of sugar bore some relationship, though whether my treasure was recompense, reward, bribery, I never felt certain, even to this day. I was, however, quite certain that I could judge, by the quality of confection I was offered, which of these callers were clever and which were fools. Similarly, a woman of my acquaintance recently boasted to me that her child, a boy of six, is endowed with a remarkable sensitivity, that his first reactions to adults are infallible, and even in those cases where she previously came to her own conclusion about a person, she does not hesitate to yield to the boy, his magical ability to see hidden natures in a few minutes of childish intercourse. I hear such claims all the time. I think it rather a spreading delusion, that somehow children see the world and its rulers clearly. Faith in the pure heart and innocent eye of the child is a worsening symptom of something quite awry in our world, a sheepy loss of confidence in ourselves as adults. Soon we shall be calling them to testify in courts of law, donning the black cap due to their claims. I tell you, as someone who makes her daily wage in make-believe, the simple truth: children install fully imagined characters behind a single physical trait or event: the lady with the too-big nose is a witch, the man who scolded me is cruel. Soon enough the world populates itself to suit their temperaments. The fearful child fills the world with menacing adults; the trusting, with the initiators of fairy-tale adventures. Credulous parents in turn adjust reality accordingly, banishing friends and embracing strangers at their darlings' whims.

Still worse, our unexamined memory of our own childhoods convinces us that the wise children we meet now must be right, for we recall those adults *we* knew in colors only a child could have painted: maids with superhuman strength, able in darkest night to carry and dispose of a corpse all by themselves; lecherous, drunken glaziers; jolly fat women who battle ghosts; dimly recalled fathers, spied from an upstairs window as they fled the house in tears. We gaze backwards, enchanted by the characters we created, and in turn credit our own children's description of similar caricatures. They in turn will grow to believe they were right, and on and on.

"I love Papa."

"And he loves you, my darling girl, I do not doubt it."

"He does. And so we shall marry someday."

Do I remember saying this to my fragile and jealous mother? Yes. And, further, I recall she laughed at me, not the laughter of a mother enchanted by her daughter's confusion, but the scornful laughter of a rival in a temporary, perilous position of dominance. Yet no sooner do I write this than I am certain the memory is impossible, for that is a comparison I could not have made at the time. I was but four years old, so what could I have known of rivals and scorn? I think it far more likely that her laughter in my memory has been tailored to dress a role she was not playing then, but which I grew to understand only later, in other contexts. Memories are injected after the fact with subsequent wisdom. Such is the treachery of this path upon which you have so thoughtlessly set me, waving your gossamer promises of certainty and truth.

My memories imply that I could move about the house silently. The stairs did not creak beneath me; the doors did not moan at my touch. I stood within ten feet of the adults, and they did not hear my breath. I stole fragments of their stories and heated conversations, gave their words to my rag doll and my invisible friends, restitched new stories from the spare fabric. Do I credit adult obliviousness or childish stealth? I cannot say. They, conversely, were clumsy and loud, as is appropriate for giants. Their voices echoed between rooms, heedless of walls and ceilings, as is typical of gods.

The only true gods and, in turn, the only true ghosts. We understand them only gradually, in stages, as we pass the years they passed before us, a lesson they conduct from beyond the grave, guiding us one epiphany at a time to our own death (when our spirits are decanted to haunt our own children in turn). Their younger selves, whom we never knew, suddenly appear in our looking glasses, the inconceivable people they were before they conceived us. These fantastical creatures puzzle us, shake off the creased costumes of age to preen again in the garish plumage of restored youth. The converse is equally true, of course. Our children reach a certain age and present us, as a gift, memories of ourselves when we were that young.

I walked freely amongst them, as if I were the spectre. I listened, for example, to the tale of the Burnham family the bright morning Anne told it to my mother in the park, frightening the wavering woman back into a proper client's behavior. I heard the story retold a dozen times over, as Anne often used it to tame other clients when, in later years, I assisted her in her work. But I know I heard it first in the park, squatting behind the bench upon which she and my mother sat unaware. That morning I believed in Mr. Burnham, hanging himself from my mother's ceiling to atone for his unspeakable crimes against a child.

However, I recall with quite equal clarity Harry Delacorte and my mother embracing in our parlor, his limbs encircling her, slithering into her dress. How clearly I can see his hand darting between her legs and then climbing up her back to grasp her hair, so the entire scene should be viewed with salty suspicion. Or perhaps not, since a three-year-old might well conflate two hands, one at the head and one at the waist, knowing of no reason why one would stop at that lower juncture rather than continuing on to caress my mother's lovely hair, an obvious goal. And I can see a gleaming white square with curved sides cast by the old gaslight in our parlor onto the pomade of Harry Delacorte's black hair. The tautness of the skin on my mother's neck as she turned her head sharply to the left and held his burrowing face in her straining fingers still smudged black from the hearth poker she had bent down to collect from where he had dropped it on the rug with the green vines and red grapes, my father's voice ringing from the next room, "Harry, where have you secluded yourself?": unimpeachable details, it must have happened just so! And yet . . . how would I have been in the parlor unobserved at that age at that time of night? I suppose I could have stolen in and out, witnessed such a thing, but the mechanics—how I came to be standing there, escaped from my nighttime restraints; how none of the actors (embracing or patiently cuckolded in the dining room like a French *farceur*) noticed my arrival, spectatorship, or departure; my recollection of feeling only mild interest and no surprise at the sight—

these moving parts jam and fling unheated sparks, implying the machinery of dreams, built to obey different physical laws.

I suspect, instead, that I collected mild ingredients for this spicy *soufflé* much later, for Harry visited us quite often in the months following my father's disappearance. He came first as an inquisitor, daily stopping to see if Joseph had reappeared, plainly puzzled by Anne Montague's quiddity and ubiquity. Later he came as a family adviser, later still as my friend, offering me, as I grew older, the occasional fragment of my father's history, told from the perspective of a condescending chum. Still later, he was transformed yet again, and, as I write, it only now occurs to me that I have transposed Harry's much older hands and lips from my body to my mother's, smoothing them and darkening his hair (later a most unreflective gray) to serve creative memory.

I recall playing on the floor of my mother's bedroom. After my father's absence, my presence was again welcome in that adult enclave. Nora, strong and silent, served tea to Anne and my mother, laid clean sheets on Constance's bed, requested a few shillings for replacement bed linens, collected buckets of filthy water, her arms scratched and bruised, her face cut. What had been done to Nora? No one remarked upon it.

"Where can Joseph have gone?" Constance asked, only briefly awake for the first time in the two days since her husband had left her serving lemon cake to Douglas Miles. Battered Nora blew a kiss to me, winked, and left the room.

"I cannot say, my most darling friend," replied Anne, though she believed she knew in detail what she assumed Constance must surely have known in principle: that Third and some anonymous accomplices had assassinated the villain in an alleyway on Joseph's accustomed route between the Labyrinth and Hixton Street, and had the next day generously refused Anne's offered payment for the act. (" '*Coriolanus.* I thank you, general / But cannot make my heart consent to take / A bribe to pay my sword: I do refuse it,' " Third recited, forced to cite a major character for such a sentiment, Anne having swept into his morning

pub exulting, " 'Messenger Two. Good news! Good news! The ladies
have prevailed!' ")

"Do you think your science has banished Joseph as well as the manifestation?" Constance persisted, yawning behind her teacup.

Anne smiled upon this necessary playacting. "I think it not impossible. We must simply wait, take each morning in turn."

"When the child comes, and I die, Anne, will you take him and Angelica? The house is yours if you wish it. Will you take my orphans?"

"Safe, safe with me, if such a thing should come to pass."

"You will not let Joseph have them? If he should return?"

She will play her part to the very end, Anne must have thought with
excusable irritation after all she had engineered for the love of her
friend. She begged me to have him murdered, and I did not flinch, and
now she will lounge and pretend it never happened, will not allow this
secret to cleave us together.

Yet when I asked him directly, in my own prose, years later, Third
only replied, " 'Porter. Men's fame accrues too readily for deeds / They
claim without just cause.' " Was he only loath to boast to his victim's
daughter? Or had Joseph eluded the actors' ambush, for that day he had
left the Labyrinth early, leading Miles to my mother?

Constance had no orphans, of course, not for many years, for quite
soon after Joseph's disappearance, her monthly visitor announced his
approach with his usual bombastic overture, sending Constance into
fits and the household into disarray with the violence of his demands.
But this time, her regular tyrant arrived with the nimbus of a savior,
carrying a pardon for which she had dared not hope: when he awoke
her in the night, the seal of her amnesty was glossy black in the moonlight, and she called out in joyful relief. Nora was there for her throughout, strong and silent, tea and linens, a cool cloth to the head and a new
set of cramp bones from Ireland.

The visitors came frequently, bearing questions, then less often, bearing condolences, and then not at all. No one ever suggested to me that

my father's life had ended in my mother's arms, and that Nora, furious at her own abuse at his hands, hauled his body off her mistress and away from the house, with or without the assistance of former actors, while Constance lay unconscious or delirious. And you cannot expect that my clear mental picture of this scene represents an unimpeachable memory or a four-year-old's unimpeachable testimony. To the contrary, I was repeatedly told my father had gone away of his own volition, and would someday return, if he so wished. I even saw him leave from my tower window, weeping no less. Coroners, friends, employers, police, and even Dr. Miles were unable to conclude otherwise. Dr. Miles's written statement to the court attested that self-destruction was not inconceivable, as the subject had been overwrought in the week prior to his disappearance, launching insupportable, paranoiac accusations against his wife, which, in retrospect, more likely reflected the vanished man's own inclinations and unnamed guilt rather than any disturbance of the perfectly competent, not to say charming lady. Harry chimed in to say he thought self-destruction unlikely, but had to concur that old Joe had lately been quite out of sorts, even more morose than his gloomy norm. Harry even retold the secondhand story of Lem, in all its contradictory implications.

Across our home fell the faint shadow of the court's ruling: the missing man had displayed ample evidence of an idiopathic melancholy commensurate with a preponderant likelihood of self-destruction or deranged abandonment. And then one more visitor called: the bank manager responsible for distributing the plentiful jointure Joseph had provided the stationer's girl.

My mother taught me to credit all our good fortune to Anne Montague's science. "Our friend saved us, my love." I slept, undisturbed. Constance, too, regained the ability to sleep, safe for perhaps the first time in her life. All of Anne's knowledge—the incantations, the rose petals laid in careful circles, the herbs rubbed along the windows—had served. The hideous fetch and its human master had been banished, it mattered not where. The three of us lived, secure and happy, served by Nora, in the cleansed and loving house on Hixton Street.

His absence complete and certified, still he came. As Constance grew stronger and more certain that all was truly answered for, now and again she would dream of him and, in the first moments of waking, would even hear in the low comforting breath to her side the sounds of the gentleman who had strolled into Pendleton's and lifted her up and away from toil and tedium. Blinking in the dying black, she would smile at him, safe from this distance, and hold more tightly the large hand under the blanket, comforted by the solidity of her friend and protectress, stained by none of man's darkness.

Did I see him wrap her cut hand, then twist it, his finger in her face, demanding how the fire in my room had begun? Not if I would have had to climb the stairs on my own bandaged, throbbing foot. So she must have told me, later, that this had been the scene upstairs while I slept in fields of ligerphants. Yet I remember no such conversation.

I do remember that butterfly, on holiday one August evening. Of that I am certain. I recall my mother's anger at my father for encouraging my interest in the mutilated insect, though I do not of course know what the sight of it brought to her mind, what associations or memories of another day, another butterfly, another father. I was not too young to note that I was the proximate cause of my parents' mutual anger. She was disgusted with my father and with me. Her repulsion did not escape my notice, and I remember worrying how to regain her love. And so I fell ill. Slightly ill? Terribly ill? Imaginatively ill? I know the answer is of significance, and I know it is lost irretrievably.

My mother's attentions were so unremitting that I scarcely noticed them, only their absence, as one only notices air when it is thin. But my father's regard—even a glance of disapproval or contempt—was a prized rarity. I went to great lengths to win his affections, while knowing that my efforts must remain discreet, for my mother would not have wished for me to please him overly. One morning, when my mother was downstairs, I tried to wake him by blowing in his ear. I stood next to his bed, my naked legs cold. I needed both of my arms to push the thick crimson curtain aside. I blew and the black hairs that lined his ear swayed. He batted, from his sleep, at the disturbance, and actually, if I recall correctly, he struck me in the eye with the back of his hand, though he did not awake. If my mother later asked me about the mark on my face, I feel certain I would have protected him and the sweet secret memory of making him swing wildly in his dreams because I had tickled him.

I recall him shaving his beard and the new father who lifted his raw, dripping face from the basin and caught my eye in his looking glass. He spoke of forgiveness for his father and with obvious pride in their rediscovered resemblance. Did Constance understand him to mean that she should forgive her own father? Or forgive Joseph for behaving like her father? For by the end, he had failed Constance. He had been no prince, no savior, not even a hot-blooded Italian, neither friend nor protector. He was only (and increasingly) a father, which role Constance had learned early to view with great suspicion.

I rather think a true haunting is less a sudden infestation of transparent pests than a settling of ingredients, the boiling over of a concoction that has been heating for years. All at once the steam melts the surface of things. Perhaps to some in the house, the arrival of invisible forces or visible ghosts is almost unsurprising. They have long felt that something dark was coming, or was already at work in the house's joints. It is as if they have felt uneasy but are unable to put that feeling into words, and so the feeling finally puts itself into ghosts instead.

In the fumes of our overheated house, impressions of years past began to sprout in Constance's mind, as mushrooms through damp soil, until, in this accelerating crisis, everything she saw burst with brightening, approaching memory: the window in her child's new bedroom, her husband's smell at night, the sight of his newly shaven face, the sight of a glazier's tool on a table in his laboratory, the coincidence of two similar, inverted names.

Vague but painful memories, strange associations, juxtapositions of the tiny details that form the scenery of both memories and dreams. She looked upon the window in my new bedroom and was reminded of the small window in the room where she spent so many hours as a child: a round window, divided by wood into eight segments, like the slices of a tart. Six of the panes were clear, but two—off-center—were colored, one red as pulped cherries, one the ugly muddy brown of a failed green, an early effort at glass-staining by her father, a glazier. As a child with little else to occupy her she would notice the change in the window as the day progressed, from the slightly tinted black just before dawn, brightening throughout the morning then darkening through the afternoon, until the reflections of candlelight appeared as yellow cones against its colors and the trees beyond. The window was the eye of God, because "The eye of God is always watching you," her mother used to say. "Even when you are alone He watches you." But at night, when the candles were out, and she could not see His eye, perhaps God blinked or even slept, when the air became thick, and her eyes burned from a nameless odor, and whiskers would scratch her face.

The odor had no name for years, as she was too young to call it whiskey and did not smell it at the Refuge, or in her flat with Mary Deene, or even after she had wed Joseph, for he never drank it. But it returned one night, entered her home on her husband's clothing, the very night before he banished me from my childhood paradise.

Her dreams were an attempt not to *recall,* but to *erase* what had come before, to scrub away the villain: she dreamt of pressing *herself* against my wardrobe, as if there were no agent in such an action, who had ever pressed her against her own wardrobe. Moved by invisible forces, she flew into furniture and straw. Thrown and turned, she fled and huddled in weeds and woods, but always fled *nothingness,* invisible but omniscient dread, or disembodied and golden smells, such as clung to her husband that night, until, in her dreams, nothingness itself was an enemy perpetually in pursuit.

She waited outside my room and remembered her own mother waiting. She saw me pretend to be asleep when my father entered my bedroom, and she recalled doing the same. She saw a grozing iron on a table at Joseph's laboratory, a glazier's tool she had not seen since she was a little girl, and his laboratory seemed all the more inexplicably sinister for it. When I turned four, she daily and with terrible new clarity recalled her own life at that age. When Joseph in jest called me "a wicked girl," it reminded her of Giles Douglas calling her "a wicked girl" in a voice quite terribly free of jest.

She told me these stories, years later, finally giving voice to the memories she had so long attempted to forget or convert to mere nightmares. By the time she spoke, it was all a muddle. She confessed to me, as I do to you now, that she was rarely certain which were accurate recollections and which recalled dreams, which were fantasies projected backwards and which were fantasies of her childhood projected forwards and taken for the truth. The combinations of perspective become too complex to produce a comprehensible picture, as if geometry itself suddenly fails. And, further, she may have wished to justify, obliquely, her actions to me. As a result, truth was thrice filtered—through wish, memory, and honesty—and yet you promise me that when I know the truth, I will be freed of my own painful complaints. You recklessly promise and you promise, and I can almost see the appeal of driving a serrated blade into your side.

Constance remembered the sound of a man making water and then approaching her bed with the words "Are you awake?" She did not move. "Are you awake, girl?" She pretended to brush noisy hair from her sleeping eyes. "You cannot trick me. Open your eyes. Open them. You're our girl, ain't you?"

Her relentless pursuer was able to discover her when she hid in the tall grass in darkness, swoop her in the blink of an eye to her bed without waking her. A magic enemy, able to read her silent thoughts, he said: "God is watching you always. He knows what is in your heart. When you lie, it wounds God's flesh and makes His angels cry." He knew all. He could hold her face under the chin, tipping her head back, examine her, and draw all her secrets, all her hiding-holes, from her eyes. "I know where you've been. I see it all over you."

Her mother, in stark contrast, was not magic, had only an ineffectual love but no wizardry and so could not read her secret thoughts. She was forced instead to demand answers: "Where have you been? Answer me!" She greeted the child's morning returns from her hiding places in the garden with rage and thrashed her. "The devil is in you, sure as anything, he's in you." Once, perhaps twice, her father came to stop the beating, but that was worse: "Now, she's just a little thing, there's no need," and he pulled her screaming mother off her.

"She's got the devil in her, that one does, don't think I don't know," her mother insisted, shaking her arm free of him.

"That may be. But we'll just have to treat him as best we can in there."

Her mother backed away from Constance (in his grip now), unwilling to stand her ground, to fight for the girl. "Then let the devil have her," she said, and turned to other work always ready to occupy her when necessary, her own tears drawing a comforting veil. How easily she surrendered her worthless Constance to the devil! She abandoned her to the devil inside her that drew the one outside her. If the devil was in Constance, why would her mother not stay and thrash him out? "Please," Constance cried, but her mother left her alone with him.

"It would explain things, of course, if the devil had been in me. I would cause those around me to act foully. My father grew more foul the closer he came to me. I used to wish my mother would work harder at her task." To thrash her was to protect her was to expel the devil was to keep her father away.

She remembered hiding, a constant event in her girlhood, "keeping the devil from those he would tempt." She remembered running from an implacable enemy, and, having put some distance between them, she stopped for breath. She knew he was approaching, as she could smell that aroma, not unpleasant in itself but the prelude to inevitable pain. The sky, gray and yellow, churned all around her, and the buildings were too far to reach. Even if she could escape that far, the buildings had no locks, and only locks could stop him. She must hide, out here in the open, under the churning butter and cream of the clouds, amidst the furze that scraped open the scabs it had only yesterday planted on her arms. She was yet another small animal alone in this open space, but she was not without hope, because she could change her color and appearance. Excited at this realization, she tested her abilities: her skin and nightclothes became yellow and gray to match the sky. Before a tree, only her eyes shone out blue, for her skin and gown became streaked brown bark. Safe.

But then the smell was nearer. The strength of it disoriented her ability: her skin churned yellow and gray but her nightclothes blanched silver with moonlight, and her feet ran clear, the wavelets of the brook. She had lost all control over herself. The smell was ever nearer. The smell was deafening: she could not hear or think or act in range of it; only fear coursed through her veins and made them brittle. And then, there at her feet, she saw a hiding-hole, an imprint in the soil, shaped precisely like her, as deep as she was thick, precise indentations carved and waiting for her nose and chin and eyelashes. All she need do was lie down and disguise her back. Surely that would not overtax her strength. The smell scratched her throat, and she coughed, though she strained to hide the sound of it, and her eyes watered. He could not be far.

Hide, don't breathe, disguise your back as brown earth. She turned her head to peek, though she knew she should not. She would have been better not to know: her nightdress, white as cloud, fluttered in the breeze, revealing her bare, scratched legs. Feebly she tried and tried, weaker and weaker: the back of her gown turned the faded blue of some other sky, then the colors of the stained glass in her bedroom, then a trickle of stream, and all the while—though she lay facedown in her hole—she could see him standing above her, laughing at her fading tricks of disguise. The ache began gently but quickly turned to flames, and she saw him burn her dress and then her flesh.

She recounted all this to me as if it were one recollection. I did not know when we had crossed the border into the country of dreams, but clearly we had arrived. At the end of her life, when she was most content to talk and talk of Anne and Joseph and the Refuge and Giles Douglas, that border was poorly patrolled. She recounted the same stories, blending plausible and impossible, tragic and dreamy, in new combinations. Once, for example, she had succeeded entirely in eluding her father, but with the most dire consequences. Out in the long grass, she hid in the narrow shadowy space between an oak and the wooden fence that ran a length between her family's land and a neighbor's. (She was never entirely sure of the fence's length or the size of anything, when she related these slivers of her most distant past; all remembered landscape is disproportionately large.) There were better hiding places, near the stacked hay, but she feared its needles, which she was certain would pierce her eye if she crept too close, so this night she squatted, and her little toes and soles were as hard and thick as a man of sixty's. This night his voice was kindly at first, though she knew it was only the tricksy evening voice, softer, wetter: "Where are you, girlie? Your mother and I are out here in the dark looking for you, see? Us two, we're out here trying to find you. Don't want you to catch your death of cold, our girlie sleeping in the muck, eh? Can you hear me? Course you can, so say something." But when Constance did not reply, his tone coarsened. "Where are you, you little slut? You don't hide from me. I'll always find you. Best I do, before a giant owl what'll come and pick you up, carry you off, pick out your eyes for her babies." She lay back against her pillows and looked at me: "He was right, of course. He always knew what I would feel or think. I remember the warm liquid gathering around my feet. I couldn't stop it, and I didn't dare move my arms to lift my skirts. Mother would whip me the next day for that."

"If I tell your mother you're out here hiding from me, she'll whip you blue." He had let drop the pretense that her mother was with him. "But I can protect you from her, you know. I'll tell her we went for a stroll, you and I."

The girl squatted still, her feet cold in her own filth, biting her bleeding lips so her teeth would not chatter. When at last he was silent, still she did not move until she had ten times counted ten in her head, touched the tip of each finger against her thumb five and fifty times more. She fell backwards at last against the fence and fell asleep there, mercifully, did not rise again until the gray broke. She returned to the house, ready for her beating, but it did not come. She did not see her mother or her father, only her sister. "Did Mother look for me?" she asked.

"Only George did. He said he had a secret for you." But that morning George was still asleep, and though he did wake a few more times before he died, he never was able to tell Constance a secret, and the frightful suspicion that tickled her nape was confirmed by her father a few days later: "Do you suppose yourself clever? George is ill because of you. He and I were out in the cold and dark looking for you, and look at him now. Your mother's favorite, you know, and after Alfred her heart is breaking. Are you pleased with yourself, girlie?"

She learned at that early age a nonsensical law: resisting a man's seductions would lead to the death of a loved one, and the heartbreak of others.

"Have I been so wicked as this?" she must have asked herself again and again as her sufferings grew worse in the weeks before my father vanished. So here, then, is a pretty question for your weak science: did she feel worse because events grew worse, or did events grow worse because she felt worse? And if it was this second arrangement, what was it that stoked her anguish to ever greater intensity? If she was being pursued by black memory, then as she felt the hot breath of her pursuer approaching from behind, she saw visions in front of her to justify her mounting dread. Haunted by the inadmissible images of Giles Douglas, she drafted some other haunting to explain her fear, memories evolving into ghosts.

Or not. Perhaps Giles Douglas (if that was his name, if he existed, if he was a glazier, if he was a slave to drink, if he was not some neighbor or even a child's garish fantasy) committed none of the violence that she sometimes nearly but never perfectly recalled. Perhaps her father was a gentle man, and perhaps Constance was simply born prepared for disaster, always warning against it, to deaf ears tired of her stories and her fears, born frightened, and when disasters did not arrive she created them, for nothing could explain her fear other than something frightful.

When, precisely, did she begin to loathe and fear Joseph Barton? Not when he said he loved her. Not when he wed her. Not when he took her so roughly that she bit her lips and cheeks until they bled. Not when she grew and carried and lost the bloody bits of his children. No, she detested him only when he became a father to her daughter and she found herself a mother. Only then did she realize what she had done: she had found a man unlike Giles Douglas and had transformed him into a man all too horribly like Giles Douglas.

Or not. Perhaps we have only a woman accustomed to living in large groups, first her family, then the Refuge, who isolates herself and devotes herself to a dull husband who does not merit the attention and cannot support her emotional needs, and so she in turn devotes herself instead to the new child, after years of painful failures, and the husband takes offense at the natural transition of affections, and neither can hear the other's voice across the widening spaces between them. Or not.

Very little evidence remains of Joseph Barton's life—a bearded face in a tarnished silver locket kept in a drawer amidst military ribbon; his name (already having traveled from Italian to English) further converted to the Latin *bartoni,* a species of bacterium, a kind gesture on the part of Dr. Rowan (after his own name, Harry Delacorte's, and several others' had already been decapitalized, latinized, immortalized).

As objectively as I am able to report, I might say that Joseph's manner, gesture, and aspect so completely reflected slowness that one would be forgiven for mistaking him for a man soon to fall fast asleep. You rightly ask why Constance believed him ruled by his Italian humors, simmering with desire. I think rather that he was a man of no great fire at any point in his life and most likely tamped down his Vesuvial eruptions with little difficulty at all. This is not to say that her suspicions of him, or Anne Montague's, were impossible.

And so I have circled back to where I began: there was a ghost. I have never seen one, but many have and do not wonder much at the sight of them. Constance saw her ghosts, and, in her efforts to protect me (for which I have no choice but to honor and love her, and from that honor and love, *believe* her), she struck down the man who invited that ghost into our home, and she evicted the phantom at the same instant.

Or, my father was a seducer of children, and he was murdered to protect me, thanks to the wise woman who became my second mother, whose love for me I do not doubt and who guided me to my career and all the limited joy that I have found in life. And in honor and love, I *believe* her, a conscious act. But I clear my throat because there remains one perhaps unimportant point of recall I must quietly mention: I have no memory whatsoever of my father behaving as anything but a father or a stranger to me. That hardly acquits him, but neither can I convict him to sate your childish appetite for conclusions.

When Constance sobbed and asked if Anne did not believe her, and Anne insisted that of course she believed Constance's every word, then who was the finer actress? They dined after the theater when the last of Joseph's hopes for himself were being dashed in York. Anne was trying to secure Constance's unwavering custom, perhaps even her affection at that early moment. But was Constance not trying to win something that night as well? If Anne's diagnosis was only half correct, then Constance *knew* her husband was acting evilly towards me and did not for a moment see ghosts, but was more than willing to *pretend* she did, so that Anne would rescue her from "them," and all the while Anne was pretending to see ghosts in order to protect Constance from having to see the far more hideous truth. Dr. Miles understood something, in his tale of the Russian soldiers (retold over sherry and cake to an enraptured Anne Montague), about the capability of a wronged wife to act with all cunning for justice. He understood something, too, about pinning down the facts.

Or, I gather the scarce and disconnected fragments of Joseph's life, and I conclude he was tormented by a wife daily madder and more maddening, provoking him to provoke her to provoke him in their every conversation, action, assumption. I imagine a man who saw in me, it is not impossible, the material for a better companion, someday, who felt a sad sort of love for me that was neither paternal nor romantic nor practical but some parti-colored and misshapen hybrid, which affection led his pursuers to conclude he was guilty of actions that justified his forceful removal from civilized society.

Or my mother was driven by a haunting of a different nature, pursued by a band of ever-approaching memories, the horror of which she would have done anything to evade or turn from her vision. They tormented her until my father appeared one night, his hair matted from the mist he had walked through for hours, his breath fiery from the whiskey in which he had bathed his self-pity, and he spoke the name *Constance* in the wrong tone of voice, at the wrong moment, his eyes hooded, and his resemblance—fleeting, allusive, venomous—to Giles Douglas sealed his fate, and she slew the father who caused her pain precisely because her own mother had not slain him. Perhaps.

And you—arrogant, seductive—promise me that in all this I shall find the answers to my sorrows, frustrations, failures, bitter victories, and foul loves, all of which you describe not as my life but merely as symptoms. (Though what life remains to me without these symptoms, I cannot conceive.) You promise me certainty soon, just a little farther on, but under uncertainty there is only more uncertainty. We are excavating muck without bedrock, laying our foundations on swamp mud, pestilent and boiling and bottomless, a Venice of a life, and sinking fast. What can we build when we shall never, never reach the end of our backwards work? I am left quite alone now, cast loose by Anne's death, as she and I were cast loose by Constance's.

I cannot explain all the events that I know actually occurred. If *this* happened, then *that* did not. If *that* happened, then *this* did not. If each of the players performed his own unconnected drama, then it is only in the intersection of those dramas that my life can be seen, through the latticed spaces where light can pass between three stories laid over each other. And yet when I lay these stories atop each other, no light does pass and no space remains. All my knowledge consumes itself. What I witnessed, what I was told, what I wished for, what I dreamt: I do not claim there are no distinctions here, only that I cannot distinguish them, and you have helped me not at all. Are you shocked that I now hate the thought of you and your manly promises of certainty?

A man whom I only slightly know invited me this past weekend to watch him massacre some fowl on his grounds. I traveled out of London to a house on a lake. He preened, rather, my host, strutted around his marked territory, puffed out his chest, made darting movements of the head until I well understood his taste for avian slaughter and quite wished to explode his plumage with a rifle.

At supper, licking from our lips the fruits of his bloody toils, he challenged the assembled party to tell a ghost story, as the weather grew only mildly inclement, and some weak and distant lightning flickered, and, more to the point, the table's conversation had long since grown fetid. This challenge appears lately at nearly every evening whenever a mild rain threatens. Have you noticed it, too? No one has the slightest thing of interest to say anymore, at least in my circles. Certainly the men are bores, and so the women are expected to titillate with creaking floors and untied corsets. I won, of course, with a tastefully done version of my mother's life.

"Of course, you can busy yourself with rehearsing such things, not being burdened by a husband or children demanding your attentions," sniffed a lady whose own effort at a ghost story was openly laughed at and whose husband had once very much demanded my attentions until, I grant her, I did find his company an untenable burden.

The assembled guests, while generally idiots, were at least quiet while I entertained them. "Oh, God. Is it about you?" asked one of the other pointless wives at the end, rushing headlong into the obvious and quite missing the pleasures of the story. "Are you the horrible little girl?"

"Bella, please," muttered this one's husband, a man whom I once found promising, but whose presence has since developed into an efficient method of self-torture. "Don't be a cow."

"Don't you *dare* talk to me, with her sitting there all pleased with herself," replied Bella, who is, professionally speaking, rather a cow. "I am through here. I am going to see to the children," and off she huffed and puffed upstairs to assure herself that my father's freely ranging libido was not squirming against her wee innocents.

But you, sir, will—I am certain—accuse me of having avoided my unsavory assignment to write about my girlhood. You will throw up your hands at my unwillingness to assign blame, even to assign truth, to distinguish between spectres and seducers, paranoia and conspiracy, murdering wives and murdering actors. You will leer at me and complain, "How, my dear lady, are we to *cure* you if you are unwilling to confront the Matter of the Past?"

How easily, sir, we could have agreed these many moons and pounds and fleeting kisses ago that I punish men because I wish to punish my father for what he did to me. I know it sits in your texts, on the first page, but I do not wish to punish him. I feel he was unjustly punished. If given the opportunity, I would possibly have taken pleasure in punishing him for being a man, but not for being my father. "Fine," you reply. "If he is innocent of these charges, then your mother was simply an hysteric." And I tell you, no. I am fully capable of believing at one and the same time that my mother was truly and literally haunted, and that my father was innocent of that haunting. "Very well," you continue (you see, dear doctor, how little I require your actual company—you have taken residence in my head, in a small, well-appointed suite, where I can visit you or lock you away at my pleasure), "then we can agree that this interfering figure, the spiritualist, was in the wrong, for it is she who convinces your weakened mother that her enemy was your father, and she does so for naked gain, both material and, if I understand you, for, for . . ." and here, bashful, you cough and blush, grasp for some Latin to drape over your naked Greek. But again, no. I owe Anne Montague a debt—many debts—and I will not, cannot, convict her of perjury or malfeasance at your bullying male insistence. No, I am able to balance my father's innocence and Anne's entirely correct certainty of his guilt. I have no recollection of his guilt; I have no doubt it was possible.

"Come, come, woman! How can you say with equal conviction that your father did not seduce you and that he deserved to be murdered for seducing you? That ghosts did not seduce you and that your mother saw them do it? While the objective truth of an event does not signify if the patient *believes* the event occurred, you are not accepting a belief in *anything,* only in *everything.* What game is this?"

You are frustrated with your patient, Doctor. She lies at your feet, as you insist, but still she does not submit to your will. She resists your honorable efforts to deliver her from her suffering. She spoils your mounting anticipation of success, certainty, judgment, conclusion. She is ungrateful. She is flighty. She plays games with words and sense when you would teach her something of value. Why will she not, for her own good, act as you wish? You would seize her, she so irritates you in her willful ambiguity. You would seize her in your arms and show her you are right. Calm yourself, Doctor!

I only mean to say that since I have no recollection of any of it— neither seduction nor abstinence, neither ghosts nor hysteria—perhaps this is not my affair to judge or take as my own. Perhaps these lives are not mine to use to explain my life in its late summer, nor is their bright light the means to scatter the shadows in my heart. These incidents are the property of others, only theirs.

And so you sigh like an actress, snap off your spectacles and polish them furiously and say, "Well, then, let us discuss *your* culpability in the matter," ever eager to strap to my back the hypertrophied conscience your most successful customers bear the rest of their lives, those stricken limping camels you call *the healthy.* "You do not recall your father seducing you, though you can eloquently fantasize your mother's feelings being seduced by her own father. You do recall giving testimony of some sort of attack on your young person, but do not recall ever specifying your attacker. You recall encouraging your mother in her beliefs, the spiritualist in *her* beliefs, and your father in *his* beliefs. Are you not then"—and here you will finally modulate your prosecutorial voice and hoist instead an unconvincing tone of scientific inquiry—"perhaps, rightly or wrongly, holding yourself responsible for some of these events and now suffering your symptoms as a variety of self-imposed penalty?"

Did the little girl here and there exacerbate conditions? Unavoid-
ably. Here she favored her father's company, there her mother's, knowing full well in her young way that with each rotation of preference, she
was hurting one and delighting the other. She exaggerated her fears to
win her mother's attentions, and mocked her mother's fears to win her
father's amusement. She may have sometimes said quite precisely what
Anne plainly expected her to say. She may have told her mother, "Don't
worry, Mamma. If you die, I will make a fine wife for Papa." She may
have here and there played the coquette, and been richly rewarded for
it by any of her three parents. And so she is to blame for igniting the
conflagration that followed, is she?

"We shall at the end see the roots of all your complaints deep underground as though the earth were a pane of cleanest glass." Such a
treasure you recklessly promised me at the beginning of our time
together, as all men do when their appetites are keen and fresh. And
this foul end is where you have led me, this gray hell of loneliness and
self-reproach and circular appetites. I have clearer vision than ever,
yet find my—what shall we say? my inclinations, practices, weaknesses, all the resulting unease—more heightened than ever. I have
approached these people with all the craft I can summon, and I cannot reach them. I stop no closer to them than an object resting on a
looking glass is to its still-distant reflection. I find no comfort, only a
machine of four jagged wheels, their interlocking teeth made only
for each other, fitting with hardly a sound, each driving the others
onwards.

And you! You held my hands, then burnt my long hours and my
money, fingered my wounds, keeping them fresh. So like a doctor. I am
miserable and you are bored. I weep and you consult your watch. Do
you wonder that we shall see no more of each other? Confess: you want
no more of me either. Your promises unfulfillable, my fascination fading, you ache to summon from your waiting room—with your seductive scientific mien—the next pretty hysteric.

The author gratefully acknowledges the help of Lee Boudreaux, Julia Bucknall, Gina Centrello, Tony Denninger, Professor Norman Fruman, the work of Peter Gay, Mike Levine, Peter Magyar, Mike Mattison, Douglas McDougall, Libby McGuire, justifiably legendary editor Daniel Menaker, Eric Oleson, ASP, DSP, FHP, FMP, MMP, Mihai Radulescu, über-düber-agent Marly Rusoff, Toby Tompkins, Donna Wick, and, of course, Jan.

ABOUT THE AUTHOR

ARTHUR PHILLIPS was born in Minneapolis and educated at Harvard. He has been a child actor, a jazz musician, a speechwriter, a dismally failed entrepreneur, and a five-time *Jeopardy!* champion. His first novel, *Prague,* a national bestseller, was named a Notable Book of the Year by *The New York Times,* received the *Los Angeles Times*/Art Seidenbaum Award for best first novel, and has been translated into eleven languages. His second novel, *The Egyptologist,* was both a national and an international bestseller and has been published in twenty languages. He lives in New York with his wife and two sons.

ABOUT THE TYPE

This book was set in Garamond, a typeface originally designed by the Parisian type cutter Claude Garamond (1480–1561). This version of Garamond was modeled on a 1592 specimen sheet from the Egenolff-Berner foundry, which was produced from types assumed to have been brought to Frankfurt by the punch cutter Jacques Sabon.

Claude Garamond's distinguished romans and italics first appeared in *Opera Ciceronis* in 1543–44. The Garamond types are clear, open, and elegant.